W9-CLY-315

PRAISE FOR *THE LAST PAINTING OF SARA DE VOS*

'Gliding gracefully from grungy 1950s Brooklyn to the lucent interiors of Golden Age Holland and the sun-splashed streets of contemporary Sydney, the novel links the lives of two troubled, enigmatic, and hugely talented young women, one of them an artist, the other, her forger. A page-turning book with much to say about the pain and exhilaration of art and life.'—**Geraldine Brooks, author of *People of the Book***

'As this story of art, beauty, deception, and the harshest kinds of loss ranged over continents and centuries, I was completely transfixed by the sense of unfolding revelation. *The Last Painting of Sara de Vos* is, quite simply, one of the best novels I have ever read, and as close to perfect as any book I'm likely to encounter in my reading life. One of those rare books I'll return to again and again in the coming years.'—**Ben Fountain, author of *Billy Lynn's Long Halftime Walk*, a National Book Award finalist**

'*The Last Painting of Sara de Vos* is a story told in layers of light. From afar, this novel is so beautiful, the prose so clear and vivid, that it seems effortless; on closer examination, one sees the rich thematic palette Dominic Smith has used. This is a novel of love and longing, of authenticity and ethical shadows, and, most compelling, of art as alchemy, the way that it can turn grief to profound beauty.'—**Lauren Groff, author of *Fates and Furies* and the *New York Times*-bestselling *Arcadia***

'In *The Last Painting of Sara de Vos*, Dominic Smith moves effortlessly between his seventeenth century artist and those who fall under the spell of her work more than three hundred years later. Smith is a writer of huge gifts and his descriptions of the painting and of those who fall in love with it (and with each other) are rendered with wondrous intelligence and keen wit. The result is a novel of surprising beauty and piercing suspense. I couldn't stop turning the pages even while the last thing I wanted was to reach the end.'—**Margot Livesey, author of *The Flight of Gemma Hardy***

'Highly evocative of time and place, this stunning novel explores a triumvirate of fate, choice, and consequence and is worthy of comparison to Tracy Chevalier's *Girl with a Pearl Earring* and Donna Tartt's *The Goldfinch* . . . Just as a painter may utilize thousands of fine brushstrokes, Smith slowly creates a masterly, multilayered story that will dazzle readers of fine historical fiction.'—***Library Journal* (starred review)**

'An outstanding achievement, filled with flawed and fascinating characters.'—***Booklist* (starred review)**

THE LAST PAINTING OF SARA DE VOS

ALSO BY DOMINIC SMITH

Bright and Distant Shores

The Beautiful Miscellaneous

The Mercury Visions of
Louis Daguerre

THE LAST PAINTING OF SARA DE VOS

Dominic Smith

ALLEN&UNWIN

SYDNEY • MELBOURNE • AUCKLAND • LONDON

First published in Australia and New Zealand by Allen & Unwin in 2016
First published in the United States in 2016 by Sarah Crichton Books,
an imprint of Farrar, Straus and Giroux

Copyright © Dominic Smith 2016

All rights reserved. No part of this book may be reproduced or transmitted in any form or by any means, electronic or mechanical, including photocopying, recording or by any information storage and retrieval system, without prior permission in writing from the publisher. The *Australian Copyright Act 1968* (the Act) allows a maximum of one chapter or 10 per cent of this book, whichever is the greater, to be photocopied by any educational institution for its educational purposes provided that the educational institution (or body that administers it) has given a remuneration notice to the Copyright Agency (Australia) under the Act.

Allen & Unwin
83 Alexander Street
Crows Nest NSW 2065
Australia
Phone: (61 2) 8425 0100
Email: info@allenandunwin.com
Web: www.allenandunwin.com

Cataloguing-in-Publication details are available
from the National Library of Australia
www.trove.nla.gov.au

ISBN 978 1 74343 995 1

Internal design by Sandy Cull, gogoGingko
Set in 12.75/17.5 pt Granjon by Midland Typesetters, Australia
Printed and bound in Australia by Griffin Press

10 9 8 7 6 5 4 3 2

This project has been assisted by the Australian Government through the Australia Council, its arts funding and advisory body.

The paper in this book is FSC® certified.
FSC® promotes environmentally responsible,
socially beneficial and economically viable
management of the world's forests.

For my father, Lanny Smith, with love and gratitude and hope.
Here's to your next ten thousand walks on the beach.

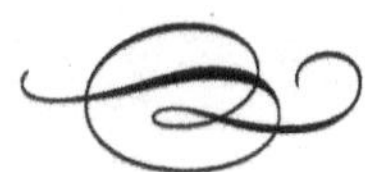

AUTHOR'S NOTE

During the seventeenth century, the Guilds of St. Luke in the Netherlands controlled all aspects of professional artistic life, including who could sign and date paintings. Guild members included the likes of Rembrandt, Vermeer, Frans Hals and Jan van Goyen. The historical record suggests that as many as twenty-five women were members of the guilds during the seventeenth century. But only a small handful of those artists produced work that has survived or been correctly attributed. For more than a century, the paintings of Judith Leyster were attributed to Frans Hals.

One gap in the historical record concerns Sarah van Baalbergen, the first woman to be admitted to the Haarlem Guild of St. Luke. She gained entry in 1631, two years before Judith Leyster. None of Van Baalbergen's work has survived.

Although this is a work of fiction, the novel uses such historical gaps as a springboard for invention. For the sake of storytelling, it fuses biographical details from several women's lives of the Dutch Golden Age.

THE LAST PAINTING OF SARA DE VOS

***At the Edge of a Wood* (1636)**

Oil on canvas

30" x 24"

Sara de Vos

Dutch, 1607-16??

A winter scene at twilight. The girl stands in the foreground against a silver birch, a pale hand pressed to its bark, staring out at the skaters on the frozen river. There are half a dozen of them, bundled against the cold, flecks of brown and yellow cloth floating above the ice. A brindled dog trots beside a boy as he arcs into a wide turn. One mitten in the air, he's beckoning to the girl, to us. Up along the riverbank, a village is drowsy with smoke and firelight, flush against the bell of the pewter sky. A single cataract of daylight at the horizon, a meadow dazzled beneath a rent in the clouds, then the revelation of her bare feet in the snow. A raven—quilled in violet and faintly iridescent—caws from a branch beside her. In one hand she holds a frayed black ribbon, twined between slender fingers, and the hem of her dress, visible beneath a long gray shawl, is torn. The girl's face is mostly in profile, her dark hair loose and tangled about her shoulders. Her eyes are fixed on some distant point—but is it dread or the strange halo of winter twilight that pins her in place? She seems unable, or unwilling, to reach the frozen riverbank. Her footprints lead back through the snow, toward the wood, beyond the frame. Somehow, she's walked into this scene from outside the painting, trudged onto the canvas from our world, not hers.

PART I

Upper East Side

NOVEMBER 1957

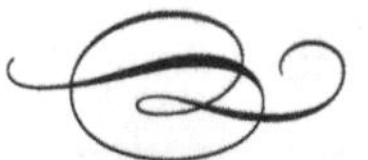

THE PAINTING IS STOLEN the same week the Russians put a dog into space. Plucked from the wall right above the marital bed during a charity dinner for orphans. This is how Marty de Groot will tell the story in the years ahead, how he'll spin it for the partners at the law firm and quip it to comedic life at dinner parties and over drinks at the Racquet Club. We're dipping shrimp in cocktail sauce, working Rachel's best china out on the terrace because it's mild for early November, you understand, while two thugs—middlemen disguised as caterers, let's say—are swapping out the real painting with a meticulous fake. He'll be particularly proud of that last phrase—*meticulous fake*. He'll use it with friends and insurance agents and the private investigator, because it sets up the rising action of the story, suggests that a prodigy or mastermind has been patiently plotting against him, just as the Russians have been conspiring all these years to colonize the stratosphere. The phrase will also help disguise the fact that Marty didn't notice the beautiful forgery for months.

What he'll omit when he tells the story to most people is that *At the Edge of a Wood* has been in his family for more than three centuries, bequeathed to him on his father's deathbed. He won't mention that it's the only surviving painting of Sara de Vos, the first woman to be admitted, in 1631, as a master to a Guild of St. Luke in Holland. And who could he tell that he liked to stare up at the girl's pale and cryptic face while he made slow, contemplative love to his melancholic wife in the years after her second miscarriage? No, he'll keep all that to himself, like a private faith to a fickle god. He's agnostic but prone to bouts of wild superstition, a personality flourish he tries to conceal. He will come to suspect that the painting's disappearance has caused Rachel's long depression to end and accounts for his firm finally making him partner. Or that the cursed painting explains three hundred years of gout, rheumatism, heart failure, intermittent barrenness, and stroke in his bloodline. Wherever the painting hung—in London, Amsterdam, or New York—the previous owners, he comes to realize, never lived past the age of sixty.

THE RENT-A-BEATS are Rachel's way of trying to rouse herself back to the living. Feeling bored by the prospect of gently drunk patent attorneys in French cuffs, with conversations about real estate and Nantucket sailing jaunts, she'd remembered an ad she'd clipped from an alumni magazine and fetched it from her recipe box. *Add zest to your Tuxedo Park party . . . rent a Beat. Completely equipped: beard, eye shades, old army jacket, Levi's, frayed shirt, sneakers or sandals (optional). Deductions allowed for no beard, baths, shoes, or haircuts. Lady Beats also available.*

If they were going to raise money for the city's orphans every year—it sounded Dickensian, even to her—then why not let the city in, bring up some grit and color from the Lower East Side and the Village. When she called the number in the ad a woman with an adenoidal voice answered, apparently reading from a script. For a flat rate of $250, the woman promised without inflection, you can have two artists, two poets, and two intellectuals show up at a designated time. Rachel imagined a basement in Queens where divorcées with headsets sat like African violets under fluorescent lights. She imagined out-of-work actors trawling in from Hoboken with her address written on a matchbook. The woman asked, "How many Beats would you like, ma'am?" and "Do you prefer the women in Mexican shawls or bolero jackets?" By the end of the call, Rachel had chosen their complete wardrobe, right down to the ballet flats, berets, sunglasses, and silver earrings. That was weeks ago and now—on the day of the event—she wonders if the whole idea isn't in bad taste. A Russian dog is orbiting the planet and she fears her little prank will be judged as frivolous and unpatriotic. She broods about it all morning, unable to tell Marty that a troupe of bohemians will be arriving at nine sharp, during after-dinner cocktails.

MARTY HAS PLANNED SOME FUN OF HIS OWN, a little demonstration for his guests and colleagues. He keeps it to himself while Rachel bustles among the caterers. By five, all three floors of the prewar penthouse smell like lilies and bread and it jolts his senses awake. He stands by the French doors on the top floor, out of the way, watching the rooms burnish with late-afternoon light. There's a fleeting sense of nostalgia and satisfaction as dusk pours through the space. Everything seems impossibly solid and real at this time of day and year, every object flushed with significance. Growing up, he'd always found this room distant and museum-like. The woody, gloaming interiors in the background of seventeenth-century Dutch portraits felt oppressive, the lacquered oriental boxes seemed austere and aloof, but now that these things belong to him he finds comfort in staring at them in that hour before the first lamp is switched on. A life contained, parsed into objects. When he closes his eyes he can smell the linseed oil in the seascapes or the Turkish prayer rugs that somehow smell like warming hay. He pours two fingers of single malt and anchors himself in the Danish leather recliner—his Hamlet chair, Rachel calls it. Carraway, the ten-year-old beagle, comes trotting from down the hallway, scampers across the parquet floor, his metal tag jangling. Marty drops one hand and lets the dog lick his fingertips. And that's when he sees Rachel through the doorway of the galley kitchen, moving among the caterers in their crisp white aprons. Head bent, one hand idling her pearl necklace, she's conferring with such diplomacy that it could be a matter of national security they're talking about instead of rice pilaf and wild salmon. It occurs to him that she's always been at her best in the throes of preparation—a trip, a dinner, a party. Lately, there's been the quiet fatigue they both ignore. She's constantly on the verge of a breathy intake of air and whenever she walks into a room, it seems she's had to pause out in the hallway to first gather herself up, like an actor walking onstage. Sometimes, when he comes home late from the office, he'll find her asleep in the living room with all the lights out and Carraway curled beside her. Or he finds empty wineglasses around the house, in the library, beside the bed, and Russian novels tucked between cushions or left out on the terrace to bleach and dog-ear in the weather.

She catches his eye and comes toward him. He rubs behind Carraway's ears, smiling up at her. The last five years, he thinks, have taken twenty years off the clock. He turned forty in the spring, a capstone to his stalled-out career and their inability to bring children into the world. It occurs to him that he'd started everything late—law school, a career, the first overtures toward a family. Inherited wealth held him back, stunted him until his early thirties. Seven years, up or out, was the conventional wisdom for aspiring partners at the firm, and now he is in his seventh year. He sees it in Rachel's gaze as she draws nearer—*Why did we wait so long?* She's eight years younger than he is but less resilient. Not frail, but cautious and easily bruised. For a suspended moment he thinks she's approaching with a staid, wifely kiss, one of those rehearsed gestures she occasionally plucks from the folds of her depression. Instead, she tells him not to get dog hair on his dress slacks. She passes close enough that he can smell burgundy on her breath and he suddenly wonders what the caterers think of her, then despises himself for caring. He watches her as she heads down the hallway toward the bedroom and disappears. He sits there until the room bloats with darkness. Eventually, he gets up and walks room to room, switching on the lamps.

A LITTLE BEFORE SEVEN, Hart Hanover, the building doorman, calls up to tell the de Groots that he's sending up Clay and

Celia Thomas, the first of their guests. Marty thanks him and remembers to ask Hart about his mother, a woman quietly dying of cancer out in Queens. "Soldiering on, Mr. de Groot, thanks for asking." Hart has been the doorman at the corner of East Eightieth and Fifth Avenue since before Marty's father bought the penthouse in the late 1920s. The narrow, fourteen-story building has only six apartments, and each of the residents treats Hart like a kindly uncle fallen on hard times. Marty tells him they'll send down a dinner tray from the caterers and hangs up. He and Rachel take the stairs to the lower floor and wait for the elevator. The managing partner and his wife are always the first to arrive and the first to leave, a couple in their sixties who host summer dinner parties that end while it's still light out.

The elevator doors open and the Thomases step out onto the black marble floor of the foyer. Rachel always insists on taking coats and hats herself and there's something about this ritual, this pretense of domestic humility, that gets Marty worked up. The housekeeper, Hester, is probably up in her room watching television, since Rachel made a show of giving her most of the night off. He stands there watching his wife take his boss's camel hair overcoat—it's too warm for such a coat—and Celia's cashmere shawl. In the first moments after arrival, Marty remembers how uncomfortable Clay always looks when he comes over. Clay is cut from a lineage of pious New England Brahmins like a slab of blue slate; he's from a bloodline of clergy, intellectuals, and taciturn privilege. He seems to silently begrudge Marty's inherited wealth, works his jaws a little like he can taste iron in his mouth every time he comes over. Marty suspects this is the reason he still hasn't been made partner—his triplex with unobstructed views across the Met and Central Park offends his boss's sense of patrician restraint.

Clay thrusts his hands into his tuxedo pants and leans onto the balls of his feet, his face brimming with forced good cheer. He looks to Marty like a man who's been out chopping firewood in a dinner jacket, invigorated by a moment of bracing contact with the elements.

Clay says, "Did you add a new floor to the place, Marty? I swear it gets bigger every time we come over!"

Marty offers up a chuckle but refuses to answer. He shakes Clay's hand—a gesture he would never make at the office—and kisses Celia on the cheek. Behind his guests, he sees Rachel half-engulfed by the shadow of the coat closet, running her hand over the plush of Celia's shawl. She might go into that closet and never return, he thinks.

"He made us trek all the way north along the park," Celia says.

"Let's get you both a drink upstairs," Rachel says, guiding them toward the stairwell.

Clay removes his heavy spectacles and rubs the lenses with a handkerchief. In the lamplight of the hallway Marty notices an angry red welt on the bridge of Clay's nose and thinks of a country parson on the brink of a fiery sermon.

Clay says, "If we're financing orphans, I thought we should walk. Plus it's a beautiful night. We'll taxi it back, don't worry, darling. I'm warning you, Marty, I'm famished from that walk. Ready to eat like a Viking."

"You're in luck," Marty says. "Rachel's hired every caterer in the state."

They arrive on 14 and walk down the hallway toward the terrace, passing the closed doors of the bedrooms. Marty gets this quirk from his dead father, a Dutch banker with a strong preference for the separation of public and private space. Marty even keeps his favorite books in the bedroom instead of the library because he considers them a kind of confession. As they pass the kitchen and come upon the great room, Marty can hear the string quartet starting up outside and above the terrace wall he sees the apartment towers across the park lit up like ocean liners, stippling the darkness above the tree crowns. He hears the faintest sigh leaving Celia's mouth and knows it's the sound of envy. He thinks of the Thomases' sober stone house with its narrow windows and the chalky smell of a rectory. Clay clears his throat as they survey the terrace banquet tables piled with hors d'oeuvres, the pyramid of glinting ice and shrimp.

Swallowing, Celia says, "As usual, it looks wonderful, Rachel."

"All I did was make some telephone calls."

"Hardly," Marty says. "It's been like planning the Normandy invasion around here for weeks. Anyway, we thought we'd capitalize on the weather. Feel free to be inside or out."

"Steer me toward a gimlet and a handful of peanuts," Clay says.

Marty hears Clay jangling some loose change in his pockets and pictures him standing before an austere bureau or secretary, plinking quarters and dimes into his tuxedo pants. He's certain there's a penknife in one of those trouser pockets. He says, "Sorry, Clay. You might have to settle for brie and shrimp." He throws one arm out, gesturing to the terrace.

The doorbell chimes and Rachel hurries down the hallway before Marty can stop her.

AT TWO HUNDRED DOLLARS A PLATE, the Aid Society dinner attracts roughly the same sixty people each year—uptown lawyers, surgeons, CEOs, philanthropist wives, a retired diplomat. It's always black-tie and assigned seating, little place cards in calligraphy on ten round tables. Once a year, Rachel calls a Japanese artist in Chelsea with her guest list. Three days later the place cards arrive in an envelope made of rice paper. Marty keeps a seating chart, a trick he learned from a friend who runs the European art auctions for Sotheby's. He puts the wealthiest guests nearest the silent auction table and instructs the catering staff to replenish their wine-glasses every fifteen minutes. This strategy has made a decade of hosting these dinners for the Aid Society the most profitable on record. It yields wildly inflated auction bids on Caribbean cruises, opera tickets, fountain pens, and subscriptions for *Yachting* magazine. Marty once calculated that Lance Corbin, an orthopedic surgeon who didn't even own a boat, was paying $120 for each issue of his maritime monthly.

The dinner tables are laid out with lilies and antique silverware in the great room, overlooking the terrace. Because it's so warm, cocktails, champagne, and dessert can be served outside, but Marty insists that dinner take place inside, where the lighting is better for signing checks, where Dutch and Flemish genre paintings and landscapes suggest, if not orphans, at least an atmosphere of underprivilege—the peasant hauling an animal haunch into a stone cellar in bad weather; the tavern revelers throwing spoons at a cat; the Avercamp of red-cheeked peasants skating on a frozen canal.

When Rachel calls everyone inside to dinner, the string quartet switches from Rossini sonatas to Bach concertos and adagios. As usual, Rachel and Marty sit at separate tables to maximize their interactions with guests, but several times during the meal Marty notices his wife looking absently into her wineglass. Clay Thomas tells his annual stories of being a World War I medic, of playing soccer with the Italians in a field of mud. Marty routinely swaps out guests from this table but always puts himself dutifully on the Clay Thomas roster. Until he makes partner he'll pretend he's hearing these war stories for the first time every year.

AFTER DINNER AND THE AUCTION, the guests drift back out onto the terrace. A long table has been set up with flutes of champagne, tiers of profiteroles, ramekins of crème brûlée, Belgian chocolates. As in past years, Rachel leaves the important mingling to Marty. She can never find her way into the banter of the men, or the partners' wives, who all send their children to the same schools and colleges, so she's content to find the outliers. The sister of the important socialite or the out-of-town cousin of some charity board member—these are the people she's most comfortable with, the ones who don't ask if she'd ever wanted to start a family. Marty accuses her of hiding in her own home, of having cramped, awkward conversations with total strangers. He tells her that the partners think she's aloof instead of shy and fragile. From the corner of the terrace, from the trailing edge of a conversation about the stray mongrel the Russian scientists found on a Moscow street, Rachel can see the ornate clock on the wall of the great room and realizes the Rent-a-Beats will be here in less than half an hour. She surveys the crowd to calculate how the troupe might go over. She can't decide if she's trying to add levity to the evening or ambush the entire event. If she's misread the situation then she'll meet the bohemians in the foyer, pay them their cash fee, and send them back into the night.

The temperature has dropped ten degrees and many of the guests have reclaimed their coats. Earlier, during cocktails, Marty built a fire in the outdoor brick fireplace, and she'd watched as Clay and the other partners took turns offering counsel, drinks in hand. At one point, Clay put on a pair of asbestos gloves and took up a cast-iron poker to rearrange the logs at the center, telling the younger men that they needed more blue flame and air at the base. Now there's a huddle of them by the replenished fire, lawyers with cigars and loose metaphors talking philosophy, urban decay, client billing. Through the French doors, she watches the caterers ferry the dinner plates toward a clearing station they've set up in the back hallway, the old servants' corridor that flanks the rear bedroom doors. Marty used to call it bedpan alley and claimed he could remember his senile Dutch grandmother—a heavy gin drinker—putting her "thunder pot" out there for the servants to fetch. But there were no servants, just an overworked housekeeper who had decommissioned the corridor years before and who didn't find the bedpans until the smell came through the walls. There must be a dozen caterers back there by now. She has the idea that she should go and check on things, make sure there isn't broken glass or waiters drinking from the bottle, but then she notices Marty conferring with Hester. She'd more or less given Hester the night off, after the flowers were set out, because she wasn't getting any younger, so she wonders whether Marty pulled the poor woman from her bedroom.

Hester walks from the terrace toward the library and then returns wheeling a metal cart, a sheet draped over the top and a tangle of extension cords trailing behind. By this time, Marty is holding Carraway in his arms and looks as if he's about to say a few words to his guests. A few glasses of wine and he turns into his father, ready to speechify at the slightest provocation. When they go badly, these speeches are tone-deaf and sentimental. He's gotten weepy-eyed over less than orphans before, so Rachel fears the worst as guests begin to gather around. A Bach adagio peters out from one corner of the terrace, then abruptly stops.

Marty stares a moment at the faces in the firelight, tenses his bottom lip. "Well, I thought I would say a few words . . . Thank you to everyone for coming and for supporting such a good cause. As usual, we raised quite a sum tonight."

He pats Carraway's hindquarters as he holds him in one crooked arm, his free hand holding a cigar.

"As you all know, this week the first living creature was launched into space orbit on a one-way journey . . ."

Rachel takes up a glass of champagne from a passing tray. She thinks, *Is he really going to segue from space orbit to orphans?*

"I'm told that when the dog eats the last of her food rations in a few days, the final meal is laced with poison, or that there's a gas for euthanasia that's released. Apparently, this is how the Russians treat their canine space explorers . . ."

A tremor works its way into his voice as he trails off. A few of the partners sip their drinks, staring into the embers of the fireplace. Rachel wonders if they're averting their eyes in embarrassment or patriotic reflection.

"Now, I can't help thinking about our little beagle Carraway here and thought we could involve him in this historic moment."

By now, Hester has brought up a kitchen chair and Marty gently places the dog in a sitting position. He uncovers the cart to reveal his ham radio set from the library, complete with headphones and a chrome-plated microphone.

"As it happens, Sputnik Two is giving out the same signal as the first one, so if I can find the right frequency we should be able to hear the Russkie mongrel orbiting above us. According to some of my ham radio buddies in Chicago, the signal should be within range right about now . . ."

Marty looks at his watch and moves Carraway's seat closer to the microphone. "I'm going to let Carraway listen to his competition because he could use a little wake-up call. Let's face it—I can barely get him to walk in the park in December."

This gets a genteel chuckle.

Rachel looks out across her guests. The women are smiling at Carraway as he nuzzles the metal gauze of the microphone. The men are less enthused, side-mouthing comments to each other. Marty brings the contraption to life, flipping buttons and turning a large dial in the middle. A lick of static comes in, then a stray newscast from Canada and a burst of polka, before they finally hear the signal—a bleeping, underwater tone. The pinging is almost painful to listen to, a lunar plink that contains quiet, Soviet menace.

"Do you hear it?" Marty says. "That's them."

By now the guests have edged closer and Rachel sees the men transfixed, cigars limp at their sides. For a full minute they listen to the signal. Marty plugs in the headphones and places them around Carraway's ears, lowering the volume. The beagle flinches and barks. Marty tells his guests that the microphone is off, that he's not licensed to let the dog make noise on his call sign, that he'd get thrown out of the ham fraternity, but pretty soon guests are encouraging Carraway to give the Russkie dog some hell. "Tell them we're coming after them," one of the partners calls. Marty pretends to open up the microphone and with all the commotion the dog begins barking and yapping. Finally, Marty gives Carraway a peeled shrimp from a nearby table and lets him scamper back inside and everyone claps and cheers for the little patriot. Marty makes a toast to space exploration and the rising star of America. Rachel turns and over the rim of her glass she sees the Rent-a-Beats coming onto the terrace through the French doors, Hester trailing behind them in exasperation. She imagines Hart Hanover's confusion in the main lobby, the intercom call that Hester intercepted, and now she watches the Beats approach—America's answer to the cosmic aspirations of the Russians. Bearded, braless, barefoot freedom. There are six of them: three men and three women. One of the men—a Marxist poet or vegetarian philosopher—looks genuinely outraged by what he sees out on the rooftop.

THE BEATS WORK THE EDGES OF THE CROWD—conversations about art shows in abandoned electrical substations, about pancake dinners in cold-water lofts on Thompson Street. At first, they're congenial enough and even Marty has to admit this is a clever idea. The sandaled women sip red wine and dance exotically by the fireplace. One of them teaches a partner's wife how to do the fandango and the quartet has come back out onto the terrace to improvise. The bearded men in corduroy jackets and peacoats strike up conversations with the uptowners, taking an anthropological interest in the rituals of these obscure, affluent northerners. They flatter and defer, chuckle at a dentist's nervous jokes. A woman wearing dragon earrings exchanges business cards with an investment banker, only her card is embossed with the word *Woe* on the front. For fifteen minutes, no one can get over this deft party trick, and Marty comes up behind Rachel to tell her she's livened things up nicely. But then Marty sees one of the men—in a red beret and army surplus jacket—holding a small group of guests hostage in his living room. From out on the terrace, he can see the man standing on an antique chair while holding up the de Groots' fruit bowl before his vaguely terrified audience. Marty begins to move toward the house when *Woe* suddenly accosts him with a plate piled with shrimp. He wonders why the caterers haven't pulled all the appetizers by now. Were these bohos going to get food poisoning out on his rooftop? "My real name's Honey," the woman says, "and I intend to eat my body weight in crustaceans. You must be the host. Glad to meet you, host." She's drunk and barefoot, wearing a flowing skirt that looks to be made from old Amish quilts. Marty offers her an anemic smile and strains to see what's unfolding inside the apartment.

"Why on earth is your friend standing on a chair?" Marty asks.

"Benji? Oh, he's high as a kite on Benzedrine. He'll fuck that fruit bowl if you don't watch out."

Marty feels himself clench as he heads toward the mayhem. The Spanish music is laced with guffaws and olés as he rushes through the glass doors and veers right.

"Take this Bartlett pear, ladies and drones, succulent and overripe with sensuality, slumming it beside a Red Delicious . . . it's waiting to be elevated to its highest calling." The man plucks the pear from the bowl and brings it to his mouth, biting so hard that it sprays everywhere.

"Excuse me, I think we've had enough," Marty says.

The man looks down from the chair imperiously, his beard morseled with pear flesh. Marty knows nothing about amphetamines but knows a deranged lunatic when he sees one—the man's pupils are as big and as bright as pennies.

"Is this the head square?" he asks his audience.

"I think I'd better call the police," Marty says. He can sense other guests coming in from the terrace, quietly fanning out behind him to watch.

The man shakes his head, incredulous. "You're paying for this, sport. You thought the sideshow would just come and sip your champagne, read some poetry about hitchhiking and sleeping in the woods, and then we'd quietly slip away. Negative assumption, amigo. Flawed logic, compadre. We are guests now in this beau monde museum and we're off-script . . . your shadow side and demons have been dogging you your whole pathetic life, brother. Now they're here. Pleased to meet you."

Honey stands beside Marty and says "Easy now" to the crazed man, as if to a riled horse.

"We've paid for your cab fare back," says Rachel from somewhere in the crowd. "We'll get you all in a taxi with some leftovers from the caterer."

This condescension makes the man on the chair tilt and gesticulate, a street corner evangelist warming to the Apocalypse. "Oh, that kills me. We don't want your fucking tinfoil sack lunch, Lady Macbeth. We're not here for the food or the wine . . . we're here because Amerika with a *k* is about to suck the phallus of Uncle Russkie and we want you to all see what a pinko commie dick looks like up close . . ."

At that moment, Clay Thomas comes bustling through the crowd. Later, Marty will think that he looks no angrier than a man woken abruptly from a nap. He seems put out, but there's nothing like violence in his manner. En route, he takes off his jacket, unclasps his cuff links, and rolls up his sleeves, like he's about to do the dishes. But as an old Princeton welterweight, Clay is limber and martial on his feet. Marty is about to ask him whether they should call the police when he finds himself holding his boss's dinner jacket. Without looking up at the man, Clay positions himself behind the chair and pulls the legs from the back, forcing the beatnik to lunge into a squat on the floor. He drops the fruit bowl en route, sending apples and pears under the furniture.

"What the hell, old man!"

Clay shoves the man once, hard, in the chest. "It's time for you all to leave."

The man in the beret stands his ground for a moment, his eyes walled back, his hands limp. It seems equally possible that he'll smash an antique vase over Clay's head or run from the house in narcotic terror. Honey and the other Beats gather in the hallway and call to their comrade in plaintive voices.

Rachel says, "The police are on their way."

He considers this, mulls it through a mental fog. Eventually he leans back on his heels and relents, following his friends down the hallway. Clay comes after them as they head into the stairwell. Marty uses the intercom to call down to Hart Hanover and tells him to make sure the intruders leave the building when they get to the main lobby. After making sure they get into the private elevator on 12, Clay appears back on the top floor to a hearty round of applause. Marty claps along, but he feels slighted and embarrassed. He just watched his sixty-year-old boss toss the Beats out like a bunch of profane teenagers causing havoc in a matinee. To make matters worse, Rachel had actually paid for this humiliation—called up and ordered it like room service.

Clay stands beside Marty, rebuttoning his cuffs. He takes his dinner jacket back and puts it on. Clay says, "You invite the lions to a dinner party and sometimes they bite."

Marty knows the gracious thing to do is thank Clay for handling the situation, but he can't. He watches the Thomases walk down the hallway. Other guests begin nodding their goodbyes and slipping out after them. Rachel is nowhere in sight and the guests are met by a chagrined Hester at the coat closet, her eyes averted. When the last of them have left, Marty stands for a moment with his back against the elevator doors. Hester says good night and he climbs the stairs before fumbling his way in the dark toward his bedroom. It's not until he's undressed, standing naked in the light coming from the en suite bathroom, that he thinks of this day as a cruel hoax. Rachel is turned toward the wall, feigning sleep. He's still buzzing with embarrassment, feels it throbbing in his knuckles and teeth. He stares up at the painting, hoping to be lulled by its frozen quiet. The girl is so frail, mired between the woods and the icy river. The skaters' faces and hands are pinked from the cold. He looks at the dog trotting on the ice, chasing after the boy, and thinks of the Russian mongrel pinwheeling through space. It'll be many years before he discovers that the dog died shortly after leaving the atmosphere, that the high pressure and temperatures were too much for her to bear. He'll look back on the dead space explorer and the forgery hanging in plain sight and see himself as impossibly naive. Right now, though, he notices that the picture frame is slightly askew, dipping about two inches at the right corner. He straightens it before switching off the bathroom light and climbing into bed.

Amsterdam/Berckhey

SPRING 1636

IN THE LONG UNRAVELING OF HER LIFE, Sara will always come back to the leviathan. It is not the cause of Kathrijn's death and all that follows, but it is the omen that turns their days dark. A spring Sunday, the day blue and cloudless. Word has come that a whale has beached itself in the sandy shallows at Berckhey, a fishing village near Scheveningen. Villagers have tethered it to cables and lugged it ashore where, for two days, it has lain moaning through its leathery blowhole. Buckets of seawater have been doused over the monster's hull, to delay its passage long enough for scientists and scholars to take a proper inventory of it. To Sara's husband, a landscape painter by training, this is a rare chance to capture a spectacle and render it with precision. The springtime markets bring a swift trade in canvases and this will surely fetch a boon price. But on the sandy track toward the coast, Sara realizes that half of Amsterdam is making a pilgrimage to see this harbinger from the deep. Barent will have plenty of competition from sketchers and painters and engravers. Sara is also a member of the Guild of St. Luke, though she often helps Barent with his landscapes, grinding pigments and building up the underlayers. Barent's seascapes and canal scenes are popular among burgomasters and merchants; they fetch twice what she makes for a still life.

They ride in the back of a neighbor's wagon, a painting field kit and a wicker basket of bread and cheese at their feet. Kathrijn is seven and dressed as if for seafaring—a cinched bonnet, sturdy boots, a compass hanging from a chain around her neck. Sara watches her daughter's face as they follow the caravan of carts and men on horseback, out into the polder and toward the grassy dunes. When Barent told them about the talk of the leviathan in the taverns, about his desire to go paint the washed-up animal, Kathrijn's face filled with enormous gravity. It wasn't fear, but steely resolve. For months, she's been plagued by nightmares and bedwetting, by terrible visions in the small hours. "I must come see that, Father," she said earnestly. Barent tried to change the subject, commented that it was no excursion for a girl. For half an hour, it appeared this was the end of the matter. Then, over dinner, Kathrijn leaned over to Sara and whispered in her ear: "More than anything, I want to see the monster die." Sara was slightly appalled by this grim thought leaving her daughter's delicate mouth, but she also understood it. A monster had washed up from the deep of the North Sea to die in plain sight, tethered with ropes and cables. All the ravages of the night, the demons and specters that had kept Kathrijn awake for months, might be vanquished in a single afternoon. Sara patted her daughter's hand and returned to her bowl of stew. She waited to talk to Barent about it at bedtime and eventually he relented.

When they crest a hillside that overlooks the coast, Sara is certain that the whole idea is a terrible mistake. From a distance, the animal looks like a blackened, glistening pelt left to wither in the sun. It is surrounded by scores of people, all of them dwarfed by its bulk. A few men have climbed onto its enormous side with measuring rods and wooden pails. A ladder leans beside one of its twitching fins—broad as a ship's sailcloth. As the wagon makes the final trek down to the beachhead, their neighbor, Clausz, says that when he was at sea he once saw a whale eye pickled in brandy. "Big as a man's head, it was, and brined up in a bell jar with all the rest of the captain's specimens from the south latitudes." Sara sees Kathrijn's eyes go wide and she tucks her daughter's hair behind her ears. "Perhaps the two of us can go take a picnic while Father paints," Sara says. Kathrijn ignores her and leans toward Clausz sitting on the box seat. "What makes them come ashore like that?" The neighbor adjusts the reins and gives it a moment's thought. "Some say it's a messenger from the Almighty, an oracle. Me, I'm more inclined to say the beast just lost his way. If it can happen to a ship then why not to the fish that swallowed Jonah whole?"

They ride onto the sandy flats, tether the horses to a tree stump, and trundle their belongings down to the site of all the commotion. They set up a base of blankets and baskets. Barent puts together his easel and strainer. He's asked Sara to work at his side and grind pigments; she will also make her own sketches that can be used back in their workroom. "I was thinking I would paint from the water's edge, perhaps with the beast's head in the foreground." Sara says this arrangement should work nicely, though she believes the scene will carry more drama if painted from above—the enormity of the glassy ocean for scale, the fish marauded by antlike city-dwellers, the shadows shortening in the noonday sun. Barent might even sketch until dusk and then commit the final impressions in the waning light. But recently she's learned that Barent prefers her ideas in the service of his own, so she says nothing.

While Barent scouts out a spot for his painting—no more than a dozen feet from the nearest artist—Sara and Kathrijn join the circling crowd. The air is heady with fishrot and ambergris, a sweetly foul odor. Kathrijn plugs her nose and holds Sara's hand. They get a few admonishing stares from the men in leather aprons who are at work with their measuring rods and pomanders. Sara garners from overheard conversation that an official from Rekenkamer has established claim to the animal and will put the carcass up for auction. She hears: "By noon tomorrow, the devil's bowels will burst out in all this sun and a foul pestilence will cloud the air." The blubber oil will be sold to the soap works, the teeth used for carved ornaments, the intestinal unguents exported to Paris for musky perfumes. One red-faced chap with a logbook is arguing with a colleague over the length of the devilish beast's *unmentionable*, a difference of two inches on a confirmed length of three feet. They debate it with scientific candor, calling it a *sexing rod* and a *clamper* in quick succession. Sara is glad to see that Kathrijn is oblivious to the conversations of the men—she scrutinizes the hulking mass from under the rim of her bonnet, perhaps drawn into the whorl of her own nocturnal visions.

The tail is the width of a fishing trawler, spotted with flies and barnacles and greenish parasites. The whale is slightly curled in on itself, like a sleeping cat, and before they know it, mother and daughter have wandered into an alcove of festering stench and the much-debated three-foot phallus. Kathrijn's piping voice says, "Look, a giant sucker has attached itself to his belly," and this gets a rowdy laugh from the nearby men. Sara takes Kathrijn by the shoulders and guides her toward the head. A villager asks them if they want to stare into the eye of the beast himself, for three stuivers each. He's propped a ladder against the jawbone and anchored it in the sand. Kathrijn looks up at her mother plaintively. "You can go up, but I prefer the view from down here," Sara says. She pays the man his fee and watches as Kathrijn climbs slowly up the ladder. Sara imagines the eye backlit with bafflement, a dumbfounded predator looking out from the dark cave of his own skull and mind. She imagines Kathrijn staring, awestruck, into the abyss of that eye and coming back down, now at peace with the hauntings of her dreams. But Kathrijn's plodding ladder climb and the stilted way she leans over the eye socket suggests a girl carrying out a penance. She hoods her gaze and stares into the whale's eye for a long time, then climbs slowly down onto the beach, refusing to say a word about what she's encountered.

The rest of the afternoon is taken up with sketching and painting. Sara works beside Barent on a blanket, preparing his brushes and pigments, watching him work up passages of translucent green and gray, stippling in veins of yellow ocher as the light changes. There is something mysterious and commanding about his work, an intensity that evades her in the constrained view of a still life. They work for several hours, Kathrijn at their side with her own sketchbook—the pages brimming with leaves and shells and horses. Barent and Sara have no desire to be present when the animal finally expires or its innards rupture, so they make a plan with Clausz to be back on the road well before dusk. Barent captures as much of the scene and light as he can; in their workroom he will fill in the intricate details of the whale from Sara's sketches. Kathrijn makes little forays down to the water's edge with sticks and wildflowers. After several trips, Sara realizes her daughter has lashed together a tiny wooden raft and carefully placed some flowering heather on top. Not a funeral pyre exactly, but something to commemorate the whale or float her visions away. The earnest superstitions of seven-year-olds never fail to amaze her. Not thirty feet away, villagers debate the deeper meaning of the whale coming ashore—approaching flood or famine or Berckhey burning to the ground. "God turn away evil from our beloved fatherland," one of the fishermen keeps muttering.

The trip back to the city is less crowded. An hour from Amsterdam, they stop on the outskirts of a small village for a snack. A peasant family has set up a roadside stand brimming with salted cod, apples, and cheese. There is a ragged-looking boy, about Kathrijn's age, helping his parents with their stall. Kathrijn, somehow emboldened by her excursion at the beach, asks if she can be the one to buy their food. Barent gives her some money and she steps down from the wagon with the wherewithal of an East Indian trader. She handles the money with care, selecting some apples and wedges of cheese. The peasant family enjoys her manner so much that they send their own son in to conclude the transaction. Everyone is chuffed by the sight of the two seven-year-olds caught up in roadside commerce—there's even a little haggling over which apples are perfectly ripe. Sara watches it unfold from up on the wagon. The only note of discord is in the boy's sickly eyes, a tad yellow and drowsy. His hands are well washed and his clothes are clean. Nonetheless, Sara will remember his eyes.

This will be one of the moments Sara tallies when Kathrijn is overcome with fever three days from now. By then, Barent will have worked up the whale scene in meticulous detail—from the ivory serrations of the monster's mouth to the leather ties on a fisherman's jerkin. Kathrijn will pass quickly, on the fourth night, her fingertips blackened and her skin crazed with welts. Sara will watch as the only child God has granted her withers and retreats. In the throes of his grief, Barent returns to the painting for months on end, adding figures and actions they did not witness. It becomes so dark and foreboding that they fail to find a buyer for it at the markets. A hooded figure stands on the bow of the enormous head, his back to the painter, plunging an ax into the blackened flesh below. The sky is overrun with lead and smalt. Sara stops painting altogether until winter arrives and the canals freeze over. One blue afternoon, she sees a young girl trudging through a snowy thicket above a frozen branch of the Amstel. Something about the light, about the girl emerging alone from the wood, rouses her to the canvas. Painting a still life suddenly seems unimaginable.

Brooklyn

NOVEMBER 1957

A WOMAN STANDING IN A SMOCK at dawn, grinding pigments and boiling up animal glue on the stovetop. It's the 1630s, as far as Ellie Shipley is concerned, and canvas can only be bought at the width of a Dutch loom—a little over fifty-four inches. She reads by candlelight, like a method actor, and makes obscure errands into the supply chain that is the stock and trade for period conservators and forgers alike. Cold-pressed linseed oil that does not cloud, oil of spike and lavender, raw sienna, lead white that fumes for a month in a cloud of vinegar. She paints in her kitchenette, where the northern light washes through her grimy windows and the view gives onto the streaming traffic of the Gowanus Expressway. She sees commuters on the city-bound buses, metal ribbons dotted with faces. She wonders sometimes whether those glazed passengers see her makeshift studio as an afterimage. In their mind's eye they see her bent over the stovetop and think she's stirring porridge instead of melting animal hide.

The smell itself limits her social life—an atmosphere of oxide and musk. Set above a Laundromat, the apartment has its own weather: a tropical monsoon during business hours and a cooler, drier climate at night. The ceilings carry watermarks and the corner above her bed fluoresces with a delicate brocade of mold. In her final year of an art history Ph.D. at Columbia, Ellie hasn't brought anyone home the entire time she's lived in this apartment. She should be living near the university, but she inherited the absurdly low rent and the lease from a departing student who'd grown up in Brooklyn. Despite the commute, she never quite materialized a Manhattan address. When she writes newsy letters to her parents back in Sydney, she tells them she lives in Greenwich Village, and has to remember to mail the envelopes on her way to the university. She writes about clubs and restaurants and art exhibits she's never visited. She studies reviews in *The New Yorker* and works backward to find a glimmering handful of details. Her father's a Sydney Harbour ferry captain, her mother a school secretary, and she can never decide whether these letters are written out of spite, to remind them of the smallness of their lives, or if they're musings on a life that's escaped her grasp. She has traveled halfway around the world, she thinks, to live in studious squalor. Her dissertation on Dutch women painters of the Golden Age sits unfinished in her apartment, a half-typed sheet of paper mildewing in the mouth of a Remington. It's been months since she worked on it and she sometimes finds herself staring at the machine's bullnose profile or the chrome-plated carriage return, thinking: Remington also makes rifles.

A few years ago, as a sideline, she began consulting in art restoration and conservation. She had always been good at the technical side of painting and it was easy money. Before art history, she studied at the Courtauld Institute in London and trained for a career in conservation. But despite her being the youngest and most talented of the student restorers, the plum museum jobs always seemed to go to older, male graduates, to the men who sported cable-knit cardigans and Oxbridge accents. Being Australian didn't help her chances, either. Museum curators treated her like a novelty, a bright spark from the colonies who might find a place as a private tutor or restoring for a small regional collection. And so, about to turn twenty-one, she drifted toward America and art history, toward a department that had two women on its faculty. Three years into her Ph.D., after she'd taken her exams, her supervisor—Meredith Hornsby, an art historian specializing in the Dutch Golden Age—started to feed her restoration assignments. Hornsby favored Ellie because she was the only dissertation student not writing about some aspect of the Italian Renaissance. A British dealer named Gabriel Lodge had been looking for someone to authenticate and touch up old masterworks.

Gabriel Lodge took her out for tea a few times and asked to see photographs of her restoration work. An exile from London and a promising career at Christie's, Gabriel wore a rumpled, moth-colored suit and carried a worn attaché case that looked like it once belonged to an embassy diplomat. He had a shambling, distracted air, but then he'd be seized by a question or a notion and his eyes would dart back to her face. Over his Earl Grey, he quizzed her about ground recipes and glazes and thread counts in baroque canvases. He hummed and nodded, held a magnifying glass up to her photographs. Apparently she passed these tea shop auditions, because within a few weeks a damaged seventeenth-century painting showed up on her doorstep.

Sometimes the paintings came to her and sometimes she went to them. She signed nondisclosure agreements and was chauffeured to private collections in the city, Long Island, and Connecticut. She killed off afternoons locked inside overdecorated rooms with her wooden case of pigments, oils, and brushes, refinishing a square inch of canvas according to another painter's style and palette. Or a courier showed up at her apartment with a neglected seventeenth-century Flemish or Dutch portrait and she spent weeks repairing it, relining the worn canvas or restoring layers of ground and glaze. Sometimes they paid her hundreds of dollars for a day's work, but she found herself unable to spend the money. Because she would have gladly done the work for free, it seemed ill-gotten. The money also felt like a tangible payback for years of being ignored by her male tutors at the Courtauld Institute. To spend it was to dilute its power.

By the time Gabriel came to her with the commission for *At the Edge of a Wood*, she had saved close to ten thousand dollars—so she technically didn't need the money. He said the present owner wanted an exact replica made but couldn't bear to part with the original. She remained skeptical and told him that copying an artwork was not the same as restoring it. But when he produced three high-resolution color photographs of the painting in its frame she felt her breath catch—it was unlike anything else painted by a baroque woman. Here was a winter landscape with the glaucous atmosphere of an Avercamp, the delicate grays and blues and russets, the peasants skating through the ether of twilight above the ice, but with this stark and forlorn figure standing at the tree. She was the onlooker but also the focal point, the center of gravity. This was no village frolic before the onrush of night—a common Avercamp motif—this was a moment of suspension, a girl trapped by the eternity of dusk. The girl had been lavished with very fine brushwork, the hem of her dress frayed by a hundred filaments of paint, each one half the width of a human hair. The painting's atmosphere, even in the photographs, was incandescent, hushed. It somehow combined the devotional, religious light of a monastery portrait and the moodiness of an Italian allegory.

Gabriel talked at her while she studied the photographs, working the surfaces in tiny circles with her eyes. She felt a prickle of recognition as he talked. It was like seeing her first Vermeer at age twelve on a school trip to see a traveling exhibition—the flush of that beautiful and melancholy light coiled at the base of her spine and had to be carried through the world. Gabriel told her that not only was Sara de Vos the first woman to be admitted to a Guild of St. Luke, but this was also her only surviving work. Because the painting had been privately held for so long, it occupied a small but cultish position in the art world. Over the centuries, very few art historians had actually seen it—or even knew about it. Now she could observe it in extravagant detail with the photographs and find a way to copy it. "An unbelievable honor," he said. Dutch women didn't paint landscapes in the seventeenth century—that was the general understanding—because the genre required long hours spent alone outside, a clear impediment to the Holland housewife of the Golden Age. But Sara de Vos seemed to be the single exception, a trained still life painter whose only surviving work was this harrowing outdoor scene. Both her father and husband were landscapists, so she'd spent her life around the form. It was clear that Gabriel had studied up; he may have even rehearsed his monologue on the way over to Brooklyn, another passenger mumbling to himself on the subway. This was a landmark painting, a historical oddity, and Ellie was being asked to work up a faithful copy of it for its rightful owner. This was the pitch from Gabriel that would stay with her. She told him she would think about it, but the truth was she had decided to do it within seconds of seeing the photographs.

ONE OF THE PHOTOGRAPHS was taken front on, from a distance of about eight feet, one closer from the side, and the final image was a close-up of the girl leaning against the tree. It was clear the images had been taken by a trained photographer. The clarity and focus suggested a tripod, and color film was expensive, beyond the reach of most amateur shutterbugs. Someone had obviously given very clear instructions on the shots to take, knowing that a side image in raking light would reveal much of the painting's texture.

The exact dimensions of the frame and stretched canvas were written in pencil on the back of the head-on photograph. Ideally, the painting would have filled the entire photograph. But for some reason the photographer hadn't zoomed in all the way, so that a mahogany headboard and two pale cotton pillowcases were visible. It looked to Ellie like the image had been taken from the end of an unmade, king-size bed before noon, and the shadows suggested slanting winter light. She should have been focusing on composition, texture, and color but instead she first tried to deduce everything she could about the owners. Who would put this beautiful desolation above their bed? Her eye kept being drawn to the twin indentations on the beige cotton pillows. She could tell the husband slept on the right side of the bed because the pillowcase retained the heavier memory of his head. It was this unexpected human element that gave the exercise, at first, a sense of voyeuristic intrusion. She was plundering a private, domestic realm.

She did a lot of pacing that first week, letting the rationalizations tick over in her mind while she walked barefoot through the equatorial climate of her apartment. She was merely being paid to reproduce a painting and wasn't privy to all the ins and outs of Gabriel's dealings and, besides, there were collectors all over the world who copied their own masterpieces for the sake of security. It was often the copy that was on display in the part-time Tuscan villa or Paris apartment. Whatever the circumstances, she was a degree removed, at the outer edge. A conservator for hire. This was her stance. Then, one night, she woke with a pounding headache and stood naked drinking a glass of water in the darkened kitchenette. She could feel the photographs, like a presence, from across the room. Fetching her robe from the bathroom, she came back and switched on her work lamp. Methodically, she unclipped the frontal photograph from the easel, laid it flat against her drafting table, took up an X-Acto knife and a straight edge, and sliced the bottom fifth of the image away—the incriminating strip of pillowcase and headboard and plush wallpaper. The work had begun.

THE PUZZLE OF HOW to build and age a copy was a house with many hallways. Some passages were well lit and others impossibly dark. She sourced a larger and badly damaged Dutch seventeenth-century canvas from a dealer and planned to cut it down to size and strip it back to the ground. She'd spent many hours perfecting baroque recipes for animal hide sizing only to realize the best method for this project was to obtain a canvas of roughly the same age and leave its underlayers intact.

She had a good rapport with a venerable antique framer on Lexington and he often called her when a renowned dealer brought something in for reframing. It was always under the guise of her evolving restoration business, of studying works that never circulated in public, but she could tell Maurice thought something was amiss when she came in with sketches of the frame. "Where is the picture itself?" he asked. She told him that the measurements and hand-drawn cross-sections were precise, that she would place the stretcher into the frame and do the backing herself. He looked at her warily and then she produced a copy she'd made of the head-on photograph, only she'd cut out the image inside the frame with a razor blade. Maurice held it up and from the other side she could see one of his bespectacled eyes blinking inside the cutout. "The client won't let me show anyone the work itself. I've signed papers," she told him. The Frenchman lowered the photograph, looking betrayed, but finally he said he could match the gold leaf and the profile. She said, "The painting is Dutch, 1630s, but it looks like a later reframing. Is it eighteenth century?" Maurice flexed the photograph toward the window and said, "Seventeen-nineties, Parisian-style. Though it looks like they skimped on the gold leaf."

The seventeenth-century Dutch built their canvases the way they built their ships—one carefully engineered step at a time. The sizing, grounding, sketching, dead coloring, working up, and glazing. The badger brush to smooth layers and blend forms. Some of them waited a year for the oils to dry and then applied a resin varnish. Obscure problems for the Dutch painter became her own—how to produce stable oranges and greens, how to approximate purple by glazing blue over a reddish underpainting. What she didn't know about Sara de Vos's technique she would invent based on what she knew of her Dutch contemporaries.

As an added precaution, she combed the small but vitriolic literature of fine art forgery. It was a welcome reprieve from her dissertation research at the Frick Art Reference Library, where she'd spent months poring over three-by-five black-and-white photographs of Dutch paintings. At the Columbia library she sat in a carrel and read forgery memoirs and manifestos, little screeds designed to take on the snobs of the art world. It captivated her and sometimes made her blush, as if she were translating the *Kama Sutra* instead of writing down how to game auction houses and the ratios for old-world gesso.

> Find damaged, discarded frames at auction houses and trace the lot number or other identifying marks. Call the houses up and ask what painting had once been in the

> frame and what it depicted. The bastards keep meticulous records.

> Van Meegeren added Bakelite to his pigments to age them before fobbing off his fake Vermeers to Göring.

In the writings of these technically brilliant but often neglected artists she recognized her own recurring anger at being overlooked. Her parents had lost a son before the two girls were born, Ellie the second of them. Long before they ignored her at the Courtauld Institute and the loneliness of the art scholarship at the Catholic boarding school, she could remember a house full of silences. Her father, when he wasn't piloting a ferry across Sydney Harbour, hunkered down in a small ketch he moored on the Parramatta River. He walked down to the dock behind their weatherboard house in Balmain each night after dinner, leaving the girls to their homework and their mother's weather-induced migraines. He slept most nights out there. From her bedroom window, Ellie could look out and see the tiny cabin lights of his boat swaying with the tide. It was no surprise, then, when she did everything she could to get the attention of the priests instead of the nuns at boarding school. She painted the most intricate, mythic landscapes for Father Barry, her art teacher—scenes that were heavy with alpenglow and Arcadian woodlands and engorged rivers. None of her early landscapes looked remotely Australian. The light and the foliage were distinctly European, despite the fact that she'd never left Australia. It was all absorbed from color slides and art books. "The old country is in my blood," she would tell Father Barry. Then, on weekends, she shoplifted at the nearby Woolworths, shoving lipstick and batteries into the waistband of her tights. When she won the school art prize in her final year, she crossed the stage to shake Father Barry's hand with an air of quiet vindication; then she made the mistake of looking out into the audience to see her mother sitting alone.

SHE PEELED BACK the antique canvas with diluted solvents, working in small circles, one inch at a time. She saved the old varnish as she stripped it off, squeezing the cotton swabs into a mason jar. To the naked canvas, she applied a thin coat of fresh ground but retained the surface signature of the original. Next, she sketched with pale chalk before dead coloring with raw umber mixed with black. The actual painting was slow and painstaking—a week on the woods, a week on the sky, two weeks on the frozen river and ice skaters. Each passage had its own technical puzzles. The bright yellows flecked into the scarves of the ice skaters were oddly textured and she eventually decided on mixing a little sand into chrome yellow. After the transparent glazes, she bleached the painting under an ultraviolet light for a week and cured it for a month in the furnace room below the basement stairs of her building. She worked a spiderweb of cracks into the canvas from behind, using a soft rubber ball. She used a spray gun to mist the picture with the antique varnish she'd set aside. A favorite dealer trick was to pass an ultraviolet light over a canvas, causing the oxidation in the old varnish to fluoresce. That ghostly blue-white apparition was a direct product of age.

BY THE TIME GABRIEL SHOWS up at her apartment one night in November, she has finally admitted to herself that she's painted a forgery. A month into her commission, Gabriel had begun talking about the swap and the organizer, laid out a trail for her to follow to its natural conclusion. He still does legitimate art deals, she thinks, but this must be his lucrative sideline. She suspects she knew from the very beginning what she was taking on, but somehow she'd sliced away her own ethical objections with the bottom fifth of the photograph. What surfaced in its place was a burning ambition to get every detail exactly right, to make contact with the woman behind the haunting vision.

Gabriel stands in her doorway, holding what looks to be a canvas wrapped in brown paper. In his other hand is his battered attaché case. Ellie has made the mistake several times of thinking it might contain dossiers and important memoranda instead of a spare handkerchief, a yellowed apple, a drugstore novel, a leaking fountain pen, and a cracked magnifying glass.

"Where are the horses?" Gabriel asks.

"I don't get it."

"Smells like a glue factory. Can I come in? I have something you might like to see."

She moves away from the doorway and Gabriel steps inside her apartment. The entranceway leads into the kitchenette and the living space and he hovers between the two rooms. He looks cautiously at the books and papers towering against one wall, then peers into the kitchenette where ice trays and mason jars brim with inks and oils.

"Should I make us some tea?" she asks, adjusting her glasses on the bridge of her nose.

"Only if you promise not to poison me."

"I would never."

"And you have Earl Grey?"

"I started buying it especially for you. But it's a tea bag, is that all right?"

Smiling, he says, "I'll stoop just this once." He sets the frame and the attaché case down by the table.

Three buses whiz by on the expressway, trailing squares of gauzy light behind the curtains. The sound of their engines is deafening and Ellie watches Gabriel as he brings two cupped hands to his ears. There is something disarming and childlike about him, a boy borrowing clothes and mannerisms from a fussy uncle. She eyes the brown paper rectangle from the stovetop. The back burner is reserved for food and the kettle; the front is for warming chemicals and starches.

"How did it go?" she asks, then wishes she'd waited until they both had their tea. She's not good at this game of tact and understatement.

Gabriel ignores her. "I'll take one cube."

"I know."

She pours the steaming water into two mismatched mugs, adds a sugar cube to his, and keeps hers black. She's used tea in her undertone tints before and she finds herself thinking about tannins as she stirs in the sugar. When she comes into the living area Gabriel sits down at the small Formica table. He repositions the case and the brown-papered frame closer to his feet.

She lets the tea steep for a moment. "So?"

"I don't involve myself with the transaction itself. I leave that to the organizer." He blows across the rim of his cup. "But apparently it went well."

"That's good." She's heard him mention runners and organizers and she suspects the former work for the latter.

He takes a handkerchief from his pocket and dabs at his brow. "You should consider cultivating orchids. My shoes are growing tropical mold while I sit here."

"It's not ideal."

They both sip their tea.

"Are you going to show me what's in the brown paper?"

"You'll spend a thousand hours on one canvas but you can't finish a cup of tea."

"Is it something to restore?" The word *restore* seems loaded now.

"That won't be for a while." He looks down at the wrapped canvas. "We were hoping to keep it here for a few days. I'm about to secure a new storage unit in Chelsea, but I'm between spaces just at the moment. Long story. Anyway, I don't think anyone will be combing this stretch of Brooklyn looking for an obscure Dutch masterwork."

Her cup is poised an inch from her mouth. She wants to ask who Gabriel means when he says *we*, whether there is a silent partner, some Latin American or European financier, or whether this is just an affectation he's picked up from his drugstore detective novels. But the thought dims away in the surge of something else—"May I see it?" The plaintive tone in her voice suddenly annoys her, so she reaches down under the table and lifts the frame onto the table.

Gabriel takes another sip of his tea. "Merry Christmas."

"I'm worried about the humidity. My apartment's sweltering."

"It won't be for long. Perhaps you can keep it wrapped in your closet."

She rests the frame on its side and begins to undo the tape, careful not to tear the brown paper. As the first sheets come away from the backing she can smell resin and the maritime inflection of old wood. Gabriel clears the mugs and art history journals from the table, standing at her side. She places the painting faceup and crosses to the wall to switch on the overhead light. The room blanches and she sees Gabriel blinking fussily. She comes back to the table and leans over the painting, her face just inches from the canvas. This is her way of taking in a new work. She has no interest in the composition from ten or twenty feet—that will come later. What she wants is topography, the impasto, the furrows where sable hairs were dragged into tiny painted crests to catch the light. Or the stray line of charcoal or chalk, glimpsed beneath a glaze that's three hundred years old. She's been known to take a safety pin and test the porosity of the paint and then bring the point to her tongue. Since old-world grounds contain gesso, glue, and something edible—honey, milk, cheese—the Golden Age has a distinctively sweet or curdled taste. She is always careful to avoid the leads and the cobalts.

What she does next is mentally compare her own layers and lines to the composition before her. She paints the canvas in reverse as a sustained thought. It's like undressing a woman, she thinks, an aristocrat cloaked in yards of lace. There are a few improvisations and influences that Ellie didn't fathom from the photographs. The sky, for example, is more like

Rembrandt's than she'd realized. And there are unexpected places where the paint rises in clots and flakes.

"How did you fare?" Gabriel asks quietly from behind her.

Ellie straightens and realizes she's been holding her breath. "Unless they have them in the same room and stand three inches from the canvas, there's no difference at all." She looks at the rough, bright yellows wrapped around the skaters' necks. Something about them catches in her mind.

Gabriel brushes a wrinkle from his sleeve. "Well, I'll leave you two lovers together."

He lifts the briefcase onto the table, snaps the clasps, and opens it up. Today, instead of a sad apple and a KGB novel, there's a folded manila envelope and he hands it to her.

She refuses to take hold of the money. So Gabriel sets the envelope delicately on the table and heads for the door. She hears his careful footfalls in the barely lit hallway and waits until he's out of earshot. For a long time she stares down at the painting, then carries it into her bedroom and props it against her dresser. She watches it for hours, until she falls asleep, mesmerized by the girl at dusk, the frozen river flashing silver and white each time a car passes by on the expressway.

Amsterdam

WINTER 1636

SHE'S SUPPOSED TO BE PAINTING TULIPS. But when Barent leaves each morning after breakfast, Sara climbs the stairs to her attic workroom and removes the other painting from a recess in the wall. This is the same room where Kathrijn took her final breath, where her fingertips turned black and the light ebbed then vanished from her eyes. It took a mere four days for her small body to become a husk wrapped in linen. The entire bed, Kathrijn's body secured to it with ropes, was lowered from the hoist beam and taken away on the back of a covered wagon. That was almost a year ago, but Sara still can't walk into the attic without her throat swelling with grief. For half an hour, before the composition of a painting steadies her thoughts, she feels unmoored—a woman pacing under the eaves, her hands clenched behind her back, furious with God.

Then she wills herself to the work at hand. Today, she places the stretched canvas on an easel by the window, flanked by a flower study. She sits on a stool with her back to the big double window, running her gaze across the frozen landscape. The icy river and the sky seem too pallid to her. In both, she wants the inflection of a deeper tone and color, something pushing behind all that white. During the dead-coloring phase, she'd underpainted the entire canvas with raw umber and black, but now she fears she used too little. The lead white in the snow seems uniformly cold and flat. She studies the area around the girl at the birch. She wonders sometimes if she isn't painting an allegory of her daughter's transit between the living and the dead, a girl trudging forever through the snow. It seems maudlin, even to her, but she lies awake each night, listening to the old wooden house tick and moan, retracing her own brushstrokes like the tenets of some delicate and inscrutable Eastern philosophy. The enigma of the brushwork and the passages of light startle her. But it also seems to wick away some of the ungodly anguish. For days at a time, she can think of nothing else but the painting.

Through the windowpane she can feel the cold at her back. She gets off the stool and prepares her palette for the day, mixing the pigments and oils in bowls and stone mortars. White lead, smalt, yellow ocher, a touch of azurite. The diffusely lit clouds—the sun like a candle at the end of a dim hallway—form a dome over the entire scene. This morning she had planned to retouch the sky and snow, getting the colors just right, but it's the girl's face that keeps drawing her attention. There is a semblance of Kathrijn—the high cheeks and forehead and green eyes—but it's different enough that Sara worries she will forget what her daughter really looked like. How is it possible that there are no portraits of her, that there's just a single charcoal sketch that captures nothing of her essence? She has painted countless still lifes, even tried her hand at austere wedding portraits back in her apprenticeship days, but she never once turned her gaze and her brush to Kathrijn. She never thought to commission a friend to work up a portrait of her daughter. She swallows, standing before the canvas, and closes her eyes for a long moment. She sees Kathrijn's face at age five or six, that look of earnest concentration whenever she floated a sabot on the canal, or the doting smile when she put a doll to bed. She's terrified such memories will dwindle and fade, that one day she'll wake up and remember nothing but the smell of Kathrijn's damp, salty hair at the seaside.

For hours, she experiments with the eyes on separate pieces of stretched canvas. A friend of her father's, a portrait master, used to say the problem of the illuminated eyelid kept him awake at night. Now she knows why. But it's the suggestion of light being reflected into the eye socket and the root of the nose that seems infinitely more difficult than painting the catchlight on the eyeball itself. There are moments when Sara feels as if everything she has lost is contained in those green eyes, as if she's painting Kathrijn's fleeting tenure on earth in that miniature, ocular world.

BARENT WANTS TO GET THEM out of debt on the spoils of tulipomania, the craze that's sweeping the provinces like some blue-lipped fever. He wants Sara to paint three identical compositions—a vase brimming with tulips in mottled light—so they can sell them in the spring, just as the first bloom of yellow crowns begins to spike through the sod. After spending months on his leviathan painting and then failing to find a buyer, he began selling quickly painted, unsigned landscapes in the taverns. When word of the illegal sales got back to the guild they were both fined, then suspended from its ranks for failure to pay. The scandal spread like poison, making it difficult for either of them to attract paying students. In desperation, Barent took a job with a bookbinder and strains by candlelight to paint at night. He comes home each day with new schemes, smelling of glue and paper. At dinner, when he tells stories of tulip speculators coming into their wild fortunes, Sara notices a new tone settling in, the hawking voice of a peddler. He recounts legends of tulip bulbs changing hands ten times a day, the man who traded twelve acres of land and four oxen for a single *Semper Augustus* bulb wrapped in muslin. Or the whore in Flanders who took her payments in bulbs, seeds, and crowns. The United Provinces are now shipping more tulips than ever before, he says, outranked only by gin, herring, and cheese. Then there are the tales of East India traders and Haarlem bleach-girls who've made it big in the flower market and retired to stone mansions on the coast.

At the end of these stories, he asks Sara for an update on her tulip paintings and she exaggerates their progress. She understands the gravity of their situation, but the truth is she has no feeling anymore for flowers. Besides, she resents the fact that every shipwright and chimneysweep in the Low Countries now wants to trade tulips and buy paintings. The flowers will make them rich; the paintings will tell their guests that they know beauty when they see it. For the most part they buy the paintings like so many tables and chairs. Only a few, the burghers from Delft and the foreign diplomats, have any eye for the work itself.

One night, Barent takes out an envelope at dinner and hands her a colored sketch of *Semper Augustus*. "Since they won't be blooming for months, I wrote away to a botanist in Leiden. A professor at the university."

Sara studies it in the halo of the lantern while Barent reads the professor's letter.

"Can you work from this?" he asks.

"I think so."

"He says the flame-like streaks are called rectification."

She says, "They dream up ways to make it sound holy and important." She sets the picture down and returns to her bean soup.

"He says that he can send us some grafted bulbs for a price. The daughter offsets bloom within a few years instead of the usual seven or so for a seed to catch."

She says, "Apparently he's also trying to get rich with tulips," but the phrase *daughter offsets* tugs at her mind. She sees Kathrijn in her attic bed, her lips murmuring and white. Bringing herself back to the room, she watches Barent rereading the letter in the light under the chimney canopy. He sits wrapped in his dressing gown, his face gaunt in the speckled firelight of the peat-box. All winter the house has been insufferably cold. She jokes that he wears seven waistcoats and nine pairs of trousers to bed, that she can't remember what his natural silhouette looks like.

After he finishes the letter, he presses it inside the pages of a leather-clad ledger. Whenever they sell a painting, he brings out the ledger and makes an entry. Each time, he reminds her that she is never to sign or initial her work. The paintings are stored in the attic until the spring markets or private sales that happen when the days turn warmer. *Dutchmen don't buy paintings when they're cold* is one of his axioms. All these paintings will be sold anonymously—ships tossed in a storm, a field at dusk, her tulips—each canvas wrapped in felt or wool blankets and sold from a stall or tavern. As Sara sits with her feet on a box-warmer, she wonders how many hurried, unsigned paintings they will have to sell before they can finally break free. She suspects there are dozens of debtor names at the back of Barent's ledger and another dozen that have never been written down.

Upper East Side

MAY 1958

A SPRING HEAT WAVE. Marty leaves a French restaurant in his shirtsleeves on a Friday afternoon, his jacket over one arm, hat in hand. He's a little drunk, the aftertaste of anise and steak heavy in his mouth. When he pushes through the big wooden doors and steps out onto Fifth Avenue, the city hits him in the chest, like he's pushed open the door to a foundry. The light dazes him for a moment—a burst of acetylene coming off the metal and glass and pavement. He can smell burning tar and sees that a road crew is filling potholes at the corner, much to the displeasure of the honking, idling cabbies. The scene is captured in the storefront window of a venerable old jewelry shop—a jittered filmstrip of men leaning on shovels against a bed of black velvet and diamonds. Marty sees his cameo flicker across the window. He could buy Rachel a celebratory gift, but then he's half a block away and it's already an afterthought. Two doormen commiserate about the heat under a canopy and they nod to him as he passes. He's always had a soft spot for doormen—his father used to call them the city's blue-collar admiralty. He can feel the sidewalk burning through the leather soles of his shoes and little blasts of air waft up his trouser legs and blow hot against his shins. He crosses to the park side of the street, for the deep shade along the stone wall. Clay was insistent that he take the rest of the day off, so he heads north along the park, away from the office.

He tries to remember Clay's exact words when he'd made the announcement, the partners already softened by Beaujolais. Something about partnership being like a marriage, only the hours are longer. Everyone nodded or gently laughed or absent-mindedly loosened a watchband. All except Roger Barrow, a senior partner and the other patent attorney, who studied the dessert menu. Clay presented Marty with new embossed business cards and an engraved Cartier pen. The small gift boxes were wrapped in papers from an infamous contract the firm had handled and bound with red legal tape. Marty told them the symbolism was not lost on him and then they all toasted his career. On Monday he would be moving to the upper floor, to the office with a view across Midtown instead of the next building's cooling station. Gretchen, his secretary, would also have a window and he would remember to bring her flowers for the new desk. Something that said new beginnings. He notices the sidewalk tulips are already gone, vanquished by the early heat.

The streets are full of people returning from long lunches, ad execs with loosened ties and secretaries in plaid skirts and knotted silk scarves. He smiles at the women as they pass, his mind still lingering on the right platonic flower for Gretchen. He remembers that yellow roses are the flower of friendship.

The sidewalk girls are chatty with weekend plans, their cheeks flushed from the walk or the drinks with lunch, and he thinks he can smell perfume burning off behind their earlobes, tiny recesses of citrus and jasmine. A few of them smile back, their faces inscrutable behind outsize Greta Garbo sunglasses. Is it flirtation or just neighborliness in the dappled shade of the elms? He puts on his hat and tugs the brim down so that it lowers and frames his view, removes the ambiguity in the girls' faces. The world is bifurcated, exists only from the waist down. From the procession of anonymous shoes and stockings and skirt hems he tries to deduce something about the person. But when he tries to confirm a suspicion based on the cut of a suit or the buff of a shoe top, he's frequently wrong. A pair of battered shoes cracked along one seam end up belonging to an aristocratic old man instead of a dockworker. Rachel says he suffers from a kind of blindness, that when he walks into a room he notices the windows instead of the people and the furniture.

He thinks about how to tell Rachel the good news. In the last few months she has become lighter and happier, recounts her days to him at dinner with jokey asides. He wonders if the old childless ache will ever go away, or whether it will always be on the periphery, a knife blade winking in the sun. Still, there's no denying the new atmosphere in the house. They've even made love a handful of times and afterward talked about the future instead of the past. Something has lifted and he's been aware of it in himself. Not luck, exactly, but an upswing, a sense of being pulled along by some force he'd thought was indifferent but is, in fact, capable of benevolence. During client meetings he's noticed himself sounding more confident and shrewd. He'll say something smart or prudent and have no recollection of the preceding thought ever forming. Gifts out of nowhere. And then there are the parking spots that appear out of the void of Midtown, or the vacant booths in restaurants. He thinks of these as good omens, as portents, and they seem to fine-tune his senses, as if his body is being made to pay attention to his own wild good fortune. Walking along he can feel the nuances of the street, the sticky air against his palms and neck, the subtle weight of his tiepin on his rib cage, the syncopation of jazz from a passing car radio. He can discern the conversational drag between two pedestrians and know that one of them feels overwhelming guilt. For half an hour, he's clairvoyant and fond of everything around him.

INSTEAD OF GOING INTO his building lobby, he walks across the street and climbs the stone steps of the Metropolitan Museum of Art. Early on in his law career, after a deadline, he would sometimes take a taxi to kill off his lunch hour in the museum. He could have eaten lunch with Rachel in the apartment, but he chose to mill around the collections instead. His father had told him stories of working as a young banker in Amsterdam and eating a sandwich in a medieval courtyard that was entombed by modern apartment buildings. It was important to walk among your own thoughts, he seemed to be saying, to plunk down on a bench somewhere and let the world roar along without you for an hour. It's been years since he's been inside the museum, even though he and Rachel live across the street and have remained members and donors. He's pretty sure there's a gold plaque from the Iron Age that he helped procure—a scene of gilded winged creatures approaching stylized trees.

He produces his membership card from his wallet for the girl at the front desk and enters into the great hall. Under the arches and domed vaults, tourists are consulting maps and guidebooks, a Texas-sounding family deep into a standoff between medieval armor and pre-Columbian gold. Marty used to skip the pageantry of the first floor and steal off to a bench on the second level. He'd sit before a Rembrandt or a Vermeer and feel guilty about it, as if he'd gone straight to the postcoital cigarette. Most of the time he wouldn't even be thinking about the paintings themselves. He would stare up at them and loop through a cross-weave of associations, an obscure challenge of a new patent application he was filing and then a sliver of memory, a day at the beach with his grandparents eating salted cod at Scheveningen, the chill of the North Sea against his bare legs. The thoughts would rush in but eventually strip away, peel back to reveal a kernel of bare sentiment. Eventually, if he sat there long enough he would feel the brute force of nostalgia or a sense of loss or elation and it always seemed to be emanating from a particular painting. Rembrandts, no matter the depiction, brought to mind the desolation of winter, the loneliness of blue afternoons. He would walk back slowly to the office in a funk, brooding and distracted in client meetings the rest of the day. Maybe that was why he'd stopped coming.

Today he walks up the cool, wide stairwell and wanders back to a small gallery that houses the Post-Impressionists. He's never been much of an admirer of Van Gogh or Gauguin, but there's something about this weather that makes him want to stare at the indigo shade of a South Sea island and a dark woman's breasts. He anchors himself in front of *Two Tahitian Women*, sets his hat and coat on the leather bench beside him. It looks so modern in its assuredness that it's hard to believe it predates modern cinema, the automobile, air-conditioning, the neon sign. Two girls stare at the viewer, a corona of green and yellow playing on jungle foliage behind them. Both of them stand bare-chested—the girl with the tray of mango blossoms is naked from the waist up and the one on the right has one breast exposed above the neckline of some improvised garment. They are looking toward, but also past, the viewer, as if a child or animal might command their attention outside the frame. It's a sensual gaze but also knowing and vaguely accusatory. It reminds Marty of certain Manet nudes, Olympia on a daybed staring out from another century, one arm crossed in front of her breasts and crotch, creating a boundary the viewer cannot cross. The shading in the Gauguin is heavy with violet and russet, almost nocturnal in its saturation. He hears a few footsteps clicking around the wood floors and he becomes conscious of how long he's been sitting there staring up at those three uncovered breasts.

He walks out to the balcony that overlooks the great hall and then decides to find a pay phone and call Gretchen, to tell her the good news. There's a small bank of phones by the coat check on the first floor, but he has to break a dollar at the museum gift store to make change. He finds half a roll of mints in his pocket, pops one in his mouth, and tries to remember his own office number. He dials the main switchboard and asks for Gretchen. She picks up on the second ring and his name surprises him with its formality—*Marty de Groot's office*.

"Put me through to Marty de Groot right now. That big lummox is going to hear a piece of mind." He says this in his best Russian drawl—a submarine captain on a vodka binge.

"I've never fallen for that. It's not even a Russian accent. It sounds like you've suffered a head injury."

Marty lets out a big, minty guffaw. "You're right. Not once in five years."

"How did the partner lunch go?"

"Did you know?"

"Know what?"

"That we're moving upstairs on Monday."

"You made partner." It's both statement and question.

"Yes, just in time for space travel."

He hears her breathing and smiling into the phone. "That's really wonderful news."

"I'm not allowed back in the office the rest of the day. Clay's banned me."

"Well, I thought something was suspicious when Mr. Thomas told me not to schedule anything for your Friday afternoon. That was two weeks ago!"

"They've been plotting."

The line goes quiet for a moment. He tries to apply his street telepathy to the phone call and discern what she's thinking. Gretchen is midtwenties, a graduate of NYU who still lives in the Village. An English major turned paralegal, she keeps an untranslated copy of *Beowulf* in her desk drawer. More than once he's caught her mouthing the hard gutturals of Anglo-Saxon to herself. Even though she reads obscure novels in the park during her lunch hour and tells stories of exotic restaurants, there's nothing bohemian about her appearance. She comes to the office dressed in impeccably modest wool skirts and demure earrings, her hair always pulled back, a tight spiral of French braids the color of cedar.

He says, "I couldn't have done it without you. Thank you for cleaning off my desk at the end of every day. And I'm sorry I never follow your color-coding system."

"You're very welcome."

He doesn't let the silence re-gather. "Why don't you come meet me for a celebratory drink? I'm lurking around the Metropolitan Museum of Art, doing everything I can to avoid the tourists in Ancient Egypt. I don't want to make my hypertension any worse."

"Have you already told Mrs. de Groot the good news?"

He knows the mention of Rachel is not incidental.

"She's visiting her sick mother in the Hamptons. I'm going to surprise her by driving up there in the morning." The lie comes effortlessly, a dead bolt sliding into a groove.

She pauses and he hears some rustling on her desk.

He says, "But if you just want to take the rest of the afternoon off, that's fine as well. I'll wander here some more."

"Sure," she says. "I'd love to meet up. Are you game to go south of Times Square?"

"The map goes dotted for me somewhere below Forty-Second."

"Meet me at Claude's Tavern in the Village in an hour."

"If it weren't so hot I'd walk."

"Do you have any idea how far that is?"

"Couple miles?"

"Four miles, at least."

They hang up and Marty digs through his pockets for more change. When he calls the apartment, the sound of Hester's voice is gruff and matronly and it's such an affront after Gretchen's warmth that he almost hangs up. Instead, he asks for Rachel and there's an insufferable delay. He wonders about Rachel's life in the house without him, whether she and Hester sit around and watch the soaps together in their housecoats. Does Hester only put on her apron at ten before six each evening, before he walks in the door? All this passes through his mind, and then he's telling Rachel that he's been invited to an impromptu partner dinner and it may go late, that he thinks the news might be very promising. She keeps saying *I hope so, I hope so, for your sake*. And then he hangs up the phone and leaves the museum. Back outside he rolls up his shirtsleeves and looks at his watch, then glances up at the penthouse of his building. Above the terrace wall of the fourteenth floor he can see the tops of the citrus trees that Rachel dutifully prunes and waters. He decides that he's going to walk all four miles down to the Village.

AN HOUR LATER, he's running late and drenched in sweat. No longer drunk, he feels the first brassy notes of a hangover wash over him somewhere in the Village. He stops strangers to ask about the location of Claude's Tavern, but no one seems to have heard of it. Near NYU, he walks by cafeterias where students mill among steam tables, the smell of stew apocalyptic. He passes Laundromats—*automatics* and *supermatics*—where college kids in Levi's smoke cigarettes and thumb paperbacks and play cards under ceiling fans. He sees big lonely men eating all-day breakfasts at Formica counters and he's convinced this is a foreign country. Storefront churches and delis, a man selling papaya juice from a quilted metal cart. Shopkeepers hauling waxy boxes of produce into the cellars below the sidewalk. It might as well be Mozambique for how exotic it feels.

Half an hour late, he stumbles into Claude's Tavern—a bricked-in basement jammed with bodies. A jazz quintet plies their music through slats of smoky neon and hipsters sway like Pentecostals. He pushes through the crowd, looking for Gretchen, the subway rumbling somewhere beneath his feet. Impossibly, he finds her sitting by herself, reading a French novel in the low-watt hemisphere of a booth. It reminds him of Rachel, briefly, and he has to push away the mental association.

She looks up. "Oh my goodness, you walked, didn't you?"

"I had no idea this was down here."

"Claude's?"

"The southern half of Manhattan."

She smiles. He rests a hand at the edge of the table but doesn't sit.

She says, "Don't you get down here for meetings?"

He has to yell to be heard. "The Wall Street firms pretend this isn't here. They put a bag over your head on the taxi ride down." He looks around and takes in the scene. "I'm going to go get us a drink. If I'm not back in three days read Keats at my funeral. What would you like?"

"Surprise me," she says. "Something clear with ice."

He jostles into the crowd and makes for the bar. En route, he watches the band play, five black men in white suits. In high school, he played the trumpet and jazz always makes him sad for the kid who was forced by his fiduciary-minded father to put down the instrument. The trumpeter swivels his horn out toward the room as he murders a fat note, eyeless under his trilby. The fleet pianist angles his ass off the bench to dig into the keys and the drummer is tightly coiled and half in shadow, his knuckles glinting above a cymbal. Marty finally reaches the bar—a barge-like colossus of wood that looks like it's been dredged from the East River. The line is three deep and he holds a twenty in the air to get some attention. He orders himself a neat whiskey and Gretchen a Pimm's Cup loaded with ice. When he gets back to the booth he sets the drinks down and settles on the other side of the table. In this light her face is softened—the delicate spray of freckles on her nose and cheeks looks like a tan.

"I'll never hear you unless you sit over here," she says. "I should have chosen somewhere else."

He smiles and makes the move. He leans toward her ear to speak, but the sudden smell of her hair forces him into a pause. Swallowing, he says, "I feel like an anthropologist in the jungles of Borneo."

"Cheers," she says, lifting her drink. "Here's to Marty de Groot making partner."

"Here's to you," he says. "Because I never would have made it without you. All those times you told Clay that I was meeting with a client when he was in a temper. Thank you!"

They clink their glasses and each take a sip.

"Pimm's makes me think I should be playing tennis."

"Is it okay?"

"Wonderful."

"You live nearby if I remember correctly."

"Yes, this is my secret life. Uptown paralegal by day and weekends in Washington Square Park."

"It seems to suit you," he says.

She smiles into her drink, her breath smoking against the ice. He has never cheated on Rachel, not in fifteen years of marriage, but there's been a lineage of near misses, office infatuations and lunches with protégées in barrettes and woolen skirts. It took him years to realize it was the flirtation and admiration he craved, not the actual conquest. But he feels something shifting in the space between them, a hesitation and nervousness that suggest he's readying to cross a new line. Even though Gretchen has always been attentive to him he knows there's a chance he's misread everything. It's possible he's followed the wrong set of clues, just like the matching of shoes to faces and lives out in the street. He makes two more forays to the bar, each time holding up a twenty to suggest a ridiculous tip. He can feel younger men glaring at him. Back at the booth, he flattens one palm against the grain of the leather and asks her questions. They talk about her childhood and her family, about road trips to Montreal and the difficulty of learning foreign languages. He knows a handful of Dutch phrases and trots them out like drunken Middle English. It gets her laughing. "Better than your Russian," she says, sipping, letting the ice clink against her teeth. He listens attentively, but he's aware of the heat coming off her stockinged legs under the table, the warm hollow behind her left knee. Her thigh is inches away and it wags toward him when she speaks.

He imagines placing his hand squarely on her leg, or touching the back of her hand, but then there's a commotion that draws his attention. The drummer has just come off a hell-bent solo, giving out a Comanche war cry at the tail end, and now something shifts in the crowd—voices pitch, somebody gets jostled. The atmosphere becomes charged. Marty can smell the room come alive with body heat and beer and something primal. He can smell the violence taking shape even before it happens—molecules heating before a lightning strike. He leans in and says to her, "We should go. I think it's about to get rowdy in here." He rests his hand on her elbow and leaves it there while she zips up her purse. As they get up from the booth, the scuffling escalates into thrown punches they can hear but cannot see through the welter of packed bodies. As they get to the stairs, Marty looks back down to see a man being hurled across the bar, shards of broken glass in his wake like ice from a comet's tail. He's surprised by how beautiful it looks and how the band keeps playing their tight, syncopated rhythms during the whole thing. Then there's a shift, something telegraphed from the stage. At the outer edge of a solo, the trumpeter gets distracted. His tone goes thin and flat, like he's developed a sudden head cold, and this is the signal to the rest of the room to start running in panic.

THEY STAND ON A STREET corner sometime after midnight. People are spilling out of clubs on MacDougal, couples holding hands and whispering boozily to each other. A few musicians heft their instruments into station wagons and pickups. Marty buys two hot dogs and they stroll under the pretext of him walking her home. The club is still ringing through his whole body, his ears buzzing under the streetlights. They stand in front of her apartment building, a stone facade zigzagged with fire escapes. "There used to be an elevator, but now they're all walk-ups," she says. "If you don't mind the alpine hike we can have a nightcap." When she says it her eyes are on his shoes and then a slight shrug works into her shoulders. He feels a surge of tenderness toward her; he wants to assure her that he's honorable and no matter what will always be kind to her. Instead, he says, "Lead the way, my little Sherpa." Climbing the darkened stairway behind her, he watches the authority of her ass swaying in her knitted skirt. He feels lust rankle through him, a pound of lead dropping into his stomach. Her apartment is decorated in a mandarin style—blond wood floors and earthen jars and books on lacquered shelves. There's a stack of novels on the low coffee table and a bedroom, faintly visible, where he sees a guitar on the wall and a scarf tossed over a lamp. She decides to make them a drink and goes to the small kitchen and begins opening cupboards filled with neatly stacked crockery and glassware. He suspects dinner parties, a circle of friends that includes bon vivants and actors and photographers. She opens the freezer door and starts in about the buried ice cube trays and how she hasn't defrosted in ages. He watches her as she stares into the diorama of snowmelt and frosted meat hilltops. The freezer ticks and breathes. He imagines pulling the wooden pin from her barrette and her cedar-colored hair falling down her shoulders. He pictures hiking up her woolen skirt from behind and pressing her into the refrigerator door. Then he notices the snapshots attached to the front of the fridge with magnets—a middle-aged couple on a country front porch; a marine, possibly a brother, in uniform; a young girl in polio leg braces leaning up against a tree beside a sunny-faced teenage Gretchen. The tableau, the sudden window into her rural upbringing, might have given his longing a new edge, further particularized his lust, but instead he feels it dissipate. He's never felt for one moment fatherly toward her until now, as she rinses off a handful of frostbitten ice cubes and divides them equally between two glasses.

When they have their drinks, they take them into the living room and she puts on a jazz album for Marty's benefit—Miles Davis's *Blue Haze*. He gets her talking about her childhood in Michigan. The sister with polio who still lives at home with her Lutheran parents, the brother who served in Korea and now runs his own appliance store in Kalamazoo. These details siphon off the last of Marty's desire.

As the album bottoms out, Gretchen asks, "You never wanted a family?"

It catches him off guard and he finds himself staring into his drink. He says, "We wanted children very much, but the odds were stacked against us. Both times we already had names picked out, two separate lists that I kept in my pocket at all times." He takes a sip of his drink and looks up at the wall.

She says, "Oh, God, I'm so sorry, Marty. I had no idea."

The sound of his first name is alive with intimacy and he hopes that tonight—the near miss—won't ruin their productive working relationship. He can feel himself folding up the old childless ache just like that, glancing one more time at her fridge covered in photos and thinking of his own blank refrigerator door.

When the silence unravels, she gets up and says she'll make him some coffee for the road. A while later he's standing in the doorway and kissing her on the cheek. "Thanks for helping me celebrate," he says. As she closes the door, she bites her bottom lip and looks down at the scuffed floorboards, slightly embarrassed by what she's laid before him.

HE HEADS WEST THROUGH the quiet of the Village and then north along the Hudson, the water dotted with fishing boats and the murmuring lights of the Jersey shoreline. He feels lightened, as if he's narrowly escaped something terrible in the world. These streets belong to someone else's map of the city, but he feels suddenly fond of them. He sees taxis going by but lets them pass. He wants to walk as far as he can before going home to begin the next phase of his life. He wanders into the flower district, where men in coveralls unload blooms from truck beds and florists are preparing their stores for business. He convinces one of the deliverymen to sell him a bunch of flowers in newspaper, but he only has a twenty-dollar bill, so he gestures for the man to keep the change and walks some more, taking in the strange sights of Sixth Avenue over the crown of his gardenias. A locksmith's window with a vein of cracked glass, a dry cleaner's with a single blanched shirt hanging in front. He stops for a moment to consider the forlorn, white shirt, finds himself wondering about the man who once owned it. Then he turns and flags down a taxi heading north.

He walks into his building lobby as quietly as possible, nodding to the night watchman. In the private elevator he takes off his shoes and carries them inside when he gets to 12. The penthouse is quiet and he takes the stairs in his stocking feet. Carraway doesn't bark and he suspects he'll find his wife and dog curled and asleep in bed. At the top of the stairs he rests the flowers on a hall stand and continues down to their bedroom. As suspected, he finds Rachel in bed sleeping, the dog at her feet. The bedside lamp is still on and she has a book splayed across her chest. He can tell that she stayed awake as long as possible and now the guilt courses through him. Although he didn't sleep with Gretchen, he briefly intended to, and now he has to carry that. She startles when he opens the bathroom door and she begins talking, though he knows she isn't awake. The sleeping tablets do this to her, dredge words from her stupefied dreams. "Nobody likes that house . . . It smells like burnt toast," she says. He stands in the doorway of the bathroom and looks at his wife's face as she talks up at the ceiling. "The stairs don't lead anywhere for one thing . . ." He lets his eyes move to the painting and the girl standing beside the birch. It never fails to still his thoughts, this moment of wintry suspension. Then he notices something odd about the outer edge of the frame. For years he's watched the antique copper nails turn verdigris inside the flesh of the wood, afraid they would eventually cause rust damage that would tarnish the canvas. He'd always thought that he would need to get the painting reframed and remounted. But now he can't see the nails. The outside edge of the frame is roughhewn and flecked with gold paint but he cannot detect a single nailhead. Quietly, he lifts the painting from the wall and carefully carries it into the bathroom. He closes the door and switches on the light. Resting the edge of the painting against the bath mat, he runs his hand back and forth, following the grain of the wood. It occurs to him that Rachel has secretly had the painting cleaned and reframed and this creates in him a moment of terrified obligation. But when he turns the painting to face him it looks dirtier than ever, the scene fogged beneath layers of antique varnish.

Sydney

JULY 2000

WHAT A SAD LITTLE PARTY. Ellie thinks it while she's standing alone in her kitchen with a tray of food in her hands. Olives and Marcona almonds, a circle of water crackers with some aged Dutch Gouda in the center. There's nothing wrong with the spread—it's the sight of those five people standing awkwardly out on her veranda that sets something off in her. They're nominally here to celebrate her recent lifetime achievement award from the Women's Caucus for Art and the new edition of her book—*Dutch Women Painters in the Golden Age*. Two female colleagues from Sydney University, her sister up from the Blue Mountains, an art history graduate student, and an old friend from her boarding school days. Three years back in Sydney and this is all she can drum up. They stand out there with glasses of wine in hand, talking about the upcoming Olympics and watching the rosellas skirl in the treetops. At least the view is good.

She ferries the plate of food out to her guests and tells them the quiche will be a few more minutes. She doesn't even like quiche, but Kate had insisted and read out their dead mother's recipe over the phone. How did she become a woman in her sixties who serves ham and cheese quiche to people she's holding captive? The gathering was Kate's idea, but Ellie did all the inviting and organizing and now she feels certain it was an imposition. Drive an hour or two on your weekend, catch a ferry over to Scotland Island, drink some cabernet, admire my view and my accomplishments. She heads back inside on the pretext of more wine. As she goes in, she hears Michael, her graduate student, trying to strike up a conversation with her sister. Kate is a retired actuary and competitive bridge player. It begins and ends with a tentative *So are you into art as well?* because Kate either doesn't hear him or ignores him entirely, already narrating one of the rosella sorties as the birds swoop down from a treetop to the tray of seeds attached to the railing. Ellie closes the sliding glass door as Michael looks down into the glassy bay. The two art historians have colonized the other end of the veranda, their backs to the view, arms folded, deep in speculation, or perhaps airing the latest campus scandal.

She sometimes wonders whether she bought this house with exile in mind. Perched among blue gums and overgrown sedge at the head of a sandstone gully, the house rises to a view of Pittwater on stilts. She bought it three years ago after fleeing her failed marriage in London and receiving a job offer from Sydney University. Everyone, her realtor included, had tried to talk her out of the purchase. He'd called Scotland Island the little piece of Sydney paradise nobody wanted to buy. But she'd changed her life to accommodate the ferry ride and hour-long commute to the city, adjusted her teaching schedule so that she went to campus only twice a week. Most of the time she loves the isolation. And the house itself—cathedral ceilings and a wall of glass overlooking the bay—always buoys her spirits. On sunny mornings, she likes to stand out on the veranda in her robe with a pair of field binoculars and observe the waterways and shorelines, the estuaries and coppery mangrove creeks that flow in from Towlers Bay. The airy, stoic house and its impractical location remind her daily that nobody has any claims on her. She has broken free. And yet here she is with an exact replica of a social life out on her veranda, but not the thing itself.

She's back in the kitchen when the wall-mounted phone rings. Her first thought is that it's the chair of her department, sending along his apologies, but instead it's Max Culkins, the director of the Art Gallery of New South Wales, calling from the airport. He's on his way to Beijing to speak at a conference. Even though she's curating an exhibition on seventeenth-century Dutch women painters that's opening next month at the gallery, she didn't invite Max to her gathering. He's an old-school art dandy in a pinstriped suit, a medieval Asia specialist who still calls himself an orientalist. Ellie had pictured him and her sister together in the same room and decided against inviting him. One less collision of worlds.

He's a little breathless on the phone and Ellie thinks of his nervous habit of wetting his lips with his tongue. It's a tic that punctuates his lectures on clan art of the Ming dynasty. "I'm boarding soon, but I wanted to share the good news. I tracked down the current owner of *At the Edge of a Wood* through some old colleagues at the Met. I telephoned early this morning and asked for the loan directly. Just like that, as if I were asking for cab fare."

She feels her chest tighten, like someone is pushing the heel of their hand between her shoulder blades. She swallows and lets the silence gather for a few seconds. The quiche is burning in the oven—she can smell it, but she's unable to move. She says, "That's marvelous news," but it comes after a long pause and the tone is all wrong. Her mind goes blank. Outside, her old schoolmate has taken up the binoculars and is scanning the bay.

A month ago, Ellie learned that a small private collection in the Netherlands had recently purchased the painting and was willing to loan it for the exhibition. It was due to arrive later in the week. The loan was proof, she felt sure, of Marty de Groot's passing, of an estate sale, that perhaps a widow had finally gotten that grimly beautiful harbinger off the bedroom wall. For a month she's felt relieved, grateful. How is it possible, she thinks, that Max Culkins has not seen the registrar's paper trail for the Dutch loan of the same painting? Then she sees an image of Max walking to the podium without his lecture notes, or the missing button from his shirt cuff, or the times he's called her Ella.

Max says, "I talked you and the gallery up quite a bit and then the chap insisted that he handle all the arrangements at his end. You have to love American philanthropy!"

Ellie coughs away from the phone to steady her voice. She is about to enlighten Max—she's certain of it for a lingering second—that two paintings of the same name, from two different hemispheres, are on their way to his museum. She might call it a baffling mix-up. But instead she says, "And who is this generous fellow?"

"A Mr. Martijn de Groot from Manhattan."

Ellie does the math: somewhere in his eighties, unless there's a male heir with the same name. Through the glass doors she watches as the bay silvers with scales of afternoon sunlight.

"Goes by Marty—a brash sort, but very generous, if you ask me. The picture's been in his family for centuries. Remarkable, really."

The carbonized smell of the quiche makes her feel lightheaded. Max says something that she doesn't quite hear—it's muffled by a boarding announcement at the airport—then he comes back in, as if through static: ". . . apparently the painting is already bequeathed to the Met. They're just waiting for the old codger to die. But this is the best part, Ellie. Marty de Groot insists on bringing the painting himself. He'll be flying out with it sometime before we open. Isn't that something?"

She feels her throat thickening with dread.

Max says, "Speaking of flying, I should head over to my gate. I'll be in touch from Beijing."

Because she's terrified of what her voice might sound like, she hums a goodbye and hangs up the phone. Her kitchen floor is plummeting for a few seconds, an elevator in free fall. She thinks, *I have invited ruin back into my life*. She stares dumbly at the oracle of the old rotary dial telephone, as if it might *unring*. She's been gone long enough that Kate comes bustling in from the veranda to lend a hand. "You're hopeless," she says in a bright, cheery voice. "You went in search of wine and now you're standing there like a lobotomy patient. Ooh, smells like a house fire in here. What have you done to poor old mum's quiche?"

Ellie is jolted into action and opens the oven door. The quiche is smoking and charred beyond recognition. Kate nudges her out of the way, slips on an oven mitt, and pulls it out onto the stovetop. "You really know how to charm your guests," she says. Then she opens the kitchen window to let out some of the smoke. "No fear," she says, crossing to the fridge. "I saw some smoked salmon in here. We'll serve that up." When she pulls the packet of salmon from the refrigerator she finally turns to see Ellie's ashen face. "What's wrong? You look like you need smelling salts."

Ellie says, "I'm getting a terrible migraine. I can barely see."

Kate's face washes with sisterly affection and concern. She touches Ellie's forehead with her wrist, as if checking for a fever. Their mother's migraines were burdensome acts of God that they both resented as girls, but Ellie's—which came on during puberty—were treated with tenderness and precision. Kate used to black out the windows of the old house with blankets if Ellie had an attack when she was back from boarding school. She used to make cold compresses and cups of tea and bring them to Ellie in the darkness of their shared bedroom. Kate says, "Go lie down and I'll bring you some medicine. I'll handle your guests and get them on the four o'clock ferry."

Ellie is shocked by the panic burning in her chest and hands and face. There's something jagged and electrical about it. The aura of a migraine, that first pulse of recognition, is nothing compared to this. She nods and says, "You've always looked after me, Kate. I'm sorry I've spent most of my life on the other side of the world." Kate kisses her cheek and sternly points her toward the back of the house.

Ellie walks toward her bedroom, goes inside, and closes the door. She sits on the bed and looks out the window, obstructed from her guests out on the veranda. A dozen yachts belly out with their spinnakers across the bay, dashing down toward Palm Beach on a steady breeze. Her mind seems to resist the immediate puzzle for a moment and so she finds herself thinking of her father. Whenever she watches the sailboats unfurl or the fishing trawlers come into the bay after a night's catch she thinks about him. He's been dead since before she was forty, but to this day the sound of halyards plinking on metal mastheads, especially at night, brings him back. There he is sleeping in his eighteen-foot ketch, anchored in the Parramatta River just to avoid the domestic claims of his wife and two daughters. Their hatchet-shaped lot in Balmain gave onto a view of the navy yards and industrial docks and she remembers the sight of her father's boat amid the hulking silhouettes of frigates and cargo ships. The darkness pulsed with the sound of ship generators and she always wondered how he could sleep through the night with all that racket. That noise was infinitely preferable, apparently, to the sound of young girls bickering or a wife calling out in her sleep.

She's incredulous that both paintings have coexisted for nearly half a century—a planet and its orbiting moon. Over the years, a few other de Vos paintings have been discovered, one of them authenticated by Ellie, but *At the Edge of a Wood* has remained the crown jewel. The private collection in Leiden had agreed to loan not only it but also another de Vos landscape she has never seen. She wonders if that one is a fake as well. While she listens to the sound of Kate corralling the guests with good humor and smoked salmon she replays in her mind the late 1950s in New York. A panicked escape, then the big push into the straight and narrow. After her dissertation was accepted by her department and some of her papers begun to be published, she took a post teaching at University College London. She had tenure in her early thirties, having walked away from the New York underworld of runners and pickers and dealers as if from a burning house, incredulous and grateful to emerge unscathed.

She didn't know all the circumstances of the painting's return, but she knew that Gabriel had both the copy and the original as of late 1958. In December of that year, Marty de Groot reached out to the public—or the forgers and thieves—like a mogul with a kidnapped child, placing a full-page appeal in the Sunday *Times* and offering a reward of seventy-five thousand dollars. The painting wasn't worth much more than that at the time. She was already in Europe when the ad appeared, and she heard about it months later. Because the painting had never been sold or exhibited, she assumed that the fake had been quietly destroyed or kept as a memento in the de Groot attic. But now, as she watches a yacht come about in a strong gust, she considers all the possibilities, follows them like the branches of some sprawling equation.

One proof entails visions of Gabriel fleeing the country with his reward to live in exile, in Morocco or Brazil, wearing a rumpled cream linen suit. Another version sees him spending years in a Rikers Island jail cell, extradited and disgraced, before teaching art appreciation to pensioners at night school. For a decade after the incident, she'd been so busy constructing a new life for herself and projecting onto Gabriel's unknown fate that she'd either ignored or denied a rather obvious and elegant solution: Gabriel returns the original painting to Marty de Groot, collects the reward, keeps the fake, and sits on it until, forty-two years later, he's cash-strapped and desperate to sell. He finds a small private museum in Leiden, thinking Marty de Groot is probably dead and the scandal forgotten. It has the audacity and simplicity of mathematical truth. And if it is true, she can't help admiring the calculated restraint of Gabriel sitting on the painting all this time.

SHE DOESN'T LEAVE THE ISLAND UNTIL Wednesday, when she has to teach and the courier is due to arrive at the museum with the Leiden paintings. Whatever she does next, she feels certain this is the beginning of how it all ends. She barely eats, drinks too much wine, falls asleep out on the veranda in a deck chair. Her dreams are lifted from a Fellini film—full of ticking clocks, abandoned houses, inscrutable strangers, doors loosed from their hinges. She is forever hearing the sound of turbines, of jets coming in to land.

Early one morning she wakes in a panic and decides to send Max Culkins an e-mail. She wishes she hadn't incriminated herself by saying *marvelous news* on the phone to him. He will soon discover the paper trail—not to mention the paintings—and wonder why she hadn't told him.

Dear Max,
Hope you're enjoying the conference in China. I'm embarrassed to say that I was a bit out of it the other night when you called. People were over and I was distracted. Anyway, somehow we seem to have two copies of the same de Vos coming to the gallery for the exhibition. A double-up on the New York picture. No idea how that happened . . . but I'll get to the bottom of it. Probably a faulty attribution out of Leiden. By the way, Leiden also claims to have another de Vos landscape. So we'll see. Anyway, let me know if you want to strategize.
Best—
Ellie

After she sends the e-mail, she wonders if the word *strategize* is too cold and calculating. She waits to see what will happen next. Max never responds directly, but later that day she gets e-mails from the curatorial staff that suggest they are all in the know. One e-mail from Mandy, the registrar, has a subject line that reads "The Same Painting Twice." The body reads: *I think Max wants to tread lightly in case rumour of a forgery gets out before the exhibition opens. Also, the poor old sod's retiring next year, so everything is hush-hush. We're under strict instructions not to let on we know anything with either of the lenders. Max says he'll handle it personally when he gets back from China.*

Ellie has bought herself some time, recovered from the ridiculous use of the word *marvelous*, but now there's the looming matter of Marty de Groot crossing the international date line. She morbidly tries to conjure the worst of the headlines if she's exposed. The national papers might go with something restrained like "Feminist Art Scholar Forges Her Way to Prominence," while her hometown tabloid, *The Daily Telegraph*, would settle for "Art Maven Uncovered as Crook."

She has visions of federal police—she doesn't know why they're federal—showing up to a lecture she's giving on Frans Hals. They wait at the back of the auditorium until she's done, politely escorting her across the quadrangle without handcuffs. Or she sees herself being called into a meeting with her faculty dean and a plainclothes detective. She finds herself dialing up her modem to connect to Internet legal advice sites, conducting searches in the middle of the night, researching the statute of limitations and international extradition treaties and case history for forgeries. There's no reason to be concerned about a criminal case, but she feels hollowed out by the specter of Marty de Groot's arrival.

The threat of being found out makes her want to take stock, to peer into the corners of her life for broader deceits. Is she a fundamentally flawed person? She fixates on small lapses, as if they might reveal something larger. Unanswered e-mails, promising students she could have given more attention to, art reviews she's published that could have been more evenhanded. She tries to uncover a bread-crumb trail of moral failure, a trail that perhaps began with her forgery, or even before, with the shoplifting excursions at boarding school. But the trail peters out after 1957. The truth is she became tirelessly disciplined and scrupulous as an academic; she forever felt the aftermath of her decision to copy the painting for money, experienced the fact of having been spared as viscerally as survivor's guilt. She was always trying to make amends. Her art-dealing ex-husband, Sebastian, liked to make gentle fun of her at dinner parties, because in two decades he'd never seen her speed or jaywalk or take a shortcut on her taxes. What's happened to that convict blood of yours, he would chide, and she would smile demurely and think about her undeniable role in the theft of a landmark painting.

AS SHE CASTS ABOUT for evidence of her flawed character, she happens upon something unexpected. At the edges of her carefully managed life, at the center of her thin social circles, is a kind of shocking loneliness. It's been there for years, even back in England. Up until now she'd thought there was liberation in solitude. She could stay in town after lectures, go see a foreign film at the Dendy, and not worry about bumping into ex-lovers or lapsed friends while eating a large popcorn in the glimmering desolation of a weekday matinee. Until Sunday afternoon, she'd thought that was real freedom. Now it seems to her like a narrow and stingy way to live.

Then she recalls the solo sightseeing trips she's done over the last three years, the tours of the old stomping grounds. A gleeful tourist in her own haunted homeland. How to explain those? The pub in Balmain where her father held court, the family lot down by the navy yards. Her first year back, she roamed the city as if struck by nostalgia. She's at a loss to explain the dozen or so trips she made across the harbor, shadowing her father's ferry routes to Manly and Taronga Zoo. This was a man who barely knew she breathed the same air that he did. The one time her father let her ride along in the wheelhouse of the *South Steyne* she got terribly seasick and clutched her sketchbook the whole time. This was before the nuns and the priests, before the onslaught of puberty. During the summer the harbor smelled of kelp and iodine and she couldn't wait to get off the boat in Manly. She snuck off for a quick swim in the roped-off area beside the terminal and a lightning tour of the shark aquarium and the Fun Pier. She'd taken some money from her mother's bedside table (had the moral failures started as far back as that?) and was determined to put it to good use. Half an hour later she emerged from the Ghost Train breathless with fear and hurrying back to make the scheduled departure of her father's boat. She stood on the dock in her damp swimsuit as the *South Steyne* pulled away, the water churning and foaming in the ferry's wake. It was two hours before his boat returned. She sat patiently and watched bare-chested boys dive for coins from the giant wooden pylons. Her father never mentioned the incident, but she never forgot the sense that the world—and her father—was indifferent to her actions and inclinations. The clocks didn't stop running just because something struck her fancy. He never asked her to ride along again.

All this floats about her—another time and city. A lifetime has elapsed but this is where things began, where the lamps were lit and the curtains drawn. Ellie the forger took root somewhere here, but *where*? The old house in Balmain with its bullnose veranda and loose-framed windows was leveled years ago, a brick cube of apartments in its place, a rogue banana tree and a flaming jacaranda the only visible reminders of that time. Everything has moved on, but she has come back in search of the brooding teenage girl who smelled like acetone. The past is more alive to her than the present, she realizes, and the thought is suffocating. The invitation to curate the exhibition for the Art Gallery of New South Wales was supposed to be her way forward, the beginning of widening her circle of friends and acquaintances, of rejoining the ranks of the living. Instead, it's become the way back to the wreckage of the past.

ON WEDNESDAY AFTERNOON, after delivering a lecture on Judith Leyster, Ellie receives a phone call from the art gallery, letting her know that the Dutch courier has arrived at Mascot airport with the two paintings from Leiden. She estimates there are about twenty-four hours before the packing cases are opened and her forgery is carefully removed. Over the past few months, as the paintings for the exhibition have trickled in from the lenders, the protocol has been perfected—the museum van with security guards and the collections registrar meet the courier, the cases are delivered to the museum for safekeeping, the courier is taken to his or her hotel, and everyone reconvenes the next day for the opening, allowing the paintings time to warm back up to room temperature after many hours in the hold of a plane. She tells the curatorial assistant that she'll come over to meet the courier and to expect her shortly. Normally, she waits until the opening of the cases to meet the couriers. These people are usually curators or conservators from the lending institution and they arrive harried and jet-lagged, rif-fling through binders of paperwork and eager to be off the clock for the first time in days. But because they have personally overseen the packing at the other end, Ellie knows they have intimate knowledge of the paintings inside. She wants to see for herself what the Dutch courier knows.

Usually she leaves her car in the faculty parking lot and takes the train to the St. James station for the short walk through the Domain, but today she bustles out onto King Street to find a taxi. The city streets have taken on a mineral sheen after a downpour and everything smells of iron. While she waits for a cab heading in the right direction she reminds herself to take note of the light, the flush of pink over in the west. She's forever telling her students to notice the light, but for three days she's seen nothing around her. She hails a cab and climbs in. Something about the Olympics and the city's state of readiness has been in the papers, and the taxi driver delivers a monologue about the city being caught with its pants down around its ankles. She looks out the window and notices the sections of Cleveland Street gone to rot, the filigreed metal balconies of the shambling terraces like rusted lacework, the grimy tiled pub facades, the windows of the Lebanese restaurants filmed with grease. This is old Sydney, her father's town of grit and mildew. The driver is talking about the general lack of courtesy in the early days of the twenty-first century as they near the gallery. She has him go around the back to the loading dock and pays the fare.

A handful of store men are milling around the loading dock in dustcoats. The museum employs two full-time packers, two installation technicians, and a carpenter. They all work for Quentin La Forge, a meticulous man in his sixties who calls himself Chief Handler. Everyone else calls him Q. When Ellie arrives, she finds him sitting in his glassed-in office, bifocals perched on his head, dunking biscuits into a cup of tea and picking through the newspaper. Over the past year, while the exhibit has slowly fallen into place, Ellie has learned to kiss the papal ring of the shippers and handlers. They mean the difference between timeliness and inexplicable delay. She brings them Mars bars and hands out movie passes when one of them has a birthday. In her planner, she's written down their full names, mobile phone numbers, and birthdays. Q's office is a fortress of industrial-green filing cabinets and laminated diagrams on the walls that chart the Dynamic Cushioning Curve or the insulation properties of various woods and polymers. Q is roughly Ellie's age but of another time—a man of pressed handkerchiefs and pomade who smells of wood glue. He wears a navy dustcoat with his monogrammed initials above a pocket crammed with mechanical pencils.

She plunks down in the cracked swivel chair in front of his neatly arranged desk. He looks up, nods, takes a soggy bite from a dunked Scotch Finger biscuit.

"So they're in transit?" she says, trying to keep her voice steady.

"What's in transit? Venus? I need a few more specifics, love."

She knows better than to broach a delivery schedule without the requisite three minutes of chitchat. But as they sit there the paintings are en route, she thinks, clearing customs or wending through traffic. She pictures her forgery like some embezzled diamond, sitting snug inside its vapor barrier, encased in layers of glassine and plywood.

She says, "The ones from Leiden."

Chewing, Q says, "Yeah, Mandy and a few of the guards went to meet the Dutch chappie at the airport." He says this with a casualness she finds infuriating. A Caravaggio could come into Mascot and he'd dunk his biscuits and prefer to talk about the weather, horse racing, the footy, really anything but the actual purpose of his job. He could be packing and unpacking plastic souvenirs for all his apparent curiosity. Early on, she'd made the mistake of transposing this apathy to the work itself and remembers her first time watching him build a custom packing case. It was a thing of beauty—every joint, batten, and corner pad perfectly made and aligned, his little wooden trolley of brass fixtures and trunk handles and his hot-melt glue gun at his side as he worked with a headlamp. He listened to the Goldberg Variations while he worked patiently for hours, his attendants fetching him certain chisels and fine-toothed files and cups of tea.

It's also clear to her from his lack of interest that he's not in the loop about a potential forgery coming through his loading dock. Ellie has spent her life around museums and knows that the curatorial staff and packers are vaguely suspicious of each other. The curators and Max Culkins have kept the news from the men in dustcoats.

She wants to ask him what the ETA is, but instead she asks, "How are the grandkids?"

"Yeah, good, took the whole tribe to Bondi on the weekend. We all ate fish and chips at the Icebergs and I even conned one of the boys into a swim."

"Bit cold, isn't it?"

"Rubbish. Gets the heart pumping."

This small talk goes on for a few excruciating minutes. Ellie notices that Q rarely asks about her weekends and plans, as if her island hermitage and childless, divorcée status makes her life inscrutable and a bit unsightly. After a while, the carpenter—a quiet man named Ed—comes into the office to report the arrival of the van from the airport. Q nods and picks up the telephone on his desk and calls upstairs to the head of conservation to announce the news. He says, "The cases are here with the Dutchman." He hangs up the phone, drains his cup of tea, and stands behind his desk. He pats down his dust-coat, checking the pockets, then remembers the bifocals resting above his forehead. He lowers them into place, squinting into the lenses as they suddenly magnify his pale brown eyes. On the side of a filing cabinet hangs a clipboard with the receiving checklist and the signature pages. Q grabs it on the way out and Ellie follows along.

The van has reversed and beeped into the loading bay and two guards get out to open up the rear cargo doors. Mandy, the registrar, is the next to get out, and then a scruffy, long-haired man with a goatee and a tattoo on one forearm emerges in jeans and a T-shirt, holding a small backpack and a bulging manila envelope. Ellie is standing beside the handlers and she hears Q say to his men, "Our courier looks like he's out on parole from Long Bay." The men laugh quietly. Ellie crosses behind the van to get a better look and sees two identical wooden cases, each with caution labels in multiple languages. Mandy and the courier come up the stairs and she introduces him as Hendrik Klapp. He shakes hands with everyone.

"How was the flight?" Ellie asks.

"About six hours too long," he says, opening his envelope of papers.

Q steps forward to assert his domain. "Hendrik, what's your affiliation with the private museum in Leiden?"

"I oversee handling there, among other things."

"Excellent. So you know how these cases were put together? Perhaps you have some diagrams?"

"I made them and packed the art myself," Hendrik says. "Down to the last nail."

Q looks at his underlings, gives them a stagey wink. "I do hope there are no nails."

"Of course. I was using an expression."

The hostility between Hendrik and Q is immediate.

Hendrik says, "Even though the cases are about one hundred pounds each, I recommend using a hydraulic hand truck to remove them from the vehicle. The cases are fitted with skids on the bottom."

With his backpack, surly disposition, and his pale, gaunt face, Hendrik looks like he's auditioning for a film role as a Dutch hacker. Ellie suspects he doesn't mean to sound arrogant or bossy; it's just the curse of a certain nonnative English speaker, a kind of mechanical efficiency that comes off as rude. But she also knows Q and his men aren't making any such calculations or allowances. Hendrik has become a scab on the knee of a Wednesday afternoon and they're eager to pick at it.

Ed goes to fetch the hand truck while the packer and the framer get inside the van to slide the cases to the rear. The ramp is perfectly level with the dock so that Ed can easily snug the tines of the hand truck beneath the cases, between the wooden skids. He lifts each case six inches from the ground and rolls it onto the dock. Normal practice is to leave the packing crates in the exhibition space overnight and then open them in the courier's presence for immediate hanging. But water damage to a skylight and ongoing repairs has meant that none of the exhibition space is available yet. All of the paintings will hang in storage until the gallery is ready. Ellie explains all this to Hendrik as the crates are wheeled toward the storage room. He stares at her, a look of incomprehension on his face.

Ellie can see from the outside of the cases, from the carefully planed corners and the countersunk brass screws and the barcode stickers, that these are exceptionally well made. Q is accustomed to receiving cases that sometimes look like they've been dropped from a height. She watches as he walks around the cases warily, like he's sizing up an unknown dog. Hendrik stands back with his bundle of papers. Ellie can tell that Q is impressed with the workmanship of the cases but also a little riled.

Abruptly, Hendrik says, "This is highly unusual, not putting them in the gallery space."

"We did notify your institution of the delay," Q says.

Hendrik looks down at his paperwork. "Well, I will need signatures of receipt and also to know of the security detail for the overnight period." He looks up at a clock on the wall. "I will return at this time tomorrow."

Ellie wishes, for his own sake, that he could stop sounding like a German spy from a World War II movie. Q takes the paperwork and a pen from Hendrik and studies the receipt under one of the lights. After a moment, he says, "We'll have to make some amendments to this, if that's all right. For starters, we won't know what's in these cases until tomorrow. Could be two boxes of rocks for all we know. So this part here where it lists the painting descriptions and asks for a signature, we'll have to change the wording to the cases with the barcodes you've provided. We'll sign the rest after we open our presents tomorrow. How does that sound?"

"That will be fine."

Q continues to flip through the bundle of papers. "Good. And we have our own condition report we'll use tomorrow. In addition to the Leiden one."

"Naturally."

It occurs to Ellie that these loans are never quite received with gratitude at the loading dock. It's always just another crate to unpack.

Q makes a few wording changes to the receipt form and both he and Hendrik initial the changes before signing. Mandy takes a copy of the paperwork and heads upstairs, but not before giving Ellie a knowing glance.

Turning to Ellie, Hendrik asks, "Is it possible to use your fax machine to send this to Leiden?"

"Of course," Ellie says. "I'll take you upstairs to the office. You can also speak to the head of security if you like."

"That would be perfect." Hendrik turns one more time in the direction of his packing cases and then says to Q and his men, "Gentlemen, I will see you all tomorrow."

As they walk out of the shipping and receiving area Ellie can feel the men watching them leave. She knows there will be impersonations of Hendrik at the pub in a couple of hours, that he'll be added to Q's ledger of foreign upstarts who didn't show him the proper respect.

Hendrik faxes his forms to Leiden with some country code help from one of the admins. Then Ellie takes him to meet the head of security, who suffers him with the same impatience as Q. Satisfied with the outcome and checking things off his prepared list, Hendrik says that he's ready to go to the hotel and could he order a taxi.

"We're putting you up at a small hotel in the Rocks, an old part of Sydney right on the water. I'd be happy to take you down there, if you're up for a walk. Do you have other luggage in the van?"

"This is it," he says, gesturing to his backpack slung over one shoulder.

Ellie estimates that he couldn't have more than a change of clothes in there.

"How long are you staying?"

"Just a few days. Not really enough to do any sightseeing."

"Have you been to Australia before?"

"Never."

"I'll give you a short list of must-sees in the city."

She leads him out under the arched ceilings and skylights to the main entrance and they head down toward the botanic gardens. It's only a little after four but already nearing dusk. A heavy bank of clouds has formed in the west. Through the trees, Ellie watches as a sunburst streaks through and turns the harbor from slate to sapphire and back again. She remembers how much she likes the city in winter. The pale sunshine in the mornings, the bouts of rain, the strange rockeries of sandstone and ferns along the waterfront, the smell of moss that always makes her think of grottoes and her early Arcadian landscapes. She misses painting, feels its absence like a great loss. They walk between flowerbeds of hibiscus and golden banksia and she wonders how the gardens look to Hendrik, to a Dutchman accustomed to tulips and teahouses nestled in pristine woodlands. She spent time in the Netherlands teaching and researching over the years and remembers the Dutch with fondness. She also recalls their sturdy, unflappable manner and their occasional brusqueness.

They pass through a palm grove where grey-headed flying foxes hang below the fronds, ravaging pods and fruit and dropping seeds on the leaves below. Other bats are taking off above the trees to forage for the night, beating their leathery wings into a sudden flurry. Hendrik stops walking and cranes up. Ellie was gone long enough from Australia to see it through his eyes—a colony of southern vampires marauding in the treetops. At the museum, Ellie's heard talk of some relocation program in the works, of predawn noise disturbance to stop the bats from roosting. They continue walking, past hoop pines and swamp mahoganies that were planted in the early 1800s, a fact Ellie would never share with a European visitor. The Amsterdam house she lived in for a summer researching Sara de Vos was four hundred years old, with the original gable clock still installed and working.

They talk about Dutch museums and cities, but Ellie doesn't let on she once lived in Amsterdam, for fear of an inquisition. By the time they pass out of the lower gardens, dusk has hardened the shadows between the office towers and there's an exodus of commuters streaming down toward

Circular Quay. Hendrik strides along with his backpack, Sydney's jewels—harbor, opera house, bridge—laid out neatly for his consideration, all of them in a single line of sight.

Ellie says, "It's very generous of your museum to make this loan."

"The Hofje van Foort is trying to widen its reputation."

His breath punches behind the formal Dutch name and she assumes it's to assert his authority. Or perhaps he thinks she's nervous about the pronunciation. All the Dutch she knows is strictly academic and used for parsing monographs; even during her time in Holland she found it hard to find locals who would speak Dutch with her. The running joke with her colleagues was that Dutch taxi drivers—often driving black Mercedes in dark suits, like embassy chauffeurs—spoke better English than the Australian expats.

Hendrik says, "It's good press for us. I assume we'll be featured in your program?"

"Prominently," Ellie says. A beat later, she asks, "When did your gallery acquire the paintings?"

"My employer bought the funeral scene some years ago but kept it a secret. Mr. van Foort wanted a second de Vos before showing the pair. It was like he wanted a couple to arrive at the same dinner party together."

"How romantic," she says. "And when did he purchase *At the Edge of a Wood*?"

"It came on the market recently." Hendrik suddenly seems evasive, looking down at his feet.

She pictures a much older Gabriel in a shabby raincoat in Leiden, sitting in a café with a yellowed espionage novel and a forgery wrapped in brown paper, killing time before his appointment at the private gallery. She doesn't want to sound like she's prying, so she changes her tactic. Casually, she says, "I'm so surprised about the new discovery . . . a funeral scene, you say?"

"Yes," he says, "*Winter with a Child's Funeral Procession*. An outdoor scene, painted in 1637."

"Another outdoor scene? I don't know of anything for de Vos after 1636."

"Ah, yes, well, you might have to revise your book."

This sounds like a dig, but it's hard to tell. If she asks him whether he's read her book about seventeenth-century Dutch women painters she risks sounding vain. Instead, she asks, "Where was it found?"

"Mr. van Foort keeps those details to himself. Trade secrets. I like to think it's something like Coco Chanel's old suite at the Ritz Hotel in Paris because that would be straight from a Disney movie!" He says this with sudden glee, as if he's landed a joke that's inside her cultural tent. Another thing she recalls about her Dutch friends is that they were listening to pop music a decade beyond its prime.

Ellie says, "Well, Paris would make more sense than Cincinnati, which is where two other de Vos paintings have ended up."

Without expression, he says, "You believe she stopped painting in 1636." It's not a question so much as a statement of her fallacy.

They're walking through the bustle of Circular Quay during rush hour. Ferries are filling up as she leads him across the grain of pedestrian traffic. A few buskers are performing along the handrail by the water, including a troupe of painted Aboriginal dancers. The city is built for tourists, Ellie thinks. When they get into a clearing, she says, "From a few letters and archival documents we know that Sara de Vos was raised in Amsterdam, the daughter of a landscape painter but she trained in still life. She married a landscape painter from Haarlem, lived with her husband and child for some years near the Kalverstraat. The child, a daughter, died young, possibly from the plague. We don't have death records for either Sara or the husband. The guild records are mostly destroyed for that period but we know from court dockets and auction receipts that the couple was going bankrupt after the daughter's death. Her name was Kathrijn. She's buried in a pauper's grave behind a church in Amsterdam. Sorry, I'm prattling . . ."

Hendrik looks at her for the first time in several minutes. In the falling dark, it's hard for her to tell whether it's smugness or knowing when he says, "But no graves for the parents have been found . . . so de Vos could have lived another twenty years and painted many more works?"

"Technically that's true. Though I've always suspected *At the Edge of a Wood* was the high-water mark. It might have tapered off after that."

"This new painting might throw that into doubt."

"If it's really hers."

"Well, you are the expert and will have to judge for yourself. But your theory may need some revising."

In a burst of vindictiveness, she imagines adding that, by the way, not only is the new landscape probably a misattribution, but also I'm pretty sure your *At the Edge of a Wood* is a fake I painted in my midtwenties.

But they're already on the outskirts of the Rocks and she gets distracted by the rowdiness of the pubs overflowing with office workers, some of them spilling out onto the street. Ellie points to the Russell Hotel, a stone building with a turret that hugs the corner. It's not flash by any means, but cozy, within budget, and in the thick of things. It's where they put all the couriers; the VIPs stay at one of the five stars at the other end of the quay. They go inside and stand for a moment in the quaintly shabby Victorian lobby.

Ellie says, "Everything should be set up under the gallery's account." She takes a business card from her purse. "Call me if you need anything."

"Thank you," Hendrik says.

"I hope you get some sleep. We'll send a taxi for you in the morning. Shall we say eleven?"

Hendrik looks at his watch and shakes his head. "Forgot to change my watch. Apparently I'm still in the Netherlands. Yes, eleven will be fine."

Ellie says good night and walks out onto the street. The thought of taking a taxi or train back to the university and the long drive to Pittwater exhausts her. She strolls along the quay and contemplates her options. On a whim, she heads inside the InterContinental and crosses the vaulted atrium lounge, the interior of the old treasury building, and stands at the front desk. The impulsiveness of it shocks her. A corner room with a view will cost her close to four hundred dollars, but she produces her credit card unflinchingly. The desk clerk is young,

Asian, and beautiful, and Ellie's surprised by how easily she lies to the woman, telling her she's just arrived from London and her luggage is delayed. The woman tells her that the concierge would be happy to arrange some clothes bought on her behalf if she phones down with her sizes. Ellie thanks her and takes the room key. She already knows she'll order room service and request a new blouse in the morning before heading back to the gallery for the case opening.

AT THE GALLERY THE NEXT DAY, Hendrik oversees the opening with a set of blueprints in his hands, as if he's built two miniature houses instead of two wooden boxes. He asks for a reading of the relative humidity before they begin the unpacking. Q obliges and gets to work on the bolting system with a hand wrench. He's a stickler for manual wrenches and drills, resorts to power tools only in a pinch. Ellie stands watching in her new blouse behind a yellow line, shoulder to shoulder with a handful of dubious curatorial staff and conservators. Word of the potential forgery has dashed their hopes that the other painting is a newly discovered work in the de Vos oeuvre. And there's still no official word from Max Culkins in China on how he intends to handle the delicate situation.

As Q begins to dismantle the first case, it becomes apparent that the boxes themselves are works of art. When he removes the foam-padded face board, Ellie sees the architecture as a cross-section—corner pads, a thick band of foam on the bottom, an inner case of half-inch plywood cradled at the center. Q removes the inner case and places it on a stainless-steel table. By now, Hendrik has been summoned to his side. In a rare act of humility, Q asks Hendrik if he'd like to do the honors of opening the first inner case—the equivalent of washing the man's feet. Apparently, in the span of five minutes, Hendrik has been elevated to the status of respected peer. Hendrik accepts, lamenting the fact that he couldn't bring his own tools on the plane. He crosses to Q's workbench and selects a small hammer, a chisel, and a specially designed cutter. Q raises the worktable to the appropriate height and Hendrik begins to chisel along the glued seam of the inner case. He taps away gently at the plywood corners and pries the case open to reveal another layer of polyethylene. Hendrik takes out the wrapped painting—about two foot square plus the frame—and lays it flat.

As the foam and wood and tape are all peeled away, Ellie can feel her cheeks flush. She remembers in vivid detail how she made the fake, how she built up one layer at a time. She knows the tints and textures as if she'd created them yesterday—the impasto of the tree bark, the luminous underglow of the frozen river, the bone-white of the girl's left hand against the blue-white of the snow. She also remembers the way she mishandled the bright yellows in the skaters' scarves. In the late 1950s, very few in the conservation world knew about lead-tin yellow, a pigment favored by Dutch Masters that produces metallic soaps over time. To capture the bright, gritty texture, she'd mixed sand with synthetic chrome yellow, a mistake that has weighed on her ever since lead-tin yellow was rediscovered in the conservation journals. A kind of technical remorse.

Eventually, Hendrik holds *At the Edge of a Wood* up for all to see. Ellie steps in front of the yellow line and Q permits it.

The painting is propped at a slight angle and the staff members are allowed to approach it as the lights are dimmed for better viewing. She takes in the painting from a distance of three feet. Her youthful habit of consuming a picture just inches from its aromatic surface died a long time ago. Sebastian, when they were first dating, had once called it an affectation and she could never bring herself to do it again. His offhanded comment should have been a sign of future cruelties and standards of perfection, but instead she'd quickly agreed with his assessment and was grateful for his candor. She stares at the canvas, her feet anchored in place, afraid to come closer. All these years later, it strikes her that she'd dutifully copied everything that gave the original movement and life. She'd fogged it with antique varnish to create the illusion of age, but somehow she still managed to capture the breathing presence of Sara herself.

Q has no apparent interest in the painting itself and has already turned to the other packing case. The curators are urged to stand again behind the yellow line, for reasons that Ellie can't discern. She doesn't risk disobeying Q, so the five of them—three with Ph.D.s—get back behind the line and wait to be invited forward again. Now Q and Hendrik work in unison, the younger deferring to the older, then the borrower deferring to the lender in some obscure packers' ritual. They lift the inner case out—it appears to be about the same size as *At the Edge of a Wood*—and lay it flat under the lights. As they unwrap the foam and glassine, the first edges of frame become visible—gilded and rippled, a Florentine reframing of the eighteenth century. Q looks up at the staff and nods for them to come forward. As art experts, each in their own right, Ellie suspects that none of them will talk about what they see until they've absorbed it, until they've had a chance to develop serious opinions or doubts about the potential fake and the new attribution. For all they know Marty de Groot is the one bringing the forgery.

Ellie notices Hendrik watching her as she moves closer to the painting. A dozen funeral-goers tramp down a hill from a slate-roofed church, its windows blackened against the pall of midwinter. Village children clamber along the frozen riverbank, apart from their parents, flanking the procession with several gamboling dogs. A few villagers stand on the ice, stilled by the harbinger of a child's coffin. The river and the woods and the clouds are unmistakably Sara's, but the whole scene is painted from above, as if from a steeple or treetop. She's seeing this from a height, Ellie thinks, and it lends the scene an air of detachment, the perspective of an indifferent God. Before she's finished taking it in fully, Hendrik is standing beside her, sounding rather pleased with himself. "Dated 1637 and signed in the lower left corner."

PART II

Amsterdam

SPRING 1637

AFTER THE TULIP market collapsed in early February, Barent was unable to sell Sara's floral still lifes. Dutchmen who lost everything inside the calyx and corolla of a prized flower didn't want to be reminded of their folly. With their debts mounting, Sara searched in vain for paying workshop apprentices, but without the endorsement of the guild, no students presented themselves. Eventually, she took a job with a seed and bulb export company, painting miniature flowers for their catalogue. With the extra money she sets aside a small amount each week toward the cost of making a birthday cake for Barent, something to lighten his mood. She buys one ingredient at a time and stores them inside a pot, hidden from view. Then, one night in spring, she attends a lecture by a visiting Italian painter in one of the big canal houses and leaves with a pocket full of sugared almonds. She doesn't remember the moment she decided to take the almonds for the top of the cake, but now she walks along with her fingertips grazing them, feeling a burst of guilt and exhilaration.

She walks home in the rain, bundled against the chill and fog. In this wealthy district, the baroque house facades are fronted with pale sandstone, the latticed windows flanked by bright green shutters. The footpath is a tightly packed herringbone of small red bricks, lined with lindens and elms. The casement windowsills are decorated with carved stone flowers and satyrs. She braces herself for walking back into her own neighborhood near the Kalverstraat, for the plank-board walkways and the doctor's office that displays a urinal out front, for the vegetable sellers under awnings, their cabbages rotting slightly in the rain.

After standing to paint tiny flowers all day, sitting inside a lavish canal house was a welcome relief. The lecture hosts, a pair of wine merchants from Paris, stood by while a third-rate landscape painter condescended to the gathered guests, many of them painters, talking about the need to lower the horizon to create scale and drama. She'd sat at the back of the overheated room, her shoes split along one seam, eating as much and as quietly as she could. It's the tail end of Lent and she feels guilty that she's not fasting. Apparently, the French hosts were godless and oblivious to Lent—the tables were laden with haddock slices and bowls of almonds and raisins. She dips her hand back into her pocket to feel the sugar and the dry woodiness of the nuts against her fingers.

Closer to her own neighborhood, people are preparing for the end of Lent. The children of blacksmiths and cobblers are building bonfires on corners that won't be lit for days. Taverns that amount to little more than squalid cellars and innkeepers' entrance halls are taking deliveries of wine and beer, the proprietors filling stone jugs while burly men in leather aprons roll barrels along the cobblestone. It's darker than she's used to, an hour before the watch will emerge for the curfew. The canals are black and slick and she finds herself looking skyward to place the moon. The Lenten theme of deprivation has overtaken the city; the lanterns on several bridges have been extinguished as a yearning for God.

She shouldn't be out alone at this hour and she pulls her hood down over her forehead. Barent had asked her not to go to the lecture, practically pleaded before he left the house with an air of resignation. For months, his moods have been sullen and unpredictable. The ledger is no longer taken out after dinner and he's stopped asking her about the progress of her paintings. She knows he has borrowed money from some of their neighbors—a portrait painter and his embroiderer wife—but he refuses to speak of it.

In the evenings, he comes home from the bookbindery and puts on his dressing gown and goes to sit by the peat-box. At dinnertime, they stand to pray, eat at the ugly wooden table by the window, sing grace without inflection, and pass small eternities of silence while they eat fried eggs and tasteless bread made from bean flour. When she catches his eyes she sees the look of defeat, the humiliation of what life has levied against him. Sometimes, in the middle hours of the night, she wakes to find him sitting by the fire, muttering to himself. He'll be upset with her when she gets in, but soon there'll be a cake in the house, a small respite from all the gloom. She'll set the almonds along the edges of the white icing.

Before the onslaught of the narrow alley that leads to her street, she stops at a furniture maker who has adopted the latest French styles in cabinetmaking. Her own tables and chairs look like they've been cleaved from trees with blunt axes; the furniture in his window is long-lined and supple. Walnut and mahogany varnish, with inlays of ironwood. She stops and admires the display for several minutes, her feet numbing from the damp cold. A wood-paneled room has been created with a finely made desk placed at an angle. A leathered chair has been pulled out and stationery is spread across the surface of the desk, a goose quill laid across it. It looks as if an important letter is about to be written. A silver inkpot awaits. She admires the lathework of the slender desk and chair legs, the glossed lacquer against the dark grain of the wood. The idea of making something solid and practical sometimes appeals to her. There are no figments or catchments of light to contend with. But neither is there the possibility, she thinks, of rendering the smoke of human emotion itself.

At first, when she sees her darkened house she thinks how angry Barent must be. There isn't a lantern burning behind a single window. She removes the iron key from around her neck and fumbles with the lock in the dark. A recent ordinance requires that every twelfth house burn a lantern from its exterior until ten at night, but the nearest beneficiary of this municipal wisdom is nine houses away. She closes the door behind her and steps into the cramped entrance hall. Barent is sitting beside the peat-box wrapped in a blanket. When he looks over at her she sees there is something vacant in his gaze, as if he's looking at an apparition six feet to her left. "I'm sorry

I'm so late. Have you eaten?" When he doesn't answer she says, "It's pitch-black in here." She bustles over to the lantern and lights it with some straw she dips into the peat-box. In the brightening kitchen she sees a letter on the table and an empty bottle of beer. "Thirty days," he says, distractedly, "before they come for me with a warrant from the debtor's prison." She has known this moment would come and yet it seems unfathomable. Kneeling beside him she takes his cold, dry hands in hers and kisses his knuckles. His gaze remains on the embers, shifting across some landscape she cannot see.

A WEEK LATER, Sara arranges to see the overseer of the Amsterdam Guild to plead her case. They are still hardened against Barent, but perhaps she has a chance. It's been more than a year since she and Barent were fined and suspended. Throughout the provinces, the guilds have been cracking down on illegal activity, fining members and residents who traffic in foreign imports or unsanctioned sales. Cheap panels from Antwerp—generic landscapes with red barns and brooding clouds, painted quickly, wet-in-wet—have flooded the market. It's possible to walk into a cobbler's storeroom and see a dozen of these flimsily painted scenes on each wall.

Because she doesn't have the fare for a carriage or barouche, she walks in the blustery spring weather toward Nieuwmarkt. The guild holds its meetings and archives in the Waaggebouw, a brick-and-turret weigh house that once formed part of the city's gate. Twenty-five years ago, when Amsterdam tore down its walls to expand, the Waaggebouw was given over to the business of commercial weighing and various guildhalls on the top floor—blacksmiths, painters, masons, and surgeons. Joost Blim, the chief overseer of the Amsterdam Guild of St. Luke, is a housepainter with political aspirations and at the end of his two-year tenure. He was only just coming to power when Sara's guild membership was suspended, so she's meeting him for the first time. He granted a meeting in his letter but said that due to renovations in the guildhall they would have to meet next door, in the "spacious gathering room of our illustrious friends, the surgeons."

The "gathering room" turns out to be the surgeon guild's anatomical theater, over which presides Rembrandt's *The Anatomy Lesson of Dr. Nicolaes Tulp.* Sara can't help thinking this is no accident, that the overseer wants to castigate her at the altar of St. Luke's most famous living member. Rembrandt has largely taken over the portrait scene since moving from Leiden to Amsterdam six years ago. A few years after his arrival, he was accepted as a burgher of the city and admitted to the guild's ranks.

The guild servant, Theophilus Tromp, is a wiry, birdlike engraver in a doublet. He greets her at the top of the stone stairwell, and then she's left alone in the theater while he fetches the overseer. She sits down at one end of a long wooden table, perhaps the same table where cadavers are laid out. Under Nicolaes Tulp's supervision, the surgeon's guild has been holding annual dissections in the theater and charging admission from physicians and curious laymen. The public displays happen in the wintertime, when colder temperatures better preserve a hanged criminal's body. Tulp is a man on the ascent; as city anatomist he is said to have personally signed the fitness reports of the first settlers in New Netherland. With mayoral aspirations, he regularly publishes essays in the newspaper about apothecary reform and the plague and the circulatory powers of human blood.

She has heard about but never seen the painting before and she takes it in with cold scrutiny. The name of the executed man was Aris Kindt; she remembers hearing that. A petty thief who'd been conveniently executed an hour before the scheduled dissection and portrait "sitting." Descartes was supposed to be somewhere in that shadowy audience of onlookers, though she cynically thinks he isn't in the painting because he didn't commission Rembrandt to feature him among the surgeons. What was the philosopher and mathematician thinking as he sat on one of the wooden benches? That the body was so much cabinetry for the vapors of the soul?

She notes how the surgeons are looking at the splayed anatomy textbook or directly at the viewer, as if the corpse itself is incidental. Despite the painter's lifelike depiction—the faces mired in reflection, the translucent eyes—the hanged man's dissected left hand and arm are sized beyond all reasonable proportion. His chest juts upward, barreled in rigor mortis, and his half-opened mouth is rife with shadow. At first, Sara thinks Rembrandt is celebrating the rarefied knowledge of the surgeons, but then she wonders whether the enlarged hand and the cadaver's monstrous face aren't a criticism, a protest against the harrowing of the flesh. She feels herself soften. Not toward the painting but toward the painter.

Mr. Tromp comes back into the room with a book in a kidskin cover. Joost Blim, a portly, blunt-faced man, walks a few paces behind him, head down, hands clasped over a ponderous belly. He dresses more like an aristocrat than a housepainter—long breeches with knotted ribbons, shoes fastened by rosettes, a short tunic with a slash in the back for a rapier. Sara's first thought is how much he must net each year in bribes and fines. He introduces himself and both men sit at the other end of the table.

"Thank you for meeting with me," Sara says.

"Our pleasure," says Blim. "My apologies for being delayed. I just got back from a meeting with the Chamber of Orphans. A rotten affair. You see, the regents of the City Orphanage filed a complaint with the mayor that they're being cheated out of their cut of guild sales. Now there's going to be a full audit of our membership. One of our painters or pottery bakers or engravers so much as dreams about a piece of work and some orphan makes five percent. They treat us as if we personally murdered the parents of these waifs."

Sara is taken aback by his candor and his breathy, long-suffering manner. Pleasantly, she says, "I didn't realize they receive a portion of sales."

"Oh, I assure you, madame, they have both hands deep in our pockets. To make matters worse, the bookbinders are trying to separate from St. Luke's. Cleaved in two, we are. So, you see, I'm leaving office just as a civil war is breaking out. We need a glassblower at the helm. A man with torrential lungs!"

"Goodness." She doesn't know what else to say.

It requires some effort for him to sit upright in his straight-backed chair. He puckers his mouth, choosing his words carefully. "Word among the membership is that your still lifes were quite accomplished before things soured."

She says, "It's regrettable, the way everything happened."

"There's no need for us to pretend we don't know the full circumstances of your husband's activities and the shadow they've cast upon your household. Thus our meeting today and hencewise the discussion that will ensue."

Sara can hear the housepainter straining up against his own jerrybuilt vocabulary. She pictures him at board meetings spewing legal *forthwith*s and *therefore*s to impress the handful of university-educated guild members. Sara says, "I'll come straight to the point. There are few things in this world dearer to me than painting. I would be honored if you would consider readmitting me to your ranks."

Blim narrows his gaze, then cocks his head to one side. "Officially, you are still a member of the guild, though not a member in good standing." Blim turns to the guild servant: "We have two current lady members, do we not, Mr. Tromp?"

"It is so, sir."

"And tell me, Mr. Tromp, are these lady painters gainfully plying their trade? Are they helping us to keep the orphans at bay?"

This is a man, Sara thinks, who has never painted a canvas, who has somehow convinced the world and the guild that painting a house requires expertise beyond climbing a ladder and serviceable eyesight. She bristles as Mr. Tromp flips through some pages of his book.

Tromp says, "You might say that production has tapered off since both of them married several years ago. There was a portrait commission a few years back. Nothing since."

Sara sees herself painting when Kathrijn was a baby, the small wooden crib beside the easel, one foot rocking it if she fretted, the plunge into the canvas whenever her daughter slept between outbursts of colic. She was always an unsettled child. Sara says nothing, looks from one foolish man to the other, waiting for an end to their deliberations.

"Ah, I see. And while you're in your ledger, Mr. Tromp, tell me about the fines we've imposed in the last year for illicit lotteries, raffles, and market sales. For example, innkeepers who hold illegal auctions . . ."

Tromp riffles back and forth between pages, seemingly flustered. "Too many to count."

Blim looks back at Sara. "This is not a pretty picture. I believe that's the hackneyed expression that best sums it up. Do you know why I was elected to hold this office, madame?"

"I'm not sure."

"Because when I used to paint houses I was known for never exposing a single brushstroke. I care about every single board and batten, every piece of window trim. The members thought I would bring that same diligence to the task at hand. But I'm being swallowed up, you understand. Every two years someone else takes this post and they hand down a book of scrawled numbers and recorded sales. We need an accountant, not a glassblower or painter at the helm. We should never have gotten rid of the stonemasons. They were the right kind of chiselers for this job."

Sara fears that this kind of muddling could go on all day, so she leans forward and raises her voice slightly. "I assure you, my contributions to this guild will be swift and steady."

As if stirred from a daydream, Blim cuts his eyes through the stony light at her. "Is that so? Tell me, mevrouw, have you and your husband been painting this past year?"

Sara knows this is a question laced with poison. "No, sir. My husband has gone to work with a bookbinder and I have worked of late for a catalogue company. But we would both like to paint again. Very much so."

"Do you have a work in mind that would meet our exacting standards?" He leans back so the painting behind him comes into full view.

Sara imagines trying to describe the painting of the girl at the edge of a wood. In her mind, it suddenly seems absurd—a ghostly figment standing beside a tree. She knows, in this moment, that she will never show it to anyone. Folding her hands into her lap, she gives the overseer the answer he wants: "I was thinking about returning to still lifes."

Blim looks at Tromp, then up at the ceiling, where the surgeons have painted their coat of arms. He nods, letting the idea wash over him. "Of course, the full board would have to meet and approve any work you submitted as a way of paying off your household's fines. I believe still lifes are an appropriate place for the brush of a woman. An arrangement could be made, I'm sure, if you brought us some exceptional still lifes that we could sell to clear the ledger. I believe it could be done. Do you agree, Mr. Tromp?"

"I do, sir."

"It's all settled, then."

Sara feels an immense pressure behind her eyes and closes them for a few seconds to regain composure.

"Now, I'm afraid I have to cut our meeting short on account of some urgent correspondence. Mr. Tromp will show you out. Perhaps you'll be among us at next year's dissection. Now that's not a bad line as well, if you ask me." Blim turns on his heels and walks from the room.

Tromp looks at her with an air of satisfaction, a meeting crossed off his calendar.

She pushes back her chair, scraping it loudly across the floor. As she stands, she looks up at *The Anatomy Lesson* and says, "I've never seen a hand so big for a body."

She turns to leave before Tromp can get the door for her.

THE SPRING IS HIGH TRADE for the catalogue company, a season of brisk export business. The day of her meeting, Sara goes to work a ten-hour shift, standing and squinting at the place where the long sable brush meets the paper. When she returns home in the evening, she's exhausted but also excited to tell Barent about her prospects with the guild. It might be their best chance and she's hoping to lift his spirits. The birthday cake failed to do that. Although it was beautiful—a pound cake glazed with white frosting and dotted with sugared almonds—it was also a grim reminder of Kathrijn's absence. She had died in the spring, around this time of year, a few months shy of her eighth birthday. Sara could tell, as she served Barent a big piece, that he felt sinful putting a single bite into his mouth. As if debt were a condition of God, not men, as if it were Kathrijn's birthday cake they were eating instead of his, as if Sara had stolen the entire thing from a bakery window instead of a handful of almonds from a pair of faithless Frenchmen. Dutifully, they both ate a piece, mostly in silence, and then the cake sat on the kitchen table for days, slowly going stale under a piece of cheesecloth.

It's dark when she gets to the house, though she's become

accustomed to Barent's forgetting to light the lantern out front. Inside, the rooms are cold and unlit and there's no sign of him. Her first thought is that he's already gone up to bed after a hard day at the bookbindery. She doesn't want to walk around in the dark, so she crosses to the shelf above the mantel to see if she can locate the lantern. She notices that the fireplace is cold—not an ember or shard of burning peat. It comes to her that no one has tended the hearth since the night before. She manages to flint some peat alight in the dark and takes a piece of kindling to the lantern wick. She carries the lantern toward the narrow staircase that leads to their bedroom, but as she does so she sees a note nailed to the banister. Her first thought is that Barent has killed himself—it descends with effortless terror. For a moment, she expects to climb the stairs and find him in bed, his lifeless eyes staring up at the ceiling and a rat-catcher's arsenic cake in his hand, or his body rigid and swinging from a heavy rafter in the attic. So when she first reads the note she experiences an instant of relief. Then she fathoms that abandonment is as good as death.

She remembers this feeling from Kathrijn's death, her insistence on being methodical. Wrap the body, fold the linens, send word for the coroner, hold the ragged hem of grief like a specimen between two fingers until you are alone and the windows are shuttered. She'd worked up the grief like a canvas, layer by layer, one pigment at a time. Then it would pin her in place as she filled a bucket of water or brushed out her hair. She takes the letter to the kitchen table and places it facedown, carefully fills the kettle and lights the fire. She prepares her foot-warmer, waits a minute, picks up the letter again. The stale cake is still on the table, a dome of cheesecloth and crumbs.

She uncovers it and takes an almond from the outer edge. She pops it into her mouth, then another, tasting the salt of her tears along with the flesh of each nut. Then something unravels in her chest and an enormous sob barrels through the darkened kitchen, frightening her. She knows she could scream very loudly without being heard, but instead she reaches over and shoves the birthday cake onto the floor. The clay plate hits the stone floor and shatters, the cake slumping in on itself. A brief and raucous crash followed by an immediate quelling, a hand covering a terrified mouth.

> My dearest Sara—
> By now I have made a barge on the Amstel, drifting with only the coins in my pocket. It was this or debtor's prison and I pray that mercy will prove more abundant for you than I. I will paint houses or barns or while away in Dordrecht cutting timber. When a man stops caring about his own plight there is suddenly relief to be found, a freedom undiscovered at the hearth. I cannot be forgiven and do not ask for any such leniency in the rooms of your mind. Perhaps you can sell the landscapes and seascapes at the spring market. This past year I haven't gone a day without regret, without missing our daughter as if some mortal piece were wrenched from my flesh. I do not expect much more in the days ahead, but I expect to endure it alone and for that I am thankful.
> Your loving husband,
> Barent

New Jersey

AUGUST 1958

THE PRIVATE INVESTIGATOR is an eccentric fat man who lives on a dilapidated houseboat in Edgewater, New Jersey. Despite Marty's initial hesitation, he's retained Red Hammond for nearly three months now. Red is an old war buddy of one of the partners and the law firm uses him from time to time. "A nutty slob who gets results" is how Marty was sold on Red's credentials. Since discovering the painting's theft, Marty has gone through the usual insurance and police channels, but he's been frustrated by the slow-grinding gears of bureaucracy and paperwork. They've failed to come up with a single solid lead and he's glad he had the foresight to take matters into his own hands. His insurance policy against the insurance company was hiring his own investigator. Earlier today, Red called him at the office after months of digging to tell him he'd uncovered something.

Marty takes the ferry across to Edgewater, a fishing enclave that's also home to a few pioneer commuters. It's his second time coming across the Hudson by boat to New Jersey and he's struck by what a sensational view these people have of Midtown. Manhattan looks like some ziggurat empire from out on the water, the towers flushed gold and pink in the dying hours of sunlight, a place of burial vaults and conquests. On the other side of the deck—he thinks it's starboard—he can see the Palisades running above Edgewater. They lend this sleepy little fishing town some scale, a sense of grandeur borrowed from nature. New Jersey always surprises him, a state known for its turnpikes that should be known for its coastlines and bayside hamlets. He looks down at the darkening waters, letting the wake of the ferry churn his thoughts. Why can't Red Hammond have a dingy office with a coffee-stained desk and venetian blinds like every other working private detective? He could have insisted that Red make the trek into the city, but Marty's colleagues had warned him that inviting Red Hammond into the office was never a good idea—one time he showed up eating a hot dog and sweating through his shirt in the middle of December.

The ferry ride, as picturesque as it is, only emphasizes Marty's dogged pursuit of a painting he thinks might have been poisoning his life for some time. Since discovering it was gone, Rachel has emerged from her depression to join a small but active social club, Gretchen rebounded after their near-dalliance, and he's been promoted at work. And yet the thought of sleeping under the fake for months riles him in a way that feels intensely personal. A stranger very likely stood on his king-size mattress to remove a painting that's been in his family for over three hundred years. Oblivious, he'd hunkered down like a fool every night, the wrong girl standing at the birch tree as he drifted off.

From the dock, he walks along a weedy trail that leads upriver to the listing pier where Red moors his houseboat, a converted tugboat with a rusting smokestack. Marty is still in his suit, carrying his briefcase, feeling absurd as he walks up the rotting gangplank. Red is in the stern, loading up a little runabout. On their first meeting, Red motored across the Hudson to pick him up at a Midtown yacht club, the big man jackknifing his small wooden boat from the stern while stockbroking yachtsmen looked on with mocking curiosity. Red is jocular, long-winded, and enormous. He wears plaid shirts as big as picnic blankets.

Red turns from the stern and squints toward Marty in the falling light. "I've got a bucket of minnows and a cooler of beer for us to share."

"I'm not dressed for fishing."

"No matter. I've got overalls hanging in the bridge. On a hook to the left of the door. You go snug into those and we'll be off. I've got *mucho revelaciones* for you."

Marty resigns himself to being held hostage in the boat and goes to change. This is the cost of doing business with a man who's spent decades following cheating spouses and thieving employees. All that solitude and suspicion has made him immune to social cues, to the look of disinterest and mild annoyance that Marty can feel on his own face.

When Marty climbs into the runabout Red admonishes him to stay low. They cast off and motor downriver toward the Narrows and the Staten Island marshes. At Marty's feet there's a cooler, a few rods, a pair of giant tongs, a canister of gasoline.

Marty looks back over Red's silhouette to see the city lights firing up above the darkening river. They hug the western shoreline, pass the Statue of Liberty at a distance, and motor into the Jersey Flats, where there's a graveyard of boat hulks, old ferryboats, and tugs lying half-submerged.

Red says, "Most New Yorkers don't remember the rivers are even here."

"I suppose that's true," Marty says cautiously. "Although on a bad day you can smell the sewage outlays as a strong reminder."

"If you ask me, Marty de Groot, the contamination of both rivers is greatly exaggerated. I eat whatever I catch. Some of the best clam beds and eel breeding grounds a grown man could want." Red picks up a rod and baits its hook. "These hulks are the perfect place for eels to breed."

"You couldn't pay me enough to eat an eel or fish from this river."

"Eels scavenge at night," Red says. "Bottom feeders looking for dead fish."

"So what did you find out?"

Red breaks open the cooler and hands Marty a can of Rheingold. The metal rim smells like fish and iodine. Red opens his own can and sips it meditatively, ignoring Marty's question.

"The Germans from Staten Island come out here in December and take home buckets of eels. And then there's the rivermen from up my way, around Edgewater, who still go clamming, even though most of the beds are condemned. There's even a Shellfish Protector who carries a .38 revolver on his patrols like a small-town constable. I'm not making any of this up."

"I believe you."

"Every now and again some family living in a marsh shanty eats a toxic cherrystone and it's Old Testament food poisoning."

Marty sips his beer, feigning patience. "Tell me about the painting. You found a trail?"

Red hands Marty a baited rod and insists that he cast off. The river plinks and laps at the sides of the wooden skiff.

"On a particularly quiet night," Red says, "you can hear the eels scraping against the hulls below."

Marty stares at him with all the disdain he can muster. "This is not my idea of a night out."

Red smiles coyly, looks at his rod, then begins: "As you know, we hit a dead end with the catering company. They hired extra help for the event and three of them worked under false names because they were immigrants without the necessary documents. These might have been the people who swapped out the painting and got the original out of the house, who knows. The Rent-a-Beats all checked out fine. A little commie and subversive, but fine nonetheless. Then I got this idea one night when I was out fishing . . . to research the frame of the fake and maybe work out where it was made and whatnot. So I study the Manhattan phone book and call around. I visit ten frame shops before it's all over. Turns out there's this Frenchman who runs a framing shop up on Lexington, in the Sixties, and his family's being doing this for generations. Tells me that his family has frames in the Louvre and the Met, that he used to sell frames to Vanderbilts and Carnegies. Little old dandy in a three-piece suit and work apron. Cheese crumbs on his shirt-front. On the walls there's every fancy frame you could imagine.

I show him pictures of the forgery frame and he says it's not one of his, but I can tell something's not quite right. I have a sixth sense for evasion. So I get him talking about the family framing empire and he tells me about making his own gesso from gypsum that hails—that's his word—from the white cliffs of Dover and he adds it to rabbit-skin glue. Pretty soon he's making me a cup of tea and I flatter him into submission. As a solitary animal I know loneliness when I smell it and I'm warming up his engine with a kittenish purr. Before long, maybe into the second cup of tea, he confesses that he did build a frame for a regular customer who came in with a photograph of a frame like the one I showed him. He won't give me the name, though, because he fancies himself a priest or shrink or attorney. Client privilege or some such. But I could tell it was personal, that these two had a rapport."

Marty says, "That doesn't really narrow it down."

"I'm not finished with the story. But nothing's biting here, so let's take a little jaunt."

Red pulls up the anchor and yanks the ripcord in the little outboard motor, which sputters to life. They head north again, angling back along the shoreline. Red opens a fresh beer and offers Marty one, but he refuses for fear of encouraging further digression. They cut across the current and Marty's arms get wet from spindrift.

Marty says, "I have to get home to my wife."

"Of course," Red says, lowering the anchor again. "Now, I ask the old gentleman for a tour of his premises and he's only too happy to oblige. He shows me his workroom with its antique chisels and pliers and he tells me how he does things.

I learn about his little operation, how he numbers the jobs and keeps a logbook. The whole place is buried under dust, but he's running a tight operation on paper. Handwritten receipts, dated entries in the log. Runs the place like a medieval monk. So eventually I'm able to get a peek in his logbook while he's helping another customer and I go back to the months before the robbery. I flip the pages looking for reoccurring names but he's got the handwriting of an epileptic nun. I can't tell his *g*'s and *j*'s and *s*'s apart. I get a little irritated—I've spent two hours in there by this point—so I shove the whole logbook under my jacket and walk out of there while he's in the back room."

"That seems a little drastic."

"I intend to mail it back when I'm all finished with it. Now, today I studied the log, combed the data, looked for patterns in the old man's cursive. I seem to have found a lead. The same name appears five times in the ledger in the year before the theft. That makes me think an art dealer or restorer, maybe someone who works for a museum. These are not cheap frames and they're mostly antiques. How many Flemish panels does one person have to frame in a single year? So I start cross-referencing the name Jergens with art dealers and restorers but hit another dead end. I call around and not a single one of them employs a Jergens. Then I notice that a few days after Jergens appears in the log there's always another name, a certain Shipley from Brooklyn. Now I know there's some fine houses in Brooklyn, but this framing shop seems very old New York to me. So there was something about Shipley that smelled like a clam left in the sun. And why was Shipley always coming within three days of Jergens? Then it came to me."

"I have no idea what happens next."

"Maybe Shipley is coming to study whatever Jergens brings in and uses it as an excuse to bring something of his own in. What if the old man tips Shipley off and he comes in to study Jergens's paintings. What if they're colluding, the Frenchman and the forger?"

"All this from the log entries? It seems like a stretch."

"I'm thinking the Frenchman makes the frames for the forger in exchange for a cut of the profits. Probably none of it's provable, but the logbook contains a list of client addresses. So I now have a solid location for Shipley."

Red hands him a scrap of paper in the half-light with an address scrawled on it.

Red says, "I plan to stake out the apartment in Brooklyn. Since I'll need to hire another person to work in shifts, I'll require some extra money to cover expenses."

There's something about Red's deductive reasoning that Marty doesn't trust. He personally knows art collectors who have things reframed all the time, so the connection between Jergens and Shipley feels tenuous. There's also his mounting superstition that losing the painting removed some great burden, that he's better off without it, but then he's thinking about his Dutch grandfather kneeling to say his prayers under the painting every night for decades and he flushes with anger. He says, "What are you expecting to find?"

"There's always a tell. Certain people coming and going. The forger going out for meetings. We tail him until we find the hook beneath the bait."

The word *tail* reminds Marty that he's sitting in a dinghy

on the Hudson with a 350-pound gumshoe. "You can have another two-fifty for surveillance. See what happens in a week and then report back."

"Roger that," says Red, smiling down at the river.

Brooklyn

AUGUST 1958

THE END OF A BEATNIK SUMMER. Ellie sleeps out on her fire escape to get some relief from the swelter of her apartment. She smokes cigarettes and watches the street below. The sensitive men of the neighborhood, the poets and dandies, dress in peacoats and moccasins and royal-blue polos. They recite unrhymed poems about inner turmoil, perform in Greenwich Village coffee shops with atonal jazz riffing quietly below their words. Kerouac is in Florida exile after *On the Road*, a book she pretends to have read and liked. She lives apart from the campus scene, goes to Columbia only for meetings. Over the summer, she's added a single new chapter to her stalled-out dissertation and rewritten the introduction for the tenth time. A few days ago, she received a telephone call from Dr. Meredith Hornsby, her supervisor, summoning her to campus to discuss the new material.

She takes the train into the city and writes in her notebook. Instead of writing newsy letters to her parents in Sydney

—which receive brisk replies from her mother, with a *Dad sends his love* in the gutter of the aerogramme—she pours herself into compiling lists of forgery techniques. Ground recipes and methods for stripping back the upper layers while preserving the signature cracks and fissures below. Then there are the forms of imitation, the "flyspecks" that can be achieved on the back of a painting if epoxy glue is mixed with amber-tinted pigment and applied with a pinhead in a suitable pattern. Flies are drawn to the sugars in a painting's varnish and the effect is to suggest a neglected painting languishing in an attic for decades. Or the blue chalk marks on the back of the frame, partially erased by hand, that suggest previous auction sales. So much of the forger's dominion is theater and subtext, she thinks, a series of enticements. An obscure provenance, suggested by visual cues, is irresistible to a certain kind of buyer—it becomes a story of their own discernment, of plucking a second self from the folds of history.

Although she's met with a few prospective clients, she hasn't had a restoration job in months and it's starting to weigh on her. A demanding restoration would keep her mind off the thrill of copying the de Vos painting down to the last brushstroke. While Gabriel waits to find the right buyer, the painting is being kept in a storage unit in Chelsea. Once a week or so, Ellie is allowed to study it. She collects the key from a counter hand at a bakery down the street and spends an hour or two examining the painting under lamplight. She takes notes about color and composition and brushwork. She hasn't told Gabriel that Sara de Vos is now the basis of a new chapter in her dissertation. It's a risk, she knows, drawing attention to a painting that's recently been stolen and that has never hung in a museum. Then again, she thinks, perhaps her painstaking copy will go undiscovered for generations. In the meantime, she will quietly put Sara de Vos back on the map.

When Ellie arrives on campus, she finds the plaza filled with milling summer students, clusters of them smoking cigarettes on the stone steps of the Low Library. Every patch of the sunny lawn is taken up with undergraduates lazing. The scene reminds her how much of her time she spends alone in her apartment, how Brooklyn is another world away. She walks through the shade of the courtyard outside the art history department, then takes the stairs up to the top floor, where Meredith Hornsby keeps her office. When Ellie knocks softly on the open door, Hornsby is reading and smoking at her desk. As the first woman to hold tenure in the department, she dresses in a way that suggests an intrepid, pioneering spirit—somber blouses and blazers, sturdy wool slacks, mountaineering-grade walking shoes. Despite the sturdy footwear, Ellie can't imagine Hornsby ever really walking very far. From what she knows of her private life, she lives with her classical archaeologist husband on the Upper West Side and never eats at a restaurant below Columbus Circle.

Hornsby looks up from her desk, a cigarette wanly at her side, vaguely resembling—or so it seems to Ellie—Bette Davis at the end of a movie. Matter-of-factly, she says, "I'm rereading your new introduction and chapter. Question: Why are you so angry at the world?"

Ellie can feel her face getting hot. She breathes and takes a seat in the wingback chair opposite the ornate wooden desk.

As long as Ellie can remember, Hornsby starts out this way, a shot across the bow, an inflammatory question tossed off without emotion. But it's never rhetorical—she wants actual answers for her soul-scorching interrogations.

Stalling for time, Ellie takes in the room—the wall of books on art and criticism, the geraniums on the windowsill, the smell that's an odd mixture of Chesterfield cigarettes and damp upholstery. There's an umbrella stand over in the corner and it's stocked with more canes and umbrellas than Ellie thinks anyone has a right to own. She remembers hearing that Hornsby plays a formidable game of golf. "I'm not sure what you mean," she says.

Hornsby leans her elbows on the desk and rests her chin on her gently clenched fists. "The verbs alone suggest a diatribe more than a reasoned argument. I've circled them all. *Testify, manifest, declare, an attack against conventional thinking* . . . Your introduction sounds like a call to the battlements."

"For centuries everyone thought Judith Leyster's paintings were by Frans Hals. I'm trying to correct the balance."

"You can do that without sounding as if you're writing about the suffragette movement." Hornsby continues to flip pages, her Mont Blanc uncapped and poised for typographic annoyances. "And tell me about the chapter on Sara de Vos. First female member of the guild, that much we know. But your theory is that she learned landscape techniques from her father and then her husband but her still life training still dominated the composition. How in the world did you come by this idea when she has one attributed work?"

Ellie folds her arms, a little defiant. She can feel her throat tightening but wants to remain levelheaded. At first, Hornsby seemed like an ally in the department, but over the years it became clear that she was among the most conservative of the art faculty. A flag bearer for the status quo in woolen slacks. Ellie says, "In addition to combing the archives, I've spent time with the painting. The fine level of detail suggests still life and portraiture, but the landscape techniques are also on display."

Hornsby drops her hands to the desk, palms flat. "It's here? In New York?"

Ellie nods.

"How did I not know about this? Is it at the Frick?"

"No, it's privately owned. I can't say who, because I've signed a confidentiality agreement."

"Did this come to you via Gabriel Lodge? Because I've known that foppish Brit for a long time and I can't believe he would withhold something like this from me. I was the one who sent him your way for restoration work . . ."

There's a danger that an indignant Hornsby will begin making enquiries or call Gabriel up directly, so Ellie hedges her bets by saying, "No, not through him. I happened upon it during a restoration project. He doesn't know a thing about it."

"And, what, it was just sitting in their living room like a portrait of Grandpa with his hunting dogs?"

"More or less."

Hornsby looks at Ellie, a little incredulous, then she licks her thumb and turns a page of the manuscript, shaking her head. "Am I to believe, then, that you will have permission to include a photograph of said painting in the dissertation? How else will you support your detailed analysis of the technique?"

Ellie crosses her legs. She's wearing a cotton sundress that makes her feel flimsy and exposed compared to Hornsby, who looks like she just came in from a jaunt in the Swiss Alps instead of a bagel run on Upper Broadway. Ellie says, "I don't know if I can get permission."

"And then there's the matter of you giving de Vos equal weight, right up there with Leyster and Ruysch, who between them have dozens of paintings in museums."

"She wasn't just the first woman to be admitted into a Guild of St. Luke," Ellie says. "She was the only baroque Dutch woman, as far as we know, who ever painted a landscape. Her circumstances allowed her to cross over into a male-dominated world. She was a pioneer and there's bound to be other paintings attributed to her."

"Yes, but surely—"

Ellie cuts Hornsby off, her accent broadening as she gives in to her own annoyance: "We've always assumed that the Dutchmen did all the landscapes since women were boiling kettles back at home, but what if she and her husband collaborated? What if they went out into the countryside together for the outdoor scenes?"

Hornsby draws on her cigarette, her expression souring into a slight wince. "It's speculation. What do the archives say?"

"That they were heavily in debt, fell out with the guild, and that she lost a daughter. The work has an allegorical atmosphere, a bereft girl standing barefoot in the snow."

"Yes, I've read the descriptions. And the work is signed and dated?"

Ellie shakes her head and looks down at Hornsby's

walking shoes swaying beneath her desk. "The provenance is well established because it's only ever been owned by one family."

Meredith Hornsby combines a head tilt with an exhalation of smoke. "You're making the centerpiece of your dissertation a discussion of an obscure painter with a single extant work that's never been publicly exhibited." She shakes her head. "No, I recommend against it. I think you're backing the wrong horse. You're projecting onto this woman, if you really want to know my opinion."

Ellie looks into the weave of the Turkish rug and feels her mood go blank. "I disagree," she says.

Hornsby stubs out her cigarette and stands behind her desk, smoothing her wool slacks. "This is not an easy profession for women, Eleanor. You know that."

Ellie bristles at the use of her full name, a patronizing tactic she's seen employed by nuns, priests, and her own disapproving father.

Hornsby crosses to the bookshelves and brings down her slim volume on Vermeer. "When all of my male colleagues were obsessed with the Italian Renaissance I slipped in through the back door, focusing on Holland. I was an oddity to them, still am, I expect. You're in the same camp. We're swimming upstream—because we're women and because our profession knows very little of the Dutch Golden Age. I was lucky. I got in early and tracked Vermeer through the snow. He dragged me along for the ride." She flips through some pages then sets the book back on the shelf. With renewed energy, she turns to Ellie again. "Even with good luck on my side, I'm here before the men every morning and I have more students than any of them. Getting tenure was blood sport, let me tell you. A goddamn coliseum." Coming forward and leaning against the desk, she says, "It doesn't hurt if you can marry into a department somewhere. That sounds callous, but it's not entirely untrue." She folds her arms. "Do whatever it takes to rein in this dissertation and get on with the next phase of your life. No one can make a career out of a minor Dutch woman painter with one canvas to her name. Keep de Vos in the margins. That's my strong advice."

Hornsby hands Ellie the sheaf of papers on her desk. They are covered in loops and scrawled cursive.

Ellie stands with the papers braced against her chest. She notices her hands are shaking and she fights back the urge to dump the pages all over Hornsby's Turkish rug. "I don't think that's advice I can follow. I'm convinced that Sara de Vos was the most important female painter of her age."

Hornsby gives out a barely audible sigh. "If Dickens had written a single book none of us would know his name."

A little breathily, Ellie says, "But what if we found out he'd written a dozen others under a pseudonym or anonymously? Then wouldn't that be the find of the century?"

Buttoning her blazer, Hornsby says, "I was right. You are angry. And it's unbecoming."

Ellie feels as if she's just been slapped across the face by some disapproving nineteenth-century dowager. She swallows, looks down at the papers, and walks slowly toward the door.

En Route to Sydney

AUGUST 2000

SOMEWHERE OVER THE PACIFIC, Marty de Groot leaves the painting for the first time. Wrapped in a woolen blanket and cinched with twine, the painting has been bought a first-class ticket under the label "personal item." He calls it his Dutch girlfriend when somebody asks. Money at this point is an abstraction, a set of sans serif numerals too small to read on the monthly statements. There's plenty, always has been. He's ashamed he cannot remember a time in his life without the cushioned guardrails of abundance. He's up in the aisle and shuffling past the lavish buffet table of Australian fruits and cheeses and wines. Reminds him of Rachel and her rooftop soirees, the old partners dead or demented and he's still living, alone, walking down the street for bagels each morning, carrying them back to the three-story apartment warm against his chest. The first-class steward gives him a paternalistic smile as Marty edges for the toilet. It's the look you give a well-behaved imbecile, an insurance policy against cosmic malevolence. In the tiny compartment he sits down, because pissing these days is a matter of timing, perseverance, and Newtonian physics. Nila, the Salvadoran cook and cleaning lady, changes his sheets more than she lets on. She's kind for not letting on. And in return, the old man overpays her and buys her teenage son extravagant gifts. She's a single mother from Queens who comes three times a week and smells of lemon hand soap. He's happy to have her around the apartment but also happy when she leaves. She never complains about the train wreck that is the human body named Marty. She cleans and cooks for that human body. His age—is he eighty-three? Eighty-five?—is another abstraction as far as he's concerned, a tiny font he can't quite decipher. He thinks of the Old Testament and men living to nine hundred, made from clay and was that Adam or Noah?

He stands and closes the lid to flush. The supersonic *thwoomp* makes him think of certain prewar espresso machines, the big Italian jobs that used to be in Midtown cafés with chrome pull-down handles and steam pumps loud as Vespas. Barely anything reminds him of death—certainly not the high altitude flushing of bodily waste. This is one of the ironies of descending into his ninth decade—he's convinced he'll live forever, albeit with fewer functioning organs, so he has to remind himself that he's running out the clock to gain a little gravity now and then. He suspects his final monologue will be about property taxes and a transcendent fish sandwich he once ate in Far Rockaway with homemade mayonnaise. He avoids his face in the narrow mirror. Nothing good can come of that harrowing vision—a character actor hired for the day. He carefully inspects his tan shirt and lined windbreaker that he's kept on for twelve hours because Qantas likes to refrigerate the first-class cabin like they're hauling steaks across the Pacific. Nila says he dresses like a game warden, but he thinks it's more like a war journalist or bird-watcher. The field vest with a thousand pockets is somewhere in his carry-on. When did an abundance of pockets become a matter of moral principle? He wants to be zipped up and buried in the thing. His final battlefield commission.

Back in his seat the steward refreshes Marty's drink and brings him another blanket, because the old and infirm can never have too many blankets. The Qantas man wears a crisp black apron while pouring the red wine and making some low-volume small talk. Marty's hearing aid is on the fritz, so Jerome's Aussie friendliness comes in faint, buzzing waves. Marty nods and smiles and puts his hand against the blanketed painting. Where else but at thirty-five thousand feet can you drink with abandon regardless of time zones or international date lines? It could be four in the morning above Fiji, but a glass of Shiraz is just the ticket. Maybe he says this aloud, or something self-deprecating, because Jerome throws him a cheeky smile before he moves down the aisle. The lights have been dimmed and the window is awash in blackness and he can see a hairline fracture of dawn against the horizon. Darkness at high altitude, the midflight quietude, always makes him think of the bottom of the ocean. There's a submarine quality to the experience, a sense of dredging the bottom instead of scraping up against the stratosphere. The stars pinhole the dome of black, but he always thinks of looking up to a surface, of glimpsing stars through a film of water or ice.

They serve breakfast two hours out from Sydney and he relishes the tray with its little compartments, a bento box of surprises. It's not miniature exactly but scaled down 30 percent. He eats everything on the tray, right down to the fruit and yogurt. His sense of taste is going, but there's some kind of muscle memory, an echo of meals past. By now, the sun is blazing through the windows and most of the shades have been lowered. He keeps his open a crack and reads *The Times* in a wedge of white sunlight. You travel halfway around the world with your own city newspaper. This is a miraculous thing to him. He's had to ask Jerome to help him with his customs form, because apparently forms of all varieties make his blood pressure spike. His feathery, spastic block letters cannot be corralled into single boxes. His ankles are swollen, he realizes, and he begins rifling through his seat pocket for some ibuprofen and then he forgets what he's looking for and comes upon his itinerary and decides he's looking for the name of the hotel where he's staying. He must be the only person alive still using a travel agent, a woman he's never met in person who used to work for the law firm. She's a voice on the other end of a phone, a woman versed in seating plans and foreign mass transit. She tried explaining to him several times that the tickets were paperless and he said he wanted something in black and white. "Paperless ticket is an oxymoron," he'd said into the phone.

They fly toward the edge of the continent, a rim of sandstone cliffs and red terracotta roofs and olive-drab treetops. He follows the landing on the seatback monitor in front of him, checks the correspondence between the pixelated, video game icon of the plane and the scene outside the window. They come in low to land, dropping down as the oil refineries of Botany Bay come into view. They taxi and he prepares to *deplane*, a verb that would make the steward sound ex-military if it weren't for the pink carnation in his lapel. The specialized vocabulary of airports has always made Marty uncomfortable. The theater of alienation, he thinks, as he carries the bundled painting up the bridge or gangplank or whatever it's called. He's brought only a carry-on suitcase and the painting, so he sails through the baggage claim area and is among the first ones to arrive at customs. A kid in his twenties in a short-sleeve shirt with a badge asks him why the painting wasn't declared on the customs form. Marty says he's loaning it to the Art Gallery of New South Wales and this naturally complicates matters. Pretty soon there's a huddle of older men deliberating about commercial forms and protocols. Marty refuses to let them unwrap the painting but insists that they're welcome to put it through the X-ray machine. They take him up on this and he's escorted to a small lounge area with vinyl seats while he waits for them to be done. Eventually he gets the painting back and walks out into the terminal. A line of people stand against a guardrail as passengers wheel their luggage out into the tiled whiteness of the airport.

The Indian taxi driver is dressed for a blizzard, with the heat cranked, even though it's only in the fifties. Marty left a Manhattan summer and has arrived to a Sydney winter, only it feels like an early spring day before the tulips crown beside the sidewalks along Central Park. Suddenly he's being driven on the wrong side of the road. It unnerves him, even though he hasn't driven a car since before Clinton was in office. The painting is next to him in the back and his suitcase is in the trunk, now called a boot. He reads the driver—Mahesh, according to the ID clipped to the sun visor—the name of the hotel on the itinerary and he seems to know it. He asks Mahesh if he can turn down the heat because he has a valuable painting in the blanket and it's sensitive to changes in temperature. Mahesh says nothing but turns down the heat. They drive through commercial streets with warehouses and furniture stores before wending through a residential area of squat, single-story row houses with undersize tiled courtyards out front, a few potted ferns or palms in place of a yard. Closer to the city, Marty sees two- and three-story Victorian terraces with filigreed iron balconies and double doors, a distant cousin of New York's brownstones. He adjusts his watch to the local time, copying the orange digital numbers on the dashboard. It's 9:06 in the morning and he realizes he doesn't know what day it is. He'd left on a Wednesday but somewhere a day was lost, or gained, he can't remember which. "Sir, can you tell me what day it is?" The driver looks at him warily in the rearview mirror and tells him it's Friday.

The vision of a weekend spent in a hotel room, or sightseeing with a group of tourists he can't quite hear or understand, cuts through him. He's never been one to dawdle around monuments with a camera in hand or take day trips to picturesque estates. Instead, he likes to walk a city's grid, to build a place up in his mind by walking its backstreets, to stop in front of real estate agents' windows to see what a 3/2 in a decent suburb might cost. This kind of urban safari always bothered Rachel. They'd go on luxury cruises of European rivers and he'd stay below or read American newspapers in a deck chair before heading out for a four-hour walk into obscurity. She studied the literature, the maps and guidebooks, the illustrations of native flowers and birds, and tried to engage him in the deep backstory of a country or town. He didn't want to know anything before he came upon it in the street. His interests were narrow—pubs, delis, paintings in hotel lobbies, two-hour circuits of museums (never with a guide or those ridiculous headphones), local color, cheap meals on busy streets, firm mattresses with feather pillows, breakfasts served in the room. He'd wear his field vest with many pockets to carry his pills and foreign coins and dental floss. They'd been to dozens of countries together, but what he remembered was meals and hotel rooms. She used to accuse him of lacking curiosity, of not wanting to know a people's history. He said he wanted to know the people from their parks and streets and sandwiches. He wrote things down on small spiral notepads, like a reporter, and never looked at them again. He had a pocket in his field vest dedicated to ballpoint pens. Now she's gone—has it been ten years already?—and he rarely travels, because now he's in the chute. This is what he tells Nila. Soon they'll install a gurney and a home nurse who'll sponge down his privates. This is the cul-de-sac that cannot be avoided. He won't die in a nursing home or hospital. This is the final thing that wealth might guarantee. But even a rich old man has to sit down to piss. This is another thing he says to Nila to make her shake her head and groan.

"Do you mind if we go to the Art Gallery of New South Wales instead of the hotel?" he says to the driver. "Is it nearby?"

"Very close."

"Thank you."

"Yes, sir."

New York could use a few more drivers like Mahesh. They pull up in front of a typical museum facade—plinths and columns and stonework. He pays the driver and trundles up the steps with the painting and his wheeled suitcase. It's not until he comes into the main entrance and sees the security guard eyeing him that the full absurdity of this errand strikes him. He doesn't quite know why he's done this, why the idea persisted like arterial plaque. Ellie was part of the reason, but there were other parts that defied explanation, some dark and mysterious sense of circling back or making amends or just reappearing in another time zone, defying time and death. He had out-existed so many people, but Ellie was still alive and by all accounts she had made something of herself. Was he here to bear witness or to remind her how she started out? No, he thinks, he's here to pay homage to an old, scalding regret.

He tells the security guard that he's here to see the director, Max Culkins, and the guard sizes him up—the shuffling lunatic with some plywood wrapped inside a blanket.

"He's expecting me. Tell him it's Marty de Groot from New York."

A phone is picked up. A call is made. Words are mumbled discreetly into the mouthpiece.

"Someone will come down for you," the guard says, a slight change in his tone.

Moments later, a pretty assistant arrives—she reminds him of Gretchen, another name from a lost decade (didn't she marry a state senator?)—and he's being led toward the back rooms and offices of the museum. He's whisked along parquet-floored galleries where Impressionists and old Europeans hang on a periphery of light that cascades down through ceilings of wrought iron and glass. Unlike the rich grays and burgundies of the painted gallery walls, the upstairs administrative offices are stark white and filled with bookish cubicles. The assistant offers him some coffee or a glass of water and they talk about long-haul flights because she's not allowed to ask what he's carrying in the twined-up blanket. As they arrive in the executive suite, a dapper fellow comes out to meet them and introduces himself as Max Culkins. He's a man of quick wit, pastel socks, and a pale, slightly pockmarked face. He has the handshake of a diplomat or politician, one hand pressed over the clasp. Marty admires his bespoke suit, the cut of the trouser legs with a pair of lavender socks winking at the ankles as he walks back to his office with Marty in his wake. Surprisingly, there's very little artwork on the walls of his office. Behind a sleek desk hang publicity shots of Culkins being presented with oversize checks and peeking out from the shining blade of a bulldozer in front of a new wing of the museum. Marty notices that he never makes direct eye contact with the suitcase or the square of blanket, as if passersby come in here every day with their luggage and wrapped paintings. The assistant arrives with a tray of biscuits and coffee in a French press. Marty tells her that he'll take it black and she pours him a cup. She makes coffee for Max—milk with two sugars—and Marty can feel some layer of respect he'd felt for the man strip away. She closes the glass door behind her as she leaves.

"I have to say, you're not the usual sort of courier we see around here. It was very generous of you to bring the painting all this way," says Max.

"At my age you want to stretch your legs every chance you get. It also takes an hour to put your shoes on."

The director chuckles. They sip their coffees.

"My colleagues at the Met tell me that you're like part of the family."

"Call it a long courtship. They've been after my collection since the sixties and they've worked out that I'm a childless widower. I guess the odds are in their favor."

The director leans back in his leather chair to absorb the curt humor. He looks like he's taking Marty in by degrees, like a difficult painting from across the room. "I can't tell you how excited we are to have your de Vos on loan. It means a lot to us. I hope the painting traveled well."

Marty watches as the director allows himself a glance at the wrapped painting for the first time.

"I was hoping to meet with the curator and hand her the painting personally."

"Like much of the artwork, I'm afraid she's also on loan to us. Eleanor teaches at Sydney University and comes to the gallery a few times a week. She's been burning the midnight oil of late. We have some last-minute repairs being done to the exhibition space."

"When do you open?"

"Next week. You're just in the nick of time, actually. We'd almost given up."

"Sorry for the alarm."

"Not at all," says Max, smiling.

Marty places a hand on top of the painting. He sees the raised veins and the liver spots like small brown planets; he has no idea who this hand might belong to.

"Will you be in town for long?"

"I'm not sure."

"Well, we'd love for you to stay for the opening. You'd be a guest of honor. And we can show you the sights while you're here. Would you like one of the curators to give you a tour of the museum?"

"Yes, I'd like that." Marty thinks it poor form that Max is deputizing a curator for the tour. Another varnished layer of respect peels away. His hand is still on the painting and he's curious how Max will raise the issue of the actual handoff. He waits and sips his coffee.

"As it turns out, we've had a couple other de Voses come from the Netherlands and we were wondering if you'd allow us to do some testing on your painting. We have a few days before we can hang everything, so all the loan paintings are in storage."

"Testing?"

"It's a rare chance to have a handful of de Vos paintings in the same room. We have a scientist on staff who does magic with X-rays and infrared images. She can practically tell you what the painter had for breakfast on the day of the final brushstroke. I can assure you that not a thread of the canvas will be harmed. Everything is covered in the insurance forms."

Marty sees Max's shoes wagging under the table and he drains his coffee cup. It burns the roof of his mouth a little, but then there's a wonderful burst of caffeine, like warm water being poured over his scalp. "I would need to see the paperwork. This painting has been in my family since before Isaac Newton was born."

The specificity of the historical reference seems to take the wind out of Max Culkins's sails. He whistles silently and shakes his head. "A miracle, really." Then he gathers himself up again. "Right, of course, please take your time with all the paperwork. Consult your lawyers as you see fit. I'll have the head conservator come up and go over everything." Max forms a church steeple with his fingers and bites his lower lip. "I don't suppose I could grab a quick peek?"

Marty gets to his feet and sets his coffee cup on the edge of the desk. He picks up the painting and follows Max to a corner of the room where a reading table is laid out with antique maps covered in vellum. He sets the painting down and Max produces a letter opener, a tiny sword with a silver-plated handle. Marty takes it from him and cuts through the twine. He pulls back a flap of the thick blanket to reveal a bed of green felt.

"Is that billiard cloth?" Max asks.

"Good eye. I had to get the baize on mine replaced so I kept the old one for just such an occasion."

"Genius idea."

Marty pulls back the green felt and exposes the face of the painting to the room. She's in perfect condition, he thinks. Kept in a narrow temperature range except for the taxi rides to and from airports. Max sidles up in his French cuffs, the kind of shirts Marty used to wear as a law partner. He looks for something in the director's face, some recognition of history and the fluke of an old man bundling across the globe to bring him this gift. I would have liked you better if you drank your coffee black and offered me a tour, if you'd led me around the galleries in your dandy purple socks. But what Marty sees in Max's face is something else—a quiet look of consternation. "There it is," Max says, "there it is."

Manhattan

SEPTEMBER 1958

RED HAMMOND IS ON THE OTHER END OF THE telephone, filing what he calls "a dispatch from the field." He's sent Marty an envelope containing a business card and a grainy photo of a woman hunched over a kitchen table. Marty turns the card over between his fingers. *Eleanor Shipley, Art Restoration*. It's a tasteful beige cardstock with discreet lettering and a slanting phone number. It's a business card that promises artful restraint.

Red says, "From all accounts, she's a woman."

"I can see that. What did you find out about her?"

But Red is not quite ready to talk about the upshot. Instead, he wants to talk about his week of surveillance in Brooklyn as if he's just returned from the jungles of Malaysia. "I have no idea what people eat over there. I was starving, could never find a decent bagel. And no one seems to have heard of parallel parking in that particular borough. I circled her apartment for hours sometimes because some jerk refused to park against the curb. Or because people live in such small apartments that they store their clothes in their automobiles. We're talking about parked closets, stationary clothes hampers, not modes of transportation. I'm telling you that Brooklyn makes Edgewater, New Jersey, look civilized."

"What else?"

"I paid some bum to watch my car while I followed her into the city, up into the hundreds at Columbia, over to the little framing shop, then a few meetings with clients in coffee shops and ethnic restaurants."

"What kind of clients?"

"From the general auditory clues of conversation, these seemed to be legitimate restoration deals. She has this nifty little portfolio of the paintings she's restored in a binder. I like binders. You know the kind with plastic sleeves?"

"Yes, I know them. So you have no hard proof?"

"Not currently. But I watched her paint in her kitchen through the zoom lens of my Pentax. She gets up before it's light and paints in a man's shirt. I even walked onto the Gowanus Expressway, risking personal injury and a citation, so I could peer into her squalid little apartment at eye level. They should call these apartments furnished kitchenettes if you ask my opinion. You can cook while sitting on the edge of your Murphy bed. Who was Murphy, anyhow, and why the hell does he get a bed named after him?"

Marty studies the photograph of the woman standing framed behind a window. She is slender and pale, with unbrushed honey-blond hair that reaches her shoulders. Her eyes are downcast, a paintbrush in one hand. She's wearing a powder-blue oxford, open to the third button, her collarbone and neck exposed in the early light. The angle of her head conceals her face—the camera registers her forehead and a crown of unruly hair. There's something hapless and slovenly about her appearance that doesn't gel with Marty's sense of a successful art forger. The calculation, the precise mixing of pigments, the requisite nerve and pluck—these are all missing from the scene. This looks like a woman in her midtwenties who has trouble remembering to bathe. He tells Red that he'll send the final retainer payment and that he should await further instructions.

Red says, "One more thing."

"What's that?"

"I could hear that she's got an accent of some kind, though I'm not prepared to narrow it down beyond South African, British, or Australian. Boston is also not out of the equation."

"You're a real linguist, Red," Marty says. "I'll be in touch."

He hangs up the phone and looks out his window. The new office has a view that faces south, across the skyline of Midtown. On a clear day, he has a straight shot at the Empire State Building. It's late afternoon and he can see the light glinting off the limestone and granite, the way it flares when it catches on the vertical strips of stainless steel. He thinks of cliff faces and Mohawk Indians, all those Quebecois ironworkers who came down to build the city its icon. His little reverie is interrupted when Gretchen buzzes in with a reminder about his final meeting of the day.

AFTER WORK, MARTY WALKS eight blocks to the athletic club where he plays squash once a week. Because the game is mocked among his racquetball-playing colleagues, he's had to look outside the firm to find fellow enthusiasts. Marty got the game from a British expat uncle and the other men inherited the sport by similar means—athletic European fathers and zealous Anglophiles with resting heart rates in the low fifties. Like his ham radio buddies, most of whom he's never met in person, these men tend to rub against the grain of convention. They drive difficult imported cars with tight gearboxes, smoke Dunhill cigarettes that one of them brings back duty-free from Paris twice a year, and carry allegiances to outspoken ideas. Marty knows he should be driving a Ford and drinking American beer, but instead he drinks Irish porters and stouts and drives a Citroën DS-19 that spends half its life with the mechanic. Because he didn't fight in Korea or World War II, these frivolous, unpatriotic habits sometimes weigh on him.

There are four of them in the core group and they play a round robin each week to determine the overall winner. Invariably, Frederic Kriel, a Swiss-German auctioneer who's the sales director of European art for Sotheby's, trounces them all. He's tall and leonine, impeccably dressed in handmade shirts, and arrives each week in the locker room wearing kidskin driving moccasins. Marty unabashedly copies his clothes and accessories—Frederic is a barometer of elegant, masculine style. Out on the court, he unleashes a savage serve, an uncanny straight drive into the back corners, and a legendary kill shot they call the Luftwaffe. When Marty loses to Kriel by five or six points he likes to say that he's been *Luftwaffered* or *Himmlered*. Frederic is a gracious winner and takes these jibes well. He's the right amount of Swiss and German, Marty thinks, so as not to evoke a crushing defeat at the hands of an Aryan prince of the Third Reich. His eyes are a cold alpine blue, flecked with mica, and they put Marty in mind of the ice at the bottom of a Scotch glass.

The other two players are Will Turner, a surgeon, and Boyd Curry, a copywriter for a Madison Avenue ad agency. For months, Marty has been telling them of the unfolding story around the forgery and they have listened attentively and offered counsel. The group likes to ponder difficult problems, from national security to whether or not Ezra Pound should have been released from the nuthouse to the potential indiscretions that come with attending out-of-town conferences. They pride themselves on giving thoughtful advice. Because they all share a love of a marginalized sport, they often favor offbeat solutions over conventional wisdom.

Tonight, after Frederic has demoralized them all, they sit in the club lounge with imported beers in green bottles and a bowl of Spanish almonds. Except for Frederic, who's unmarried, they're supposed to be going home for dinner, to their respective wives, but they're flirting with the menu and the waitress. "A Bryn Mawr graduate with a ponytail" keeps making forays to entice them to the full dinner menu, but so far they have stuck to their guns. Unlike the basement level, where the neglected squash courts resemble concrete bunkers with flaking white paint, the club lounge is rarefied with mahogany and dead member portraits and plush leather booths. Presidents have dined here and swum in the pool with its skylight and tessellated tiles. Marty wants to ask for advice about what to do with the latest information, with the name Eleanor

Shipley, but he can't find a way into the conversation. At the end of the second beer, Boyd has floated a question about professional anxiety dreams. He likes to formalize their conversations, provide a theme or a hypothetical—who would win in a made-up presidential race; which animal, panther or jaguar, would vanquish the other beast in a battle to the death or an open-country sprint? Tonight, he's asked, "What's the worst dream you have about work?"

"Recurring?" Will clarifies.

"Could be," Boyd answers.

Frederic says, "Mine is always the same. I am standing behind the rostrum at Sotheby's and the house is full. A few employees are on the line with London buyers over at the phone bank. The next painting comes out and my vision begins to blur. It's supposed to be seventeenth century, but it looks modern and abstract. I look down at my notebook, which is supposed to contain the names of who's expected to bid and where the money is sitting, but every page is blank. I don't even know what the painting is, so how can I sell it? I just stand there until eventually one of the staffers says that they have a phone call for me. Everyone in the audience puts their paddles down and they watch me as I cross the room and take the phone."

"Who's calling?" Marty asks.

"It's just breathing on the line, but somehow I know it's the dead artist. He's so saddened by what he's just witnessed."

They pause a moment, sip their beers empathetically.

Will studies the head of his racquet, adjusting the catgut strings into parallel rows. "I have these little rituals on the day of a big surgery," he says. "I trim my fingernails and listen to a

Verdi opera in my office. Sometimes I read a few pages from *Huck Finn*. Then I go into the OR and greet everyone by name. If I haven't met a nurse I always ask her name and where she went to school. In my dream I am standing next to Harry Truman in scrubs and he's telling me, right as I sew up the patient, that I've left some gauze inside the abdominal cavity. We stand there arguing and eventually I open the patient back up and pull out a little wad of scarlet gauze."

"That's terrifying," Marty says. "My anxiety dreams are run-of-the-mill. Patent attorneys dream about filing the wrong paperwork or missing a deadline. It's the saddest thing in the world. I used to wake up in a cold sweat before I made partner. I saw myself wheeling one of those coffee carts down the hallways at work and delivering mail. My boss sometimes pissed in the coffeepot in that particular dream."

Boyd says, "I'm no Freudian but these are all very revealing, gents. In my dream I'm watching television and one of my ads comes on but it's in a different language. It sounds like Swahili or pidgin and so I hit the side of the TV set as if that will correct the language of transmission. The thing starts buzzing and warping but eventually the picture comes in and there are scenes of the Midwest scrolling by."

"What's happened to your advertisement?" asks Frederic.

"Sucked out the back of the tube. Every time I hit the set the scenery changes—a little wooden farmhouse and a red barn and a scratch of dirt with a tethered horse. And then I realize it's my childhood being depicted, back to the farm in Illinois and the horseshit town where I grew up."

"There's no way that's an actual dream," Marty says.

"Tell that to my superego."

"I think it would be your id," Frederic says matter-of-factly.

Marty raises his beer bottle in the air. "I'd like to motion to change the subject."

Boyd says, "Unless it's about an Angus steak so rare it has a pulse, I don't want to hear it. I'm hungry enough to eat the leather hide off this booth. When that classics major comes back here I'm going to order food. How old do you think she is anyway?"

"We made a pact to our wives—snacks only," Marty says.

Boyd says, "Read history: pacts are designed to be broken."

"Well, while you're sitting with that moral dilemma, I have an update on the missing painting."

Frederic says, "Go on."

"As you all know, I retained this slob of a private detective who lives in a houseboat over on the Jersey side of the Hudson. Anyway, after months of digging around and eating hot dogs on street corners, he finally delivered me a name and some photographs. Apparently an art restorer who might also be the forger behind the painting that's now sitting on the floor in my study." Marty digs through his pockets and places the business card on the table.

Boyd says, "Were we expecting this? A woman art restoration expert?"

"I don't know what we were expecting," Marty says.

Will picks up the business card, studies it under the blown-glass wall sconce, and hands it to Frederic. Marty notices how perfectly manicured Kriel's fingernails are as he turns the card over and then waves it in the air. Frederic says, "This is very nice paper. It has heft."

"That was my thought as well," says Marty.

"Are we saying the quality of the paper suggests a legitimate enterprise?" Will asks.

"No, we're not saying that quite yet," answers Frederic. "So what are your next steps?"

Marty puts a few almonds in his mouth and chews meditatively. "Well, I suppose the right thing to do is to give the name to the police or the insurance firm. But part of me wants to know who this woman is before I hand her over."

"And why would you want to know that?" asks Will. "If a burglar comes into your home and steals everything in sight do you want to read his memoirs?"

"I would," offers Boyd.

"The other thing," Marty says, "is that I have this sneaking suspicion that my life has only gotten better since the painting was stolen. I feel stronger somehow."

"Your squash game hasn't gotten any better," says Boyd, smiling. "I just had an epiphany—I'm ordering a steak. The iron levels go down in my blood and I get mean-spirited. A steak at this point is for the sake of my fellow humanity."

The waitress eyes the table again and Boyd waves her over. She smiles and begins to make her way across the room.

"Are you saying the stolen painting is cursed?" Will asks.

"That sounds melodramatic," says Marty. "Although none of its previous owners lived past the age of sixty."

"That's because they were living in a malarial swamp called the Netherlands and didn't have flushing toilets," says Boyd.

"I mean since then," adds Marty.

Frederic says, "We've all read *The Picture of Dorian Gray*, Marty, so you're not the first to imagine that a painting has supernatural powers. Every time I auction off Renaissance art I think that I'm going to burn in hell or that I'm getting secret, coded messages from God. Let me tell you something . . . it's oil and pigment on scraps of linen or hide and sunlight passing through prisms of color. What we're trying to buy, when we buy art, is ourselves. So if you ask me, part of you was stolen with that painting and you should feel outraged. And, of course, if you no longer want the painting after it's retrieved, Sotheby's would be only too happy to auction it for you."

Marty says, "I was thinking I might flush her out. Call her up and pretend to engage her as an art consultant or something."

"That would be foolish and risky," says Will.

"I think that's an interesting idea," says Boyd. "Like that waitress, you have my full and undivided attention."

Marty says, "I might have to use a false name. She might know who I am."

"Or know what you look like," says Will.

Boyd is glued to the approaching waitress, but he says, "Yes, but what's the worst thing that can happen?"

"I don't know. She leaves the country with his three-hundred-year-old painting," Will says.

The waitress finally arrives and Boyd orders a steak, rare, and a baked potato. He deliberates over the menu, enunciating his words, asking about the soup of the day and the seasonal vegetables. The other men look on with moral outrage. The waitress is wearing a black vest that gives her a certain authority, despite her age. She asks the others what they would like to order, the sound of certainty in her voice. One by one they fold. Marty orders the porterhouse and another beer. There's a moment of quiet defeat.

"How about this?" Will says. "When my wife files for divorce because I don't eat her lasagna tonight how about I just put Boyd's name on the decree."

They all laugh and sip their beers.

Frederic picks the thread back up: "Here's what you do. You know the auction house over on Fifty-Seventh, Thornton and Morrell?"

Marty nods.

"They're having an Old Masters auction next week and they've got everything out on display. You invite this supposed art restoration expert to meet you there. You see what she knows about that period, start asking probing questions. You decide whether it seems plausible."

"Do I use a false name?"

"Why not have some fun with it?" says Boyd. "A little undercover operation, some recon. We need to think of a really good name. And if on the off chance she acts cagey when she sees you then you know the jig is up and she knows your face. You abort the mission if that happens. This is sounding like Hitchcock. I like it."

"You should be writing cheap novels," Will says, "not 7-Up commercials."

"Why wouldn't I bring her to Sotheby's?" asks Marty.

"If it ever came out that I let a potential forger into the auction house they would send me to the basement archive and change my name to Clause. We call those people down there archive monkeys."

"But you're fine with me taking her to a competitor?"

"Thornton and Morrell are a niche market."

Boyd says, "I've got a fake name for you! Oliver Kitwell."

"Sounds like a London barrister," says Frederic.

"Sam Iris," Boyd counters.

"An eye doctor from Connecticut."

Marty says, "I've always wanted to be called Jake. My father's name was Jacob. How about Jake Alpert? The last name still has a Dutch ring to it and I might convince her I'm building out a family collection."

Will says, "I still think you should just call the cops or the insurance investigators. What happens if they find out you had information and never passed it along?"

Boyd replies: "This is why I want you to operate if I ever have an aneurysm, Will, because you think of every contingency. I'd like to have my capillaries in your hands." Boyd looks around the room. "Now, if my steak doesn't get here pretty soon I'm going to have the aforementioned aneurysm."

Marty laughs and drains his beer. The conversation takes a new turn and he quietly mutters, "Jake Alpert, Jake Alpert," letting it play out in his mouth.

WHEN MARTY ARRIVES HOME, his harrowing vision is realized—Hester has made a full meal and Rachel is carrying the dinner plates from the kitchen. With Carraway scampering for attention at his feet, he pours two glasses of wine and sits down at the table. Overcompensating, he says, "I'm famished."

Rachel smiles and whisks her napkin into her lap. "Hester made beef Stroganoff and green beans."

Within the hour, Marty has eaten a steak the size of his terrier. Hester appears with the laden plates and the thought of more beef, mixed with cream, puts pressure on the back of his throat.

Rachel begins to tell him about her day chasing birds in the park. Recently she joined a social club, an offshoot of the Aid Society, and they meet once a week for book club, bird-watching in Central Park, or a cultural field trip of some kind. With binoculars around their necks and fastened sunhats, they try to spot warblers or migrating chickadees—Marty has no idea what—before sitting by the azalea pond to drink a thermos of English Breakfast tea. They're all women, as far as Marty can tell, led by a British expat in corduroys who's married to a federal judge. As ridiculous as this outing sounds to Marty, he's so grateful that Rachel is back among the living and finding distraction.

"Did you discover a new species out there today?" Marty asks.

"Don't be dismissive," she says. "The park is on a major migration route." She gives a little shake of the head. "In the afternoon I went to the travel agent. Do you remember we talked about the river cruise in the spring?"

"How could I forget?"

Beside her on the table she's stacked a small pile of travel brochures. The trip is a river cruise along the Seine, stopping at villages and towns in Normandy. Marty would rather take the train somewhere, through the Alps or across Spain, stopping at the Alhambra, but he's not about to complicate things between them. She opens a glossy brochure and reads some highlights between mouthfuls.

"On day three we stop at Vernon and travel into the town of Giverny, where Monet lived from 1883 until his death in 1926. Doesn't that sound fun?" she says.

A Kodachrome image of the iconic water garden with its lilies and Japanese bridge flashes through Marty's mind and he thinks there must be better ways to spend eight days and several thousand dollars. He says, "Wonderful," choking down another bite of Stroganoff. When she's immersed in the brochure again, Marty puts another piece of beef in his mouth before pulling it back out under the cover of his napkin. He drops his hand beside his chair with the chunk of meat and feels Carraway's muzzle nudging it from his fingertips.

He empties a third of his plate in this fashion while Rachel steps him through the itinerary. He can feel his mind fogging over, so he takes a sip of ice water to brace himself back to attention. He stares at the painting above her head, a dour Flemish school portrait of a man holding his hat. Like so many of his father's paintings, it's dulled by age and in desperate need of cleaning. Jacob de Groot believed that cleaning paintings ruined their rustic appeal and diminished their power. There's part of him that wants to tell Rachel that he's got a solid lead with the private investigator, but there's a stronger part that's protective of this new information. For a month after they discovered the robbery, when the police and insurance investigators came through the house, she asked for regular updates, but now she's lost interest. He'll tell her once he knows something definitive.

Bringing his gaze back to Rachel, he says, "Impressionists from a slow-moving river, what could be better?"

"You hate the Impressionists," she says, laughing slightly.

"Not all of them."

"You once said to me, and I quote, 'Monet makes me feel like I'm queasy and squinting outside on a hot day.'"

"Did I actually say that?"

"At this very table, my love."

"Well, maybe I've changed my tune. And what better place to do it than in his old stomping grounds."

"Well, I appreciate you being flexible with this trip. I just think it'll be nice to get away from the city for a bit."

"I couldn't agree more," he says, cutting a green bean into a dozen tiny pieces.

Rachel goes back to the brochures, which have been dog-eared and underlined. It strikes him that she's eager to make a fresh start, to leave the wreckage of two miscarriages behind her. In theory, they could try again, but they made an unspoken pact after the second time, a silent agreement to never subject themselves to the brutal forces of nature again. He feels a surge of tenderness toward her as she turns the pages of northern France, the way she's willed herself back from the brink of despair. For several years he stood to lose her; she was drifting down hallways with sad, sun-bleached novels in her hands. Not really thinking it through, he says, "If you ever wanted to, I would adopt. A whole tribe of them if you wanted."

She looks up from her dinner plate, startled for a moment but then softening. She holds the brochure very still and smiles faintly. "I know you would. I just don't think that's right for us. For me."

He reaches over and touches the back of her hand. "Of course."

AFTER DINNER, Marty goes into the library to smoke a cigar and drink some Scotch behind his father's old desk. Like the paintings and the apartment itself, this was handed down, a sprawling ship captain's desk with heavy walnut legs and brass fixtures. It's a throwback to the Dutch bloodline, the shipping merchants and traders. His father's personal effects are still strewn throughout the desk, as if Jacob de Groot were away on one of his extended business jaunts instead of dead for decades. An old appointment diary, opera tickets, a pair of eyeglasses, medical scissors, typewriter ribbon canisters, a leather dice shaker. There are pullout panels and secret compartments, a recess at the back for navigational charts where a life insurance policy and a roll of cash still remains untouched. Marty's added his own effects over the years, his embossed stationery and cigar boxes, an old mouthpiece from a trumpet, but he still feels like he's sharing the desk with his father.

The talk of assumed names at the club made him remember something he's kept since he and Rachel were first married. Inside the top drawer, along with his correspondence, he finds a list of names written on hotel stationery. They'd been in Europe on their honeymoon, eating their way through France and then taking the train overnight to Barcelona, where they lay marooned on a blanket at the beach for a week. They made love every day in their hotel room with a balcony, he remembers, quietly during the siesta hours, their bodies rimed with salt, the sound of the street vendors making it feel slightly illicit. One afternoon he took a long bath with the windows flung open above Las Ramblas and jotted down all the names he fancied for children. Girls: *Martha, Susan, Elizabeth, Genevieve, Stella*. Boys: *Harold, Claude, Franklin*. He reads the names now under the desk lamp, feeling nostalgic but also wondering what the hell he was thinking with the name Claude, which seems to have a pouting and bookish sting to it. Claude is the name of a man who walks out of rooms in the middle of arguments. He'd continued to carry the list for years, folded inside his breast pocket, waiting for the right occasion to review it. But he never showed it to Rachel, because it somehow itemized their loss, gave it a tangible form. These were all the children they would never have. He puts the list away and leans back in his chair to blow smoke up at the ceiling.

The forgery leans against the bookshelves opposite. By lamplight and at this distance, he can't detect any differences from the original, the image that floats through his memory. He's made a point not to study it closely during daylight, afraid that he'll see a clear sign of fabrication—an implausible passage of brushwork—and therefore a suggestion of his own gullibility. It's only a little after eight, but Rachel has gone to bed with the dog and her travel brochures. He takes the heavyweight business card out of his pocket. On a piece of blotting paper he writes down *Jake Alpert* so he won't forget, drains his Scotch, then picks up the phone on his desk and dials the number. It rings nine times before a woman answers, sounding slightly annoyed and out of breath.

"Hello?"

"I'm looking for Eleanor Shipley."

"This is Ellie."

"Ah, yes, sorry to trouble you so late, I got your name—" He pauses, begins again. "My name is Jake Alpert and I'm looking to retain an art consultant and restoration expert. Is that something you do?"

There is a slight delay and he thinks he can hear water running in a sink. "It's not a terrific time," she says. "I just jumped out of the shower and I'm dripping wet. Can I call you tomorrow?"

"Yes, of course. Again, my apologies. It's hard for me to talk at my office."

"I can call you back wherever you like."

Marty thinks about how the small lie of *Jake Alpert* has had a cascade effect. Since he never answers his own phone, he could never give out his home or office number.

The silence unravels.

She says, "Listen, if you hold on a sec, I'll go dry off and we can talk for a minute."

"If it's not an imposition."

The sound of the phone being put down on a table or counter. He tries to listen to the ambient sounds of her apartment, but all he hears is the water being turned off. There's something oddly intimate about being on hold while she towels off. A different woman would have insisted he call back during business hours, but then it occurs to him that she's used to calls during the night, that she might operate in a world without appointment diaries and switchboard operators. When she comes back, her voice is steady and composed.

"Mr. Alpert, are you still there?"

"I am indeed." He places her accent as Australian and wonders how he could have hired the only tone-deaf private investigator in all the five boroughs.

"So what can I help you with?"

"Well, I'm in the process of building out my father's art collection, filling in holes and whatnot, and I need a good pair of eyes. There's some cleaning and restoring, but I'd also like some help with some new purchases. I was thinking Flemish and Dutch school, seventeenth century. Do you have any experience in that area? My father was Dutch, so I had an early introduction to the lowlands."

"I'm writing my dissertation on the Golden Age, at Columbia. I'm focusing on Holland, but I also know my way around Flanders. It's nice to hear of a collector who sees the potential."

"Perhaps we can set up an appointment to meet and discuss possibilities."

"That would be fine. Who recommended me, if you don't mind me asking?"

Marty keeps a pull of cigar smoke in his mouth and considers. "That's a good question. Could it have been a professor of yours that I met at a dinner party? I remember an abundance of tweed."

"That hardly narrows it down."

They both laugh at this and he considers it a small victory.

"You're Australian?"

"Thank you for not saying Boston."

"Not a thing like it. Where are you from?"

"Sydney. But I spent a few years in London before I came here. I switched from conservation to art history. Do you know the Courtauld Institute in London?"

"Of course," he says, though he's not sure he does. He pauses a moment and says, "Thornton and Morrell are holding an Old Masters auction this Thursday afternoon and I have my eye on something. Perhaps we could meet before the auction and if things work out you could come along as my trusted advisor."

"That sounds fine."

"I'll send a car for you at four sharp. What's your address?"

"Oh, that's not necessary. I can take the train or a bus."

"I insist."

He hears some clicking and thinks she might be twirling the phone cord. "All right."

She gives him the address and he writes it down.

"Good night, then, Mr. Alpert. Thank you for calling. I look forward to meeting you."

"Please, Ellie, call me Jake."

"Very well, I will."

He puts down the receiver and realizes he hasn't taken his eyes off the forgery the whole time they've talked. The light is so diffuse that the shadows register as watery outlines, barely discernible against the faintly blue ice and snow. He thinks of her painting something that is so close to being transparent, one remove from not being there at all, and for a moment feels nothing but admiration.

Amsterdam

MAY 1637

PIETER DE GROOT ATTENDS AN ESTATE auction being held by the local Guild of St. Luke. He's in town on business, but the delays at the shipyard have kept him casting about for distractions for three days. It's barely dawn when he wends along the Kalverstraat, looking for the address advertised on the handbill. The night watch is returning home with their dogs and rattles while the lamplighters refill tiny pots of oil on the hog-backed canal bridges. The wooden house, when he finds it, is hemmed in by alleyways of painting studios, blacksmiths, and two dubious-looking taverns named the Thirsty Cat and the Lion's Tale.

Inside the house, it's a rummage of dim rooms, all set at different levels. A wiry man introduces himself as Theophilus Tromp, guild servant, and directs him up a steep flight of darkened stairs. A group of speculators and bidders has already assembled in a room that's been set up for the auction, lined with furniture, wedding souvenirs, linens, and unframed paintings. The canvases have been organized thematically, propped against easels or along one wall—seascapes to the left, landscapes in the middle, and still lifes to the right. The buyers quietly mill among the objects. Some of the other men start conferring and strategizing and it becomes apparent that many of them know each other, that auction alliances have been forged on previous occasions. Pieter wonders if anyone will chase after the tulip still lifes. After tulipomania afflicted the provinces for several years, the whole thing went bust in February. During the boom years, when every tailor and glassblower dabbled in the short-term market for bulbs, Pieter had been one of the few Dutchmen who never fell victim to the mania. A ship is something I can understand, he would tell people, the formation of rib and hull, the combined logic of prow and sail. On principle, he has never invested in anything he can't explain to his wife and children. Betting on a flower's future blooming always seemed to him like betting on the motion of clouds.

He has his eye on a particular seascape—a ship tossed in a squall, besieged by foam-crested waves. On the horizon a fissure of sunlight breaks through the brooding clouds and to Pieter it suggests everlasting salvation. These seamen will not drown. The ocean is leaden and tinged with green—he's seen those foreboding waters in the middle of the Atlantic, back in his days as ship's carpenter. When the auctioneer appears he has the bearing of a functionary—myopic and with a sheath of papers in his inky grip. He insists on auctioning off the household items first and starts up with his droning, mercantile voice. Just to be sportsmanlike, Pieter bids on a rack with three canes. His house outside Rotterdam is set on acreage, and when guests come for the weekend they always admire his Malacca walking cane. One of the other bidders ends up with most of the pans and saucers, perhaps as gifts for a new wife starting a household. Before the auctioneer moves to the paintings, one of the other bidders says, "None of the canvases are signed."

The guild servant nods carefully, deliberating over his words. "Although masters are licensed to sign their works and run workshops, paintings cannot be sold outside guild statutes."

From the back of the room Pieter says, "Are we to assume the painter left behind some debts with the guild?"

The servant looks at the space in front of him, purses his lips slightly, then glances at the auctioneer, who springs into action, riffling through his papers and summoning another mercantile chant. The bidding begins with the flower paintings. Surprisingly, a manservant attending the auction on his employer's behalf buys the whole lot of them. A crown of tulips dazed by sunshine, a vivid arrangement in the splendor of a drawing room—they might as well be portraits of demons for all Pieter cares. When the bidding starts on the seascapes Pieter comes out quickly, raising his hand in ten-guilder increments. A grizzled-looking adversary with a clay pipe rises up against him and from the look of the man's ravaged face Pieter suspects he's a retired sea captain, a querulous pensioner who still wakes for first watch. Pieter ups his bid and buys the painting for much more than it deserves. The retired captain pulls on his pipe, avoiding eye contact, and settles for a grim scene of a beached leviathan, its blackened hide ravaged by villagers carrying axes and pails of fat. By the time all the paintings have been sold an hour has passed and the day has grown warm outside the attic. The closed room is stifling, smelling of tobacco and varnished canvas. The auctioneer places the goods of sale into separate piles, each with a corresponding bidder's name, and wraps the paintings in lengths of muslin for carrying out into the street. Pieter goes in search of fresh air.

He finds a back room set behind the main attic space. From the look of things it had been the artist's workroom. It faces the street with a large shuttered window that he opens, swinging it out beneath the bell gable and the beam hoist. He guesses the room was once used for hauling and storing provisions, and it now looks as if the artist has just left to fetch something. A small city of bottles and stone bowls occupies a table, an assortment of scrapers, trowels, and brushes rising from an earthenware jar. A shelf is lined with pigments, oils, and spirits. Beneath the window Pieter notices a canvas covered with a drop cloth. His first thought is that the guild member has siphoned off something for himself, some little gem that is far superior to everything else in the next room. But when he removes the cover and takes in the scene he wonders if the painting is destined for the guild archives so as to avoid scandal.

He angles the picture to study it in the light of the window, but in the harshness of sunlight the surface recedes and flashes iridescent. Pieter brings the canvas back down and props it against one wall. He stands there for several minutes, riveted by the uneasiness of the scene. He's never thought much about paintings or what they mean. He knows of Rembrandt and the craftsmen of Delft, has heard stories about portrait artists being summoned behind palace walls. Up until this moment, though, he has always thought of painters in the same light as stonemasons or engravers, craftsmen who ply a trade. This painting is entirely different, a scene so ethereal that it flinches in the full light of day. The boy waving from the ice with the dog at his heels, his scarf nothing more than a yellow crinkle, a shaving of lemon rind. The barefoot girl with her pale hand against the birch, leaning toward the skaters; the light on the horizon that is somehow both serene and ominous. Looking at the painting makes Pieter think of those wintry afternoons when as a boy he waited for dusk to settle over the house and for the first tallow candles to be lit. His father would become quiet and speculative and tell stories about dead relatives. The smell of supper would kindle from the stewpot in the flames of the hearth. The painting contains all this. It is about the moment before nightfall, about waiting to cross over.

He imagines the painting framed above his desk back in Rotterdam, sees it presiding over one wall during contract negotiations. He pictures shipwrights and underwriters staring up at that scene, stupefied into submission. There's a commotion next door and he becomes aware that he's been missing for some time. He covers the painting and puts it back where he found it. When he walks out into the hallway, many of the bidders are descending the narrow stairs with their spoils, the guild servant directing them from the landing below. Pieter enters the room and lingers by the auctioneer as the other men bundle up their supplies. He waits for the last man to leave and begins to organize his cane rack and painting. The auctioneer is entering spidery figures into a ledger and double counting the money.

"I have a cousin who's an auctioneer," says Pieter. "Mostly horses and farms, but he makes a swift living."

The auctioneer looks up but does not respond.

Pieter persists. "How did you do today? Overall. It's a percentage, if I'm not mistaken, of the total."

"What is?"

"The auctioneer's fee."

The man brings his attention back to the ledger and the money. Pieter can tell he's a practical man, that he auctions off paintings and jewels and dead men's clothes with the same impunity.

On a whim, Pieter says, "I've been following the funeral notices. I don't recall the name of the artist who passed away. Usually the guild makes a big to-do of the passing of an illustrious member."

The auctioneer looks up at him. "The guild did not publish the name."

"And, yet, a simple questioning of the neighbors would reveal that."

"As you wish, sir."

Pieter paces a little, then turns back. "Well, I can only assume that there was some sort of scandal with the dead painter." He examines his fingernails. "Perhaps it was a suicide. That never looks good for a guild."

The auctioneer begins to stack his money into a cloth bag.

Pieter says, "I notice there is another painting in the next room."

Squinting for a moment at the ledger, the man says, "That picture is not for sale."

Pieter knows from the look in the auctioneer's face that he's pressing against something. The man scribbles beside a column of figures.

Pieter says, "Perhaps it is not presently for sale. But perhaps an auctioneer might represent a potential buyer like myself with the guild in this matter. Hypothetically, and for a handsome commission, that auctioneer might tell the guild predicant or bureaucrat or whoever he is that a good reputation is worth a lot. Priceless, in fact. Scandal and gossip can ruin the standing of a guild, especially when your average monger or merchant thinks they should all be abolished. Those membership fees amount to taxes, and clearly this artist was driven to sell his unsigned work on the black market to survive and took his own life under an extremity of circumstances."

The auctioneer sits before his splayed ledger, formulating some tactic of his own. Quietly, he says, "He's as good as dead."

Pieter waits.

"From what I hear, the husband and wife were both painters, former members of the guild with debts thereto. Going bankrupt, they were selling work on the side. The guild does not permit—" The auctioneer's voice breaks off and he looks back down at the floor. "The wife is selling everything off before going to work for one of the husband's creditors. He has abandoned her and the poor wretch must now fend for herself. I'm told that the guild was considering her readmission, but now things have changed." The auctioneer stands abruptly and crosses to the door with his ledger and bag of money. "This is all I know."

Pieter says, "Tell the guild servant that I will offer a hundred guilders for that painting and with that comes discretion and peace of mind."

The man hesitates, his eyes lifting toward the window.

Pieter says, "Your commission for this transaction will be ten percent, which I think you'll recognize as generous."

"Twenty," the man says, still standing there, looking out onto the Amsterdam rooftops, his voice unabashed. "For twenty percent, sir, I can secure you that painting."

Pieter knows that he's revealed his attachment to the painting and that the balance of power has shifted. The auctioneer has plucked it from his hands like a pebble. Pieter nods but says nothing. The auctioneer disappears into the passageway and Pieter listens as he plods down the stairs. From the attic window he watches the street below, sees the guild member and the auctioneer confer. After a few moments he sees a woman approach in a long cape, her face pale and bereft, her hands clutching a small basket in front of her. The auctioneer hands the cloth bag of money to the guild servant, who shifts from foot to foot, addressing the woman. The three of them seem to be talking, but the woman's eyes are averted. At one point the servant cranes up at the narrow facade of the house and the woman follows his gaze. For a brief moment, Pieter is staring directly into her face, her features narrowed into a squint. He's not sure whether she can see him behind the reflection of the glass.

Sydney

AUGUST 2000

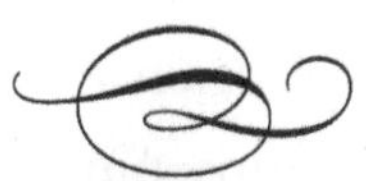

TWO MEN ARE HAULING a Kelvinator fridge over to Scotland Island in a metal dinghy. Ellie watches them from the veranda, peering through the hem of trees with her field binoculars. A small crowd has gathered at the ferry dock to watch the spectacle unfold, somebody's father or uncle too cheap to hire one of the cargo launches. It's been a few days since the Dutch cases were opened, and Ellie waits for her life to be cleaved in two by a ringing phone. It could be a call from Max Culkins, or Marty de Groot, or Helen Birch, the museum's conservation scientist.

Max's version of handling the delicate situation was to insist on thorough testing of all three de Vos paintings now that Marty de Groot had delivered his painting to the museum. When Max called Ellie he said, "Compare and contrast, back up the claims with data." His voice was casual and academic. Meanwhile, the thought of Marty de Groot walking into the art gallery fell like a hammer through her whole body. Max said that once the examination was complete and the test results were in hand, he would personally communicate with the owner of the forgery and arrange for the return of the painting. "Let me be the one to handle that," she'd said. "I feel partly responsible for this mess." But Max ignored her offer and continued in a conspiratorial tone: "They take it personally, Ellie, they always do. What if both the Leidens are fakes? They'll be very humiliated. Or, heaven forbid, what if Mr. de Groot is lugging around a bad egg?"

Helen Birch has spent several days with the paintings. A small-town veterinarian who got a Ph.D. in material science after a devastating divorce, she's the only person at the museum who wears a lab coat. Helen has the reputation of being a data person with no inherent feeling for art. She's called in like a ballistics expert to conduct examinations in microscopy, X-ray, infrared, and spectroscopy. The handful of times Ellie has interacted with Helen she's always gone away with a sense of a misplaced calling, that Helen should have become a UN weapons inspector instead of a painting conservator.

Normally, any testing would be done in the presence of the courier and after the exhibition has concluded, but the maintenance team is still repairing some water damage to the skylights and no paintings have been approved for hanging in the gallery space. Somehow, Max Culkins has persuaded the Leiden museum to permit the testing without the presence of Hendrik Klapp, who has flown back to the Netherlands.

The two men with the fridge have come to the choppy midpoint of the bay, the smaller man now throttling the outboard into a high-pitched whinny. The sound unzips over the watery basin, the sandstone cliffs bear it across the bay like the skin of a drum. The boat's gunwales are just inches from the waterline and through the binoculars Ellie can see the bigger man's mortification.

Ellie wants to believe that if it weren't for the lead-tin yellow, her replica might be considered a copy made by the artist herself, a common practice in a seventeenth-century painting studio overflowing with apprentices. But anyone with a cursory knowledge of de Vos knows that she was exiled from traditional practice and probably not inclined to copy her own work. Even the packers know about the twin paintings now, about the planet and its orbiting moon. Q and his men have taken up a nickname for the upcoming exhibition—*Dutch Doppelgängers*. They can't be sure exactly how, or when, but every curator, packer, and conservator suspects—and hopes—that someone is going to be humiliated by the conclusive evidence of a fake, either a rich American or that imperious little Dutchman with his ornate packing crates.

Ellie goes inside, pours herself a glass of wine, and comes back out onto the veranda. Her thoughts return to Sara de Vos and the funeral painting—*Winter with a Child's Funeral Procession*. It keeps pulling her back, like an undercurrent to her dread. Not only does the picture extend Sara's life beyond what Ellie has published, but it also throws into doubt her whole theory about the painter's career. Ellie had claimed in her book that *At the Edge of a Wood* was the high-water mark of Sara's career, a moment of transcendence before she might have abandoned the medium altogether. She'd speculated that the daughter's death had loosed something in Sara, a savage kind of grief that burned onto the canvas. But she'd also wondered whether it depleted something in the artist, made it difficult for Sara to move on with her life. The trail of paintings went cold, after all. She'd never come out and said that the painting was a fluke of circumstance, a historical accident, but it somehow seemed implied. Now, the new painting suggests a kind of rebirth, an artist who continued to evolve in her mastery.

She often sees Sara in her dreams—a woman in a bonnet, a sallow, slightly drawn expression, peering in through a window. But she has never allowed herself to think of Sara as a martyr or a sage. She routinely warns her graduate students not to project mysticism onto the lives and canvases of seventeenth-century Dutch painters. They're often tempted to view Rembrandt's delicate blue hazes as a sign of spiritual nuance, but she reminds them that they were more technical feats than a hungering for God. Religion had its place, but it was both practical and mercantile; it endured like a sturdy table in a polished kitchen. Here was a republic of watery provinces, cut through with sluices and canals, where the threat of Old Testament plague or divine retribution or epic floods kept men awake at night. In the face of that, the lowlanders were caught between appeasing God and appeasing their appetites. By all accounts, seventeenth-century Dutchmen were inveterate worshippers, brawlers, drinkers, and womanizers. They covered their walls with beautiful paintings for the same reason they drank—to distract themselves from the abyss. Or did Sara de Vos continue painting as a way to sharpen her view of the abyss?

The first suggestion that the Kelvinator has fallen into the bay is the sound of the crowd at the dock groaning and cheering. Somehow she misses the heavy plunk of the fridge hitting the water. She stands with the binoculars and sees a ring of widening ripples and the fridge jackknifing out of the water, sinking by degrees, the metal dinghy overturned. The two men are thrashing their arms through the water and yelling at each other. A police boat guns it across the bay from Church Point while half the crowd walks up the hill from the dock. Ellie spies one of the retirees from the island civic council, an elderly widow, standing in a sun hat at the end of an adjacent pier, her hands on her hips. She finds herself wondering whether the Kelvinator was a gift from two wayward sons and feels a terrible sense of loss for the woman.

Ellie goes inside and closes the glass doors behind her. The image of the woman on the pier and the pieced-together narrative of the fridge and the errant sons has worsened her mood. The red wine has amplified things by making her feel drowsy and nostalgic. She sets her wineglass down on the kitchen table, looks over at the phone, and goes back toward her bedroom. Ellie opens her closet. On the top shelf, there's a box of memorabilia and old journals and she gives in to the impulse to take it down and unpack it across her bed.

She begins to flip through the notebooks from her New York years and feels her cheeks burning when she sees all those scribbled notes from the forgery manifestos and manuals. There's a strain of anger burning beneath the notes that she barely recognizes. She was the least political person she knew back then, so it certainly wasn't a Marxist agenda that drew her in. She remembers being adrift and lonely, spending years on the periphery of a New York life until Marty de Groot faked his way into her life. There are other notebooks that date from her high school years and she follows the anger all the way back. She was angry at her father, then at the nuns and priests, then at the world. It built up for years, before reaching some kind of flashpoint when she was sixteen.

Her art teacher, Father Barry, had arranged for her to complete summer work experience with a venerable Pitt Street art gallery and restoration business. The Franke brothers were dealers in their sixties who specialized in Dutch and Flemish paintings, long before they were in vogue with collectors. It was Ellie's first exposure to lowland depictions of the seventeenth century outside of Rembrandt and Vermeer. Ellie spent six weeks at the firm, filling cracks and cleaning old paintings under a desk lamp, while the brothers did their best to bilk Rose Bay widows out of family heirlooms.

Jack Franke ran the gallery downstairs and Michael cleaned paintings on the floor above, an inner sanctum he protected with handwritten *Keep Out* signs. Despite the Franke family's aristocratic origins, the brothers were on hard times and always on the lookout for an easy profit. A typical ploy involved a wealthy and lonely old woman bundling up the wooden stairs for a restoration consult. She'd have a painting under one arm, wrapped in newspaper or sometimes in a David Jones shopping bag for fear of a curbside robbery. Occasionally it was something very valuable—a colonial botanist's depiction or an unsigned modernist on the ascent—but it would be in desperate need of cleaning. Dressed in a three-piece suit, Michael would make some tsking noises with his mouth before murmuring "pity, pity." Jack would be called in to offer counsel, turning to the woman and saying, "Madame, the prognosis is not good." The widow would recount the history of the painting and its appraised value, to which Jack would nod and thin his lips. "The cleaning will be like jackhammering old concrete. You see, it's been doused with copal varnish. If you leave the painting with Michael he will see what can be done." In fact, the varnish was almost always mastic, not copal, and easily removed with turpentine. After keeping the painting for a month, they would tally up a bill for cleaning that put a sizable dent in the value of the painting and talk the widow into a fire-sale price.

This was all part of Ellie's induction into the art world. When she wasn't filling in cracks and swabbing down glazes and scumbles, she was fetching the brothers meat pies and sandwiches and newspapers. They had parish connections to Father Barry and implied that they'd be happy to file a good report if she kept her head down. Standing above her worktable for hours, she'd get dizzy from the solvent fumes and feel light-headed by the end of the day. She got migraines from the eyestrain and went home to lie down in the bedroom she shared with Kate. It was summer holidays and boarding school was out, so Kate fetched her cups of tea while Maggie Shipley resented the special treatment, calling her Queen Eleanor under her breath. The rest of the time she was invisible to her parents and her closet was full of her mother's sewing projects. For Bob and Maggie Shipley, her going away to boarding school on an art scholarship was the equivalent of moving to Ecuador or dying at a young age.

During her last week at the firm, Michael Franke asked her if she wanted to have a go at a little inpainting. Naturally, she agreed and was invited into his studio, a glassed-in room that had once been a storekeeper's veranda. Canvases in various states of cleaning hung on the walls along with several clocks. A teakettle and a cooktop took up one corner. On an easel stood an eighteenth-century British landscape—a coastline with cattle grazing and some backlit clouds. Michael said the sky needed patching up and he'd already got the blend right. "Five shades lighter before it goes on is the general rule. Allowing for the varnish and drying and so on. Come on and take a stab." She liked the painting, the simple pleasure of cows on a coastal morning. She stepped in front of the easel and Michael picked up a fine brush with some paint on it. "Try to match the strokes if you can," he said. She took the paintbrush in her hand and steadied her arm above the canvas. The painter's brushwork was even and smooth, cutting horizontally across the grain of the canvas. She made contact with the picture with a light, steady stroke and the blue adhered nicely. She knew at once that she'd executed the brushwork perfectly; except for the wet tone, it was barely discernible from the original. Michael stood over her, smelling of acetone and damp newspapers. She made several passes with the brush and each one added to the carefully blended effect. She took a step back and looked at Michael, who turned his attention suddenly to a pile of paperwork on his desk. The Franke brothers weren't big on praise, so she fully expected something understated, a nod and a *not bad*. But without looking up at her Michael leafed through some invoices and said, "In twenty years I've never seen an apprentice quite bungle a painting like that. Maybe your sort is better suited for a different kind of trade." She stood there for a long time, unable to move or fathom why he was being so cruel. Did *your sort* refer to her being female, Catholic, or the daughter of a ferryman? Then he added, “It’s almost lunchtime. Go see what Jack wants. I’ll take a hamburger with bacon.” She left the workroom in tears and trudged down the stairs, not saying a word to Jack as she walked out onto the street. She never went back, but weeks later she saw the painting she’d touched up for sale in the Franke gallery window. It was her unchanged brushwork in the sky—perfectly blended and seamless within the swath of blue.

Something changed in her after that. The anger hardened, came back as a refrain. For years, that moment flickered back whenever she was cleaning or inpainting a canvas—a sense that she had no business engaging in this work. Sometimes her throat would bloat with rage. It should have been easy to dismiss—a miserable old man unable to offer a gifted teenage girl a simple compliment. The Franke brothers reported to Father Barry that she’d run off one lunchtime and the priest soured toward her after that. It was the beginning of a new era, of living on the periphery. Lying across her bed forty-odd years later, a little drunk on a Wednesday afternoon, she reads the notebooks from her teens and twenties and feels a presence in the room—a neglected, slightly gullible teenager. She wonders now if the forgery wasn’t a form of retribution, a kind of calculated violence—against Jack and Michael Franke, against the old boy network at the Courtauld Institute, against her own indifferent father. But mostly against the girl standing out on the glassed-in veranda who thought her talents were prodigious and therefore enough.

THE RINGING TELEPHONE dredges her from a deep sleep. She gets up and navigates blearily through the house, a hand against the hallway wall to steady herself. She doesn't pick up the receiver in time and the call goes to the answering machine. There's a certain satisfaction in hearing Helen formulate her words into an impromptu speech. "Ah, hi, Ellie, look, it's Helen Birch here from the gallery and I'm wondering if we might schedule a time for you to come into the lab. I've been performing some technical analysis on the three de Vos pictures and have found a few anomalies and whatnot. Perhaps I can talk you through my findings in person. Anyway, I'm ducking off for the rest of the afternoon—dentist appointment, sounds lovely, doesn't it?—but I'll be in first thing tomorrow. Just come by any time before noon if you have a chance and we'll go through the data. Okay, cheerio then."

Ellie goes back out to the veranda to see what's become of the miniature shipwreck.

Manhattan

SEPTEMBER 1958

WITH ITS FRENCH WALNUT paneling and ferns in copper planters, the auction house on West Fifty-Seventh makes Marty uneasy. It reeks of old money and makes him self-conscious, puts him in mind of venerable old steak houses and New England boarding schools. He's arrived an hour before the auction and waits for Eleanor Shipley to pull up in the car he's sent for her. The employees of Thornton and Morrell, the department heads and cataloguers, dress like pallbearers except for their vivid bow ties. The doorman has the bearing of a Renaissance scholar whose post out on the sidewalk is due to some kind of clerical mishap. Marty thinks of the jaunty, grinning Sotheby's doorman, who looks like a bouncer from an upscale London nightclub.

He stands by the front windows, waiting for the car service to pull up. The street has thinned out after the frenzy of lunch hour, a lull in the middle of an Indian summer afternoon. A florist and a watch repairman stand in front of their adjacent storefronts, chatting and smoking cigarettes. When the black Cadillac arrives, he waits for the driver to come around to open a rear passenger door, waits to see Eleanor Shipley's face revealed in the doorframe, but the front passenger door opens and a loping blonde hops out on the traffic side. A passing taxicab honks. The driver emerges in his chauffeur's cap, a little too slowly, mortified, looking down the sidewalk to see if anyone has seen this crazy bird from Brooklyn riding up front. As she passes the front of the Cadillac, she lifts her left high heel and adjusts an ankle strap while steadying herself against the hood. The driver takes her elbow and guides her toward the auction house. A few feet from the entrance she stops and cranes up at the facade, her mouth opening slightly. The driver dismisses himself and hurries to the car that's flashing its hazards by the curb. So this is his first impression of her—a tall, ungainly woman who seems oblivious to social norms and probably hasn't worn heels in a very long time. She's pretty in an offhand, Anglican sort of way—her hair pulled back tight, her features freckled, pale, and strong, a darting intelligence in her green eyes. The nose is slightly snubbed, he notices, watching the doorman greet her, an echo of brewers or weavers or convicts from the English Midlands, he thinks. But those electric green eyes suggest a devastating IQ smuggled into the colonies like an embezzled diamond. *How did I become such a deplorable snob*, he wonders, crossing to the double glass doors, then: *She has stolen something priceless from me*.

When she steps inside, he says, "Miss Shipley?"

Her eyes must be adjusting to the dim interior because she seems shocked to find someone standing in front of her.

"Mr. Alpert. Pleasure to meet you. Remember, call me Ellie."

"And please call me Jake."

He looks at her face, tries to discern any note of caution. He likes the fact that she's not wearing lipstick.

A little sternly, she says, "I have to warn you, this is my first auction. The art crowd thinks this is all a bit seedy and untoward."

"Oh, it is," Marty says, "a comedy of manners complete with little wooden paddles. You're going to love it. I'll teach you all the brutal customs. Don't worry that you're green—it's your expert eyes I want to lease for the afternoon."

"Speaking of eyes . . ." she murmurs, rummaging through an enormous leather handbag. Eventually, she produces a pair of black-framed reading glasses and perches them on the bridge of her nose, blinking as if the room is just now coming into focus.

He says, "Shall we take a stroll and see what's what?"

"By all means. Lead the way."

Marty moves to the far corner of the room, where there's a clearing in the inventory of Italian, Dutch, and Flemish Old Masters.

"Now, I like to make a quick perimeter check of the sale items before the auction. No use being bogged down by anything until you know the lay of the land. The auction catalogue is useful but prone to vagueness. There's a lot of *circle of*s and *attributed to*s and this or that school. Those are for the amateurs fresh off the boat. I prefer attribution, a provenance with some teeth. So I mentally cross the phantoms off my list as I walk around."

"You have a system," Ellie says brightly.

"The system is try not to be cheated. What do you see here that grabs you?"

She digs through her handbag again and produces something that looks like a jeweler's loupe on the end of a lanyard. She wears it like a necklace. "I'll need a few minutes. Why don't I report back once I've walked the circuit? You want to stick to Holland and Flanders?"

"I do," says Marty. "How about we rendezvous at sixteen hundred?"

"Is that four o'clock?"

"I'm joking."

"Of course."

"In fifteen minutes?"

"See you then."

He watches her step off uncertainly, both hands in the pockets of her flowing skirt. She stops in front of a painting, positions the loupe, and leans in, one hand clenched into a fist behind her back, a girl peering through a keyhole. By now a few dozen people have gathered in the salesroom and he sees her get some attention from some Upper East Side types and one of the grim-looking cataloguers in a silk bow tie. Marty begins to walk the floor. A seventeenth-century oak panel from Antwerp, *A Rocky Landscape with Christ on the Road to Emmaus* by Gillis Claesz. The estimate in the catalogue says two to three thousand dollars, but he doubts it's worth fifteen hundred. Next is *A river landscape by a lock, with elegant company on horseback and villagers on the bank*. Sometimes the titles are short essays and it always makes him wary, as if they commissioned a toothpaste copywriter to tell the viewer what he's looking at.

A winter village landscape with huntsman and travelers on a track is estimated at four to seven thousand dollars. These are all middling novelties, he thinks, and he suddenly worries that Ellie will think him an armchair collector, a weekend gallery warrior—she might beg off if she thinks her talents will go untapped. He looks over at her and sees her face just inches from the weave of a canvas, as if she's smelling the pigments. She straightens, looks over, gives him a self-conscious wave, then begins in his direction. He watches her handbag swing as she lopes across the room.

He says, "This lineup's weak. I feel like I'm at a garage sale in Newark."

A little breathily, she says, "I think I found something. There's a private collection, four pictures, and what's wonderful is that they're all from the same two-year period, but some from Holland and some from Flanders. Come take a look."

He says, "Some widow is converting her assets to cash or an heir is lobbing off Granny's depressing old paintings."

He's surprised when she takes him by the elbow, not affectionately, but a little forcefully, and leads him to the corner of the room where the four paintings lean against easels. He flips through the sales catalogue for the right entry: *From the private collection of the late Mr. J. A. Simmons*.

He says, "Thornton and Morrell specialize in the private collections of the dead or dying."

Ellie stands beside a floral still life—Christoffel van den Berghe's *Tulips, Roses, Narcissi, Crocuses, an Iris, a Poppy, and Other Flowers in a Gilt Mounted Porcelain Vase on a Ledge, with a Queen of Spain Fritillary, a White Ermine, and a Magpie Butterfly.*

"Oh, they kill me," says Marty. "It's like Charles Darwin wrote half these titles."

Ellie laughs, the loupe pinched between her fingers. "I agree, the title is a little on the descriptive side. But they write long descriptions since the painters didn't give the works names. It helps to keep them straight. Here's the wonderful thing. This is from Middleburg, a northern Dutch port city that was incredibly isolated in the first decades of the seventeenth century. Picture this lonely place sticking out into the North Sea like a sore thumb at the end of a chain of islands. Swamp and black mud channels, the sloppy branches of the Rhine. The Middleburg flower painters kind of invented this stuff, and it's long before the Holland tulip mania, so here is the most exquisite floral still life, the height of the art form, taking place on this little muddy nugget of land, miles from anything else. And virtually none of these flowers bloom at the same time, so everything you're looking at is amalgamated and invented in the painter's mind. So the year here is 1616 or so. Then, let's take a look at its neighbor."

Marty notices that her cheeks have flushed.

"So, then, over in Antwerp, Bartholomeus Grondonck is painting his only signed work, dated 1617."

Marty stares at *The Kermesse of Oudernarde*. It depicts peasants and children frolicking in a village during a festival. The light is blue-green and spectral.

"This is quintessentially Flemish," Ellie says. She puts one hand on her hip. "Look at the guy pissing against the doorpost."

This comment catches Marty off guard and he folds his arms in delight, leaning back to better take her in.

"Classic Brueghelian narrative, the innocence of children juxtaposed with the excess and debauchery of their parents. Now," she says, moving along, "we see this elegant and lush river landscape by Anton Mirou, also Flemish, not wonderful, but still interesting, and finally this divine de Momper, with his winter landscape. You can feel the bracing cold in this one. See how the horseman's mantle covers everything but his eyes and nose, making him look a little like a hangman. But there's not much wind and some pallid-looking sunshine is straining through the clouds. See the tree encrusted with frost, glimmering with ice—that's just beautiful!"

They both stand for a moment studying the tiny pendants of ice on the tree. There's a look of quiet reverie on her face.

He asks, "Are you religious, Ellie?"

She gives him a quizzical look. "Agnostic at best. Why do you ask?"

"Most people in the art world are looking for something divine in old paintings. Atheists looking for meaning and so on. When you look at these paintings there's a look of devotion on your face."

She shakes her head. "I'm terribly shortsighted. I'm sure that's it. I've been accused of daydreaming my whole life, but it's really just myopia."

He takes a step back so he can see all four paintings at once. "So which one do you think I should bid on?"

She brings her jeweler's loupe up to one eye and hunches over the de Momper, studying the brushwork and humming. She straightens and says, "If it were me, and I had the means, I'd take them all. The real value is in the collection, the fact that a single moment of the seventeenth century is chronicled, from that beautiful golden parrot tulip painted in Middleburg to this Flemish peasant frolic."

Marty looks down at the catalogue and takes a quick mental tally. The estimated price for all four is a little north of eighty thousand dollars. He swallows, flips pages, imagines briefly that Ellie knows exactly who he is and this is his punishment for trying to flush her out.

Regaining composure, he looks up and says, "What ties them together, besides history and geography?"

"For one thing, oil on copper. They're all on the same metal support. Whoever Mr. J. A. Simmons was, he didn't want his paintings to age. Apart from a few tiny dents, the paint is pristine with virtually no cracking. Good as new. Look at those jewel-like finishes, the bright pigments . . ."

"I noticed the craquelure is nonexistent," he says, then wonders if he sounds pompous.

"Metals don't react to humidity changes the way canvas or wood does."

From behind, they hear a commotion and turn to see the auctioneer making a sound check at the dark wood rostrum. A few men in overalls are rearranging chairs to make more room. A solid crowd has gathered in the foyer and gallery area and Marty suspects it will be standing room only.

"We better get in position," he says. "The socialites like to sit up front so they can be seen."

They take their seats a few rows from the front and watch as the auctioneer—a middle-aged man in a bespoke suit—continues counting into the microphone. Every once in a while he hoods his gaze beneath the lights and checks in with someone at the back of the room.

Marty says, "Notice the accent. The auction houses all hire Brits or Swiss or Belgians to flog off their art. It distracts you from the fact that this is not that different from a horse auction. I have a friend who's the auctioneer for Sotheby's and he tells me the house hires a voice coach who studies his performances. He's trained to avoid verbal tics and colloquialisms. Elocution and strong body language sell paintings, apparently."

"I had no idea," Ellie says.

Marty turns around to assess the crowd, hoping he won't see anybody he knows.

She says, "I've read that brown paintings don't sell as well as brighter colors. Is there any way that could be true?"

"Absolutely. And buxom female nudes sell better than skinny ones or males. Which seems intuitive enough. Also, size matters. If you can't fit it into an uptown elevator then it adds a layer of complication."

A few minutes later the salesroom is packed and there's a small crowd standing at the back. The lights dim in the house and come up on the rostrum. The auctioneer strides onto the little stage with his folio notebook. He takes a moment to make eye contact with the audience and smile. "Good afternoon, ladies and gentlemen. Welcome to today's sale of Old Masters. Before we begin, I'm obliged to read the rules concerning the conditions of sale." In a clipped Oxbridge accent, he recounts the return policy, the waivers and disclaimers, the commission fees. Marty notices that Ellie writes some of these down on the back of an envelope. A few of the auction house staff stand off to the side, sizing up the crowd.

Marty leans close to Ellie, close enough to notice that she smells more like acetone than perfume. "He's standing up there with a seating chart in his book. It's a map of the money. The people who RSVP get special placement so he knows where his bids are likely to come from. The rest of us walk-ins are harder to estimate . . ."

The auctioneer raises his gavel and turns it gently in his hand. "Let's begin with lot one, shall we, the Jacques de l'Ange on my right." A colored slide of the painting appears on a screen behind him. Marty flips through his catalogue to see that it's titled *An Allegory of Avarice*. It seems like a ruefully appropriate place for the auction to begin.

"In this case six thousand starting . . ."

A paddle in the front row wafts the air. "We have six thousand. Now six five. Do I see seven thousand dollars?"

Marty says, "Sometimes he starts with what they call chandelier bids. He calls out a series of bids that haven't actually come from the salesroom."

When she doesn't respond, Marty looks over at Ellie. She bites her bottom lip, spellbound; she could be watching a boxing match with that look of bloodlust. The bidding continues through Italy and back to the lowlands of the seventeenth century, the swamps and fens and backwaters that were somehow a hothouse for the flourishing of painterly technique, the whole Golden Age a fluke of rheumatic temperament and history. Marty punctuates the litany of artist names with this whispered commentary. He tells her to watch the range of bidding gestures, the finger salutes and paddle swipes, the big hand waves and curt head nods. She turns in her seat to better take in the spectacle.

When the first oil on copper goes up, Ellie looks outraged that they're being sold off separately. On the back of her catalogue she writes, *These paintings shouldn't be orphaned.* Apparently, Marty and Ellie are not the only ones who've scoped out the handpicked private collection, the brilliant depictions on four-hundred-year-old copper. Bids come from all sides in a flurry. Marty generally likes to take the temperature of the room before he makes a bid, so the auctioneer is saying *going once* on the Van den Berghe when he throws up his hand. Ellie's leg twitches as she tries to restrain herself. They're starting with the most valuable of the four paintings, the floral still life that could have been painted last week for all its color saturation. It's at thirty-six thousand dollars and Marty doesn't quite know how he's waded into these waters. The painting is beautiful in its own way, but he's not feeling the libidinal pull that usually guides him at auction. The artwork is merely a vehicle to further entrapment of those who wronged him. He stares straight up at the rostrum but scans his peripheral vision for competing bids. Someone from up the back must wink or pull an earlobe, because a staff member signals to the auctioneer from the sidelines. Ellie looks over at him, her eyes widened back. Marty leans close and says, "You're terrible at this," and then throws up his hand again without turning away from her. She closes her hands into fists.

"I see thirty-seven thousand from the gentleman at center. In the rear? Fair warning. Going once . . . Twice. Sold."

Ellie rubs the palms of her hands down her skirt front, looking down at the floor with a colossal grin.

"On my right now we have Grondonck and in this case, the bidding starts at twelve thousand. Again I see the gentleman at center, this time taking the lead. Now I'm looking for twelve thousand five hundred."

Marty whispers to Ellie: "Why don't you take over the bidding? Every time I tap my watchband you throw up your wooden paddle."

"No, I couldn't," she says.

A bid comes from the far right, a bat of the paddle from a ferocious-looking woman in a cashmere scarf. Marty taps his watchband on *going once* and there's a hesitation, a moment where Ellie seems paralyzed by some sense of etiquette or professional boundary. Marty shrugs with his hands in his lap and then her paddle shoots into the air. The auctioneer says, "And now a bid with gusto from the duo at center, excellent, and we're at thirteen thousand five hundred." Marty looks over at Ellie, but her eyes are still down at the floor. She rubs her hands along her skirt front again and when she turns them over he sees that her palms are glistening with sweat. He feels an odd mix of tenderness and satisfaction. There's a mounting affection toward her but also this grim delight in seeing her out of her element, in lifting that crown of tangled hair from the photograph and giving her cause to put on heels and show her face. It's clear to him now that she was not the calculating mind behind the forgery swap. No, she was the subject matter expert, the hired brush, the art savant who's probably never eaten an oyster or gone to a jazz club. It strikes him that he wants to teach her things and dupe her at exactly the same time. The feeling puzzles him as he sits back, the wire transfer to the auction house already made in his mind. The whole thing has already played out. The next oil on copper displays on the screen and he leans close to Ellie's ear. "Look at those poor sods tramping through the snow. Let's reunite them with their siblings." She looks up from the floor and gives him a look of sincere elation.

Leaving Amsterdam

SPRING 1637

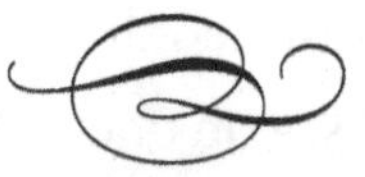

THE CREDITOR, an aging bachelor named Cornelis Groen, had commissioned Barent for a series of landscapes that were never completed. Now he's offered Sara a year of employment to work off the debt. Through the open doorway of her house, Sara can see Mr. van Schooten, the creditor's manservant, in the waiting gig, the paintings he bought at the auction wrapped and sitting at his feet. She walks out into the street and pulls the door behind her. As it catches, she stands for a moment on the stoop, unable to turn around, both hands on the green waxed door, palms flat, as if feeling the warmth of a kettle. She's suddenly terrified that she won't remember what Kathrijn looked like without the envelope of the house, without the earthly reminders of a life briefly spent. Giving herself a gentle push back, she turns to face the street. Her neighbors, many of them artists, have come out to wave goodbye.

They catch a late-afternoon water coach along the tow-canal that connects Amsterdam to Haarlem. From there, a boat takes them down the Spaarne to Heemstede, a district of burgher estates and wooded dunes. Sara looks off at the passing fields. Sometimes, when she went sketching in the countryside with Barent and Kathrijn, they would see a tiny village in this region where dogs towed flat-bottomed boats or peasants rowed out to the fields to milk their cows. Barent would tell Kathrijn stories of childhood travels with his father, a brewer stricken by wanderlust—tales of Drenthe woodcutters living in houses that were windowless and half underground, or the fishermen of Marken who lived on pilings and tarred their wooden houses against the constant damp. He'd seen heaths and forests, could describe the way the provinces were walled in by the sea on one side and the sandy moors and marshlands on the other. She pictures him out among it now, free to roam while she lives out his punishment.

After nightfall, the boat pilot leaves them at the dock in Heemstede with their stock of paintings. They wait for an hour in the cold fog. Sara glimpses a few houses through a lacework of tree branches, a stray candle burning behind a window that projects a faint halo through the mist. Eventually, a carriage rocks down the sandy road toward the dock. A single lantern bounces and sways next to the driver, a man in his thirties. Sara is not introduced to the driver, but she hears Van Schooten call him Tomas and she thanks him by name when he helps her up into the carriage. He gives her an appreciative nod, then climbs up onto the box seat. They ride a few miles along the narrow track, the fog clearing away from the river, before wending through a wood of elms and birches. They enter the estate through an iron gate. The lantern swags little glimpses into view, picks out a stone fountain and a bower in one of the gardens along the path. Beyond the dome of pale light the heavy facade and tall white windows of the house come into view. The steep tiled roof is run through with dormer windows that jut out like tiny caves in a cliffside.

The front door is carved from a solid piece of oak and bears the name *Groen* above a coat of arms—an eagle reared up and holding a sword in its talons. They pass into the foyer and Van Schooten sets the paintings against the wall. "Mr. Groen won't be disturbed tonight, but he will meet with you at breakfast. I have a small cottage at the back of the estate, but the others sleep up in the attic rooms. Mr. Brouwer here will show you up. Good night." His epic errand dispensed with, Van Schooten is out the door and she hears his boots along the gravel drive. Tomas Brouwer holds the lantern, his expression blank, before he reaches for her bundle of clothes and the painting box. Reflexively, she picks them up herself, unwilling to be parted from them. In a gentle voice, he says, "I have to take the horses to the stable, but I'll take you up first."

He leads the way across the marble floor and they pass behind the wide staircase to a narrow passageway she assumes is designated for the servants. Tomas is tall and meticulous in his movements, smells of leather and horses. His hands against the lantern are pale and thin; they seem at odds with his tending of the stables and the grounds. She follows him up the steep wooden stairs, drenched in his shadow.

"Mr. van Schooten said you are also the gardener . . ."

Tomas turns to her, smiles, and gently presses a finger to his lips. "The cook is sleeping and we don't want to be poisoned at breakfast."

They reach the attic hallway and a series of closed doors. Sara expects her sleeping quarters to be next to the storeroom, nestled beside the peat and firewood, so she's surprised to find a spacious room at the end of the house, hewn under giant crossbeams. Three dormer windows look down onto the gardens and a bed cantilevers from the wall on an iron frame. There's a small desk and an easel and a linen cupboard for her clothes. Tomas lights a candle for her and says good night. He has a kind face, she thinks, the face of a man who's spent his life around horses and roses. After he's gone she surveys the big room. It strikes her that perhaps she's been accorded special privileges, given the largest of the servant rooms, a room once reserved for a head butler. Far from smelling of sawdust and peat, the room smells of sweet woodruff and wax and lavender. She unbundles her clothes and puts on a nightdress before lying on the mattress stuffed with cotton. That first night she refuses to peel back the wool blanket or bed linens, as if this will delay her arrival.

CORNELIS GROEN IS a rheumatic bachelor in his late sixties, the son of a Heemstede founder who can trace his name back to the twelfth century. After a brief career as the inspector of weights and measures in Haarlem, Cornelis became a trader for the East India Company and eventually inherited his father's fortune and retired to the Groen estate. An amateur scientist, collector, and gardener, he wears a velvet-lined dressing gown with a pair of scissors dangling from a leather belt in case he needs to snip a stem or leaf at short notice. He also uses it to shred the tobacco for his long clay pipe that he likes to wedge beside the scissors against his waistline. Decades of unmarried life have inclined him toward his own idiosyncrasies and a misplaced sense of occasion. When Sara is summoned to breakfast that first morning, before the light has flushed the treetops, she finds him standing beneath a portrait of what looks to be his father, with a faint echo of the elder's pose—hands clasped and eyes cast into the middle distances as if contemplating a heavy burden or loss. Cornelis's eyes are a startling, febrile blue.

The dining room table has been set as if for a banquet still life—sliced apples and nuts arranged on silver trays, a loaf of bread broken in a basket, a wheel of cheese in yellow wax. Two places have been set with starched cotton napkins and hand-painted china plates. Groen turns on his heels and looks at Sara for a moment, stiffening in his joints. He is pale and tall, but also stooped in the shoulders, as if a weight is pulling on his chest. There is no formality of introductions—he speaks to her as if picking up the thread of a conversation begun in a different room. "Are you much troubled by dreams, Mrs. de Vos?"

Sara crosses the room toward him. "Not all that much."

"I had Mrs. Streek put some lavender in your linen cupboard because I've always suspected it wards off ill thoughts and troubled sleep. I liked your husband's work, but he had certain incapacities. Finishing something was one of them. I imagine he haunts your dreams and for that I'm regretful." He looks out the window that overlooks the front acres—a tendril of sunlight is edging its way into a thicket. "Every morning I stand here and watch the sun gild the trees and the grottoes.

It's like drawing a breath before the day begins in earnest. Are you hungry or could you tolerate a brief tour of the household?"

Sara hasn't eaten since Amsterdam and feels faint with hunger. "At your pleasure, Mr. Groen."

"Perhaps a few slices of apple and some herring before we walk about. But you must call me Cornelis. We'll consider this an informal arrangement, a squaring of the ledger, yes, but certainly not servitude. Dear Father in heaven, we thank you for this bounty. Please, serve yourself."

Sara sits and places some cheese, herring, and bread onto her plate. She waits for Cornelis to take his first mouthful before she begins eating. He slices and chews with great concentration.

"I've already hung your florals that we acquired, one of them in the *Kunstkammer*, the others in a barely used sitting room. You have a background in still lifes? I made certain enquiries in Haarlem. The cheese is from my own pastures. We have dairy cattle off toward the dunes in the west of the village. Forgive me for saying, but I don't think the florals are the best I've seen. A hair short of prodigious would be my approximation."

Sara looks up from her plate and wonders whether Cornelis has always been so simultaneously frank and meandering. She has the sense of listening into a conversation he's having with himself or with the room around him. She realizes now that Barent had been strangely silent about his time spent at the estate, referring to the patron simply as a fussy old burgher with too much time and money on his hands. She finishes her mouthful of bread and says, "They were painted under urgent time constraints. Sir, I wonder if we might talk about the terms of my employment. I have read the court document and contract, but I'm uncertain how I'll repay my husband's debt to you."

Groen brandishes a morsel of herring between two fingers. "Ah, let's not talk of debt. Would you pass me that butter dish, meisje?"

Sara hands him the silver dish and watches as he slathers some butter onto a heel of bread.

"Before he passed away, my father was a landscape painter and I trained in his workshop from the age of twelve. I helped my husband with his work, when I wasn't painting my own still lifes. I could continue with the landscapes if you like."

"Eat up and we'll take that tour." Cornelis looks back out toward the window and nods, as if approving of the sunlight's passage across his treetops.

THEIR FIRST STOP IS THE KITCHEN, where Mrs. Streek, a stout and ruddy Frisian woman, is scrubbing a copper pot. Cornelis enters tentatively and explains that there are actually two kitchens, one for cooking and one for "inventory and display." Mrs. Streek looks up from the soapy water and asks whether they're done with the breakfast dishes. "A second sitting is in the stars, I believe, Mrs. Streek," says Cornelis. "I'm showing our guest around the place." Mrs. Streek rinses the pot under some scalding water and says, "A guest, is it?" She never once looks at Sara, and they demurely pass into an adjacent room glinting with copper pans, pewter dishes, a glass-fronted cupboard that displays crockery and hand-painted china. "Mrs. Streek would never do more than boil water in here. I've caught her polishing the silver on her day off. Grew up with the herring mongers of Friesland so perhaps that's part of it."

They pass into a long hallway hung with Venetian mirrors. Sara glimpses a number of sitting rooms as they walk along, their fireplaces unlit and stacked with beech logs. Not a cinder in sight. They come through a reception room paved with marble, the chairs and tables covered in drop cloths. "My father hosted dignitaries when I was a child, but we've been short of occasion lately." They stop in a narrow room with rose-colored leaded windows and a small wooden table arranged with delicate china. "This is where I take the tea that the apothecary prescribes. Many years ago I imported china from the oriental provinces and I had to train them to stop painting their supernatural pagan fantasies onto the dishware." He picks up a delicate teacup and turns it in the rosin light. A white magnolia is painted on the side. "Now, let's go see the *Kunstkammer*."

At the end of the hallway is a set of double doors and Cornelis takes a key from a chain around his waist and unlocks them. "My father may have dug the first waterways in this area and commissioned a school and church, but he had no eye for beauty. He was a pragmatist, not an aesthete. He helped the local peasants set up a bleach works and they became famous for the laundry they mangled in the village. I like to think this is the least practical room in the house."

Cornelis throws open the doors with great ceremony, only to realize the curtains are drawn and his guest can't see anything but a sea of darkness. He rushes into the room ahead of her and begins pulling back the velvet curtains. The room blanches into view one dagger of light at a time. "I try to keep the light at bay so the paintings won't dull between viewings."

Sara estimates the room is about sixty feet in length, with an ornate ceiling twenty feet above the white marble floor. Except for a patch of blank wall at the far end, every inch of wall space is covered with paintings. At first, she doesn't know where to cast her attention—the walls are choked with color and a maddening variety of composition. She wants to pluck a single painting off the wall and hold it by a window, her face close enough to discern the brushstrokes. But then she begins to discern a pattern: along the left wall the landscapes flow into the seascapes before a transition to still lifes at the corner and along the back wall. The right side of the room, flanking the tall windows, is filled with portraits and genre paintings. There's a general movement from nature to objects to quotidian excerpts of a man's life, a painterly route from God's kingdom to the shopkeeper's dustbin. In this moment she feels a glimmer of affection for Cornelis Groen, for the mind that has gathered all this in one place, but then he says: "Your husband helped me arrange the paintings into a natural pattern. He arranged all these works like the notes of an opera."

She feels a sudden chill of loneliness and longing for Barent before it subsides back to steady anger. To collect herself, she walks the perimeter of the room. It's more work than she's ever seen assembled in one place and she wonders whether it rivals the court collections in Den Haag. She turns to face the back wall, from where she'd entered, and notices that it's filled with mythical allegories and histories, with rippled Greek gods and martyred saints. She shifts her weight from foot to foot, spinning slightly in place, and looks over at Cornelis, who stands by one of the tall windows. "I would recommend starting in that far corner. Many of them are from artists living in or passing through Haarlem, but there are also a few stray Italians and Flemish imports."

The teeming room, its sheer scale, keeps her in place for a moment. She resolves to look at one painting at a time and walks over to the far corner. Each work has a small plaque below with its artist, descriptive title, and date of execution. She suspects Cornelis has devised some of the more grandiose titles himself—*Serene Landscape with Heroic Figures* and *Noble Hills in Dawn Light with Great Church*. The titles given by the artists are less emphatic, like the circular oak panel by Jan van Goyen, simply called *Landscape with an Old Tree*, from 1620. The composition is straightforward—the outskirts of a small village, a few figures on horseback, a boat on a pond, a lone tree—but the atmosphere is flushed with muted browns and sepia-tinted clouds. In the foreground Sara can see traces of walnut ink Van Goyen must have used on the tree. The whole scene is wrapped in permanent twilight. She hears Groen's halting footsteps coming across the parquet floor toward her. Somehow he's left the *Kunstkammer* to light his pipe and returned without her noticing. He says, "Van Goyen studied landscape with Esaias van de Velde, who died a few years back in Den Haag. He's hanging right above him. I try to put the master above the pupil whenever I can. That was one of my ideas and your husband liked it." She looks up at *Summer Landscape*, from 1614. A few villagers walking along a pathway under feathered trees, it contains the same secretive tints and tones. The walkers are painted so faintly that the road can be seen through their bodies and Sara can't decide whether this is a defect or a flourish.

As she moves down toward the seascapes, Cornelis puffs at her side, studying her studying the paintings. Ships tossed about in squalls, or men climbing the rigging toward the Dutch flag of a lion on a rampart, twelve cannons bared at starboard. Into the still lifes with their staged meals, the glistening hearts of oysters against chill pewter, the husk of a bread roll, the rind and peel of half-eaten fruits. She sees her own depiction of the *Semper Augustus* tulip with a host of other flowers, the light pouring down from some unknown source. It's not a terrible painting, she thinks, but in all its technical competence it's rather forgettable. Nearby is a vanitas that achieves something lasting—a skull, a Bible, and a telescope arranged on a table, the pallid light and weak shadows perfectly capturing the chill loneliness of midwinter. They suggest there are a thousand dead white afternoons that wait for us all.

Cornelis crosses toward the back wall and gestures to a closed door. "There is one more room."

On the other side of the wall is a small space that reminds her of a sepulcher, a place where a saint might be buried behind an altar. Only instead of it being dank and stony, a downpour of light breaks through a ceiling of wrought iron and glass. "My father used to take his naps back here before the days turned dark." In the center of the room is a wooden table with a model village mocked up in wood and clay, painted with bright greens and dun browns. Hills and dunes have been formed from plaster and there's a narrow pathway that leads off the side of the table like a trail to oblivion. Sara stands over the tiny village and then looks up at the walls, where she recognizes Barent's landscape style—heavy skies pushing down on blanched horizons, a middle ground of stark trees and windswept dunes.

"They called it Groenstede, after my father. He built them a school and a church. A lot of the villagers worked at the bleach works or in my father's gardens. They used to throw a feast in his honor once a year."

Sara brings her eyes back to the table. "Where is it?"

"To the west, not more than a few miles. Technically, we own the land, but it's always been an independent township. I decided to capture the main vistas and build a tiny replica, to set them down in the record. I hired your husband to paint the environs and then he was supposed to render the village itself in paint before it disappeared."

"Why would it disappear?"

"In the last plague almost everyone died and the rest left. People for miles became convinced that it was a place of death, a cursed piece of ground. Now it's abandoned except for a mad-woman who refuses to leave. I'm sentimental about my father's legacy and want to make sure it's put down in the annals. I won't have any sons, you know. There's a nephew in Leiden—he's my only heir."

"And what would you have me paint?"

"I'd like you to continue on the town itself. To capture it."

Sara folds her arms. "Buildings are not my strength."

"Let me be blunt—given the village's history, there's not a painter in Haarlem who would take this commission." He smiles thinly. "So on this front consider your debt to be a strong form of encouragement."

The subtlety and refinement Sara had glimpsed in Cornelis Groen's *Kunstkammer*, in the painstaking assembly of so many paintings, now seems run through with something coarser. He turns and walks from the room, pipe smoking at his side, leaving her to stand beneath her husband's paintings.

Sydney

AUGUST 2000

HELEN BIRCH HAS MADE cupcakes for somebody's birthday and the leftovers are laid out in a Tupperware container when Ellie arrives in the conservation studio that adjoins her lab. The studio faces north, with big windows onto the Domain and a glimpse of the harbor. The room is flushed with watery light. For all the cold science and detection that goes on in here, Ellie is taken aback by the clutter—binders and books stacked in no particular order, a shelf of pigments and solvents labeled with illegible handwriting, a plastic cup brimming with brushes and cheap ballpoint pens. It reminds her of her grad school days in Brooklyn, before she left her stifling apartment and reinvented her life. There's a sun-bleached copy of Alan Burroughs's *Art Criticism from a Laboratory* on the windowsill, an early classic in the field she hasn't read since her days at the Courtauld Institute in the early 1950s. Industrial safety manuals and videos line a wooden book cart, something Helen has apparently stolen or borrowed from the research library. In addition to being the museum's chief conservation scientist, Helen is also the emergency safety officer. If a bomb goes off or someone sets fire to the Asian Gallery, she will be the one to lead the survivors to a designated meeting area in the parking lot. In the far corner of the room is a door that leads to the lab where Helen keeps her spectrometers, microscopes, and X-ray machines. Whenever she places a painting above the X-ray bulbs she puts a red cone and a caution sign out in the hallway. The other conservators affectionately call this area the fallout shelter.

Ellie watches Helen lick some white icing from her fingertips. She's got an optivisor perched on her forehead that makes her look like a welder in a white lab coat. Her hair is cropped short, almost spiked above the ears, and she's wearing a mohair sweater under the lab coat. Somehow, Ellie wasn't expecting the cupcakes. It's hard to imagine Helen cooking anything beyond chemicals at high temperature.

Helen says, "You sure you won't try one? This bugger's got buttermilk icing and a whipped cream center. I injected it with a piping bag. You know, because it's important to squeeze as many additional calories into these little bombshells as possible. I'm paying for this for a week at least."

"Honestly, I'm fine. I had a big breakfast."

"What'd you have?"

"Sorry?"

"For breakfast."

"Oh, eggs and toast."

"I wouldn't call that big. When we used to live out at Orange I'd make Keith, that's the ex, the whole grill-up sort of thing. Bacon, sausages, eggs, grilled tomato. Good old-fashioned country fry-up. Now that bastard can make his own fucking breakfasts."

Ellie doesn't know where to look. She sits across from Helen at a wooden desk strewn with manila folders and experimental data readouts. Helen keeps glancing up at her computer screen like she's scanning her e-mail in-box or a favorite baking website. Bringing her back to the room, Ellie says, "So, you got all three de Vos paintings at once? Must make testing easier."

To her computer screen, Helen says, "Yeah, the Leiden ones were in lock-up until Max got back from China. Then the other one arrived and he had a curator bring them all down at the same time. Works for me." Helen's gaze goes back to the frosted domes in the Tupperware tray. "Those are a bloody crime against humanity," she says. "A death knell for menopausal women everywhere . . ."

A little testily, Ellie says, "I've only got about half an hour before I have to go to the university."

"'Course, sorry, love, I got sucked into some e-mails. You ever get those ones from Nigeria, you know the crown princess in exile or a chief asking for money?"

"Not really. I only use the university e-mail so they screen all that out."

"Well, they must be sending me yours. My Hotmail spam folder is choked with them." Helen gets up from her chair with a clipboard of papers, takes a final lick of her fingertips, and then goes to wash her hands at a sink in the corner that sports a mounted first-aid kit and an industrial eyewash station. She scrubs her hands thoroughly in hot water, up onto the wrists, like a surgeon. She turns back to Ellie and says, "Well, let's take a look at the pictures then."

She leads Ellie toward an alcove and flips on a few light switches. Overhead fluorescents buzz to life and a bank of tungsten spotlights, mounted on black metal stands, flares up. "Sometimes I feel like an actor walking onstage. Either that, or I'm working inside a toaster oven," Helen says. The three paintings are still in their frames and lean against easels in the artificial sunlight. Ellie steps closer as the canvases brighten. The two *Edge* paintings are adjacent to each other and the funeral scene is at one end. Helen consults her clipboard while Ellie takes in the infrared and ultraviolet photographs of the paintings tacked to a cork bulletin board.

Helen slips one hand into her lab coat pocket. "Now, I've imported the X-radiographs into Photoshop, so I'll show you those last on the computer, but let's go through the initial findings. Let's start with the new painting, the funeral scene from Leiden. Appears fairly standard for the period . . . double ground, no underdrawing visible, so I'd say the artist used pale chalk since the carbon in black chalk would show up in infrared or X-ray. Brushwork and pigments are consistent with one of the other paintings and with what's known of the time period. A little more impasto than the other two, but still consistent. A few fugitive colors in use, like here she uses some copper resinate for the greens along the riverbank and it's turned brown over time. Ultraviolets show very little history of cleaning and varnishing so I'd say this one probably sat in an attic somewhere for a good while. On the back you can see tiny sediment from frass on the stretcher, so that's consistent with neglect. Like almost all paintings from the seventeenth century, the stretcher was replaced some time ago, probably in the nineteenth century, along with the frame. So, all up, I'd say we're dealing with an authentic work here. That's in the plus column for Leiden—a new work by the same artist."

Ellie turns her attention to *At the Edge of a Wood* and its copy. The artificial aging she'd done on her own canvas, the intricate spiderweb craquelure and varnishing, seem a bit showy in this light. "What about these two?" she asks.

Helen sniffs back the beginnings of a winter cold or a decade of inhaling solvents. "Here's where it gets interesting. Seems to me there were two hypotheses going into this horse race. One, the same artist or her apprentices made a replica of the work in the studio or, two, this is a later, unauthorized copy."

Ellie appreciates that she doesn't use the word *forgery*, which seems to belong to daytime television. She says, "I'm all ears."

Helen takes a crumpled handkerchief from her lab coat pocket, blows her nose, then replaces it. She lowers the optivisor over her eyes and gets up close to the fake, her hands braced against her bent knees. Straightening, she continues talking, but with the visor still pulled down her words take on a magnified, robotic menace. "In many regards these paintings are cut from the same cloth, so to speak. Canvases match the style and weave of the period, ground and underlayers pan out, pigments are generally of the period."

"What do you mean *generally*?"

She lifts the optivisor, blinking as the light hits her eyes. "You know anything about lead-tin yellow?"

Here it is, Ellie thinks, the chemical proof itself. "I've read the literature, but not in a while. Remind me." She feels her stomach clench.

"Right, then, as you probably know it was the main bright yellow up until about 1740, but then it fell off the map for a while. After they started making synthetic yellows in the nineteenth century, some of the old pigments went by the wayside. It was one of them. There's type one and type two lead-tin yellow, but we don't really need to go into all that. The reason it fell away was because it was hard to make and quite poisonous—picture fusing lead, tin, and quartz at a thousand degrees and then grinding the resulting glass up and shoving it through a sieve. Not my idea of a fun project . . . anyway, when the art world rediscovered this pigment they found out that it gives off these metallic soaps as it ages, in this case lead soaps."

Helen heads back to stand in front of the original. "See this bit here, how it gets a little pebbly in the bright yellows." She points to the bright strains in the ice skaters' scarves.

Ellie leans in and sees fine-grained distortions that look as if they're coming from underneath the paint layer. "I can barely see it."

Helen says, "Oh, it's there, believe me. Big time. Under the microscope the yellows look like sandpaper they're so rough. Maybe that's where the copyist got the idea."

"How do you mean?"

"When I run the elemental analysis on the one on the left, study the gritty yellows, it shows a fair amount of silica dioxide—the main ingredient in sand. Whoever made this one used sand to try to get the same textured feel, but the metal soaps give it away. There are no lead soaps in the fake from Leiden."

Now that the word *fake* has been trundled out Ellie finds it hard to look at Helen. "Interesting," is all Ellie can manage.

"The metallic soaps are the clincher. Do you still want to see the X-ray images?"

Ellie wants to run from the museum and go sit by the harbor for a day. She wants to quit her job and vanish for six months. But she says, "Sure, might as well."

Helen says, "The X-radiograph images just offer up some more nuance. Let's go back to the computer and take a gander."

Helen switches off the lights and they walk back to her disheveled desk. She sits before her computer screen and disrupts a screensaver of intergalactic space. Adobe Photoshop resolves onto the screen. She clicks through some menus and brings up the X-ray images of both *Edge* paintings, side by side. Because the radiographic sheets are only slightly larger than standard paper, Helen has had to use several per painting and they come up now as skeletal quadrants separated by white lines on deep blacks and grays.

Ellie leans in, aware of her own breathing, and looks between the two adjacent grids. Just as Helen begins to speak again she notices something in the underlayers of what must be the original. Helen waves the cursor around in the offending corner for emphasis. "I had a professor who used to call this an infrared ghost—a white figure trapped below the paint film. I first saw this one in the infrared images, and then the X-rays brought it out beautifully. There's no way the forger could have known this was here without an X-ray."

In the original painting, Sara de Vos had at some point painted the outline of another figure, a woman, standing at the edge of the wood. The figure appears not to be fully formed, but there was enough lead white in the skin to show up in the X-ray. It has the otherworldly quality of an apparition, a half-woman hovering in a silver-white corona. There is the faint suggestion of two eyes, hollowed out in radiographic relief, and they're directed at the girl standing against the tree. It's a woman watching a girl watching the skaters at the edge of a wood. The drama was first envisioned as the act of twin observation—a witness to the onlooker—an idea that fell away as the painting unfolded.

Helen closes Photoshop and the screen returns to a clutter of icons. Quietly, she says, "The forger was too exacting, too superficial. Only the real artist has the false beginning."

Manhattan

SEPTEMBER 1958

MARTY CAN'T BELIEVE how easy it is to open a Midtown post office box under the name of Jake Alpert. It's the only address he gives to Ellie, but even so, he's surprised when she sends him an invoice a week after the auction. Under the heading *Art Consultation—17th Century* she has charged him ninety dollars for the three hours they spent together. It galls him, because he knows he brought her an afternoon of deep pleasure as they sat in the mahogany-paneled jewel box of Thornton and Morrell's showroom, the flawless diction of the Brit auctioneer more like a holy incantation or Vedic prayer than a sales pitch. Since he can't write her a check—a bank would check his ID more scrupulously than the post office—he thinks about another meeting and handing her cash. At his desk, working through a patent lawsuit, he finds himself auditioning venues in his mind.

He invites her to meet up at a jazz club one Monday night after work. He briefly considers Birdland but he's afraid he'll run into an acquaintance, one of the many lapsed musicians he's encountered at the clubs over the years. Instead, he chooses the Sparrow, a second-tier basement club below Fifty-Second. He tells Rachel that he's meeting some of his squash buddies for a night of beer and jazz. She won't go to see bebop for the same reason he won't go to see Impressionist exhibitions—the patterns are pretty but they don't make sense. Once a month, sometimes more, he goes to a jazz club and relives his time as an aspiring trumpeter in the prep school marching band. He spent many hours listening to Dixieland phonograph records at three-quarter speed, slowing the notes so he could play along. Before his mother died of cancer, when he was in high school, this eccentric hobby was tolerated, even encouraged by his parents. But once his father became a widower, something hardened in the household and the trumpet was seen as a boyish indulgence. His father came into his bedroom one night where he was blowing scales in front of the mirror and simply said, "Enough with that thing. You won't be fifteen the rest of your life." Then he was gone, the door closed, the era over. Marty can still feel the embouchure in his facial muscles when he walks into a jazz club, the nervy tension in his jaws when he hears a trumpeter cut loose.

Ellie agrees to meet him but insists on taking a cab. He walks over from his office, up Broadway where the car showrooms are lit up as if for surgery, chrome fenders in high gloss, then he heads along Fifty-Second Street, past the sorry procession of prewar swing clubs and clip joints and Chinese restaurants. Through a steak house window he sees a ravaged old Steinway and what looks to be a sad cruise ship quartet playing to an empty restaurant. He waits outside the Sparrow and lights up a Dunhill. Within four square blocks of here, in exposed-brick basements he considers to be subterranean temples, he's seen Charlie Parker and Art Blakey and Fats Navarro ply their trade, names that mean nothing to Rachel, that might as well be obscure baroque painters. If she had her way there would be nothing in the house but Cole Porter and French Impressionists and Post-Impressionists, a soft murmuring atmosphere of crooners and blue-greens. When Marty looks at certain Cézannes he sees bluish fuzz—the powdery bloom on the skin of a Concord grape.

Ellie arrives ten minutes late and overdressed. In her dark wool coat and white beaded dress she looks like she's going to dinner theater circa 1928, he thinks, smiling broadly as she steps from the cab. He leans in the front window to pay the driver. When the cab pulls away, she says, "I was going to do that."

"Can we agree that transportation and meals are on me?"

She nods and looks up at the club's neon sign. "I'd be surprised if there's great art inside."

"There is, but not the kind you're thinking. Do you like jazz?"

"I wish I knew the first thing about it."

"I looked at the playbill. No one big is on tonight, but the place is fun. You can't leave New York without hearing some jazz."

"At the rate my dissertation is going, I'll be here for a while."

They walk inside and head down the musty carpeted steps to the ticket window and coat check. At the base of the stairs, in the threshold to the club proper, they hand their tickets to a hostess and she leads them to a booth. The interior is dark and smoky. He likes the juxtaposition of this place with the funereal splendor of the auction house, a jump-cut that suggests he's a man who might spend eighty thousand on paintings one afternoon and then hole up in some underground cathedral of jazz on a Monday night. He wants Ellie to know it's possible to belong to both worlds, that he swims in the high and the low registers of the city.

The hostess guides them toward the wall of booths not far from the bandstand. They sit and a cocktail waitress comes over. All the women who work here are over fifty, Marty realizes, as if it vouches for the club's seriousness. Ellie orders the house red and he asks for a Tom Collins and some nuts. It's still early and one of the warm-up bands, a quintet, is playing onstage, the sax player deep into a solo. Marty thinks about the time he saw Charlie Parker, a little ample around the waist, his tie loosened and barely reaching his rib cage, eyes downcast as if he could see the notes burning out of the bell of his horn. He was an apparition, junked out and holy. Every saxophone player since has seemed entirely mortal.

Ellie looks around the room. "I think I'm a little overdressed."

"They're used to theatrical types," he says, smiling.

Their drinks and a bowl of peanuts arrive.

Taking a handful of nuts, he gestures over to a burly black man in a white suit. "The emcee is a bit of a tip monger. If you stiff him he'll remember you forever. Even the musicians tip him because he introduces the bands and if they stiff him he botches their names."

"It sounds even more cutthroat than the auction houses."

"Ten times worse."

She sips her drink. "How are the oil-on-coppers doing?"

"They're beautiful, a reunited family, though right now they're all sitting in my study, waiting to find wall space."

"I'd love to see your collection some time," she says.

"Of course. I'm renovating at the moment so it's a disaster zone."

Staring into the red bowl of her wineglass, she says, "I'm sure that's an ordeal for your wife."

Marty realizes he's never mentioned Jake's wife, but neither has he removed his wedding ring. He lets five seconds of silence unravel while he considers his options. Looking off toward the band he says, "Actually, she passed away last year. I guess I haven't gotten around to taking my gold band off." As soon as the words are in the air he feels his stomach drop. He looks over to see her face fall a little, as if she's committed some error of taste.

She says, "I'm so sorry. I didn't mean to pry."

"No, no, it's fine. I'm getting back on my feet. Maybe that's why I want to fill out the holes in the collection. She usually took the lead on that front."

He takes a big sip of his Tom Collins to wash away the aftertaste of deceit. He thinks about the European river cruise in the spring, the way Rachel will lay out the brochures and ship menus across the perfectly made bed. They will eat oysters and truffles and make love once or twice, floating by the peat fields of old Europe, sunken down into its ancient rivers. She will read novels in bed and fall asleep with the light on. The predictability of it is both heartening and its own kind of ruin. He looks up at the stage where the trumpeter is on the outer edge of his solo, rising onto the balls of his feet to launch his big buttery tone. "That kid's not bad," he says.

"Are you musical?"

"I used to play trumpet in high school. Then my father made me give it up and I became a patent attorney. Now I vet other people's creations." He wonders whether he should have invented an alternative career. Jake Alpert could have been anything—a diplomat, a surgeon, a financier.

"My father tried to make me give up painting. He was uncomfortable with anything artistic, thought it was *puttin' on bloody airs*."

They both watch the emcee as he walks through the crowd lighting cigarettes, prospecting for tips with an oversize butane lighter. A few musicians with their instrument cases have set up on the bleachers to watch their colleagues onstage.

Ellie says, "So, how can I help you build the collection you want?"

"That reminds me." He takes an envelope from his pocket with the cash inside and slides it across the table. He's seen this done in movies and it makes him wish he'd ordered a martini. For some reason she refuses to look at it.

"Thank you."

"I know it's crazy, but I prefer to deal in cash. I'm the son of an immigrant."

"I hope you didn't pay cash to Thornton and Morrell."

"They were only too happy to set up an arrangement directly with my bank. Delivery happened once they got confirmation that the funds were transferred. The delivery guys looked like their doorman—arthritic old men in blazers and argyle sweaters."

"No one seemed to be younger than sixty over there." She laughs. "So what's next? Italian Renaissance? Venetian wedding portraits might suit you." She looks away from the table, as if she's made another conversational blunder.

He lets the ice clink against the side of his glass. "What do you know about women artists of the seventeenth century? Dutch women, for example."

He wasn't sure when he would steer the conversation in this direction, but now that it's happened he tries to gauge her reaction. The lie about being a widower has freed something up in him.

She looks down at the table and takes another sip of wine. "As it happens, that's what I'm writing my dissertation on. Women painters of the Dutch Golden Age. Well, before it stalled out."

"I didn't mean to remind you."

"It's fine, I'm just riddled with guilt. Every time I look over at my typewriter I feel sick. Did you know Remington makes guns as well as typewriters? I think about that every time I look at it."

"I guess I never thought about it. Did you know they invented the zipper before barbed wire? As a patent attorney I follow the history of inventions. The guy who filed the first zipper patent in the nineteenth century called it the Automatic, Continuous Clothing Closure. For obvious reasons that name never caught on . . ."

"Interesting," Ellie says, but he can tell she's not listening. She takes up a cocktail napkin and digs through her handbag until she finds her eyeglasses and a pen. "So there were a handful of Dutch women painters in the Golden Age. Maybe twenty-five mentioned in the historical sources but only a few with surviving works." She writes the following names on the napkin: *Judith Leyster, Maria van Oosterwyck, Rachel Ruysch.* She raises the pen tip and her eyes waver over the rim of her glasses to the smoky stage. The trumpeter finally comes down from his solo. "There's also a woman named Sara de Vos, but so far she's only got one attributed work." She adds *de Vos* to the bottom of the list.

Without hesitation, he says, "And these are likely to be in private collections? So if a collector like myself wanted to acquire them it's conceivable they might come up for auction at some point?"

"Most of these are in university and public museums. A handful of private collections. The National Gallery in Washington has some good Leysters. And everyone's got some Ruysch flower paintings—she lived to be very old and painted her whole life."

"Perhaps you can help me locate some. I think my wife would have liked the idea of Dutch women painters."

He's aware of the theatrically morose tone in his voice, but he also realizes there might not be another six encounters with Ellie. She will grow increasingly anxious as she's reminded of her unfinished dissertation or her forgery and before long she'll claim to be too busy to meet up. He can see it all in her careful, circumspect manner—an underground river of guilt.

"Do you have any children?" she asks.

He touches the rim of his glass. "We were doomed not to have any," he says. Somehow she's made him divulge something of his real life.

He orders another round of drinks when she gets her glass below the halfway mark.

"So, that's enough business for now," he says. "If you would do some research and let me know what you find out I'd be very grateful." He folds his hands together to indicate a change in subject. "How does an Aussie girl end up in Manhattan?"

"It's complicated. I thought I wanted to restore paintings professionally, so I spent a few years in London at the Courtauld Institute. They taught me everything there is to know about inpainting and the structure of old paintings. Though even there every professor had his own rules and none of them were in agreement. We'd all go down to the pub and argue about which way was the right way to build a loss back up in a painting. It was a very small world. So I decided to switch to art history and will probably end up teaching. I applied to Columbia and got a fellowship."

"Seems like you'll make a very fine teacher. From what I can tell, you know how to bring paintings to life."

"That's sweet of you to say." She takes her glasses off and folds them.

"And do you paint yourself?"

"Not much anymore, though I painted a lot in my youth."

She squints into her glass and he wonders just how shortsighted she is.

She says, "That sounds pretentious, doesn't it? My *youth*."

"Not at all."

She pushes her first empty wineglass six inches away from her side of the table.

"And what do you do for fun? Is there a vanguard of Columbia grad students who storm the Village every weekend, playing barefoot in Washington Square Park? Are there male colleagues in thin black ties and sunglasses, riding Vespas?"

"I wouldn't know. I'm a bit of a homebody. It's sad, really. I just find it difficult to like people." She brings the second wineglass in and takes a sip. "Who knows what's wrong with me. When I was a girl everyone just thought I was a snob, my own parents included. Dreamy kids who paint for hours in their bedrooms don't do well in Australia, at least not where I grew up." She looks around the bar again. "I'm suddenly starving."

"Let's finish our drinks and then we'll go foraging. They don't have much in the way of food here. Do you want to go have dinner and then come back? The better bands always come on late anyway."

"Only if we can get pizza and eat it out of the box. We can take it down to the Hudson and sit on a bench."

"You make the Hudson sound like Key West. I'm not much in the mood to get mugged by a juvenile delinquent or one of the winos that live down by the river."

"You're exaggerating."

"Not by much."

"It's decided then," she says.

They drink up, but she can't finish her second glass of wine. She stands up from the booth a little tipsily. Marty leaves some money on the table and they head back up to the street.

THEY CARRY A PEPPERONI pizza and some beer down to a strip of parkland along the river, the expressway traffic dulled by a hem of trees. There are a few people out walking their dogs and a lone fisherman casting into the river. They find a bench to watch the ferries and boats crossing between Manhattan and Union City. Ellie takes a slice of pizza from the box and tries to maneuver it into her mouth. The point sags down and cheese grease drips onto her white beaded dress.

"Shit," she says. Then she looks up at him. "Mind my language. I come from a family of heavy blasphemers."

"My father was Dutch and he swore like some deranged pirate from the eighteenth century."

"Shouldn't have worn this stupid thing. I hardly ever go out—that's part of the problem."

"You have to curl in the sides of the pizza, vertically down the middle. Then the tension picks up and keeps the tip from flopping."

"Nobody wants a flopping tip," she says, then, "Oh, God, I'm drunk."

"Eat up," he says.

She gestures to the ferries with her newly repositioned pizza slice. "My father's a ferry captain on Sydney Harbour. I was only ever asked once to ride inside the wheelhouse and I got seasick. Girls didn't belong there anyway, he said. He was a man who lived as if he'd been born a century earlier." She takes another bite of pizza. "I'm prattling . . ."

"My father used to make his own tonic water, boil up the cinchona bark on the stovetop. Maybe that's why we like old paintings—our fathers were trapped by the past."

Chewing, she says, "Either that or we can't get our heads around the present."

They eat in silence for a moment, watching the lights of New Jersey in the grain of the river.

She says, "I rode in the wheelhouse during a big swell. I think he wanted to test me. These slate-colored rolling waves came through the heads between Manly and the city. The ferries probably shouldn't have been running, but my father was the last one to heed caution. Even the deckhands were turning green. When we got halfway between the heads it was so bad that I had to run out on deck and throw up over the railing. I came back in drenched from all the crashing waves but my father didn't say anything, completely ignored me until that night when we got home to my mother. We walked into the kitchen and my mother just about died when she saw how I looked. When she asked what the hell happened to me, he said, 'Ellie had a little spell on board, that's all.' My torrential vomiting was dismissed as *a little spell*. That was the story of my childhood. My sister broke her arm once and my father called it a busted wing and rigged it up in a piece of torn bedsheet. To this day her arm's crooked. Her tennis ground stroke is five degrees off-center . . ."

"Your father sounds intrepid."

"That's one word for it. He served in the first war and I think part of his personality was actually shell shock. Then they lost a son before us girls came along. He was never the same, or so I'm told. Did you go to the war?"

"I'm not that old."

"I meant the second one."

"No, they wouldn't have me. I'm flat-footed with a bung knee and a side of mild asthma. Filing a few patents for the army and navy was as close as I got to the action. How's the pizza?"

"Fabulous."

"Tell me how you repair a painting."

"It'll put you to sleep."

"Try me."

She reaches for another slice of pizza. "It's not interesting, believe me."

"I'd really like to know. Please."

She looks out at the river, then down at the pizza box. "It really depends. But you have to think of a painting in geological terms. It's all about strata, layers that do different jobs. A painting has its own archaeology."

"This is why I think you'd be a good teacher."

She pulls the crust off her slice and bites one end. "The shadows and the light usually take root in the ground layer. You fill in losses with chalk and rabbit glue. You should smell my apartment. There's a French butcher in Brooklyn who sells me rabbit pelts by the dozen."

"You can't buy it ready-made?"

"It's better if you make it from scratch. For one thing, it gets you in the mind-set of the seventeenth century."

"What else?"

"Well, you cheat a little with the brushwork, building it up sculpturally and then going over it with thin layers of paint. In London we used to argue about whether or not to match the color of the ground exactly or whether you should clearly mark out your territory, let future restorers know where you'd been."

"It was an ethical issue," he says.

"I suppose it was. They made you choose sides and there were professors there who hated each other because they couldn't agree on what color to make a ground."

"I thought lawyers were petty and contentious."

She looks over toward New Jersey, the slice of pizza midway to her mouth, and blows some air between her lips. She drops the pizza slice back in the box. "I'm exhausted and still drunk. I don't think I'm going to make it back to the Robin. I'm sorry."

"The Sparrow."

"I should stop talking."

"Some other time. Do you want to take the pizza home?"

"Naturally. You're talking to a graduate student."

Marty says, "Yes, one who charges thirty dollars an hour. That's more than my dead wife's analyst and he actually studied in Vienna with one of Freud's disciples." He means it as a joke, but there's a note of hostility in his voice.

She turns her head but doesn't look at him. The pizza box sits open between them, grease stains like tiny islands on a cardboard map.

Slowly, she says, "Do you think it's unreasonable?"

"I think you know what rich people are willing to pay for mounting a little existential meaning on their walls. My wealth is a historical accident, just so we're clear."

A diesel engine thrums somewhere out on the river. The mood has suddenly been poisoned. He wants to shift the conversation back to banter, but he knows it's too late. "Let me get you into a taxi," he says. "Will you take the pizza?"

She doesn't answer but takes the box. They walk a few streets over from the expressway and he flags down a taxi. His father used to carry a doorman's whistle in his vest pocket, just for hailing cabs, and he wonders where that thing ended up. It might be resting at the bottom of a drawer in the ship captain's desk. When the cab pulls up he climbs into the back beside her before she can object. "Brooklyn and then the Upper East Side," he tells the driver.

"You don't want to do it in reverse?" the driver asks.

"We'll take the lady first," Marty says.

She says, "This is completely unnecessary."

"Let's just say I'm from another century as well."

They don't talk the full length of the Brooklyn Bridge. He watches her look out the window, shoulders turned away from him, her fingers gently drumming on top of the pizza box. Her body language suggests she's brooding about the earlier comment. He saw a flash of something back there. A quick temper, perhaps, but also a propensity for self-doubt. He rolls down his window slightly to let in some air.

MARTY TELLS THE DRIVER to wait while she gets inside her apartment building. The stream of traffic thunders overhead on the expressway. He waits until he sees the play of light and her silhouette against an upper window, then tells the driver to go ahead. A few blocks later he tells the driver to let him out and he returns on foot, his collar up, gently drunk, pulled along by something he doesn't fully understand. Each thing she divulges about her life and work is a small theft. It's like taking ornaments off a stranger's shelf, one by one, and dropping them into his coat pockets. He stops at a late-night deli and buys two cups of coffee and a pint of ice cream. Then he stands outside her apartment building, the ice cream tucked under one arm, cooling against his rib cage, while his hands warm against the coffee. He watches her silhouette against the drawn curtains, the little forays she makes between rooms. He imagines showing up on her doorstep with the forgery wrapped in paper, telling her that it's a restoration he wants her to work on, or watching her face as he describes the Sara de Vos he once owned until someone plucked it off his bedroom wall during a charity dinner for orphans. It's her future he's holding in his hands, flimsy as two paper cups. He wants to understand her life from the inside out, to feel into its corners and handle the filaments that hold it in place.

He walks inside the darkened apartment building and climbs the tiled stairway to the second floor. He knows it's the corner apartment with its windows facing north—he's always been good with direction, knows the cardinal points when he's sitting in a windowless Midtown restaurant. He knocks softly and hears her feet padding across the wood floors, moving away and then coming back. A shadow breaks up the chink of light from under the door and her voice is muffled—"Who's there?"

Quietly, but as jovial as he can sound, he says, "It's Jake Alpert with coffee and ice cream as a peace offering. He's very sorry for being an ass."

There's a moment of silence and another shift in the light under the door. "Tell Jake that I was just getting ready for bed. No need to apologize."

"Well, at least let me put this in your freezer before it melts."

"I'm sorry, it's just so late . . . I'm not dressed."

"I understand." He takes a step back from the door to make sure his voice doesn't sound threatening. "Since Rachel passed I've become a bit of an insomniac. I'm very sorry for my earlier comment. Good night, Ellie." He feels a burst of terrible shame that he's used Rachel's name, as if her actual life now hangs in the balance. He takes another step away.

There's a pause, then he hears the sound of a chain being unlatched. Her face appears when the door opens six inches. She says, "You can give me the ice cream. I'll put it in my freezer and we can have it some other time. That was nice of you."

He comes closer. "It's under my arm. I can't get it while I'm holding the coffees."

"Oh," she says, a little annoyed. She opens the door another six inches and extends her arm so she can reach below his elbow. He sees that she's wearing a flannel nightie with small birds on it. Her calves are skinny and pale, her feet slightly splayed and blunted at the toes. A girl who grew up barefoot, he thinks. When she takes the ice cream he says, "Peppermint chocolate chip."

She looks away. "I'm more of a vanilla person myself."

"I offended you and I'm sorry. Your expertise is worth every cent you charge. I wish I could come in, just for a moment."

"I'm not used to having company," she says. "The place isn't fit."

"All right, well, good night. Here's your coffee as well." He hands it to her through the doorway and she has to set the ice cream down to take it. He turns back for the stairwell, knowing that she's still there.

She says, "Five minutes is all. And you have to wait until I tidy up and dim the lights. The less you see the better. Wait here," she says.

Another small theft. She closes the door and he comes back to await further instructions. He can hear her tidying up, placing dishes in the sink. When she finally comes back to the door she's put on a man's bathrobe that has flecks of paint on the lapels. He steps inside. The windows above the radiator, facing the elevated expressway, have been opened and there's a slight breeze blowing through the humid space. A series of snake plants and philodendrons line the sill in tiny pots. He can smell the animal glue she talked about and there's the high chemistry of solvents and oil paints, and something darker that smells like shoe polish. A small wooden island in the kitchenette is taken up by mortars and pestles and stone bowls. A lacquered tea tray has been repurposed to hold every kind of brush and palette knife imaginable. A drafting table on metal legs is covered by strips of paper and charcoal sketches. She sets her coffee down on a small Formica table by the window that Marty recognizes from the photo. The living area is stacked with books and newspapers and over in one corner is the offending Remington with a sheet of her dissertation, no doubt, wilting in its Bakelite mouth.

"If the landlord ever sees inside this place I'll get evicted," she says. "But it's not easy to find apartments where they don't mind you melting rabbit pelts on the stovetop."

Marty looks over at the blackened oven and range. "I'm pretty sure that kitchen has seen worse."

She tells him he can sit down if he likes and he sits on the mustard-brown couch that faces the windows and a shelf with a record player. There's a painting resting on an easel by the window and it's covered by a paisley tablecloth. He wonders whether she has just draped it there or whether this is a habit, the masking and unmasking of her trade. He knows better than to ask about it right now, so he sits and drinks his coffee. When she brings the ice cream over there are no bowls but two spoons.

"Family tradition," she says. "My mum used to make her own butterscotch ice cream, but she made us eat out of the churn bucket. Didn't want to dirty extra dishes."

They eat several spoonfuls each, the pint between them on the couch. Marty looks around the room, taking it in. Gretchen's apartment had signs of a rich and vibrant social life—cheese knives and glassware and linen napkins for entertaining. This apartment could belong to an invalid, a shut-in with kidney stones and a fox terrier.

"I could build you some bookshelves," he said. "I come from a line of men with carpentry tools in the basement."

"It wouldn't do any good. All those spines wedged together would make my head spin."

"Again, I am sorry about what I said before."

"It's fine. You're probably right. I've been spoilt. You people pay me to do something I'd do for free. The money doesn't mean anything to me. I can't ever bring myself to spend it. It feels tainted because it comes too easily."

"That sounds rather noble. What do you mean by *you people*?"

"There are people who look at art, people who buy it, and people who make it. I'm in a whole separate category—I mend it, bring it back to life. It's not unusual for conservators to spend more hours alone with a great work than the artist themselves."

"Is that why you do it? To meditate on the work?"

He watches her shrug and leverage her spoon into the core of the ice cream. She lands a chunk and smooths it with the roof of her mouth, pulling the half-empty spoon back out. Something has shifted between them, a new candor on the end of her spoon.

"I'm not good with men," she says matter-of-factly. "I don't know what they want."

"Have you had many men in your life?"

"That seems rather personal," she says. Then, "No, not many. What was she like? Rachel?"

He flinches at the sound of her name and has to look away. "I don't want to cry, so I'd rather not say."

"I'm sure it's a terrible loss."

"It's hard to describe."

They seem to be at a conversational impasse, so Marty gets up and strolls around the room.

"You can put on a record if you like, though I don't have any jazz."

"I'll buy you some Chet Baker."

He flips through the small stack of LPs—Chopin sonatas, Stravinsky, Rachmaninoff. "Why am I not surprised by your record collection? Is there anything here from the twentieth century?" She doesn't answer. He takes out the Chopin from its sleeve and places it carefully onto the turntable. "Do you ever paint with music on?"

"Never," she says. "It changes the brushwork."

He sits back on the couch. She closes her eyes and leans back against a cushion, letting the music wash over her. She says, "Tell me about your first encounter with art. I always like to hear that story."

"My father used to tell stories of being at the Armory Show, of lining up with a thousand people to see Duchamp's *Nude Descending a Staircase*. He liked to hang out with painters when he could so he knew some of the Ashcans and their circle. He used to get drunk with John Butler Yeats, father of the famous Irish poet. As an old man John Butler Yeats was living above a French restaurant. Anyway, my father claimed that he went to the Armory Show with John Yeats and saw a woman faint when she got to the front of the Duchamp line. So that was my first encounter with art, a story about what it could do to people. Do you know that Duchamp lives in Lower Manhattan and hasn't painted in decades? He says his life is the art now."

"I didn't know that. Obviously because he's from the twentieth century." With her eyes still closed, she says, "What else?"

"I grew up in a house filled with Old Masters. It wasn't until I got to college and took some art history that I understood what my father had assembled or inherited. We owned some of the paintings discussed in the textbooks."

They continue in this eddy of conversation for a while. She throws out a murmured question and he answers at length, trying to summon interesting anecdotes from his real life, as if he can make up for so many layers of deceit. Eventually, she stops asking questions and he suspects she's fallen asleep. To test his theory he says, "Am I so boring that you've nodded off?" She doesn't answer. The Chopin and art stories have finished what the pizza and beer began. He sits very still, listening to her breathe, the ice cream slowly melting on the scuffed coffee table.

After several minutes, he quietly sets down his spoon and walks toward the short hallway, back toward the bathroom and bedroom. He walks as softly as he can, trying not to squeak the battered hardwoods. The bathroom smells of damp towels and there's a wire clotheshorse set up in the tub, a few pairs of her underwear hanging out to dry. In her haste to tidy up, she'd forgotten to close the shower curtain and there's something tender and sad about her industrial cotton underwear. He pictures her hand washing her clothes in the tub. Her beaded white dress—now stained with cheese grease—has been spot cleaned and draped over the sink. He looks back at her underwear and quietly closes the shower curtain. He's afraid to use the toilet in case the sound of it flushing wakes her, so he steps back out into the hallway and peers into the darkened bedroom, a narrow room with a single lamp burning from a bamboo nightstand. The bed is unmade, the floor strewn with clothes, and her closet appears to be filled with suitcases. A flourish of rising damp blots against one wall and part of the ceiling. He can't imagine how this is the product of a methodical mind, a temperament for finessing a canvas one painstaking stroke at a time.

When he goes back into the living area she's still slumped against the back of the couch, head back, mouth slightly open. He moves over to the easel and lifts one corner of the paisley tablecloth. For a fleeting moment he imagines his de Vos sitting there, but now he sees it's a canvas awaiting some depiction—an underlayer painted an earthy and pale red. That she thought to cover the naked canvas but not her damp cotton underwear reveals something, though he's not sure what. He drops the corner of the tablecloth and begins for the door. As he passes the drafting table with its rummage of papers and sketches, he sees a pattern that looks familiar. A narrow strip of photographic paper protrudes from under a charcoal etching. The sliced-away piece is no wider than two inches, but he recognizes the headboard and the arabesque of his own bedroom's plush gray wallpaper. The bed appears to be unmade, the pillows in plain sight, and from the shadows of the headboard rods against the wall he guesses it was taken on a winter morning, when the light spills into the room late and from the south. He puts it in his pocket and continues for the door. He should wake her, he knows, so that she can lock the door behind him. She'll wake some hours from now, and feel disoriented and vulnerable. But the thought of someone taking photographs in his bedroom during broad daylight rushes through him and he heads down the darkened stairwell in a surge of anger.

Outside, he walks several blocks until he finds a cab and makes his way back toward Manhattan. As they near the Brooklyn Bridge, the city glimmers into view—a Dutch outpost at the confluence of two rivers, an island plucked from the flotsam of history. Whenever he reenters Manhattan, even if it's just from a weekend in the Hamptons or an antique show in Queens, he can't help feeling how tenuous his grasp of the city is. He's spent his whole life here and yet there are neighborhoods that are as dark and unknowable to him as the Congo. Like his father, he's a street walker, but it's always above the parallel of Forty-Second Street and south of Central Park's upper edge. He has dreams in which he walks his dog around the perimeter of the entire island, letting Carraway drink from both rivers.

At home, Hester has turned off all the lights—her customary way of protesting his late hours—so he's forced to walk up the stairs from the foyer in the dark. To turn on a light would be to admit moral failure to the housemaid. As he enters the upstairs hallway he wonders whether Hester has betrayed them, whether she let in a photographer when they were catching some winter sunshine in the Bahamas one January. Although there must have been a few hundred people through the house in the last year, very few had been there during daylight. It could have been a tradesman, the plumber or the piano tuner with camera in hand. He knows if he confronts Hester she'll quit in a heartbeat; she has Southern notions of honor and loyalty and his wife will carry a grudge for years.

Through the bedroom doorway Rachel appears to be asleep, facing the other wall, the dog curled behind her legs. He pads down the hallway to his study and closes the door behind him. He pours himself two fingers of Scotch and picks up the telephone and dials the number on Ellie's business card. It rings half a dozen times before she answers. "I'm sorry I left without waking you," he says, peering at her forgery against the bookshelves. "It occurred to me that your front door isn't locked." He can hear her sleep-addled breathing, the sound of her swallowing to wake up. "I must have dozed off. My apologies," she says.

"I forgive you."

She breathes drowsily into the phone.

He says, "I'll be in touch soon."

"I'll have a list of Dutch works by women for you to consider."

"Excellent. Until then."

"Good night, Jake."

He puts the phone down and drains his glass. He walks out into the hallway and down to the bedroom. In the en suite bathroom he puts on his pajamas and hangs his clothes on the back of the door. He takes out the narrow strip of photographic paper from his trouser pocket and brings it into the bedroom, holding up the strip in a narrow band of moonlight. The photographer had stood at the end of the bed with the windows behind the camera. He looks up at the empty space on the wall above the headboard. During daylight, you can see the blanched ghost of the painting, the rest of the wall turned a pale sepia from the light and grit of the city. It hung there for forty-five years, since before they were married and the room had belonged to his father, who never remarried, who slept alone under the ice skaters and the girl at the edge of the frozen river after his wife had been wrenched from his grasp.

With her back to him, Rachel says something. At first he thinks she's talking in her sleep, some snippet of a troubled dream, but then the sounds assemble in the darkness with a slight delay.

"You're awfully late. How was the jazz?"

"Frederic got us all drunk and I lost track of time. There were a few decent quintets playing, nothing special."

She repositions herself and the dog has to adjust. "What's that smell?"

"The club's underground, remember? A bunker of cigarette smoke and sweaty musicians." He sits on the edge of the bed and puts the photographic strip into the drawer of his nightstand.

"No, it's something else," she says. "I can't quite place it."

"Should I shower?"

"Do you mind?"

"Not at all."

"It smells like old house paint. Like you've been crawling through somebody's attic."

"Strange," he says. "Sorry to wake you."

He gets up and closes the bathroom door behind him. In the shower, he runs the water as hot as he can stand it, letting it scald the back of his neck and shoulders. He scrubs himself with soap and washes his hair, removing the fug of Ellie's apartment.

Heemstede

SUMMER 1637

A WEEK OF FOG AND DRIZZLE. Bone-chilled and melancholic, Cornelis Groen holes up in his tearoom, plying himself with home remedies and apothecary blends of Ceylon loose leaf. Mrs. Streek carries a lacquered tray through the warrens of the great house, sets them out for his consideration beside the blazing hearth. Cinchona wine, tinctures of aloe and saffron, a compound of aniseed water for his chills. At precisely noon each day he places a sugar cube in his mouth and draws a swill of tea, warm and medicinal, down the back of his throat. Sara sits part of each afternoon in the stifling room, listening to a litany of bodily complaints. "My bones are made from ice," is a favorite expression. Groen tells stories of being a shipping merchant, of being transformed by latitudes of smallpox, scrofula, and canker. "Changed my very constitution," he says, looking forlornly out the window, "as if the humors of the body coalesced into a watery gruel." She tries to cheer him with stories of her progress preparing canvases for his desired project. She's enlisted Tomas to make wooden supports, grind pigments, and size the canvas they've had delivered from Haarlem. But there's no cheering Cornelis when he's overcome by distemper. His mind kindles in the memory of previous ailments and he feels them all over again—the swollen knuckles, the chilblains. The entire house succumbs to his sunken mood. Tomas tells her that even the horses seem out of sorts. Mrs. Streek, standing blowzily in her pristine display kitchen, cannot be summoned from her wordless blue funk. She cooks Groen's favorite meals like so much penance—mutton with prunes and mint, minced ox tongue with green apples.

The painting expedition to the village of Groenstede, the abandoned settlement out along the river, has been delayed for weeks. They wait for Cornelis to recover so he can lead the excursion, but Sara suspects he's in no hurry, that he enjoys the latitudes of illness more than health. They give him something to philosophize about, some tension in the pull of daily rope. Eventually, after a month of napping and complaining in the tearoom, he rebounds with the weather. When midsummer arrives with a morning of clear skies, Cornelis rallies in the dining room in a pair of rhinegraves and a tunic, a pair of garden shears tucked into his belt like a rapier. Tomas is instructed to ready the horses and the wagon. Mrs. Streek is given very precise dietary instructions. Sara is told to gather her supplies.

They head out of the grounds toward the back country in an open wagon, Tomas on the box seat and Cornelis and Sara in the rear. The wooden pavilion with the domed roof, the arbor where Cornelis reads poetry on sunny afternoons, the raspberries ripening along the painted fences, all this cultivation is left behind but also bundled along in the wicker baskets Mrs. Streek has prepared. Bread rolls, Leiden cheese studded with cumin seeds, strawberries with sour cream, marzipan, and wine spiced with cinnamon and cloves. Sara thinks back to meals she shared with Barent, the bean flour bread and the turnips served with fried onions. Poverty appeared first in their meals, then in their shoes, and finally in their thoughts and prayers. Still, she would trade all her newfound appetites for a single day back at the old house before things came untethered. Kathrijn floating a sabot on a canal; Barent sitting on the stoop after a day of painting, reading the gazettes and chatting with the neighbors while she made a hearty stew in the brightly lit kitchen. The past is so clear to her that she could paint it. It burns through every dream and waking hour.

As the wagon passes into a countryside of wooded dunes and bogs, Cornelis speaks about the women he might have married, about the golden mean of feminine charms. The ideal woman, he tells Sara, combines a face from Amsterdam, a gait from Delft, a bearing from Leiden, a singing voice from Gouda, a stature from Dordrecht, and a complexion from Haarlem. Although he says all this authoritatively and reasonably, Cornelis's verbal dissection of a woman makes Sara think of corpses and rigor mortis. She can't help thinking back to the stoniness of the surgeons' guild and the prospect of a cadaver being laid out on a table. Happily, he changes the subject and begins to tell her about the topsoil he imports from Haarlem for its supernatural vitality in yielding perfect flowers—narcissi, crocuses, aconite, delphiniums . . .

He says each flower name so tenderly they could be the names of daughters or lovers.

As they come around a bend in the river, Sara sees that the village lies in ruins.

Cornelis says, "The fire was deliberately set by a mob from the vicinity. Sent by burgomasters who thought we were running a lazaretto for the plague-stricken. A Dutchman cannot abide a swath of cursed ground, especially beside a river."

Sara sees the remains of a clock tower, the kind built for a chamber of rhetoric or the inspector of weights and measures. This was a town with civic aspirations, she thinks. She traces its ambition in the low brick walls that are tarred against the elements and in the neat, unroofed houses. A column of drowsy smoke comes from one of the remaining chimneys and Sara supposes this is where the hermit lives, buttressed in the flanks of the crumbling old church. She thinks about how desolate the ruins will look from one of the nearby hillsides, how she'll extend the vanishing point beyond the river to the expanse of dunes. She probes the possibilities in her mind, feels the gratifying tension of new work. It may be Barent's debt she's repaying, but the painting will be her own.

Cornelis says, "We'll lunch first and then you can begin your explorations. A painted commemoration will seal this era nicely, tie a knot from the loose ends."

They unpack the baskets and eat on a blanket. Tomas eats his cheese and bread on the box seat, preferring the company of the horses to his employer's meandering speeches about the fleetingness of time. He and Sara exchange a few knowing glances during one of Groen's monologues. When they're done eating, Tomas hands Sara her sketching kit and tells her that he'll follow a few roods behind. Cornelis removes the small shears from his waistline and goes off in search of mushrooms and edible berries. "The hermit is quite harmless," he tells Sara. "Muddled with grief and stubborn as a mule, but friendly to anyone who isn't trying to evict her."

Sara walks along the overgrown riverbank with Tomas trailing behind her, the reeds and thistle up to their waists. Her sketchpad and charcoals are wrapped in a cloth sack, slung over one shoulder. She tells Tomas she will go ahead alone, and he falls back, dashing stones into the sluggish river. She sees further evidence of the village's ambition to become a town—a network of ditches dug around the low walls, a cemetery hemmed in by evenly spaced birch trees, a gateway with rusting hinges still bolted to a thick stone wall. Honeysuckle grows wild along sills and ledges. She passes into the main square—spanning little more than a dozen houses—and walks over the flagstone toward the tendril of smoke. She can make out the remains of a stable and a barn and some mud-walled huts. The woman, when she appears in the crumbling doorway, is much younger than Sara expected. Cornelis made her sound like an old hag. In reality, she isn't more than a few years older than Sara, though her face has been roughened by solitude and weather. She holds a steaming ladle in front of her face, peering at Sara while blowing to cool whatever's intended for her mouth.

"Goedemiddag," Sara says.

The woman stops blowing. "I told him already, I'll die here properly with my feet facing east. Buried up on the hill with the others, my children among them." Her cheeks are windblown and Frisian. She wears a long smock filthy with ash and grease, a pair of leather mules on her feet.

Sara says, "We haven't come to chase you away."

"No point in that, as I say."

The woman squints into the distances beyond the river, waiting for Sara to come to it.

"I was hoping to sketch the town. I'm a painter by trade and I've been asked to put something down."

The woman considers this as she cools the contents of the ladle. "Didn't know women could be painters."

Sara smiles, pulling her bonnet down to keep the sun out of her eyes. "There are a few of us in Amsterdam and Haarlem."

"The cities are smitten with vice. I had a son, Joost, the eldest, who wanted to go off to Leiden. I told him that cards, tankards, and petticoats have ruined more than one young man. Do you know the proverb?"

"I do."

The woman sips from the ladle, one hand cupped beneath it. "It's not much, but I have rabbit stew to spare. You can sit a spell."

Sara thanks the woman and enters into the dark cool of the ruins, into the jagged memory of old rooms. These quarters must have once belonged to a priest and his family, a rectory built into the brick hind of the church. A rent of blue sky dominates the ceiling and the walls are mossed a delicate green. An overhang of slate surrounds the tarred hearth, a pair of cauldrons smoking above a low set fire. A few wooden bowls, a gruel cup, a pelt of rabbit furs laid out as a rug, a low milking stool with three legs. The only suggestion of civil society is a single cushion covered with moquette and mildewed velvet, the fabric attached with copper nails.

The woman plunks the ladle down into one of the cauldrons. "You place some tender greens down in a cellar with the trapdoor open. You remove the ladder. They can't help themselves. The rabbits jump down to investigate and you close the door on them. Wintertime is harder because there's nothing green to lure them to their own demise. The estate people used to come hunting out here with their carriages and dogs. A bounty of dune birds and thrushes and wild geese. I can barely trap a partridge these days."

The woman insists that Sara take the stool. She fills two wooden bowls with the stew, hands one to Sara, and sits on the rabbit pelts. There appears to be only one spoon—pewter and engraved with the estate seal—so the woman hands it to Sara and takes the big wooden spoon from the cauldron.

"You're very kind," Sara says.

"My grandmother had an entire set of silverware given to us by Cornelis's father, all of it engraved. This one spoon is all that remains."

"They must have held your family in high regard."

"My grandmother was in the room when Cornelis was born. Swaddled him and brought his mother ewe's milk to help her recover."

Sara takes a tentative mouthful of stew, which tastes bitter and woody. "You've seen everything change."

"Before the sickness this was a spotless concern. We mangled laundry for the summer estates and the men worked in the Heemstede mill. We had a schoolhouse with a crippled teacher from the north . . . for some reason the cripples always fared better than the sure-footed ones. She taught the boys catechism and the girls embroidered and milked the sheep and cows." She looks into the embers over the rim of her wooden bowl. "Harvest was always a happy time. The children playing quoits and knucklebones, the young couples dancing raise-the-foot."

Sara can hear the woman's grief behind her wistful recollection, hears it tightening her voice. For an instant, she appears lost to it, her face dumbfounded and coming back to the room from a great depth. But then she brims with the Frisian sense of forbearance again, some kind of rectitude and resolve that develops on the wind-battered islands of the North Sea. Sara sees how easily she could avoid the woman's burdens. She could ask to be shown the remnants of the town and repair to the hillsides to begin sketching. There's no reason to linger at the hem of this ragged wood.

But then she's asking, "How many people died here?"

The woman's lips purse. "Near a hundred. The rest left, went to settle elsewhere."

"God in Heaven," Sara says. "I will pray for them."

"I gave birth to nine children. Every one of them is now up on that hill and their souls dispatched to heaven. Their father is at the head of the table, closest to the stone fence. I still see him saying grace with his clay pipe sticking out of his pocket."

Sara pictures the children buried below the hillside of lilies, then, unbidden, there's a vision of Kathrijn baking in the kitchen, her hair pulled back, a cheek dusted in flour. A good helper at mealtime, Sara recalls, knew how to drop griddle cakes onto the smoking skillet without burning herself.

The woman says, "Not one of them was given a proper funeral and burial. Near the end, there were bodies racked by the plague, piles of clothes that had the fever burned out of them. The sound of an entire village overcome with it, the coughing like a flock of keening wild birds." She physically holds back a sob with one clenched hand against her chest.

Sara says, "I lost a daughter to the same fever. I cannot imagine multiplying that grief by nine or ten."

The woman steadies her eyes and brings her face up from the fire. "What was her name?"

"Kathrijn."

"And she passed quickly?"

"It happened in fits and starts and then all at once. I remember the very first cough. She slept up in the attic room and I lay in bed listening to the sounds of the house. It was a thin, raspy little cough, as if she were coughing into a pillow, afraid that I would hear. When she was hours away from death I sat up there and asked God to let me be the one. She was so feverish that she fell into these fits of tiny laughter, her face burning up with the sickness and shame, as if she had brought this on herself, had caught it from walking barefoot." Sara hears her voice quiver and takes a breath. "She was always going barefoot around the house, a drafty old place with stone floors. She was seven years old, almost eight, and the only child I could ever have."

The woman places her calloused hand on Sara's.

"Forgive me," Sara says. "I have no right to burden you."

"It's not a question of rights, meisje."

They continue eating their stew in silence. "How many girls did you have?" Sara asks.

"Three, including the eldest. She was sixteen and being courted by the local boys. My husband was forever finding ribbons tied to the fencepost as a sign of some secret love promise."

"We never had to contend with that, thank goodness," Sara says. She thinks of Kathrijn, part tomboy, part scrubwoman, bustling around the house in her apron and scolding Barent if he left his boots by the fire. Her nightmares kept her a child when it was dark out. She wonders how Kathrijn would have softened or hardened into womanhood, about the kinds of young men who might have come to tie ribbons on the stoop in the middle of the night. But these kinds of speculations always end in a wave of sadness and recrimination, as if Kathrijn had been abandoned to a fate worse than death. The vision always ends in their Amsterdam house, the windows dark and the fires unlit, the overwhelming smell of cinders, and Kathrijn living out eternity as a young girl in the empty house, alone and waiting for everyone else to return.

"Are you all right, my dear?" the woman asks.

Sara brings her gaze back from the low fire beneath the cauldron. "Will it ever go away? The anguish."

"Not ever, far as I can tell. I just hope the dead feel better about it than we do." She hefts herself up and goes back to the cauldron to give it a stir.

Sara can tell the woman is worn out and wishing to be alone again. She takes a last mouthful of her stew and regains her composure. In her mind, she folds up the empty house and its seven-year-old tenant like a map. She stands and gives the woman her bowl back. "I'm sorry, I never asked your name."

"Griet."

"Thank you so much for your hospitality and stories. If it's all right, I'd like to sketch the town for some paintings. I might come back once or twice. Perhaps you can give me a tour next time?"

"I'd like that," Griet says.

They walk back through the ruined rooms, the heady smell of moss in the afternoon shadows. Sara says goodbye and walks down toward the fields. She sees Tomas waving at her from the riverbank, his fishing rod in the air.

Manhattan

OCTOBER 1958

IT DOESN'T OCCUR TO ELLIE that she's being courted by Jake Alpert until she gives him the list of paintings. She has spent a week researching privately held works by Dutch and Flemish baroque women and whittled it down to just five. A Ruysch, a Leyster, a Clara Peeters, a Van Oosterwyck, and the de Vos. She wrote down *At the Edge of a Wood* and crossed it out at least a dozen times. She conjured visions of Gabriel in a damp raincoat with the stolen painting under his arm, meeting Jake under the clock at Grand Central—a scene lifted straight from one of Gabriel's dime-store espionage novels. The painting can't be sold at auction, so she assumes it's destined for a transaction in the shadows. There's a part of her that can imagine a widower being oddly comforted by the depiction—a girl at the edge of a frozen river, the world suspended and amplified by the cold. She is unreachable and bereft but also, it seems to Ellie, forever waiting, a passive witness to the living. She leaves the painting on the list that she brings to their lunch meeting on a Friday afternoon, her fingers rubbing the edges of the paper on the subway. She always has the sensation of being swallowed by the roaring dark of the first tunnel, her ears popping and the sudden appearance of her reflection on the blackened windowpane like some hangdog daguerreotype from another century. She wonders whether she normally looks so startled and uneasy, or whether she's nervous about seeing Jake. Has she dressed for a date or a restoration client meeting? The plaid skirt suggests the latter but her blouse is a bit breezy, she thinks, short sleeves and an open neckline. She buttons up her cardigan and tries to brighten her face in the reflection without attracting attention.

They meet at a Midtown Spanish restaurant where the waiters are old men with silver comb-overs and pressed white aprons. As always, Jake is impeccably dressed, wearing a three-piece suit with a burgundy tie and carrying a tan leather briefcase. When he greets her he leans in to kiss her on the cheek and she notices he smells like vintage luggage and hand soap. It's an odd gesture, she thinks, this first peck on the cheek, at once intimate and formal. She thinks of her severe face on the train and sparks up a smile. They sit and make small talk for a few minutes, about the weather and travels in Spain, before he orders for both of them.

In a low, considered voice, he says to the waiter, "Gazpacho para dos, followed by the seafood paella to share. Could we also get some rioja?"

Ellie thinks he's showing off with a few words of Spanish but likes the fact that he's trying to impress her. The waiter brings some rioja in a glass flask that looks vaguely institutional—a conical beaker with a clear handle—and pours them wine.

"Do you always order for the table?" Ellie asks.

Jake unfurls his napkin into his lap, bringing his eyes up at her slowly. "Oh, I'm sorry. That was presumptuous. An old habit."

"It's okay. You seem to know what to order. Did you come here often? With Rachel?"

"Not this place, but another Spanish restaurant near the park. We fell in love with the food when we honeymooned in Barcelona."

They sip their wine. The short stubby glasses remind Ellie of the water tumblers her mother used to keep on the kitchen counter.

"I brought you the list of paintings," she says, taking it from her pocket and laying it flat on the table. "It's a bit wrinkled."

He reaches over to pick it up. "It looks well loved."

She watches his eyes move down the list, then back up again.

He says, "Thank you for putting this together."

"Listing them is the easy part. Finding them is another question. But a good art dealer might have some leads. I looked up auction and museum records to make sure they're all still private."

"Which one is your favorite?" he asks.

"A year ago I would have said the Leyster. *A Game of Cards*. The woman is holding her own with the men, sharing some bawdy joke. She's looking back over her shoulder and just letting everything unfold. She's in charge, somehow."

He adjusts his silverware parallel to his plate. "And what about now?"

"It's the de Vos. No question."

"¿Por qué?"

She suspects he's flirting, but she also knows she has a track record of misreading signals from men. In London, there was a series of botched dates with fellow restoration students. Three dates in with an aristocratic boy from Yorkshire before she realized she'd mistaken his effeminate manners for refinement and that he was furtively gawking at the Italian waiters whenever they ate out.

She pushes all that back and focuses on the question at hand. "It's totally unique. A landscape by a baroque woman. People depicted with portrait-like details. The only painting attributed to her."

"What's her story?"

"We can't be sure, but she lost a daughter to the plague and her husband went bankrupt. That much is documented."

"And where is it? The painting."

"Hard to know. I suspect it's been in the same family for generations."

The gazpacho arrives and she hopes that he won't condescend to her with something like *Now this is a cold soup*. That would ruin everything, poison whatever flirtation is, or isn't, transpiring. She can't even work out if she's attracted to him. Does he smell like an old suitcase and Ivory soap and, if so, could that ever evoke more in her than a well-traveled uncle coming to visit? She likes his hands, the way the French cuffs rest against the bony part of his hairless wrists. His eyes are kind and vital, his smile a little raffish. But there's something self-entitled, she thinks, a man who's never known want.

"Fascinating," he says, swallowing some soup. "Have you seen it?"

"No." She takes up her spoon and swirls the surface of the soup a little, aware of him watching her. "Though I would dearly love to. I wouldn't say it's a famous painting in the art world. More like a cult classic. An enigma." She's surprised by how effortless the lie is, though she knows the real exposure is the list itself. One day, years from now, if her dissertation manuscript becomes a book, Jake Alpert might happen upon it and read the chapter on de Vos and realize she was holding out on him. The thought of her future feels like a rope around her waist, a tightening noose around her rib cage. She sips her wine and focuses on her soup for a moment to steady her thoughts.

He says, "Listen, I've got the afternoon off and I wondered if you might like to go see a movie."

She lets it hang in the air too long, so that when she answers she sounds calculating instead of enthusiastic. "What's playing?"

He wipes his mouth with his napkin, perhaps a little disappointed. "There's a Fellini over at the Paris Theatre. *Nights of Cabiria*."

She puts her soupspoon down. "I don't really understand Fellini. I always feel like I'm watching someone else's demented dream in black and white."

He laughs. "That's a relief, actually. I was trying to be more cultured than I am. Rachel used to drag me along and I was dutiful. How about *Gigi*?"

"The musical?"

He nods.

"Sounds like fun."

They finish their soup and the paella arrives in a big pan with handles, shrimp tails and clam shells sticking out of the saffron-colored rice. The waiter serves them and refills their wine and she hears Jake whisper *gracias*, an affectation that has become endearing in the span of half an hour.

When they leave the restaurant there's a downpour and of course Jake has a compact umbrella in his briefcase. She takes his arm and walks beneath the open umbrella, worried about the garlic aftermath of the paella, trying to talk out of the side of her mouth, facing away from him. He walks closest to the curb, a gesture, like the cheek kiss, that smacks of chivalry and old money. They walk over to Broadway where a movie palace on hard times is still showing *Gigi* with faded posters out front to prove it. Jake buys their tickets and while Ellie stands out at the curbstone, craning to look up at the Art Deco facade with its gold lions and chevron-painted tiles, it occurs to her that here is the life she has written about and fabricated for her parents. Lunch at a Spanish restaurant, wine from a glass flask, a wealthy widower taking her to see a matinee on a rainy weekday afternoon. Her life suddenly seems interesting and full, as if a glaze has shocked a muted underlayer into color.

Jake comes back with their tickets and says it's about to start. They go inside the musty, cavernous lobby, the dingy red carpet and the pendant lights and the tired concession stand, the 15-watt gloaming as heavy as a fog. She loves everything about this place. They buy a bag of popcorn to share and two Cokes and go inside the theater itself, where a handful of people sit watching previews in the underwater light, the pale blue-white ribbons of the projector rippling above their heads. They sit in the middle, an entire row to themselves. He nestles the popcorn between them, holding it for her on the armrest. When the film starts she's immediately won over by the costumes and the sets and the music. Paris in dappled light, the upper classes frivolous about marriage and serious about love, Maurice Chevalier dancing in a boater and powder-blue suit. She's faintly aware of the plot beneath all the musical and visual confection, the girl who is being groomed for life as a courtesan, the lackluster options that fan out before her, but the darker themes seem like a distraction, the struts beneath a beautiful bridge. Several times Jake grazes her hand at the rim of the popcorn bag and she wonders whether his attention is mere loneliness, a widower reentering the fray with a younger woman. She tells herself to make no assumptions, that keeping a man company is not the same as keeping a man's interest, a sentiment that seems like something her mother once told her. How did they ever make love, come to think of it, Bob and Maggie Shipley, with her dad spending his nights out on his boat? On-screen, Gigi flirts and drinks champagne with an older man, apparently oblivious to her own intoxicating sexual charm.

When the movie finishes he puts her in a cab and pays the driver and she doesn't protest. He kisses her again on the cheek, thanks her for the list, asks her to send him an invoice, and then she's driving home in the rain, the afterimages of the movie and the melodies floating through her mind, a warm floaty sensation that she always gets after a good matinee, a sense of waking slowly to the quotidian world and its demands. She hopes the driver won't make small talk and he doesn't. Brooklyn is gray and ambient, the whir of tires on the road, the yellows of headlights. Even her apartment, when she gets home, feels softened and less cluttered. She tells herself it *was* a date and puts the kettle on the stovetop. While she waits for the water to boil, she hurries down to her bedroom and opens the closet. The de Vos—now on Jake Alpert's list—was recently moved back into her apartment, this time in an airtight case. Certain complications developed at the Chelsea storage unit and with the bakery key, Gabriel reported, but a sale, he felt sure, was imminent. She assumes it's all part of keeping his inventory on the move. She lays it flat on her bed. How remarkable, she thinks, the way paintings trap light and time. Father Barry used to call it starlight, the passage of pigments on canvas across the centuries. Feeling inspired for a moment, she goes to the typewriter table and begins to jot down some dissertation ideas on a notepad. She needs a chapter on the Guilds of St. Luke and the apprenticeship model.

When the phone rings she knows it's Jake Alpert because no one else has called her since the summer, not since Meredith Hornsby summoned her to campus for a browbeating. She decides to let it ring four times before picking up. "I had a wonderful time," he says. "Have you ever been to the Cloisters? I was thinking we could go on Sunday afternoon." For the first time, she allows her imagination to brim over and she sees a Metrocolor montage of her new dating life. They'll meet for drinks in the Oyster Bar at Grand Central and she'll lead him through a tour of the Frick and they'll picnic in the park. She'll cut her hair to make herself look older, wear lipstick in the middle of the day, learn how to cook eggs Benedict. She'll move to Manhattan and start reading again for pleasure and they'll go ballroom dancing. All the colors in this vision are milky and washed out, softened not by rain but by a delicate blue haze. It's Rembrandt meets Metrocolor. She sees the new palette taking shape, the beginning of the life she's been lying about in her letters for years. "I would love to," she says. "It sounds fabulous." She can't remember ever using the word *fabulous* before.

Sydney

AUGUST 2000

MARTY SHAMBLES ACROSS the sandstone campus in his field vest, his pockets filled with Aussie dollar coins and banknotes, with toothpicks, an acorn, a roll of antacids. Something about their money he likes, the frontier gold coins, the wild colors and the bush motifs on the notes, the outlandish-looking animals on the coat of arms. Sydney is easy to like and for several days he's been walking and cabbing-it around with a pocket-size map. Sightseeing has never been his forte—that was always left up to Rachel—but he likes to launch out into an unknown city with few bearings, exploring the grid or the serpentine alleyways, and see where he ends up. For two days he's wandered through the Central Business District and out into the leafy innards of Georgian sandstone and postwar redbrick, along the little scrubby bays and mangrove inlets of the harbor. He took a ferry across to Manly and back, saw the steel blue of the Pacific through the sandstone jaws of North and South Head. He ate a hamburger with an egg tucked inside on a hilltop above Bondi Beach, washed it down with a very thin banana milkshake that seemed as exotic and outlandish to him as tapioca. His walk is loose-kneed and a bit shuffling, but he can clip along at two miles an hour, a pace endorsed by his doctor. When he tires he flags down a taxi and makes notes in his small Moleskine. When he was still driving, hunkered down into his sixties, he took up the habit of reading street names and commercial signage aloud, a bewildered tone in his voice, as if no one had any business naming a place Dick's Accessories or Krumholz Drive. It drove Rachel around the bend and he thinks of her when he finds himself doing it in the back of a cab, flummoxed by the Aboriginal words—*Woolloomooloo* and *Woollahra* and *Kirribilli* and God knows what. The drivers look at him blankly or give him a charitable laugh.

Sydney University is High Church in an Anglican sort of way, a croft of leaded windows and wheat-colored stonework. He sees echoes of Cambridge and Oxford, of British imperiousness. He scrutinizes the campus map handed to him by a security guard at the main gate. The auditorium is circled in yellow highlighter several times because the old and the infirm need a little extra help. Early this morning he'd asked one of the front desk clerks at the hotel to help him with an Internet search in the business center. He told her that the ham radio and the pacemaker were inventions he knew something about, but the World Wide Web was a sea of white noise to him. Under his direction, the woman brought up the University of Sydney website and located Professor Eleanor Shipley's faculty profile, complete with course schedule and building locations. He made a point of not looking at her faculty profile picture, because he wanted his first glimpse of new millennium Ellie to be in person.

It's not until he gets close to the lecture hall that he has second thoughts. He rarely thinks of death, but when he does it's usually in the context of inconvenience—a stroke at thirty thousand feet, a heart attack in the barber's chair, the fatal onset of colitis on a foreign park bench. For the most part, he stopped traveling oversees as a courtesy to the future strangers who might one day find him sullied and expired beside one of their national monuments. What he thinks now is that he won't live much longer and this is an errand he's always meant to run—a settling in the ledger of regret. He sits down to catch his breath before going into the lecture hall. Whatever shape Ellie's life has taken on, he knows this will be an intrusion. Here comes Marty de Groot, the wrecking ball of the past.

He scans the hedgerows and building facades for omens and portents, for signs of cosmic sanction. As he's gotten older, his superstitions have grown increasingly mystical and apocalyptic. In his forties, he was briefly convinced that the missing painting had rescued him from premature gout or death, that the men in his bloodline had been cursed by its presence. This theory was disproved when the painting was returned. Not only has he lived into his eighties but also his marriage endured and there were decades of relative happiness. If not actual and abiding happiness it was at least contentment buoyed by occasional moments of bracing pleasure. Still, despite all this inductive proof against nameless cataclysm, there's always been a quadrant of his thinking reserved for the world's signs that prophesy ruin. A digital clock face with three identical numbers aligned suggests bad luck for the rest of the day, an acorn in his pocket prevents him from being struck by lightning, looking away when an ambulance wails by prevents fatal injury befalling him. He's never killed a bee that's flown into his house because he knows it will invite a troublesome stranger onto his doorstep. He can see all these beliefs as irrational, understand that they rise through the layer of primal murk buried below the hippocampus, but none of that stops them from angling his thoughts toward misfortune. So as he looks at the lecture hall he waits for a sign, for permission to enter. Eventually, it comes in the form of two coeds walking toward the building, two girls wrapped in bright scarves holding hands and chatting excitedly about some scandal. Marty can't remember girls holding hands during his college years, but there's such a look of good cheer on their faces, such fellow feeling burning in their cheeks on a blustery afternoon, that he's convinced of his mission. He gets up and follows in their wake, moving into the dark chill of the building, across the wax floors and into the auditorium itself. He gets a few stares from university students who are dressed in tattered clothing and who look like teenagers to him. He sits down in the back row and settles himself with an antacid.

Marty sees her for the first time in more than forty years across the valley of raked wooden seating. She seems small down there, standing behind the lectern, her hair long and completely gray, pulled back at the seams in the manner of academics and archivists and feminist poets. He thinks of the old-fashioned word *handsome* when applied to women. She's dressed in navies and creams, in a wool skirt and knee-length boots and a copper necklace that seems from another time. As she leans against the lectern she raises one boot, brings it onto the toe as she looks out at her ragged charges. When she begins talking it's clear how comfortable she is up there. She speaks about the Vermeers in intimate tones, as if she's talking to a fellow devotee, to a confidant who's made a pilgrimage to unravel these mysteries. A pretty little lecture, he thinks, the coaxing of poetry from the passage of light. Something about *tronien* and the invented person. Very nice.

TWO DAYS AFTER HER encounter with Helen in the conservation studio, Ellie gives an undergraduate lecture on Vermeer and his use of light. This part of her course on the Dutch Golden Age always coincides with the heart of a Sydney winter, when the maritime light angles low and from the north. As an assignment, she asks her students to pay attention to the way winter sunlight slants across Victorian sandstone in the afternoons or the rosin, almost pink light that brims off the Pacific in the mornings. They're supposed to keep a journal of their observations—a light journal—but they are mostly blind to the subtleties of illumination. It's like noticing their own heartbeats or breathing for the first time. They take the tawny hues of Sydney's bushland in summer, or the somber warm light of the city in winter, for granted. So she starts out her lecture by putting several Vermeers up on the projection screens in the auditorium and walks them through the fall of light.

"In *Woman Holding a Balance*, we are spectators to the passage of light. Arthur Wheelock describes the light as spilling in from the window, behind the thickest part of the orange curtain. You see it cascade down toward the table, bathing the gold and the pearls. Blue drapery, folded in shadow. The light is northern and amorphous. It gently guides the eye. Our gaze goes to her hand at the edge of the table, then up her forearm toward her face. It could be reverie on her face, her eyes downturned, nothing to distract us from the balance between her fingers. Wheelock says it looks as if she will never move and you can see it. She's suspended in time. Vermeer wants us to believe that the light is still pouring down, her pinky still extended."

She looks out into the auditorium where sixty or so Bachelor of Arts students take notes or make asides or fidget with their mobile phones. For two days she's had the sensation of seeing her own life as a painting under an X-ray—the hairline fractures and warped layers that distort the topmost image. She sees her private history, the personal epochs and eras in foreign cities, with a keen, clinical detachment. They have all led to the cracks on the surface and it's time to take responsibility for those flaws. Last night, she drafted two letters of resignation, one to the museum and one to the university.

Lead-tin yellow radiates from the next Vermeer she shows her students, *A Lady Writing a Letter*. "We think her garment is all gold and yellow, trapped in the light from the window, but the lead-tin yellow is only in the highlights—a series of bright invitations to the eye. Most of the fabric is muted and overrun with delicate grays. In his way, Vermeer is asking us to complete the painting in our minds. He paints in a suggestive rather than a descriptive mode . . . We're the ones who complete the image."

There are a few head nods out in the auditorium, a pen held against a lip in consideration. Ellie thinks about the new Sara de Vos painting of the child's funeral and the way it extends the artist's life beyond the known and documented. Had she taken Hendrik a little more seriously, had her ego not been riled, she would have asked detailed questions about the painting's provenance. Just this morning, she spent several hours in a research database scanning for mentions of funeral images in the seventeenth-century catalogue—there were many, but none that matched the new scene. After the library, she'd walked across campus to her office and typed the two drafted letters on her computer—one to Max Culkins and one to the chair of her department. Both letters outline the reasons for her resignation but refer to the transgression as "an unfortunate slip of moral conscience" instead of a calculated forgery. By way of explanation, she typed: *I was twenty-six and deluded about how everything worked in the world, including myself.* She suspects she has let herself off too lightly in these letters. The thought of them sealed and addressed in her purse under the lectern tugs at her attention every few minutes. She's decided that she won't send them until she has personally returned the fake to the Leiden archive and accepted responsibility for it. Even if it ruins her financially, she will reimburse them for whatever they paid for her copy. If she were to send the letters now Max Culkins wouldn't let her within a mile of those paintings. It lightens her mind knowing the letters are written and sealed.

She looks up at the projector screens. "Next, let's look at Vermeer's *The Girl with the Red Hat*. The Dutch term for this kind of painting is *tronien*. These are busts or heads, and the figures are often wearing exotic hats or clothes. The person is usually invented, rather than depicted. This is a small painting on a wood panel and it's possibly experimental in nature, a way for Vermeer to perfect the use of small blurred points of light."

A male student in a wool cap throws up his hand near the front of the auditorium. "Her mouth is slightly open. Is she about to say something?"

Ellie says, "An open mouth was a sign of sexual availability in Dutch culture at the time. A signifier of sorts."

"So Vermeer's basically perving on her . . ." the student says. He gets some encouraging laughter from the back.

Ellie is about to fire off a rejoinder when an older man's American accent comes through the semidarkness of the back row. "He's projecting onto her, no doubt, if she ever existed to begin with. By the way, Bub, he wasn't much older than you when he painted this. So show a little respect."

It's East Coast, she thinks, probably New York or New Jersey, the kind of accent that pronounces *human* as *yewman*. For a few moments, she doesn't connect the voice with her memories.

The auditorium cranes to see who's put the smartarse in his place with such gusto. Ellie wonders whether a visiting academic has decided to sit in on her class and no one bothered to tell her. Or perhaps this is the new university chancellor, an American scholar she's never taken the time to meet and who has a reputation as a disciplinarian. Irrationally, she wonders whether he's dropped by to hear one of her lectures before he fires her for academic misconduct. She sees an old man in a khaki vest shuffling toward the rear exit. She tries to bring her attention back to her lecture notes, then looks squarely at the boy in the wool cap. "All art contains desire. Vermeer's just being a little more honest about it than some of the others." Then there's a fleeting profile as the old man closes the auditorium door gently behind him. No matter how transformed by age, it's a face she could never forget. She stands behind the lectern in silence for a long moment. Eventually she puts a new Vermeer slide onto the screen and forces herself to talk about light.

Heemstede

SUMMER 1637

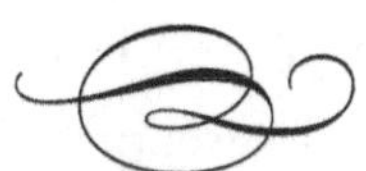

SARA WANTS TO GIVE Griet's children a proper burial, at least on canvas. Painting the girl by the frozen river had been a companion to her grief and she wonders if she can offer Griet some solace. She thinks of her winter scene hanging above a merchant's desk or in an austere sitting room, a thousand hours and shades by her hand. It was never meant to be decorative—she'd somehow never imagined it hanging on a wall—but burghers like Cornelis had a habit of transforming the world's objects. A burial shroud or a human bone from the Orient was a thing of dinnertime curiosity and philosophizing. An occasion for comment. She feels unable to paint a well-proportioned image of the ruins in falling light. It feels like a lie, like an affront to Griet's torment.

She thinks of the portrait commissions that arrange the dead for a widow, the children plucked from the afterlife to sit neatly at a kitchen table arranged with apples and copper pans. Or the husband ported back to the living, a hand on his paunch as he blazes with good health by the hearth. Why not rebuild the turrets and the mud-walled huts? Why not capture the procession leading down from the church in the late dusk of high summer? She sees the candles burning behind the rose-colored windows, the pallbearers trudging along in rolled shirtsleeves.

She makes sketches in charcoal, rejoins the lines and lintels, but then finds herself unable to paint the scene on a sized canvas. After checking her proportions and reconstructions against Cornelis's scale model, she realizes that the fault is one of atmosphere, not composition. Despite its being midsummer, the lushness of the full foliage feels orchestrated and false. It reminds her of a still life, of striated tulips in a painted vase, of curling lemon rinds against wood grain. Beautiful perhaps, but also an insult, she thinks, to the buried dead up on the hill, to the hundred or so souls who prattled with fever before they drew their last earthly breath. No, it must be in winter, the trees bare, the river frozen. Out of plague season, yes, but true to the desolation of the spirit. She tells no one what she's painting. For all Cornelis knows it's a summer landscape with a picturesque village in the twilight. Perhaps that's what Barent had promised long before the whale and the apple—the comfort of nostalgia at dusk. She can't bring herself to do that.

Each Saturday she returns to the remains of the settlement and sits with Griet for an hour before making more sketches. Tomas takes her in the wagon and she sits up beside him on the box seat. He fishes on the riverbank until she is ready to return to the estate. She takes Griet little gifts from the main house—cinnamon cakes and sugared almonds and bottles of beer. Griet complains that such luxuries are wasted on her, but each time she unbundles them with relish. She tells stories of the town. The traveling bohemian who blew glass, who walked over the dunes one day and decided to stay. The courtship rituals of the young men, the way they used to climb a girl's roof and attach a green branch to the ridge beam or carve their beloved's name in a tree trunk or write it in the sand of the riverbank with a stick. "All the men were gamblers," she tells Sara. "They wagered on the outcomes of marriages and battles during the war with Spain and whether a child would be born a son or whether the river would freeze one winter over another. They even bet on who would die from the plague and who would live. Handing over a fistful of stuivers on your deathbed was considered a way of going out with good humor and grace."

"You had six sons?"

Griet nods. "The youngest, Jakob, was only six when he crossed over. He was the last to go."

Sara imagines the boy's death. She sees her funeral depiction taking shape. Nothing in the world is more sinister than a child's coffin.

ONE AFTERNOON SHE CLIMBS the old stone tower with her rucksack to see the view. Griet has told her that it was meant for the burgomaster and official town business, that a bell used to ring out storm warnings and proclamations when the town was at its height. Cornelis calls it the Tower of Weights and Measures. The view from the top is a circle of trees and a flank of grassy dunes, the river a tin-white ribbon under the sun. The horizon is cloudless, the color of chalk, the sea a gauzy blue line to the west. She imagines the landscape in the full of winter, the geese gone from the riverbank, the light diffuse. Tomas waves at her from the reeds, his fishing pole kept perfectly still. She waves back at him, marveling at how small he looks. In the distance she can see the green polder off toward the coast and the glinting crosshatching of the drainage canals. She will turn everything she sees white and brittle, change the sky to a field of smelted lead.

As she unpacks the camera obscura, it strikes her that she has never painted exactly what she sees. Surely, this is the way of all art. The painter sees the world as if through the watery lens of a pond. Certain things ripple and distort while others are magnified and strangely clear. Rembrandt, the famous and adopted son of Amsterdam, ignores the shocking newness taking shape all around him. He ignores the quayside markets of exotic animals, the armadillos in wooden cages, the Hungarian bandmaster striking up an orchestra from a houseboat lit with paper lanterns. Instead, he mostly paints in the unbroken lineage of portraits and histories.

She doesn't mean to paint from God's perspective—that would be a sin of vanity—but the height inflects the scene with something godly and omniscient. She positions the camera obscura on the ledge of the stone wall. Sixty feet in the air, she bends down to hood her gaze through the eyeholes. The world blinks, sways in two, then comes back into sharp relief. Everything converges toward the pinnacle of the ruined church, the vanishing point cutting through the bright ether of the sky. She looks through the darkened chamber and then draws some charcoal lines on her paper. The camera obscura has a narrowing effect, allows her to see shadows and lines and the dapplings of sunlight as pure geometry. The crenellated wall beside the church becomes a necklace of alternating shades, a plait of dark and light.

WHEN SHE RIDES HOME on the box seat, Tomas complains of never catching any fish. He claims that the river is barren just here, that the trout never school in places that carry a stain. Changing the subject, he asks her to explain the camera obscura.

"I saw you using it up on the tower," he says, staring out at the late afternoon above the horses' heads.

Tomas has an inexhaustible curiosity for all aspects of the painting trade. He stretches and sizes her canvases to her specifications, grinds her pigments with the utmost care, down to the last shard of lapis lazuli or flake of lead white. He has this same exacting manner with horses and plants, she has noticed. Shodding a horse or grafting a rose resembles an act of ritual under his steady hands. On more than one occasion, she has thought about painting his portrait just to capture the boyish earnestness of his gaze and the dexterity of his hands.

She says, "It's a small dark chamber. Picture a room where you look at the outside world through a hole in the closed curtains. It frames everything into view, throws a clear image onto the back wall."

"Why is it necessary?"

"It tricks the eye. You look out at the countryside and you see the whole thing run together. The obscura lets you see the shapes and colors in isolation. Everything is captured."

Tomas reknuckles the reins and considers. He says, "It does some of the looking for you."

"Yes, it does," she says brightly.

"I'd like to look through it sometime."

"Of course."

They ride along in silence for a while. The uncultivated bogs and heaths out by the village make Tomas talk of all the work he has to do over the summer. She likes the sound of his voice—it's unhurried and careful. The trimming of the hedgerows, the pruning of the fruit trees, the chopping of the winter firewood. His hours spent fishing are the only times she ever sees him at rest; he seems happiest in the throes of daily work.

As they near the stone fence around the inner acres, his mood changes and he asks, "What happened to your husband?"

Sara has been in Heemstede several months and it's the first time anyone besides Cornelis has asked about Barent. She had assumed that her employer had said enough about her situation to settle gossip and speculation among the household staff.

"Forgive me," he says after a moment. "I have no right to ask that."

"We were very poor after we lost our daughter. He couldn't make a living so he left me holding the docket."

He considers this, looks off at a wooded croft, the trees burnished with northern sunlight. "That is not an honorable thing to do, if I may say so."

"You may. No one has ever wronged me so."

Tomas pulls up the horses and gets down to open the gate. Cornelis insists that every gate and door be closed as a precaution against the intrusions of untamed nature—wind, humidity, malevolent humors, wandering animals. As he sets off for the gate, without looking at her, Tomas says, "I'm glad you came to us. We all are."

Sara smiles to herself as he carefully unlatches the gate.

SHE WORKS ON THE PICTURE for the rest of the summer, mounting a burial one brushstroke at a time. In the boy's coffin she hopes Griet will see the whole town honored and memorialized. She is nervous to show Cornelis because she suspects he wanted a bucolic scene with ruins or the reconstructed village hunkered majestically against the dunes. Reforming the buildings turns out to be the easy part; they offer the certainty of straight lines and strict perspective. The difficulty is in the onlookers down on the frozen river and the funeral procession itself. She paints the villagers in thin, translucent layers of paint and plans to build them up slowly into full color and vitality. But one night she leaves her work for the day and returns to it the next morning to find a new effect in place. The bodies and clothes of the villagers have silvered and dimmed away slightly, the pigments absorbed back into the canvas. It's a fault in the sizing and grounding of the canvas, either her mistake or Tomas's, but the effect is pleasing to her. She recalls the picture *Summer Landscape* by Van Goyen and rushes down to the *Kunstkammer* to view it again. When she returns to the attic she decides to continue building up the layers of the funeral-goers and onlookers, but she will stop just shy of making them full-bodied and completely opaque. Their dark winter clothes, their hands and faces, will be faintly transparent, the lines of the landscape barely discernible but nonetheless visible behind their bodies. These are not ghosts, she thinks, but figments of a woman's unspeakable grief.

Even though she has only worked on a single painting all summer, Tomas continues to bring her carefully stretched and sized canvases. He prepares them out in the stables and brings them to her three and four at a time, placing them like an offering below the eaves of her attic workroom. Several times she has gone out to the horse stalls and seen him at work—standing in his breeches over the cauldron, boiling the pelt clippings into glue until it all has the texture of honey, smearing it meticulously onto the stretched canvases with a palette knife. She'd shown him the process only once and handed him a written recipe. When he handed it back to her she realized he couldn't read. Now she has enough prepared canvases to work a year without pause.

On the afternoon that she finishes the funeral painting he knocks tentatively on her door and she tells him to come in. Stepping inside, his eyes averted—he never looks at her work unless he's invited to—he places three more canvases at the far end of the room.

"You'll have me painting for the rest of eternity," she says.

"Are they all right?"

"Perfectly made, but there's no need to make more. I'll teach you how to do the grounding next."

"I'd like that."

She stands by the window, brush in hand, and looks back at the funeral scene. She dries the end of her brush on the sleeve of her painter's smock. "Tomas, would you come and tell me what you think of this?"

He brightens whenever she uses his first name. This is something that she notices. He walks slowly toward the window, hat in hand. She's surprised by how much she wants him to like the painting, by the sound of her own heartbeat thrumming in her ears. When he turns to look at the canvas his face turns grave, an expression of genuine sorrow darkening his features. He moves his face close to study the brushwork, just the way she has taught him, then stands back a few feet to take in the totality.

"I was thinking of taking it to show Griet before presenting it to Mr. Groen. Do you think she'll like it?"

His mouth looks as if he's swallowed a bitter almond and she fears the worst. She has labored for months over an epic failure.

He says, "I'm no expert."

"You have eyes, don't you? You have a heart and a mind." There's a hint of exasperation in her voice.

He gives her a gently admonishing look, then comes back to the painting. He looks at it from several angles, cocking his head each time and biting his lip. Quietly, he says, "We are rising and looking down from a great height. How did you do that?"

"All those sketches from the tower."

He swallows and folds his arms across his chest. "I can feel the cold in my hands."

"Is that all you have to say about it?"

"I was raised to feel things and not speak them."

"But if I made you say something, what would you say?"

In profile, as he stares at the painting, he could pass for a man moved to prayer. "It will make her weep," he says. "It's the saddest and most beautiful painting I've ever seen."

She's overwhelmed with a feeling of tenderness and gratitude toward him. He turns to look at her and startles, as if he sees something new in her gaze. He looks down at the floor, runs his hand along his hatband. For the first time it occurs to her that Tomas might be courting her, however coyly, that all these canvases are a ploy, two dozen perfectly sized excuses to be in her presence. She feels her breath tighten up against her rib cage.

He says, "Tomorrow we'll start the grounding lessons, then?"

"Yes," she says. "Come up here tomorrow and we'll get started."

He bites back a smile, buoyed along, a little jaunty now on his feet as he walks over to the door and closes it behind him.

Manhattan

OCTOBER 1958

A MONTH OF DINNERS, LUNCHES, matinees, and museum walks. But Ellie remains confused about Jake's intentions until he invites her away for a weekend. In the fall, she agrees to go antique hunting upstate and stay overnight in Albany. He arranges to pick her up at her apartment early one Saturday morning, so they can hit the estate sales and antique shops before noon. The weather has turned—Indian summer has given way to chill mornings and cold nights. She wraps herself in a scarf and heavy wool coat. While she waits, she double-checks her luggage and becomes conscious that her suitcase is one size too big for a weekend getaway. Right-size luggage seems like an extravagance of poststudent life, a distant shore she's still rowing toward.

Jake raps at her door and when she answers he's standing there with a framed painting wrapped in brown paper and masking tape.

"What's that?" she asks.

"Your new assignment. It needs a good cleaning and some inpainting."

"Can I take a peek?"

"It'll be waiting for you when you come back." He takes her hand and leans in to kiss her cheek. "We need to get a head start on those Albany widows. They've been up since four planning for the ancient blood sport of antiquing."

Ellie smiles and sets the painting beside the front door. Jake grabs her suitcase and doesn't say anything about its size, for which she's grateful. He leads her out into the hallway.

At the curb, his night-blue Citroën looks almost sardonic in the morning light—its raked hood and sleek headlights give it the dreadnought grace of a shark. She thinks of the grey nurse sharks that sometimes followed her father's ferryboat across Sydney Harbour. They've taken taxis up until now so the unveiling of the car feel momentous, like she's seeing a new side to him. He puts her suitcase in the trunk and they climb in. When he starts the engine, the car shudders and rises a few inches with a pnuematic sigh. She looks over at him and he grins. He says, "They call that the kneel." A moment later, he puts on a pair of driving gloves and gives the horn a light jab—it sounds French and adenoidal—and they pull down the street.

"What do you think of the car?" he asks.

She likes the way he asks her opinion about everything, even if she doesn't know the first thing about cars or music or half the food they eat. She looks over the molded dashboard and the instrument panel with its needle-thin dials and clock-face odometer. The steering wheel has a single spoke and the brake appears to be more of a push button than a pedal. "I'm not sure whether it was designed by an engineer or an avant-garde theater director."

He likes this answer, she thinks, finds it sporting and witty.

He says, "The French like a bit of theater in their automobiles. They pour their souls into them. Did you know that Citroën was part of the French Resistance during the war? They sold trucks to the Nazis but they lowered the oil markers on the dipsticks so the trucks just died out in the field, burned up their engines."

"I like this car already."

They pull down Thirty-Sixth Street to get on the expressway, past the plumbing supply store and the boarded-up florist and the rusting stairwells. From inside the car, she can't help feeling like an aristocrat touring the proletariat. He's wearing a pair of driving moccasins and they're cut from the same leather as his kidskin driving gloves and his watchband—she's always noticing his clothes. That kind of accessorizing on a different man might seem foppish, but on Jake it seems natural and masculine. Sometimes his clothes and mannerisms make her feel clumsy and flat-footed, but most of the time she likes to watch him do things with his hands—the slow and precise gestures, the easy way of folding his arms across his chest when he's listening to her go on about paintings. She looks out the window and sees a gaunt man leaning in a doorway, his breath smoking as the early light braces the length of the street. She thinks about her parents and grandparents, about the hardscrabble brood of relatives in Dubbo and Broken Hill, about the impossibility of her driving in a Citroën with a Dutch-American blue blood named Jake Alpert. While his family passed down baroque and rococo paintings, hers passed down a set of tarnished souvenir spoons, complete with lacquered and wall-mountable display rack. Her mother's pride and joy, right above the kitchen sink and the view of rusting oil tankers where the Parramatta River flows into the harbor.

Driving north they talk about childhood exploits and transgressions.

He says, "I used to feed my father's horse an apple right before he'd go riding on weekends. I was terrified of horses so it took all my courage just to stand there with my flattened palm. I can still remember the feel of its soft muzzle against my hand."

"The horse was direct competition," she says. "You wanted that animal, and therefore your father, to be stricken by horse flatulence. It makes perfect sense to me."

He throws out an easy laugh, his leather gloves turning walnut in a streak of autumn sunlight.

She says, "At the boarding school I went shoplifting whenever I could. I'd steal lollies—candy—and batteries. I kept a transistor radio under my bed and listened to this wonderful show after lights out called *Is It Ours?* They'd play a piece of classical music by an unnamed Australian composer and then one by an anonymous European. People would call in to guess which was which. They almost always thought the better ones were European."

"What does that say about Australians?"

"That we don't trust our own talents. That anything foreign or exotic is automatically better and more refined."

They drive through the gold-and-russet foliage of the Catskills, stopping at small towns with stone courthouses and redbrick fire stations. People dress differently up here, she notices, the men in hats and suspenders, the women in brown woolen dresses. There are municipal bandstands painted white and willow trees presiding over ample walkways. The Citroën gets some stares from the locals as it wends through backstreets—an alien predator of the deep in search of estate sales and antique shops going out of business. They look at old church doors and leadlight windows and dusty mountains of Persian rugs. Ellie scopes out the artwork, but it's mostly decorative and of little value—seascapes, riverscapes, portraits of stern ministers and their patrician wives.

By noon the day has grown warm. They drive on to the next town, the radio playing, the windows down, Jake's gloved hand patting the side of the car in a way that makes Ellie think of him patting the flank of a horse.

Somewhere along the Hudson, between towns, he says, "I've been thinking about our list of prospective Dutch women's paintings. I think I'd like to acquire the single de Vos first. Wouldn't that be something?"

She looks out at the scenery, scrutinizing a little wooded dell of noonday twilight. The car flashes into sunshine and then passes into these coppery green depths under the trees. In an instant, the temperature drops twenty degrees then warms again as they dash back into daylight. She thinks of ten-second days and nights, of miniature deaths. "That would be something," she says casually. Her mood glazes over and she feels faintly dizzy. It reminds her of being on her feet for eight hours at a stretch while restoring a painting, the acetone and close work suddenly going to her head like the blade of a knife. "If you can find it," she says.

Jake adjusts the radio dial, moving the red needle between licks of static. "I've begun to make some discreet inquiries. Put out the word to fellow collectors."

She squints into the trees, letting her eyes go loose so she can slacken the colors from their shapes. She swallows to steady her voice. "That can be part of my brief, if you like. To research private collections and write letters of inquiry."

There's a long pause.

"Your *brief*," he says finally, without looking over. "Is that all this is to you?"

There's a moment of dappled quiet, the air siphoning and whistling in through the open windows.

He says, "I expect there'll be an itemized invoice at the end of the weekend. Send it to my PO box, will you?"

She's shocked by how mean he sounds. Around a bend, it looks as if winter has already burnished up along the riverbank, throwing the elms into skeletal relief. She reaches across the dashboard to touch his gloved hand on the steering wheel, the leather grain warming in the palm of her hand. She's careful not to pat the back of his hand, because she doesn't want to console or patronize.

"That's not the way I see this," she says. "Not anymore."

She takes her hand back, but the words still burn in the air between them. She's not sure if she's surrendered something or claimed something. His face softens.

He says, "I spoke out of turn. Forgive me."

Trying to regain some levity, she says, "Forgotten already. Now, let's strategize about lunch."

He puts his foot down on the accelerator and the Citroën revs into the next octave, pulling them through a stretch of dun-brown fields, the shadows choked and violet up along the rocky hillsides.

They stop for a late lunch at a restaurant run out of somebody's house—a big Victorian with a screened-in porch. It's a makeshift affair, with a parlor of white tablecloths and, in the backyard, picnic tables and wooden chairs set up by a stream. They sit out on the porch and eat sandwiches and chowder at a wicker table before retiring to a line of rocking chairs so Jake can have a smoke. She feels that something has shifted between them and wonders what will happen next. The inscrutability of men, she thinks, not mysterious so much as unreadable. She watches him blow smoke out toward the trees, the way he studies the middle distances as if his childhood were right there in the clearing, as if the teenage trumpeter were practicing scales out in the woods. He's a brooder like me, she thinks.

In the old Dutch section of Albany, they find an estate sale in a three-story house that appears to be sinking into an acre of delicate moss. It's midafternoon and the best items have been thoroughly picked over. A son or nephew of the deceased walks across the naked wood floors—the rugs have all gone to a single buyer—and shows them what remains. There's a handful of oil paintings from the nineteenth century, all of them badly fogged by age and antique copal varnish, some Quaker sideboards and china cabinets, and an array of knick-knacks, some of them heaped into cardboard boxes. Jake asks if they can wander around and the heir tells them to take their time. They go upstairs to the top floor, where the rooms are cavernous and sun-scrubbed, up above the tree crowns. In an enormous bedroom a four-poster bed takes center stage, a hulk of wrought iron and solid carved mahogany. "The deathbed," Jake whispers to Ellie. She takes a landscape painting down from the wall, scrutinizes its seams, and slants it into the light. Turning it over, she examines the back, trying to decipher the blue chalk marks from the auction house and the condition of the relining.

He calls her over to an adjoining bathroom with a claw-foot tub, tiny white mosaics, and exposed copper pipes. The mood is one of convalescence, of warm mineral baths on white afternoons. The double windowpane above the tub is crazed and studded with tiny whorls of distortion that warps the view of the Albany skyline. She wants to tell Jake that the view through the warped windowpane reminds her of Picasso's *Still Life with a Bottle of Rum* because she knows he'd find that amusing. But she doesn't and instead she leans over, one foot inside the tub, letting the old glass buckle the sightlines and magnify the colors of the afternoon. Her first thought, when she feels his hand at her waist, is *Here it is*. "Be careful," he says, "these floors look rotten and that tub could fall through to the basement at any moment." But his hand stays there even when she straightens and turns. She finds herself standing in the tub and Jake Alpert leaning forward to kiss her, blinking into the cubist light of the window. A strange moment to choose, she thinks, with the bathroom smelling faintly of iodine and bath salts. This is part of the inscrutability, she thinks, a man's absolute blindness to timing.

The kiss itself is staid, almost platonic, but his hand rests on her hip and his thumb loops into the outer edge of her skirt pocket, pulling her forward.

She says, "I wondered when that would happen." Then, a second later, "Or if."

He backs away far enough to put her into focus. "Me too."

On a whim, Ellie lowers herself down into the tub, her hands along the smooth edge. She lies back, fully clothed, the satin lining of her coat a shock of blue against the white enamel. She looks up at the stenciled tin ceiling, then out the window, and says, "You could do worse than getting old with a big tub at your disposal. When I was a kid, to escape the household, I used to read in the bathtub for hours. The year I turned eleven took place with me and the Brontë sisters half-submerged. The pages would get as wilted as my pruned fingers and toes. All the great scenes from literature are watery in my mind—and they play out to the underwater sound of my own heartbeat."

"I'm not sure I should be picturing you naked in the tub as a prepubescent girl."

"Agreed," she says, not looking at him.

They hear footsteps on the rickety wooden stairwell and she extends her hand up to him so he can help her out. She straightens her clothes and they go back out into the bedroom where a middle-aged man and woman come through the door, their coats doubled over their arms, both of them smiling politely. The man says to Jake, "Find anything good?" and Jake says, "We're still on the hunt." They walk back out into the hallway and as they go down the stairs she can feel him behind her, his hand gently at her back. She thinks, *Everything has changed.*

THE FAMILY-RUN HOTEL he's booked is a big sunny Tudor-style house in a cul-de-sac. The check-in procedure is a mixture of mild interrogation and stilted small talk, the husband in his shirtsleeves and the wife in an apron. The woman keeps running her sparrow-boned hands down her front, dusting off patches of flour. She's baked a pie from frozen cherries, she tells them, and this gets an approving nod from her offsider. Ellie thinks of how the world is governed by couples, how unmarried women make good academics because they've been neutered by too much knowledge and bookish pleasure. The world hands them a tiny domain it never cared about to begin with. There's only one room key on the counter and she stares at it as the wife discusses breakfast times and the inventory of board games in the den. The husband excuses himself to the raking of leaves and soon they're climbing the stairs. When Jake opens the door to their room she sees there are two twin beds, each under an eave, and this poses a slight awkwardness. He seems not to notice. She looks over the room while he goes downstairs to bring up the suitcases from the car. The bathroom is swallowed up by lavender hand towels and doilies and ornate fixtures; there's even an embroidered cover over the vulgarity of the spare toilet paper roll. She comes out of the bathroom when she hears Jake back in the room with the suitcases.

He says, "Let's get unpacked and have a glass of wine. How about it?"

She watches as he lays his suitcase on one of the beds and unlatches the lid. Everything she suspects about the rich is contained in the silk-lined interior—an abundance of carefully organized spaces, a leisurely life organized into discreet compartments with tasseled zippers. A handmade shirt, trousers, socks folded around a pair of Italian loafers, a leather shaving bag. He produces a vintage bottle of red wine from the swaddle of a yellow cashmere sweater, but she's still looking into the inner sanctum of his suitcase. Her suitcase faintly resembles the crumbling green Gloucester bag her mother keeps in the wardrobe with her wedding dress rolled in mothballs. He goes into the bathroom to fetch the two tumblers from the sink and proceeds to open the bottle with a corkscrew he's brought along. She's pretty sure it has its own dedicated pocket in the suitcase.

Ellie puts her suitcase onto the other bed but refuses to open it. He hands her a glass of wine and even this gesture, of drinking a '47 burgundy out of water glasses, seems rehearsed, like he's done it before. Maybe this is why the rich are so good at self-deprecation, she thinks, because it offsets the perfection of their clothes and houses and lives.

They sit in the easy chairs by the fireplace and sip their wine.

"Should I light a fire?" he asks.

"Not yet. Maybe we should take a walk before dinner."

She drinks her wine too quickly and feels it flushing up into her earlobes.

He says, "I hope you don't mind that we're sharing a room. The rest of the house is fully booked."

"It's fine," she says. "I intend to pin a blanket in place as a partition." She wonders if he'd planned to kiss her sooner, before this afternoon, to pave the way for this new intimacy.

"I can sleep in the bathtub if you like."

"That would be appreciated."

He looks down into his glass, smiling into a pause before another sip.

They try to talk about dinner plans and what a night in Albany might offer, but the conversation falters into long silences. She wonders how he will get out of the easy chair in a way that's remotely graceful. He'll stand to top up her wine, then perhaps hold her glass while he leans over to kiss her again. Novelists have this same problem, she thinks, Dickens and Austen and everyone since: how to get people in and out of rooms, up and out of chairs. That problem doesn't exist for painters. She knows they've been building toward this for months—a glittering trail of glances and innuendo—but now that it's here she feels a stab of panic.

When he eventually stands, halfway through their second glass, there is no pretext or subterfuge. He's driven from his chair in the middle of her scrambling sentence about Sunday country drives to the Blue Mountains. It's ungainly, an unchecked impulse, and he almost knocks over his glass in the process. Then she's craning her head up awkwardly as he kisses her from above, his winy breath in her mouth, his hand with the dead woman's wedding band cradling her head. Nobody tells you how to kiss him back while convincing him through some unvoiced nuance or telepathy that he's throwing your neck out of joint. She tries to stand, but he seems to be pinning her in place. Eventually, when the kiss peters out, he puts his hand down inside her blouse, straining against the buttons, and she can feel her heart drumming into his hot palm. Again, there's something odd about the timing, something forced and off-kilter. To break the moment, she takes hold of his wrist and he goes slightly limp, straightens, and walks back to his easy chair and his wine.

These erotic sorties—if there are more of them coming—already seem exhausting. She'd prefer to just be done with it, to meet the change of season at the door. She drains half her second glass of wine and says, "You asked me that first night in my apartment whether I had much experience with men."

He brings his gaze back from the window but says nothing.

She forces herself to look directly at him. "Well, the truth is, if you really want to know, I've never been with a man. Not properly, anyway." She's eleven again, her pruned hands trembling in the bathtub as Mr. Darcy dances with Elizabeth Bennet for the first time. "You'll be the first."

He looks into the tightly woven rug instead of her eyes, blinking and nodding soberly, like he's just received news of a distant cousin's death. "I had no idea," he says, sitting up straight. "It makes sense, though. You've never been married, so . . ."

The earnestness kills her and she can feel the mortification like a wave of nausea. She has to sip her wine and let it rest against her tongue for a few seconds before she can talk. She's looking at the darkening wallpaper behind his head when she says, "Most of the women I know lost their virginity before now. I'm late to—what's the expression?"

"The races? The party?"

"One of those."

A gash of darkness at the window. She wishes now they'd lit a fire. At least they would both have something to look at. An enduring silence guts the room. Eventually, she says, "I shouldn't have said anything."

"No, no, I'm glad you did. It means a lot to me."

He seems to consider saying more, but his thoughts trail off and now he's looking over at the blackened window and scratching the side of his neck.

She wants to scream.

Instead, she says, "I think I'm going to take a bath and freshen up before dinner."

"Excellent idea," he says. "I might take a walk around the neighborhood." He gets up out of the chair, pushing himself with both hands. "Will you be ready in half an hour?"

They both know what he's asking and she feels the question fall through her. Is it a look of resignation or tenderness on his face and why can't she tell the difference?

Against all her impulses, she says, "I'll be ready."

He walks gingerly over to the bed, grabs his anorak, and heads for the door. From the lamplit hallway he turns to look at her one last time before closing the door.

Over at the bed she opens her battered suitcase and lays out the negligee and lace underwear she bought in Manhattan the day before. She'd carried them back to Brooklyn on the train, neatly folded in tissue paper in a thin white cardboard box, certain her fellow passengers knew what was inside. *I've kept it as long as I care to*, she'd wanted to tell them. She takes her satchel of toiletries into the bathroom and runs the water into the tub. It takes forever to warm up, but soon she's soaping herself and rinsing off with a metal bowl the housewife downstairs, the woman of frozen cherries, keeps by the basin. She stands naked in front of the steamed mirror, finding her reflection with the watery wipe of her hand. She didn't wet her hair so she brushes it out, cleaning the brush into the toilet bowl and remembering to flush. Wrapped in a towel, she walks out into the room and closes the curtains. She puts on the negligee and feels it cool against her skin. The lace underpants, on the other hand, are immediately uncomfortable, riding up in the back. She wishes now that she'd brought her paint-spattered bathrobe to cover up at the beginning of things. The truth is, every time she imagines sex it's with a big window behind her lover, blurring out the lines of his body in an impressionistic starburst.

She peeks through the curtains to see a rind of purple and orange against the western sky. She straightens the beds and pours the remaining wine into her glass. Now she tests out a number of positions for his entrance—sitting on the edge of his bed, reclining in the easy chair, standing over by the window. The wine has blotted out her initial humiliation, but she can't imagine feeling actual desire. All of the positions seem rigid and pretentious. She sits back in the chair with her wine and wishes she hadn't noticed that her toenails need trimming, or that the hairs on her arms have darkened now that summer is gone. On hot sunny days, she sits out on the fire escape with lemon juice rubbed into her arms and scalp, bleaching herself. She drinks down the wine and waits. The darkness outside has bloated against the windowpane and she can see herself framed and looking back into the room. This slightly baffled doppelgänger is always following her. She realizes he's been gone at least an hour. The thought of dressing again to go find him, of putting her coat over her negligee, demoralizes her beyond belief. Hasn't she already offered herself up like a bag of peaches at the tail end of the season? No, she'll wait, she'll wait, until he walks through the door.

When he comes into the room thirty minutes later, he brings the scent of the night with him, a smell of wood smoke and damp leaves. He makes no apology and instead walks over to her in silence and takes her hands. She stands, and it's immediately clear that he will take control, that he's worked out some strategy for her deflowering while walking under the first evening stars. He kisses her forehead, then her mouth, then gently slides the straps of her negligee over her bony shoulders. It drops at her feet with a soft ripple. He kisses her collarbone and then her breasts, gently, one then the other. She closes her eyes while he trails his lips down her stomach and removes her underwear, the lace scratching against her thighs. She wants to undress him, but she doesn't, because she's not sure if she's supposed to. Taking her by the hand, he leads her over to the bed and settles her on the edge, tenderly, while he peels back the lavender bedspread and reveals the shock of white sheets. His hands on her shoulders as he leans her back, her body flat and exposed. There's an instinct to curl up and face away but she doesn't, she keeps her legs relaxed while he undresses beside the narrow bed. It's a child's bed, she thinks, in a dormer room with windows, perfect for a daydreamer or a girl with hobbies. She brings herself back, trying to keep everything relaxed and visible. She's conscious of her knees and her cold feet. Her mother's feet, a little big and flat. He leans over her, naked, his mouth on hers, one hand pressing into her. After a minute or so, she reaches up to take hold of him because frankly she needs a job to do, something besides this waiting, half in terror and half in love, her heart like a swollen hand balled in her chest and her throat like burning metal. But he brushes her hand away gently, his other hand tight between her thighs. When he finally lies down on top of her she feels his weight and then everything seems to happen at once. He says nothing the whole time and she wishes there could be a moment of levity, some acknowledgment of the strangeness of him on top of her, her legs splayed like a frog's, her wrists pinned to the bedsheet, but there's no joke or kind word of encouragement. She had hoped, or imagined, that they would still be themselves during sex, and perhaps that will happen, but for now he's a stranger, a sinner in church with a look of grim devotion on his face.

When she wakes some hours later, the room has been swallowed by nightfall and Jake is gone. By the clock on the nightstand it's still relatively early, before nine, but it feels like the middle of the night. They never ate dinner, she realizes. She has the sensation of coming to in a strange house, unmoored, finding herself inexplicably—at least for a few seconds—naked and lying in a twin bed. When the recent past flares up again she rubs her forehead where a hangover has already taken root. She gets up and turns on a lamp. Her outfit from earlier is draped across a chair and she notices how comforting the rough twill of the skirt is against her thighs, how reassuring she finds the tension in her bra straps. She wraps herself in her coat and goes out into the hallway and down the creaking wooden stairs, trying to favor the strip of carpet in the center. A din of pots and pans comes from the back of the house. She looks in the living room and the den, half expecting to find Jake Alpert reading the newspaper or playing checkers with a fellow hotel guest. But there's nobody to be found. She drifts back toward the kitchen and sees the aproned wife drying some dishes with a hand towel. The woman turns and seems startled to see Ellie in the doorway.

"I'm just doing the last of the dishes. Your husband said you were feeling unwell."

Ellie can feel herself blinking in confusion.

"Have you seen him?" she says.

"Your husband?"

Ellie stares at her, nodding.

"No, but I did hear that exotic car of his popping and rumbling in the driveway. He went out quite a while ago. Seemed to be in a hurry."

"Thank you," Ellie says.

She moves through the rooms of the house, the tartan furniture marooned in lamplight.

Back in the room she turns on the overhead light and it makes the gritty feeling behind her eyes flare up. He must have left hours ago, she thinks, and her mind ticks over with possibilities and speculations, the drugstore run or the engine trouble out on a country road. But why didn't he wake her or leave a note? She's a light sleeper, so he must have dressed silently or in the bathroom, not turning on a single light. She slumps down on the unmade bed and stares at his suitcase on the other bed before she moves toward it and unzips the lid. She begins to go through his things, thinking at first that she'll put his clothes in the dresser. Do you put things in the dresser for an overnight trip? She has no idea what the proper etiquette is, so she just arranges everything neatly out on the bed. The leather shaving bag is kidskin, so soft and smooth it feels like an organ being removed from a warm body when she takes it from under the cashmere sweater. With everything laid out she runs her hands through each compartment and sets a few pennies and a stray button onto his pillow. Inside the cashmere sweater is a label hand-sewn into the collar. At first she thinks it must be the name of a European menswear store in Manhattan—*Martijn de Groot*—because there's also a 212 phone number printed on it. But then she finds the initials *MdG* monogrammed onto a pajama shirtfront and realizes that Martijn de Groot must be a person, not an uptown menswear store. She stares at the name and number for a long time, deciphering each letter and digit.

She walks back downstairs with the number written on a piece of paper and asks the housewife if she can make a long-distance call to Manhattan. The woman says she'll have to time it and can only guess at the charge, but she shows her into the office where a big black phone sits on the desk. Ellie picks up the receiver and asks the operator to connect her. After a few rings an older woman with a Southern accent answers—"De Groot residence."

Absurdly, Ellie says, "I'm looking for Jake Alpert."

The sound of a dog barking in the background, then: "You must have the wrong number, miss."

"I'm terribly sorry. Who lives here? I may have written down the wrong number."

"This is Marty and Rachel de Groot. Good night."

The line goes dead, the receiver still in her hand.

SHE BARELY SLEEPS, waking every few hours to stare at the ceiling. She feels numb, hollowed-out. She sleeps in her clothes on top of the bedspread beside the emptied suitcase, her coat still on. All of his things have been thrown onto the floor, but she can't remember doing it. In the morning, she carefully packs up both suitcases and trundles them downstairs. She pays for the room and the phone call in cash and asks the wife if she would mind driving her to the train station. The woman is consoling and discreet, has her husband bring around the station wagon but insists on driving on such a delicate occasion. Her manner suggests that either Ellie's husband has run off or he's shown up in a morgue overnight. Ellie wants to tell her *He's not my husband*. Outside, it's pouring, and the woman drives to the train station ten miles under the speed limit, confiding her own marital burdens. "Sometimes he goes a week without speaking to me, a blue streak or whatever, but then he comes around. In the beginning you don't know everything and then, by the middle, you know too much." She hugs Ellie on the platform, tipping a porter to make sure both bags get safely on the train. In Ellie she has seen her own narrow escapes from marital oblivion. She waves goodbye, one hand clutched at her stomach with a crumpled tissue.

Ellie rides next to a window, stunned by the veracity of the moving landscape. Other people's lives flicker by—headlights through the drizzle, a tractor swaying out in a sodden field, a couple wordlessly sharing a sandwich on a covered station bench. The same five white farmhouses scroll by. Every time she woke up in the night her fists were clenched, but now she feels weak with bafflement and hunger. She hasn't eaten since lunchtime the day before—that scene in the rocking chairs by the stream is already receding, the lines soft as a Vermeer. The landscape floats by in her peripheral vision. Had it not been for the name tag and monogram she might have spent half the night calling every hospital and police station within fifty miles. She rubs the situation over in her mind, looking at it from different angles. She hadn't yet fallen completely in love with him, but she was hoping to be dragged along in its wake. She sees herself standing behind a high window, overlooking a yew maze and trying to solve its inner passages. The whole thing has been put together with too much artfulness and care to simply be a married man cheating on his wife. It's a thing she feels outside of, a shapeless configuration of larger forces and events.

AT GRAND CENTRAL, as she's leaving the express train, she makes the conscious decision to leave both suitcases behind, and it gives her an odd sense of relief as she walks, unencumbered, under the enormous zodiac of the vaulted ceiling and makes her way to the subway. The lace underwear, the monogrammed pajama shirt, the tasseled zippers, all of it headed back upstate or into the storage catacombs below Grand Central. She arrives back in Brooklyn around lunchtime and has no recollection of the painting until she sees it leaning by the front door. Her future has arrived, wrapped in brown paper. Nothing has come together yet, but there's a sidling premonition so that she approaches the painting warily. Placing the painting facedown on the Formica table, she untapes the corners so that it's the back of her forgery that she sees first—the worn relining, the stained wood supports, the ghosting of insect frass that suggests an attic somewhere in the painting's history. She can feel her pulse in her eyelids, feels it buzzing in her thumbs. She gently turns the picture over and studies her work, sickened but also relieved to have the copy back in her possession, to have solved the mandala that's held her transfixed for eighteen hours. Slowly, she walks back into the bedroom and pulls the original from her closet and its case and brings it into the living room. Side by side, from a few feet away, they are absolutely painted by the same hand. But as you step closer the roughened passages are different and the yellows in the copy are not as vital. She thinks about Martijn de Groot's careful restraint, the way he lured her one step at a time—the auction, the jazz, all that wine—and she can't help admiring his cunning. Was this a jaunt of the well-heeled, to track down the forger and handle the entrails of her life? Was it her virginity that finally made him feel like enough had been stolen in return? She had left the door wide open for him to plunder her life and he did it flawlessly. When would she receive the call from an investigator or detective asking for information about the original?

She sits there for an hour or so, studying the two paintings before wrapping the original in the fake's brown paper. She calls Gabriel at the gallery. "I seem to have both paintings in my apartment."

"What exactly are you talking about, dear?"

"The de Vos. The copy and the original."

"How is that possible?"

"When you get here, the original is the one wrapped in brown paper."

"Stay there. I'll be right over."

But she doesn't stay there. She walks through the apartment, from room to room, taking a mental inventory of everything she's going to leave behind. It shocks her to see how she's been living. The blooming damp above her bed, the sprawl of dirty clothes, the towers of books that are slowly being mutilated by mold. It's not self-loathing, exactly, because she hates this version of Ellie Shipley's life with as much vigor as if it belonged to a separate person who's wronged her. Whatever destruction she's summoned from outside, she's sure it will track her down. But for a month, or six, she will quietly go about the business of resurrection, of reclaiming the reasons she came here in the first place. She takes her passport and her bank account passbook from her dresser, puts a small photo album in her handbag, grabs her thesis manuscript, and packs the Remington into its travel case. A last look from the door at the two paintings, one concealed and one open-faced, before leaving the door unlocked and the key under the mat. She will write a letter to her landlord and a letter to her dissertation committee. In three months, she will come back to defend her dissertation about Dutch women painters of the seventeenth century. The only remaining question is where she will go in the meantime. The taxi waits while she goes into her bank branch and withdraws as much money as they will allow, an even ten thousand dollars. She doesn't want to put the cash in an envelope so she sinks it to the bottom of her bag. And it's not until she's at the airport that things fall into place. She pictures a loft apartment overlooking the Prinsengracht, or a room in a house near the Kalverstraat, in the neighborhood where Sara de Vos lived and possibly died.

The ticket is printed with her birth name, Eleanor Shipley, which has always seemed too formal for a ferryman's kid, but now it seems strangely comforting. She flies through the night with the Remington in the overhead compartment, arriving in Amsterdam on the edge of a blue dawn. She exchanges money at the airport, dollars for guilders, erasing her old life at the exchange booth window. A taxi takes her to a hotel near the Leidseplein, and by noon she walks the few blocks over to the Rijksmuseum. She stays there all afternoon, taking a slow walk of atonement under the searing depictions of the Dutch Golden Age. Then, at dusk, she walks back toward the hotel. She stops at a boutique on one of the narrow, kinked alleyways and buys three new outfits. She stays an hour and parts with a hundred dollars in cash—it's more than she can remember spending on clothes at one time. Back at the hotel, she showers and puts on the guest robe and orders a steak from room service. She takes the Remington out of its travel case and places it on the little wooden desk that overlooks the tramline. She works through the night, trying to summon her way back into the seventeenth century, typing the next chapter on hotel stationery.

MARTY ARRIVES BACK in the city before midnight, overcome by remorse. The storefront synagogues of the Lower East Side, the granite and limestone cathedrals of Midtown, these all put him in mind of worship, of earnest hours spent on the knees beside widows of unspeakable woe. He has always wanted to believe in something greater than himself, but the God-fearing genetic code ran cold by the time he was born. His Calvinist grandparents had bundled their terrified faith over from

Holland, erected shrines to it that ended up in every high-ceilinged room of the penthouse—the lowland paintings and embroideries were balms against the total depravity of man. As was money. The family fortune had been milled from cloth—sailcloth in the seventeenth and eighteenth centuries and treasury-grade rag cloth in the nineteenth and twentieth. Banking was never discussed in the house; to do so was to elevate it to the status of idolatry. Instead they pretended the money came effortlessly and quietly from above, flowed across the centuries like a hallowed ancestral spring. He thinks about the glimmer of benevolence he first felt when the painting went missing. The cosmos bestowed him with small favors, with parking spots and insightful rejoinders. Then he'd seized upon the slight, rubbed it like bronze, the attack against his household and his bloodline and his ego, as if he'd painted the scene himself. Everything turned ashen after that. He'd lured her out of the woods like some rawboned animal and now he has blood on his hands.

He drives into the Upper East Side feeling weightless and stunned, a fixed point in space behind the headlights, unable to control the drift of his thoughts. He thinks of Russian satellites pinging through the plasma of space, loosed above the continents like a handful of dice. There's a new Sputnik mission up there now and he can't recall whether there's an animal tucked inside the probe. The previous dog, Laika, apparently burned up in the atmosphere upon reentry. What a savage and surreal end to a street hound's biography. The lights of the dash are a pale and luminous green and they have a habit of dimming when he stops at a light and the engine idles. At a standstill, the sound of the motor churning reminds him of a fat man clearing his sinuses. He has no idea why he drives such a ridiculous car. Staring up at the red light he sees Ellie waking alone in the dormered room of the Tudor hotel. The magnitude of what he'd done kept him from sleeping or packing his things. A single speck of blood on the bedsheet as he got up in darkness and took his clothes out into the hallway to dress. He drove three hours without stopping, the radio off, the wind cold and gushing through the open window. The light turns green and a taxi honks. He understands that he will never forgive himself.

Along the park, he realizes he can't face Rachel, so he drives to his office, circling back toward Midtown. The streets are mostly empty, the storefronts peopled by mannequins in rust-colored outerwear. He parks in the garage below his building and calls up for one of the security guards. A big man with a billy club stands smiling when the elevator doors open in the lobby, a people person glad for the company. "A little late to be working, isn't it?" he says. Marty says something about leaving some important documents in his office, then he leans in with a confiding tone. "I'm on the outs with the wife, so don't come looking for me if I bunk down on my office couch." The security guard knows just that situation, he says, and presses the elevator button with sudden discretion. Marty is startled by the brisk little bell when the doors open. When the doors close, Marty slumps against the back wall of the elevator and puts his face in his hands. He closes his eyes and feels the climb in his stomach and then his ears.

He unlocks and relocks the front lobby and the dignified client sitting area, filing back to his corner office in semidarkness. He takes a brief inventory of Gretchen's desk—the sharpened pencils and the blotting paper and the miniature souvenir drum he brought her back from Jamaica one year. He shuffles into his office, switches on the lamp, and pours himself a drink. Reclining on the stiff designer couch he stares out the big windows. He's never been up here at night and there's a sensation of being fortified behind glass, of something solid between him and the mercantile canyons of the city. The office buildings are phosphorescent through the darkness, effulgent with a smoky light that reminds him of dry ice. It occurs to him that everything outside the window is a mirage, that everything in his life is festering with untruth. He gets up and sits behind his desk and begins to write a letter with a ballpoint pen on a yellow legal pad. At first he thinks he's writing to Rachel, because he's asking for forgiveness and itemizing his wrongdoings, but by the third page he understands it's to something or somebody he's never met—the Russian dog turning in the voids of space or the two unborn children they lost years ago or the man he might have become, the trumpeter with a big buttery tone that never wavers.

Sydney

AUGUST 2000

MARTY DE GROOT IN A RENTED TUXEDO. Earlier in the day he bought a pair of black dress shoes on Pitt Street and now they pinch and rub as he nears the gallery. He's worked up two blistered heels by walking the mile from the hotel, passing under the figs and palms of Hyde Park with his chilled hands in his pockets. He thinks of his father and his old dead boss, Clay Thomas, of inveterate walkers who footslog through the night air in dinner jackets and cuff links. He never set out to become one of them, but here he is, a rambler in formal wear. The museum director offered to send a car for him, but he refused for reasons that elude him. Was it because Max Culkins took his coffee weak and milky and hadn't personally shown him around the gallery? He's been known to slight a man for less.

At night, the gallery is floodlit and austere, a Greek temple hovering through the trees. The colonnaded pavilions and sandstone columns could belong to a courthouse, Marty thinks, if it weren't for the bright, vertical banners. They billow and flutter in the cold breeze, rivers of silk above the entrance. *Women of the Dutch Golden Age*. The lettering is so big that Marty can read it without his bifocals, which he forgot anyway back in the hotel room. He managed to source a new battery for his hearing aid, but he's had to turn the volume down to soften the brash auditory impulses of everything around him. He takes the broad stone stairs slowly, trying not to aggravate his feet. Surviving his eighties is predicated on a thousand contingencies—so why are there no Band-Aids in his trouser pockets? Old age is having the name of a chiropractor in your wallet. It's cutting out coupons for the zeal of discounted, small commerce and the practice of fine motor skills. It's talking unabashedly to the nightly news. His hearing aid warbles just below actual hearing. The sonic world of the foyer and vestibule comes at him distorted and from a distance, as if someone's moving furniture underwater.

The exhibition is in one of the smaller galleries off the main vestibule, but the reception lines the long entrance court, people mingling under the blackened skylights. Despite its billing before the Olympics, the turnout is good. And the fact that there are no Dutch heavyweights—no Vermeers or Rembrandts or Halses—has brought out a serious, scholarly crowd. No frivolous socialites here, just the true-blooded art patriots and critics. There's an artsy, masculine style that Marty recognizes from decades of attending openings: longish gray hair raked below woolen berets and Greek fisherman's caps, horn-rim glasses, hand-tied bow ties the color of tropical fish, collarless shirts with Nehru jackets, goatees and Van Dyke beards. The women wear batik shawls and indigenous-looking earrings, dark dresses with slashes of color. He realizes he's misread the formality of the evening, because he's the only one in a tuxedo, a rental at that, dressed like a sound engineer at the Academy Awards. He'd expected at least a few black-tie types, but the men are all bohemian dandies. Even Max Culkins is wearing a vest and a cashmere scarf.

He heads for the table filled with flutes of champagne and takes a canapé from a passing waiter. Hors d'oeuvres at openings are always highly salted, he thinks, to encourage drinking and the slackening of aesthetic standards. A string quintet plays some Bach or Vivaldi (he can't decipher which) on a low stage. He scans the crowd for Ellie. It's been two days since he sat in the back of the auditorium, admonished one of her students, and then fled before the end of her lecture. Not so much out of cowardice, he thinks, but as a reprieve from the inevitable. By now, she must have heard from the gallery director that Marty de Groot had shambled into his office, straight from the airport, with a seventeenth-century masterpiece wrapped in billiard cloth. *Baize* was the word he was trying to remember earlier—it drops into the mind slot with a satisfying clink. At least now she'll be braced for the encounter. If he had any compassion at all he'd get on a plane instead of hobbling around the exhibition with bleeding heels and a forty-year-old apology.

He finishes his champagne and heads toward the exhibition gallery. Because he doesn't have his bifocals and his hearing aid is dialed down, he moves cautiously, his champagne flute held out like the prow of a ship, parting the waves of bookish dandies and lesbian artists in velvet waistcoats. He infers from one of the museum staffers that no food or drinks are allowed in the exhibition space, so he drains his champagne and hands the glass to a nonplussed museum guard. Inside, he treads gently across the parquet floor to begin a slow perimeter check in one corner, starting with Judith Leyster. The Leysters hang against the starkness of the white wall, stippled into soft focus. He has to lean in close to make out the composition and then it's too grainy and pixelated, a topographic map flaked with lead white. He's tempted to go ask one of the other two octogenarians he spotted if he can borrow their tortoiseshell reading glasses. He recognizes Leyster's *The Proposition*—the fur-hatted scoundrel leering over the sewing woman, his hand cupped with money. But in *The Last Drop*, as the half-shadowed drunkard throws back his flagon, Marty fails to make out the skeleton that's been summoned back to life. For a full minute he thinks the skull in the skeleton's bony hand is a loaf of bread being proffered by a maid.

He moves on to the Van Oosterwycks, the vanitas and portraits and floral still lifes, but they're little more than gashes and rhomboids of color. Dispirited by his eyesight, he retreats for the entrance court and the champagne table. He picks up another flute and looks out into the whorl of mingling. He feels flattened out, burrowed inside himself. Somehow he's daydreaming about all the dogs he's owned in his lifetime, naming the lineage of terriers to himself as he faces down the repeating archways, when the formalities start up. He feels the air pressure change in the room behind him and he turns to see Max Culkins and Ellie up on the little stage, the quintet carrying their instruments off into the attentive crowd. A round of applause, then Max's speech stripped of meaning and studded with moments of pantomime—some chuffed remarks, tepid laughter, then all eyes on Marty de Groot hiding in the back. He suspects he's been thanked for trundling the painting all this way. He raises his champagne flute modestly and arranges a kindly smile. What passes between him and Ellie, who's now at the microphone in a mauve dress, cannot be called eye contact. He can see her pale face framed beneath her gray hair and a posture that suggests she might be making glances in his direction, but he can't make out her exact features or expression. He catches a few words from her speech, *art is our most universal* something-or-other. He looks into his champagne flute and finally turns up his hearing aid.

ELLIE SEES HIM AT THE BACK OF THE ROOM—the only man in a tuxedo—and knows instantly that he's not here to plunder her life. As she talks about art as the great window into culture, she brings her eyes again and again to his slumped shoulders. In her dreams, she'd conjured the melodrama of him unmasking her in public, but now she sees a man ravaged by age, shrunken and sallow-cheeked, still dapper but a little wobbly on his feet. *This* is the man who held her life and affections in his palm all those years ago? She's never seen anyone after a four-decade hiatus before and the effect is startling. The husk of the younger man is still there, in the aristocratic nose and jawline and the elegant hands, but his balding scalp has the consistency of blotting paper and his skin is the color of weak tea. It's the chromatic certainty of death. She's surprised to feel a burst of pity. She'd always imagined him suspended in recollected time—an energetic adversary, the virile blue blood in driving moccasins, his cashmered arm out the window of the speeding Citroën. Wasn't the promise of immense wealth a cryogenic cloister in which to grow old? Couldn't decades of eating the best foods, taking the best vacations, and sleeping in the finest beds prevent the slumping of the frame and the spackling of the skin? All these years, she has kept him in his forties. It opens out before her during her speech, a backdrop to her words about the role of seventeenth-century women in Dutch society. *Sara de Vos was somehow able to cut against the grain, to find her way into outdoor scenes because of her unique circumstances. With the new funeral painting, there is also strong evidence to suggest that she continued to grow and strengthen in her art.* She says all this while realizing that even the old Brooklyn apartment has remained hers, preserved exactly as she left it in the autumn of 1958. The windows flung open, the mason jars brimming with solvents, the ceiling mold fluorescing at night, the expressway traffic streaming behind the curtains. Her museum of squalor and anonymity. She went back to New York numerous times for work but never once went to see the old neighborhood. As far as she was concerned, Brooklyn was the graveyard where she'd buried her twenties.

When her speech is over she steps down from the stage and decides to be the one to approach first. That weekend with him in upstate New York has never stopped replaying and unraveling in her mind—the tartan furniture of the quaint hotel, the narrow twin bed where he took her virginity under false pretenses. She had offered it up because she was tired of carrying her virginity around like a penance and Jake Alpert seemed like a safe bet, a widower reentering the fray of the living. She'd imagined courteous and patient lovemaking, an attentive older man, and instead she got a grim, silent impostor. She never got over the feeling of violation, but now something shifts in her as she comes toward him. When he looks at her she sees that it's regret, not vengeance, that's brought him halfway around the world. It's a look of bruised self-loathing as his eyes lower then come up gently from her feet. His face changes and she sees something entirely familiar—that odd mixture of tenderness and playful attention from half a century ago. He smiles and gives a slight shrug.

Max Culkins is suddenly at her side. He makes introductions when they're standing just a few feet away from Marty and the champagne table.

"Eleanor, I'd like you to meet our gracious benefactor of the beautiful de Vos, *At the Edge of a Wood*. Marty de Groot, this is Eleanor Shipley, the curator of the exhibition."

Marty is pretty sure he's bleeding through his socks. He wants to have a Scotch and lie in a warm bath. Even without his glasses, having her this close makes it hard to breathe. He says, "So I hear. I managed to turn up my hearing aid during Ellie's speech. May I call you Ellie?"

"Of course," Ellie says.

Max fetches three glasses of champagne. They stand through an awkward silence as the crowd mills toward the gallery.

Max makes a toast. "To Dutch women of the seventeenth century."

"Hear, hear," Marty says.

They clink their glasses and drink.

Max says, "Mr. de Groot here has quite a collection of Flemish and Dutch masters. Ellie, your assignment for the evening is to convince him to leave us a few things that the Met doesn't want."

"I'd rather not ask for crumbs from the table," Ellie says. "I'd rather convince him to give us something the Met wants very badly."

Marty idles a finger on a button of his tuxedo jacket. His fingernails are still manicured and white. "The Met is slowly poisoning me and they send spies to check on my ailing health. Do you think you're up for that kind of curatorial espionage?"

"We'll do our best," Max says, a little uneasily. Somebody catches his eye in the crowd. "Well, if you'll excuse me, I must head into the gallery and make the rounds with the donors and journalists. Marty, I'll leave you in Ellie's capable hands."

Ellie and Marty watch him disappear on the other side of the stone vestibule.

Ten seconds of silence. The sound of dress shoes on parquet flooring.

He folds his arms, the champagne flute jutting from one elbow, exposing the gold lion heads of his cuff links. She notices that he still wears the same cologne—an alpine and citrus telegram that arrives from 1958. He rocks gently onto the balls of his feet, about to launch into something, then he drops back and stares mutely out into the commotion. She takes a step back, turns her shoulders toward the champagne table.

In a low, steady voice, he says, "For what it's worth, I didn't come here to ruin your life. You should know that at the outset."

She says nothing.

He blows some air between his lips, as if he might whistle into the gaping silence.

She says, "How do you know you didn't ruin my life forty years ago?"

"From what I can see, you never looked back."

"I looked back, believe me," she says.

"That makes two of us."

She surveys the entrance court, the art groupies and laggards who are more interested in the free food and bubbles than a roomful of masterworks by baroque Dutch women.

Then she turns back to him: "Did you come all this way just to reminisce about old times?" Her voice takes on an edge she doesn't like, so she dampens it with a sip of champagne.

"Is there somewhere we could talk privately? Also, I'm in desperate need of some aspirin and some Band-Aids."

Ah, the sense of easy entitlement, as if she's got pills and Band-Aids in her purse. It sets something off in her and she stops trying to temper her speech. Louder than she intends it to be, she says, "How is it even possible you're still alive?"

Instead of flinching he leans in, enjoying his own response. This is the other Marty de Groot, the guy with a thousand quips and rejoinders in his pockets like tiny scraps of colored paper. "Wheat germ and beta-blockers for the most part," he says. "A miracle combination. If FDR hadn't been so run-down with hypertension, Stalin might not have taken Eastern Europe at Yalta. Do you ever think about that?"

She finds this infuriating. "No, I've never thought of that. Not a single time."

Quietly, he says, "They say regret eats you alive," then he looks down at his hands. "But, actually, it *keeps* you alive. It gives you something to push against. That's why I'm here. To apologize. I wronged you and I've never been more sorry about anything in my life. I kept waiting for a sign, for a way to cross paths again. Then I got the call from the museum . . ."

He's still looking down at his hands, as if the past is pouring through his fingertips. His eyes are still sad and dark, she thinks, when they're not in the service of banter. She remembers the eddies of reflection, the quiet beneath all that brash worldliness. He says, "Also, I thought you'd like to see the painting again after so many years. You know it better than I ever did."

It occurs to her that he still doesn't know that the fake has surfaced. How could he unless Max has divulged the museum's embarrassing situation? After much lobbying and letting Max drone on about his potential legacy and his retirement, Ellie was able to convince Max to let her be the one to return the forgery to Leiden. The painting is now in the basement storage closet, waiting to be packaged in the morning. She'd lied and said she needed to do some quick research in the Netherlands anyway. But she'd assumed Max would quietly let Marty de Groot know of the museum's *pickle* with the Leiden shipment. That was just the word he'd use, she was sure of it. But from the relief on Marty's face, he's oblivious to the fact that the loaned painting and its double have brought her life and career to a crossroads.

He says, "Would you give me the chance to explain myself? Can we go somewhere?" He pulls up his trouser leg and shows her the dark stain on his sock. "I've lost a gallon of blood from these Italian shoes. They're made of fucking wood, as far as I can tell."

"Aren't you too old to be swearing like that?"

He waves a dismissive hand, still looking at his feet.

She says, "It looks painful. Follow me."

She leads him to an elevator and they go down to the loading docks and the packing area. She knows Q has an industrial first-aid kit in his office. The fluorescent lights blink on and Marty sits down gently in the swivel chair. She refuses to tend his wounds, such as they are, so she hands him a few Band-Aids and some Panadol and watches him with folded arms. He lifts one leg and gingerly takes off his shoe and sock with a sigh. His bloodied heel looks as if it's been grated and she can't help wincing. He says, "I can't get the Band-Aid to stick." It's the voice of a child, she thinks, plaintive and willful.

She ducks out of the office and fetches a few paper towels from the packers' break kitchen. When she comes back she hands them to him and digs through the first-aid kit for some antibiotic gel. After a few minutes of watching him blot his heel she eventually gives in and squats down in front of him. He doesn't smell old at close range, that's the funny thing. He smells like a walk in the woods, like breath mints and cologne and vintage luggage. It baffles her. "Let me do it," she says impatiently.

She dabs the heel and holds it there before applying a thin film of clear gel that tints red as she rubs it gently around. Away from the heel, the skin of his foot is pale and somehow untouched by eight decades of walking the planet. There are no calluses, no unsightly toenails. She's always assumed ruined feet and orthopedic footwear were inevitable in old age. Perhaps this is what a cocooned life might yield—ageless feet. Annoyed, she goes back to the first-aid kit and opens a packet of cotton gauze. Placing the gauze over his heel, she unpeels a Band-Aid and presses it down.

She tells him to take off the other sock and shoe. "I have to admit," she says, "I don't mind the sight of your blood."

He brightens—she can feel it in his body even though she doesn't look at him. She repeats the brisk triage on his other foot.

Looking down at his bandaged foot, he says, "I never forgave myself for what I did to you. I'm so very sorry for it."

Something about the candid, fluorescent light of Q's office allows this to reach her. Her face is suddenly hot and she doesn't know where to look.

He says, "For what it's worth, I really was in love with you, Eleanor."

She looks at him squarely over his kneecap, determined to keep her voice under control. "It was unbelievably cruel. I thought I was going to marry Jake Alpert and have a weekend house in Connecticut."

He looks away and the room goes quiet.

Eventually, he says, "I'm not going to justify anything I did, that's the first thing. But you might want to know—"

"Know what?" she says.

"The context."

"An odd word choice."

"Agreed." But he decides to continue. "Rachel and I were reeling from two miscarriages and my career as a lawyer was lunging toward its mediocre highpoint. Patents were a trifling puzzle to me, they meant nothing. Inheriting money ruined me as a lawyer, maybe as a person. Thank God I never stepped into a courtroom. I was bored and unhappy, looking for something to get me out of bed in the mornings. When the painting went missing it gave my life a ruthless kind of focus. I manufactured quite a display of indignation, talked about it until I bored everyone senseless, hired a private detective, and we tracked you down in your apartment."

Swallowing, Ellie says, "Oh, God, that apartment . . ."

"I thought I would just bait the trap and then hand you and that Brit dealer over to the police. Then something odd happened." He places one hand on the back of a bandaged heel, his lips thinning.

Ellie takes in the wall of hanging clipboards and the industrial-green filing cabinets. There's a chance, she thinks, that he might cry, and she wants to avoid that spectacle for both their sakes. But when he continues his voice is suddenly animated.

He says, "Not only did I fall in love with this odd little Australian art expert who was way too young for me, with the way she talked about paintings as if they were extensions of her own flesh and mind, but also I liked myself around her more than I could remember. She buoyed me up. So, I courted her—and my new, better self—as if my life depended on it. None of that was fake . . ."

He says all this to the side of her face as she studies the walls.

Then he says: "But then the deceit set in, of course, eventually burrowed in like a cancer. I'd never had affairs but I always felt like I was one phone call away from crossing over. So we dated, and I plotted because I was arrogant and stubborn. It was such a wild, audacious plan. And who the fuck were these people anyway stealing paintings off my wall? So I brought your forgery over that weekend we went upstate, knowing it would be there when you got back. That was supposed to be the unveiling. And then there we were in that sad little hotel upstate and you offered yourself up to me. And it was more than I could take. But I went ahead and took it anyway . . . and it's dogged me ever since."

It's oddly comforting to her that he's carried this burden with her name attached to it. She'd imagined herself to be the only one trapped like a speck in the amber of the 1950s. But then something else is pushing down on her and she turns her back to him, walking around the room. She looks up at a wall of graphed coefficients. Beneath the remorse and the sense of betrayal she suddenly feels a cavernous and familiar sense of shame. It is so familiar that she wonders if, in fact, it has ever *not* been swirling there at the pit of her stomach. She understands that she continued to paint the forgery for years in her mind, that she was forever tending the canvas because it was the last time she'd painted anything at all. She would summon it at her desk or on drives to the country with Sebastian—it would glimmer into view through the unsettled light of a dream—and it never failed to hold her attention. The shame was not merely in copying it but in the fact that it was the closest she'd ever come to creating something lasting. The forgery didn't stop after she'd handed off the canvas, it continued into the unfolding of years—the plush academic job, the marriage to an art dealer, the publications and curating of exhibits, none of these spoils would have been offered if anyone knew what she'd done. She'd walk into London galleries and antique stores convinced she'd run into Gabriel with his battered attaché case and that everything would come undone, in an instant. She understands it now in Q's bright, meticulous office. She never stopped painting the beautiful fake.

Marty says, "That was a dark period in my life."

"You stayed married? Did your wife ever find out the whole truth?"

"It took years of therapy—a grim Freudian with Danish leather furniture—but we came back from the brink. I never took her forgiveness for granted, but neither did that look of betrayal ever go away when she looked at me. I became faithful, if you can believe that. It was like I'd had a near-death experience. The death of the soul, if that doesn't sound like too much."

"It sounds a little much," she says. Then she softens, comes back to his side. "For what it's worth, there's nothing I've regretted more in my life than painting the de Vos. I never stopped looking over my shoulder, waiting for that ramshackle life to hunt me down."

The air shifts between them. The silence, when it regathers, is unhurried.

He says, "Well, excellent, we have regret in common. I tried to make amends. The whole point of the reward and the newspaper ad was an apology. That money was meant for you. I imagined you making a fresh start to . . ." His voice trails off. Then, he says, "What happened to you after you left?"

"After the copy—" She begins again. "After the forgery, I went to England, where I was the most law-abiding citizen in the world. I admonished my ex-husband for taking bogus deductions on his taxes and never drove above the speed limit. I acted like a goddamn saint. It's laughable, really."

"So you married."

She nods.

He smiles weakly. "Children?"

She shakes her head. "I wasn't cut out for that." She looks over at Q's desk, at the cups of sharpened pencils and the goldenrod shipping forms. Something occurs to her. "Why were you heckling from the back of my lecture hall the other day?"

He grins. "That punk in the wool cap had it coming."

"He's all right. Just naive."

"You spoke about the Vermeers like old lovers."

"They are, in a way."

The conversation falters again.

The thread is lost, he thinks. What else is there to say? You carry grudges and regrets for decades, tend them like gravesite vigils, then even after you lay them down they linger on the periphery, waiting to ambush you all over again. The world is full of noise again. He can hear the mechanical gears of the industrial clock on the wall. He has always liked plain, white-faced clocks with red needlelike second hands.

She says, "I want to show you something. Can you walk?"

"I'm not putting those shoes back on."

"Well, you'll have to come barefoot."

She stands and grabs Q's key chain from a hook on the wall. Q and Max are the only ones beside security with keys to every room of the museum. She leads him to a set of storerooms. He hobbles behind her, swearing under his breath.

"Did you know that almost every museum has a room full of fakes?"

"I didn't know that."

"They come in over the years. Bequeathed or sold to the institution. Every year the technology gets better and most museums keep finding fakes in their own collections. They've had them hanging for years a lot of the time. Of course, they feel compelled to take them down and keep things under wraps."

She jiggles the storeroom door handle and tries a different key. She can hear Marty breathing beside her. The lock gives and she pushes open the steel door. Inside, it smells of aluminum and plastic sheeting.

She says, "They don't want the fakes drifting into the open market and burning them seems a little draconian."

She turns on the lights and the cluttered room sputters to life. The copy of *At the Edge of a Wood* has been propped up on a shelf, facing out. It's surrounded by other paintings, some of them wrapped, some naked. A masterful Manet, a Julian Ashton, a Cézanne, a Picasso, a Brett Whiteley.

Marty blinks and says, "I left my eyeglasses back at the hotel. I can barely see my own hand. What am I looking at?"

"My beautiful lie, Marty. It showed up just before you kindly brought us the original."

He cocks his head, as if listening to a voice from another room. He didn't know his exact intentions when he decided to loan the painting, but this eventuality now seems hardwired into the fabric of possibility. His act of repentance was also, it seems, an act of malice. He remembers that day in 1959 when he met the British dealer at an uptown restaurant. The shabby little man had the original but not the fake with him; he said they'd destroyed the copy after the advertisement had appeared in the newspaper. He made a show of a manila envelope full of ashes and strips of canvas. Marty had asked about Ellie and he'd said that she'd gone back to Australia. It wasn't Marty's concern what happened to the fake, after all. The reward had been intended for Ellie—a sum of atonement, a payout against his own guilt—but now that this man was staring at him with bread crumbs on his lapels there was no backing out of the arrangement. He might have run out of the restaurant and thrown the painting into the East River. So Marty took the painting into the men's room, unwrapped it, and studied it. The antique copper nails he remembered were gouged into the flesh of the frame. But what if that too had been manufactured in the interim and this was still a fake? He doubted his instincts even as he came back and put the cashier's check on the table with the bitterly ironic word *reward* printed on the memo line. The foolish Brit said he would have preferred cash, to which Marty said, "I don't pay thieving cunts in cash." The whole episode was over before Marty's rare steak arrived. He remembers eating alone because he sure as hell wasn't going to share a meal with this weasel. Of course the fake was kept and resold. Of course the past was still alive and throbbing in the veins of the present.

THEY SPEND AN HOUR talking in the closed museum restaurant, looking down through the big windows at the Woolloomooloo docks. From the darkened waters of the harbor, buoys flash blue and green, tossing shards of light back and forth from Bradleys Head to Garden Island. Ellie knows all the names and the ferry routes; her childhood is written into the crags and coves and bays. She tells him he should make it over to the zoo before he leaves and see some of the old houses in Mosman. She brings him up to speed on the other de Vos painting, the child's funeral procession, because he confesses the gallery was a blur of colors loosed from their frames. She tells him she's leaving for the Netherlands in the morning to return the fake. He asks her lots of questions: the name of the private museum in Leiden, what the funeral painting depicts in detail. She says, "When I'm over there I'm going to do some digging. I want to find out what really happened to her."

Marty says, "Will you write to me and tell me what you find out?"

"I'd be happy to."

"And not by e-mail. An actual letter."

"On paper."

They look out at the darkened parkland that leads down to the harbor.

She says, "You were the first man I fell in love with."

He catches his breath and says, "I can't imagine."

"You knew exactly how to reel me in."

"Because I was smitten myself. I'd stare at your exquisite forgery in my study at night and plan our next encounter. I think I fell for you the first time we met at the auction house, the way you talked about the paintings. I bought those four copper paintings just to impress you. Cost me a fortune. I don't think I even knew what I was bidding on."

"Do you still have them?"

"Of course."

She smiles at this, staring at his reflection in the wall of glass.

From the entrance court, they can hear the sound of chairs being folded up, of the event winding down.

He says, "I'm suddenly very tired. I think it's time this old man got to bed. I'll be up in a few hours with jet lag."

They discuss possibilities for getting Marty back to his hotel with his bare feet and blistered heels. He refuses to put his shoes back on.

"Which hotel?" Ellie asks.

"I'm drawing a blank, but it's nearby. Somewhere I have my room key with the name on it."

She says, "I have an idea. Stay here and I'll be back."

She returns after a few minutes with a wheelchair from the guest services and coat check area. "Hop in. I'll give you a ride back to the hotel."

He looks mortified. "There's no way in hell I'm letting you push me through the night in that thing. I have exactly twenty percent of my dignity left and that ride would cost me a good deal more than that."

She laughs and flourishes a hand down the chrome sides of the chair, as if it's a prize on a game show. Now he's the one laughing.

"I'll go barefoot," he says.

"We do have taxis in this country."

"Walk me back," he says.

They put his shoes in a brown paper bag from the restaurant and leave the wheelchair beside the counter. Back out toward the entrance court, the gathering has petered out; only the diehards and the drunks are still at it. The catering company is ferrying small plates and champagne flutes into plastic bus tubs. Something flashes through Marty's mind and he gently touches Ellie's elbow as he pads along in bare feet. It's the hand pressure one reserves for dancing. "How did they get the goddamn painting out of my house in the first place? And who took those pictures? Your accomplice never did tell me that."

His hand is still on her elbow, now on the pretext that it's helping him stabilize. She's surprised that she doesn't flinch, that there's no electrical jolt. It's somehow consoling to both of them. She puzzles at it while she tries to answer his question: "The sad truth is that I have no idea. I knew nothing about the logistics. I really was the paintbrush for hire."

Marty lowers his face in contemplation. "The same private detective who gave me your name and address told me that he thought it was the catering company we used for an Aid Society dinner we had in November 1957. He thought they did the swap, but we never could prove it."

From under the archway that leads into the exhibition gallery, Max Culkins looks at them incredulously as they approach. Marty sees them through his eyes—the old barefoot blue blood, the cuffs of his tuxedo pants rolled up, hobbling along with a brown paper bag and a curator's elbow. Marty nods at Max, who's being buttonholed by an elderly female donor by the looks of it. Marty gives him a salute.

Marty says to Ellie, "Wait, I want to see the new de Vos."

"I thought you couldn't see anything."

"You can describe it to me."

Ellie turns for the gallery and they pass Max Culkins in the archway. Max and the donor stop talking to take in the spectacle. Max says, "Is everything all right, Ellie?"

"Mr. de Groot is having an attack of gout, but I'm getting him back to the hotel."

Marty suppresses a smile. He can tell Max Culkins wants to break off and interrogate them, but something about them shuffling across the parquet floor is so surreal that he's rendered speechless.

They continue on to the section devoted to the de Vos paintings. They stand directly under the funeral scene.

After a moment of contemplation, she says, "It's a funeral procession, but they're carrying a child-size coffin down from a darkened church. The clouds are brooding and cumulous. You know the Dutch use the word *wolkenvelden* to describe these skies. It means cloudfields. The river is frozen, just like in your painting. She became preoccupied with winter and ice, just like Avercamp did. There are children and onlookers clambering alongside the procession or watching from down on the ice. There's a village downriver, but no smoke or firelight. It's a deadly calm. The most unusual aspect of the painting is that it seems as if the entire scene is painted from above."

"How do you mean?"

"As if she's painting from up a tree or on top of a tall house. The whole perspective is from up on high, the vanishing point out beyond the frozen fields. It's signed and dated in 1637. We thought she might have been dead by then. Or at least that she'd stopped painting."

He almost says, "I could come with you, you know. To Leiden. I'd buy us first-class tickets. We'd scour the countryside looking for her trail." He stares up at the painting and imagines her response. She would say something witty but definitive: "We both know that would be interesting for about three hours."

After a few more moments in the gallery, they head out toward the main entrance. Max Culkins is nowhere to be seen, just a few security guards checking their watches. They clear the vestibule and foyer and walk out into the street. They take the footpath along Art Gallery Road, heading toward the city.

Ellie says, "Watch your step. I feel like junkies come to the Domain to shoot up. You might step on a needle."

"I can't see my feet anyway, so you'll have to keep me from ruin."

He still holds her elbow with the slightest amount of pressure.

She says, "That's a lot of responsibility. Did you remember the name of your hotel?"

Marty digs through his trouser pockets for his room key. He hands it to Ellie to read—the Sheraton on the Park.

They reach the end of the Domain and St. Mary's Cathedral looms above the tree crowns. The twin spires make Marty nostalgic for a strand of faith or religion he's never had. He says to Ellie, "Can we cut through the park?" and she says, "I don't fancy being mugged while I'm walking with a gout-stricken old man." They walk past St. James station and make the left turn onto Elizabeth Street. The streets are mostly empty, but they get a few wary glances from bundled passersby. Sydney on a blustery August night. They reach the Sheraton Hotel and he finally lets go of her elbow.

"This is the end of the line," she says.

He says, "It's silly, I know, but I'd love to say goodbye with my eyeglasses on my face. All night you've been nothing but a bright whir that smells like jasmine."

She contemplates making him go up to his room to fetch his glasses while she waits here. But then she decides he's a man in his eighties who's trundled all this way to set things right, who only has a finite number of elevator rides left in his lifetime, who couldn't be an imposition in a hotel room even if he tried. He hasn't been neutered by time exactly—there's still a tiny high pressure weather system that hovers between them—but his potency moves in and out, at the edges of reception, muffled then surging then gone.

They ride in silence to his suite on the top floor. She opens his door with his key card because apparently it's part of her new role. Would this have been her lot if she'd married a man fifteen years her senior?

He stands clutching his shoes in the paper bag, scanning the bedroom for his glasses.

She says, "I'm actually glad you came. It settled something for me."

He looks blankly over at the television.

Ellie spots his eyeglasses on the nightstand and hands them to him. When he puts them on he blinks and stares at her for a long moment.

He says, "You don't look a day over twenty-five."

"I wouldn't go back to my twenties for anything."

"I don't blame you. No matter. Your sixties seem eventful enough."

She looks around the hotel suite, then back at him. "It would be a lie if I said all is forgiven."

"Let's not lie."

"But everything is how it should be. How's that for wisdom?"

He laughs at this a little, blinks back a tear in his left eye. He says, "It wouldn't be in the right spirit of things to make a fuss. So, goodbye, then. Please take great care of yourself. I consider you an extraordinary person who happened my way."

She's shocked by the overwrought feeling in her chest. She says, "You take care as well."

There's a moment where a hug or a kiss on the cheek seems plausible, but then it vanishes. They shake hands slowly before she turns for the door. He closes it behind her, checks the lock, and moves slowly back to the bed to undress. He knows he won't be able to sleep, so he turns on the television and flips through the channels. Eventually he turns off his hearing aid and puts it on the nightstand, but he leaves the TV running. Nila gets on his case when he does this, lies up in his room with a glass of seltzer water, the television murmuring and his hearing aid off, the hour and the day dialed down to a slight impulse. A whole afternoon in this near-soundless, silvery-blue light. It's when he gets his best thinking done—the past and the present coagulate into something that makes sense to him. He carries the past around like a bottle of antacids in his pocket. You outlive your wife, then your colleagues and friends, then your accountant and building doorman. You no longer attend the opera, because the human bladder can only endure so much. Social engagements require strategy and hearing-aid calibrations. Every sports coat you own is too big because you continue to shrink, your shoulders like a rumor behind all that fabric. You are waiting to die without ever thinking about death itself. It's a face at the window, peering in. You live in three rooms of your twenty-room triplex, whole areas cordoned off like cholera wards. You live among the ruins of the past, carry them in your pockets, wishing you'd been decent and loving and talented and brave. Instead you were vain and selfish, capable of love but always giving less than everything you had. You held back. You hoarded. You lived among beautiful things. The paintings on your walls, the Dutch rivers and kitchens, the Flemish peasant frolics, they give off fumes and dull with age, but connect you to a bloodline of want, to shipbuilders and bankers who stared up at them as their own lives tapered off. Like trees, they have breathed in the air around them and now they exhale some of their previous owners' atoms and molecules. They could last for a thousand years, these paintings, and that buoys you as you drift off, a layer just above sleep. Skimming the pond, Rachel used to call it, or was that something you once said to her? You should turn everything off in the room, but you don't. You let the lamps burn all night.

Heemstede

WINTER 1649 / SUMMER 2000

A WEEK OF SNOW FOLLOWS a storm from the north. The meadows and tree branches are glazed with ice. Just before dusk, Tomas and Sara watch the whitening from behind the chill windows of their stone cottage in back of the main house. When Van Schooten finally retired and went to live with his ailing sister in Utrecht, Tomas was promoted to estate manager. Shortly after, he and Sara married—in the spring of 1638—and moved into the cottage. Cornelis, now in his seventies, has never liked the fussiness of titles (*head butler*, *scullery maid*, *footman* . . .) so he still calls Tomas the stableboy and Sara the visiting painter. She tutors some of the wealthy children during the summer retreats from Amsterdam and Haarlem, teaches them the principles of perspective, how to paint flowers and barns. In the winter, she helps out Mrs. Streek, who finds the stairs a painful bother. She stocks the pantries and cleans the upstairs rooms, brings Cornelis his meals when he's in a funk of melancholia and sulking by the fire in his tearoom. Although she occasionally sketches, the truth is that she hasn't completed a canvas in years. Somehow that practice was swallowed up in the new workaday, domestic routine. She's happy—she would be the first to claim that state or emotion—but she misses the tension of an unfinished work, the sidling glances of a world looking back at her.

They spend much of the spring and summer out of doors. Tomas is fond of expeditions to collect mushrooms and mosses, to pick wildflowers or catch trout upriver. The foraging is a pastime he learned from Cornelis and Sara suspects he's trying to keep the collecting flame alive now that the old man is housebound. One season Tomas spent every waking moment hauling lumber out to a secret location on the estate under Cornelis's direction. Their employer had asked him to build an observation hut to keep watch on the eastern border of the estate—the neighbors were threatening a boundary skirmish—but then Cornelis forgot all about it. So in June of that year Tomas laid claim to the tiny outpost and announced to Sara that he'd built them a *zomerhuis* overlooking the coastal dunes. Whenever it's warm and the mood strikes, they trundle out to the one-room cabin, a painted wooden jewel box on the seaward side of a bluff. Sara prefers the stone cottage and the comfort of her own bed, but she indulges Tomas's frontier spirit. They cook fish on open coals, swim in the river, sleep on wadded cotton and sheepskin. He erects neat piles of heather and the webcap mushrooms that Sara uses for dying yarn. These earnest little offerings remind her of Kathrijn. As he ages, Tomas is forever turning seven again.

Sometimes she spends a few hours with her sketchpad, looking down toward the North Sea. It's been years since a subject seized her by the nape of the neck. After the funeral procession there were other works of ambition, a handful of grapplings, but then the hunger died off in the easy contentment of daily life. She wonders about it sometimes while she sketches, feathering a gossamer cloud or blurring the amorphous line of the dunes against the blanched sky. She's surprised that it doesn't weigh on her more, this carefree quality of her days. But she sleeps easily and deeply, the sleep of a farm hound who's spent all day outside. She looks forward to the darkness, when everything is hushed and Tomas tells stories of boyhood escapades and seafaring uncles and cruel spinsters. A little flourish in the design of the *zomerhuis* is that there's a removable panel in the slanted roof. Tomas likes to make a show of opening up the room to the night sky above their makeshift bed, to present his wife with this rectangle of stars and planets. Here, he seems to be saying, I have assembled all this for you. But she suspects that he never quite finished shingling the roof. She lets him exaggerate his stories and talk her through the five constellations that he knows before they drift toward sleep. This seems like the truest kind of love to her.

She's thinking about the impossibility of warmer days while she stares out at the brittle world from the cottage window, at the pendants of ice hardening along the barren fruit trees, the vapor of hoarfrost against the fence palings. Tomas interrupts her daydreaming—she's staring into and through the fogged windowpane. He kisses her cheek and tells her there's a break in the weather. *Ice-skating at night*, when he says it, sounds like an invitation to wonder.

ELLIE DRIVES DOWN from Leiden in a rental car. The Netherlands in August is a vision of symmetry and Calvinist restraint, the greening fields perfectly square and run through with sluices and irrigation canals, not a rise anywhere to bend the sightlines. The Dutch love to repair to the countryside in the summer, take up residence in caravan parks and jerry-rigged dwellings no bigger than a sunroom. They ferry across to the wind-ravaged island of Texel or the dunes of Zeeland to spend a month reading barefoot in a tent. Or they drive into Germany and France with their pull-behind trailers and an end-of-days supply of toilet paper and tinned soup, afraid of what they might find outside their own province of watery domestication. Have they ever recovered from their intrepid seventeenth-century preoccupation with slaying everything wild? And yet they long to be free, barefoot, outspoken, immersed in nature, can't wait to make this annual pilgrimage to camp under the stars. She wants to share these observations with her Dutch passenger, but she knows he would take offense. Instead, she looks out at the gentleness of the countryside and considers how much has happened within forty-eight hours, how her life has been reshaped. She left Sydney just as a winter southerly buster was lashing the coast and now she's driving a rented Peugeot with Hendrik at her side and her own forgery in the trunk.

THE STORM CLEARS JUST AFTER nightfall and a full moon emerges from behind a cloth of weather. Tomas sharpens their skate blades with a file he uses for shoeing horses, makes them sharp enough to slice an apple. Sara packs along some walnuts and dried fruit and a kidskin bag of spiced wine. They bundle up in their woolen caps and mittens and scarves, their skates looped by the laces across one shoulder, and walk out into the cold, their breath like smoke. The freeze has settled deep into the landscape, sent splintered ropes of ice out along the leafless arbor vines, stiffened the hinges on the metal gate. They head for a western branch of the river, a spot where it widens a few miles from the village ruins. It's a favorite summertime fishing spot for Tomas, a deep pool of rocks and eddies where the trout like to congregate. The snow is halfway up their calves as they walk along through the woods. The moonlight comes through the treetops in flickers and starts. Sara stares up as she tramps through the snow, glimpses the moon and a few stars dulled by its milky aura. It makes her realize that she hasn't seen a cloudless sky in months.

They come down to the frozen riverbank, the ice thick and almost translucent where the snow has blown clear. There are patches of such clarity that she can see warped reflections of the night sky. The reeds are empty husks, gone the color of driftwood; they rattle and clack in the light wind. The couple stands together, his arm around her shoulder. She looks down into a window of clarified ice and thinks of the sluggish fish moping at the bottom, drifting in the slurries that run cold along the mud, of the way she and Tomas might appear to them as a two-headed beast through the frozen lens of the river. Tomas throws a big rock out into the center to test the hardness of the ice. It makes a satisfying thunk. There are Dutchmen who categorize the tenor of that sound and classify it against degrees of hardness. There are men who, during epic freezes, skate from Leiden to Amsterdam in a matter of hours. They sit on the cold stones to put on their skates and each take a sip of spiced wine to warm themselves through. Sara is the first to get to her feet and glide out onto the ice. She keeps her hands behind her back and kicks off with one leg, heading upriver. Tomas is forced to follow, calling after her as he copies the lines of her blades. She turns to face him, skating backward, her face flushed with wild good cheer. "Come on, you old mule," she yells, "I'm going to skate all the way to the sea."

HENDRIK NAVIGATES THEM toward Heemstede with a tattered road atlas. He tells her that this district was once filled with old estates and summering aristocrats from the cities. "Now it's filled with tired old bed-and-breakfasts and villas where nouveau riche German tourists can bunk down with their entire brood." She looks over and sees that he's still clutching the piece of fax paper he'd been holding when she first arrived. He's an odd accomplice for this errand, but she feels herself softening toward him.

When she arrived at the private gallery in Leiden, he'd stood in the threshold, the fax paper clenched like a winning lottery ticket. Given their interactions in Sydney, she was expecting him to be aloof, even a little hostile, but he was in thrall to something that made him seem boyish and friendly. He explained that an anonymous buyer from America had offered twice what they'd paid for *At the Edge of a Wood*. The wire transfer of funds had gone through just hours before, after

Hendrik had tracked down the owner of the collection by phone in Switzerland. "When I got your e-mail that you were coming here to return the painting I was very confused," he said. "But now it all makes perfect sense. The buyer has instructed you as his private courier. You have come to tender the paperwork and receive original signatures before you deliver the painting to America. My employer returns tonight." The halting, World War II spy diction was still there, and so was the patchy goatee and the four earrings in his left ear, but on his own turf, he no longer seemed especially stiff and dogmatic. Perhaps he now had nothing to prove. She came inside the three-story brick canal house, too flustered to take much notice of the chandeliers and hanging artwork. Only in Holland does an archivist answer the door to an opulent brownstone dressed like an anarchist. She asked him whether the painting would be safe in the trunk of her rental car. "We'll watch your vehicle from the front window. My bicycle is chained right in front of it. Shall I make us some tea?"

He told her to keep an eye on the street and went to make the tea. She stared out the window, letting everything settle over her. Surely he thought it was odd that they were returning the painting a few days after the exhibition had opened. Ten minutes later, he was pacing in front of the window, cup and saucer in hand. "Mr. van Foort is prowling through old Swiss attics," he said, blowing across the rim of his teacup, "like an old hungry tiger looking for an easy kill." After a few moments of such talk, something occurred to him and he got up and returned with another piece of fuzzy gray fax paper. "This one came through in the middle of the night, marked for your attention." Hendrik handed it to her facedown, as if to suggest he hadn't already read its message.

> I trust you will know what to do with the painting, Ellie, now that all the claims against it are settled.
> Very truly yours, MdG

She could tell that Hendrik had no clue as to its cryptic meaning and he knew better than to ask who *MdG* was. The art world honored anonymity, upheld it like a rank of purity. Hendrik said, "The buyer from America must want the picture very badly if he wouldn't let it hang for the exhibition." He smiled to himself. "Perhaps he doesn't want the public to see his private jewel." Hadn't van Foort questioned the logic of the return? Or was he possessive enough with his own acquisitions that he could relate perfectly to this zealous American buyer? She sipped her tea and waited for the words of confession to come out of her mouth. She waited for the moment when she would produce the fifty-page material analysis report by Helen Birch, the head material scientist at the Art Gallery of New South Wales, that proved beyond all question that the painting in Ellie's rental car was a fake created in the twentieth century. On the long-haul flight she'd imagined what she would say to Hendrik and his employer. She would apologize and take full responsibility. She would ask them how much they wanted as compensation, to take the liability off their hands. She might even repeat a line from one of her sealed but still unsent resignation letters—*Eventually, I was undone by time and circumstance and lead-tin yellow*. In the northern light of the plush sitting room, this explanation seemed melodramatic and false to her. The truer statement was that she'd used the de Vos canvas as a testing ground for her own thwarted talents, that she was reckless and lonely and angry with the world, that she craved a kind of communion, to find a layer beneath the glazes and scumbles and lead white where Sara herself still trudged through the fog of antique varnish, racked by grief but somehow dispensing painterly wisdom. *For a thousand hours, I wanted to think with Sara's mind and hands and shut everything else out.* These confessions were much closer to the truth, she thought. But there was no audience in her life—least of all Hendrik—for this brand of self-examination. Who besides her actually cared why she did it? It was certainly no longer Hendrik's problem. He and his employer had been neatly removed from the equation.

She suddenly wanted to be alone in her hotel room where she could take in the enormity of what Marty had just done. With three lines of smudged fax ink he'd not only taken the fake off the books but also given her permission to get on with her life. She felt a moment of fearlessness but also anger that she was getting off so easily. Instead of confessing, she found herself asking questions about the provenance of *Winter with a Child's Funeral Procession.*

Hendrik looked out the window and said, "My employer keeps all those records in his office. All I know is that it came from a widow in Heemstede who was selling off the family inheritance one oil painting at a time. She couldn't keep up with the maintenance of an old house or something."

Ellie watched him pacing at the window and wondered how deeply his ambitions ran. She said, "Perhaps we could partner together on something related to de Vos. While I'm here I'm going to do some additional research, see if I can connect a few more dots."

He turned to her. "Don't you have to get the picture to America?"

"I have a few days. I'll put it in secure storage."

He looked back out the window. "Partner how?"

She said, "What if we could set the record straight about what really happened to her? We know she continued painting after Amsterdam and there must be more to find out. Perhaps we could coauthor a paper on Sara de Vos? On her final chapter."

He cut his eyes at her through the sitting room, the halo of a sunlit canal behind his head. "That is a record that you largely created," he said. "Your career is built on hers." He said it a little testily, but she also understood from imagining his days toiling for an absentee employer, from his rusting bicycle chained to the metal spikes of the front fence, that he was at loose ends, underutilized and waiting to break into the major leagues of public museums. A joint paper could be his ticket out of this enormous, unvisited brownstone.

"That's true," she said. "But now I want to set it right." She felt emboldened, like she could say anything. She was twenty-six again, at the beginning and full of ambition. "How old are you?"

"Thirty-two."

"Do you want to keep curating paintings that no one ever gets to see?"

He emptied his teacup and looked out the big window.

She said, "Your career passes in a flash. Take it from me."

From behind, she saw him take in a big breath and let it out slowly.

When he turned, she saw a different person looking back at her. He was trying to hold back a big grin.

"Follow me, please," he said, leading her toward the stairs with a set of keys in one hand and his cup and saucer in the other. They went upstairs to the owner's *kantoor* and he unlocked the door. "He documents everything," he said, "right down to the name of an art collector's cat."

Now in the rental car, she looks over at him as the Spaarne comes into view, the riverbank dotted with linden trees and wooden boathouses painted bottle green and sky blue. He navigates with his outdated road atlas, tells her that the driveway to the bed-and-breakfast should be "appearing before us in approximately three hundred meters."

THE COLD AIR BURNS her cheeks as she skates along, pushing into long glides, her hands behind her back, the sound of her skate blades like the sharpening of a knife on a whetstone. She wants to skate for miles, to fall until midnight into this bracing pleasure. The bare trees glitter with ice along the riverbank, a complement to the winking stars. The night feels unpeeled, as if she's burrowed into its flesh. Here is the bone and armature, the trees holding up the sky like the ribs of a ship, the ice hardening the river into a mirror too dull to see the sky's full reflection. Everything flits by except the sky and her thoughts, both of which seem to widen and gyre in a loose, clockwise procession. She thinks of paintings and meals and Kathrijn, one somehow leading to the other, then Barent and Tomas, then her mother knitting by the fire, then a bowl full of oranges in winter light. Everything is strung together on the line of her skates, swooping curves and perfect delineations of her wistful thinking. She is light upon the ice, a weightless passenger.

Tomas skates many yards behind her, no longer calling out, but occasionally letting out a howl of laughter or exhaustion. She has half a mind to skate all the way to the village ruins and sing at the top of her lungs until Griet comes out of her hermitage to see what all the commotion is about. She forgets for a whirring moment that Griet is dead, her bones bleaching in the frozen earth beside her children and husband and neighbors. Toward the end they brought her to the house and Sara nursed her during the final weeks. A slow winnowing, so unlike the outward rush of Kathrijn's death. She would come into the guestroom to find Griet vanished from the feather bed and sleeping on her animal pelts by the open window. She died as she lived, like a Spartan or a mendicant. Sara misses their conversations, the stories of the old village. She turns around to ensure Tomas is still within eyeshot and sees him coming around a bend in the river, both arms up, waving like a goose trying to take flight. She laughs, skating backward, her breath smoking in front of her face. There are pockets of time, she thinks, where every sense rings like a bell, where the world brims with fleeting grace.

For an instant she doesn't know that she's fallen through. The river, under all that ice, is a burning flood. The moonlit sky replaced by a dome of shattered white glass. A searing underworld of distorted shape and sound. It's only when she tries to take a breath that she knows she's been swallowed up.

Her hands rake above her head, as if she's trying to climb a ladder. Everything dims away as she sinks toward the cold sludge of the riverbed.

Her feet are two leaden weights, her pockets full of stones. She kicks her feet but can't feel anything below her. She can hear Tomas's skates cutting and scraping along the ice above. And then she hears her own voice—not a garbled scream but someone moaning in her sleep from a dark room at the bottom of the river. The sound terrifies her. She sees her own panic rise in the stream of bubbles and understands that everything she wants is up above, through that jagged rent in the ice. The glimmering night has been wrenched cruelly from her grasp. It seems so impossibly far away. Her vision blurs; a dead tree limb looms through the murk. She coughs and feels the river burning inside her chest. Then everything slows. She can see elegant spirals of current passing above her, bearing fish and flotsam downriver. She can see stars embedded in the ice, a second muted sky with its own constellations. Tomas is there, lowering a long tree branch into the water, plunging his face into the icy water, his voice vibrating as he moves between realms.

THE WIDOW—Mrs. Edith Zeller—runs the bed-and-breakfast without any flair for hospitality. Wealthy Germans and Amsterdammers show up, materialize out of her guest register, and she sets them loose on her overdecorated, cold rooms. If the plumbing goes south in the winter, or there's a dip in reservations, she sells off a painting or an antique desk. It's been that way for years. Antiquity pays for maintenance; tourists pay for the utilities and the petrol in her car. A cash-poor widow sitting on millions in accumulated wealth. Ellie sees all this in the way she signs them in, sees it on the wallpaper blanched with the ghosts of sold-off paintings, in her instructions and laminated signs for brief showers and turning off the water while brushing teeth. The widow somehow carries the burden of inherited wealth. They are shown to their ground-floor rooms. Ellie's is narrow and a little threadbare, makes her think of convalescence and bedpans—a washbasin on the bureau, an embroidered hand towel, a view of the summer garden gone to seed.

At dinner they broach the subject of the funeral painting, gently interrogate the widow about how she came by it, how long it had been in her family, et cetera. Mrs. Zeller has warmed them up a stew of root vegetables and smoked sausage for dinner and Ellie wonders whether they'll be charged for these days-old leftovers. They eat in one of two disheveled kitchens, the dining room closed off to guests long ago. The widow recounts the stages of household decline as if they were acts of God—the plague of ruin and dustcovers when her father died, the eternal cold and damp of the upper rooms when she and her mother couldn't afford kerosene or firewood, the dwindling of the spirit as she lost her own husband and her children moved away. A banker in England; a concierge in Paris.

"Where did your picture collection come from?" Ellie asks.

"Some came from a distant uncle on my father's side and others were bought by my father himself. During the second war there was looting and German soldiers all around here. The old families tried to hoard their treasures with neighbors and in old barns, to keep their heirlooms hidden from view. A lot of the paintings disappeared."

"The painting we bought years back," says Hendrik in Dutch, "the child's funeral scene. Do you have others by Sara de Vos?"

Mrs. Zeller chews and thinks. "I'm afraid I've never heard that name."

Ellie feels a wave of sudden fatigue, a burst of jet lag. "Do you mind if we look through your collection?"

The widow looks up from her bowl of stew. "It's spread all over. Some in the attic, some in the sitting rooms, some who knows where. My lawyer in Heemstede township makes up the papers when I make a sale. I think he took an inventory at one point."

They finish their dinner and speak no more of paintings. Later, when the plates have been cleared and half the lights in the house have been extinguished, Mrs. Zeller brings some extra towels down to their rooms. The towels are stiff and rough and smell like lemons. Ellie thanks her, stands out in the hallway to chat with her before bed. Out of nowhere, Mrs. Zeller asks her whether they'll be going out to see the ruins tomorrow. "Out by the old settlement. A nice spot for a picnic," she says. "In the Netherlands we have many ruins but very few castles. The Dutch do not like lords and ladies." Ellie wants to bring up the Dutch adoration of Queen Beatrix but instead she confirms what she's just heard. "What ruins are those?"

"The old village," the widow says.

"From the painting?"

She nods but then appears suddenly wary and frightened. Ellie wonders, not for the first time, whether she has dementia.

Hendrik has come out of his room to listen in. In Dutch, he says, "Mijn vrouw, are these the ruins of the village in the painting? The picture of the funeral procession."

The widow says, "The whole town was buried out there. I will make you cheese sandwiches for a picnic lunch." She says good night and walks down the long hallway.

SARA WAKES IN the thin blue hours of the night, the big house dark and bloated all around her. She's marooned in firelight, in a narrow feather bed in the tearoom. She knows this is the place where Cornelis tends his melancholy and imbibes the Orient one cup at a time. She's burning up beneath a mountain of blankets, her hair drenched with sweat under a cotton bonnet. She tries to sit up and throw the bedspread off, but she falls back with exhaustion. A fire is ablaze in the hearth and she sees Barent slumped in a chair, the folded pages of a gazette across his lap. It takes her a moment to realize that it's Tomas sitting there, that this is a different time, a different life. She has been dreaming of Barent, of following Kathrijn through the woods and into a cave. There are afterimages when she closes her eyes. Black tulips and gleaming ribs of ice. She sits up in bed again and looks out the window at the snowdrifts. She's very thirsty, but she doesn't want to wake Tomas. She sees them swimming together across a placid lake, then they are fording a river beside a field of running horses. She wakes again from another dream.

In the morning there is a doctor from Haarlem and Tomas at his side. The physician wears an apron with a tiny island of blood on the hem. Is it mine? she wonders. She wants to ask, but speaking requires formidable strength. She glimpses her frostbitten toes, the blackened nail beds. They are no more hers than the milky glass apothecary bottles on the mantel or the slurries of melted snow pooling in the orchard. She looks at her hands, overcome by a sense of relief—these bony pink fingers alone are mine. She points to a goose quill and a half-written letter on the writing desk, one of the sad epistles Cornelis writes to foreign correspondents. On the back of it she writes *I want to be in my own cottage, in my own bed.* The doctor says she cannot be moved. But there is the matter of the blood on his apron and the way it pulls crimson from the wintry light. It's in the shape of a reared lion, just like the provincial flag. Emissaries have been sent for her; they will come bearing myrrh and tulip bulbs wrapped in muslin, the daughter offsets of *Semper Augustus*.

ELLIE AND HENDRIK bicycled out to the ruins earlier in the day, dutifully packed along their cheese sandwiches and macintosh squares for a picnic. Now Ellie has returned alone, her forgery removed from the frame and stretcher, folded into triangles in her backpack like a flag she's about to unfurl. Hendrik thinks the painting is back in Leiden in safe storage until she flies to America. For a fleeting moment she thought they would find the high perch where Sara stood to paint the funeral scene. Instead they found mounds of rubble and brickwork, the occasional base of a chimney, a lintel or casement, but nothing revealing. Still, this is hallowed ground, a place where Sara had passed through or lived. The broken headstones in the cemetery are mostly illegible, a few engraved dates and names blackened with age. This sense of ceremony—burning the canvas down by the river—is probably misplaced.

She has always been an atheist and mistrusted the rituals of the believer. But there's something about the idea of setting it alight as a kind of offering to Sara de Vos that appeals to her. From under the widow's kitchen sink she has brought matches and lighter fluid. She spreads out the canvas on the riverbank and douses it with fluid. When she strikes the match there's an after-burn of sulfur in the air. The corners of the canvas blacken and curl. She watches the layers of paint buckle, the image stripping away into striations of smoke. The canvas chars in the corners first, in the places where the paint is thinnest. When the bright yellows of the skaters' scarves catch, she sees something flare like a tiny starburst or an incineration of glass. It's beautiful to watch it kindle slowly against the grass of the riverbank. As it burns, she wonders if she will ever paint something of her own again.

ON THE THIRD DAY OF FEVER, she asks for a hand mirror and a hairbrush. She sits up in bed and brushes her long dark hair out, holding each length between her fingertips. The face in the oval frame belongs to a stranger. Cheeks ablaze, wind-chapped lips, a look of fatigue about the eyes. She hands the mirror back to Tomas in disgust and says, "Do you remember how to size and ground a canvas?" Her voice has recovered, but it remains low and hoarse, some damage to the throat is what the doctor says. He looks at her impatiently, arms folded. "It's how I won you over. Of course I remember." She holds her hands up to show him the size and requests a ground of warm, earthen tones. "Are you sure you're well enough to paint?" he asks. "The doctor forbade any form of exertion."

She sinks back down to the pillows and closes her eyes. "I'll paint in bed just to keep you happy."

A prepared canvas appears beside the bed that afternoon. It's a foot square, mounted on a wooden strainer made from fence palings. The ground is a little darker than she'd like—more russet than warm clay—but it's well made, pumiced smooth and even. On the bedside table are the ground pigments that make up her palette: white lead, smalt, yellow ocher, a touch of azurite. She can't imagine how long she's been asleep. Tomas is beside her again, bearing soup on a tray. "What are you going to paint?" he asks.

She shrugs and looks out the window. The bare elms are streaked with twilight up on the hill. "Nothing with snow or ice in it."

He smiles, touches her shoulder, and leaves her to eat and work.

She knows this will be the last thing she ever paints. It briefly overwhelms her with the magnitude of choosing the right subject. Before that first line of pale chalk, before the underdrawing fleshes out into shapes and proportions, there is a stab of grief for all the things she didn't get to paint. The finches wheeling in the rafters of the barn, Cornelis reading in the arbor, Tomas bent over his roses in the flower garden, apple blossoms, walnuts beside oysters, Kathrijn in the full bloom of her short life, Barent sleeping in a field of lilacs, the Gypsies in the market, the late-night revelers in the taverns . . . Every work is a depiction and a lie. We rearrange the living, exaggerate the light, intimate dusk when it's really noonday sun.

Then she begins, banishing the feeling of remorse with gentle lines of pale chalk. Her hands are unsteady, so she first practices on the back of the canvas. She settles on a pose and a depiction before turning the canvas over. She paints a series of lines and textures for an entire afternoon, retooling her hand and her eye. There are bouts of exhaustion, hours where she sleeps with the canvas laid faceup, across her chest, one layer drying at a time. She wants to paint something she has never set down before, something true. Her fevered dreams are overrun with the berry-black eyes of the fish along the riverbed, the scraping of Tomas's skates up above, the pallid moon through the window of ice. Her skin burns with the memory of it. Sometimes she wakes herself up with her own moaning. Opening her eyes is to come ashore again, to find the stone cottage abundantly solid and straight-edged. She paints another hour, then stares out the window for long stretches. One day, sometime near dusk, Tomas rides his horse up to the window and smiles at her from across the big mare's white-diamond forehead. It's called a star, she remembers, this marking on a horse's head. She wants to remember the names. She wants to remember him looking back at her in the twilight.

ELLIE TAKES A FLASHLIGHT and a pair of gloves up to the attic rooms. As she climbs the narrow staircase, the smell of damp is a living thing. It catches in the back of her throat, a visceral reminder of Brooklyn. She fears the worst, that even if there are dozens of paintings up here—squirreled away from the Nazis, is the widow's claim—that they'll be damaged beyond repair. The rooms are littered with newspapers and desiccated insects, the walls blotted through with continents of mold. Boxes of mildewing books and clothes, a crate of wooden toys. No one has been up here for a very long time. She continues down the passageway toward a triptych of north-facing windows opaque with grime. Pigeons appear to be nesting in the roof because the floor is splattered with their droppings. Cut into one wall is a crawl space with a little wooden door. She opens it and shines her flashlight into the musty interior, but there's nothing inside but exposed electrical wiring and cobwebs. She goes back out into the hallway, opening each door. In a tiny room she finds some mutilated luggage and begins to open tattered suitcases and trunks. There are yellowing black-and-white photographs from the 1920s, snapshots from family vacations and postcards from foreign hotels. Children brimming with smiles beside statues in parks and running along northern beaches. Inside a metal trunk, wrapped in a twill blanket, she finds eight canvases, each one rolled and coiled with a ribbon, the tiny puncture holes visible along the edges where they've been carefully removed from a stretcher. She cinches her gloves and spreads out the blanket. She unrolls each canvas and finds something to pin down its corners with. Before long she has a spread of Flemish, Dutch, and English paintings, a few from the nineteenth century but a few also from the 1600s. There's one that feels familiar to her, something about the brushwork and the light. A young woman is sitting at an easel but turned toward the viewer. It's an open, youthful face, her dark hair pulled beneath a bonnet and her chin set against a broad disc of lace collar. Despite the loose brushwork and the easiness of her pose—elbow propped on the chair, one hand holding a paintbrush like a quill—she's dressed formally. A working artist would never wear a crimson velvet dress and a high church collar to paint in. She has dressed herself for something momentous. In her left hand she clutches the wooden palette, a dozen brushes, a piece of cloth. Beside her is a half-finished canvas resting against the easel—a young man on horseback framed by a leaded window, peering in, the angling northern sunshine like a corona around his head. He appears to float through space, to radiate off the canvas and into the artist's workroom. She is still young, the painter, despite the date of 1649 in the lower left corner. She is twenty again and just starting out, turning to take us in as we come through the door, her lips parted as if she's about to speak.

ACKNOWLEDGMENTS

Special thanks to Professor Frima Fox Hofrichter for her expertise on Dutch women painters of the seventeenth century; Stephen Gritt, director of conservation at the National Gallery of Canada, for his insights into the technical aspects of art restoration and conservation; and, Ken Perenyi, master art forger, for vetting my fabrications.

Forgery techniques are derived from interviews and from details found in three sources: *The Fake's Progress* by Tom Keating, Geraldine Norman, and Frank Norman; *Caveat Emptor* by Ken Perenyi; and, most important, *The Art Forger's Handbook* by Eric Hebborn. The chapter that contains a night fishing scene on the Hudson River draws from reportage about eels, shipwrecks, shellfish, and the Shellfish Protector found in Joseph Mitchell's iconic *New Yorker* essay "The Bottom of the Harbor." The advertisement for the Rent-a-Beats in the first chapter is taken from Fred McDarrah's 1960 real-life ad in *The Village Voice*.

Deep gratitude to the late Wendy Weil, for her guidance and wisdom, and to my agents, Emily Forland and Gaby Naher, for their encouragement and expertise. Many thanks to my editors, Sarah Crichton and Jane Palfreyman, for their faith and insight, and to my early readers—Karen Olsson, S. Kirk Walsh, Michael Parker, and James Magnuson. And a big thank-you to Jeremy Pollet for being my driver, tour guide, and lunch date in and around Edgewater, New Jersey.

A final and enormous thank-you to my wife, Emily, and my two daughters, Mikaila and Gemma, for always believing in me and helping me steal the time to write.